BLOOD
ATONEMENT

S.M. FREEDMAN

BLOOD ATONEMENT

DUNDURN
PRESS

Publisher: Kwame Scott Fraser | Acquiring editor: Elena Radic | Editor: Shannon Whibbs
Cover designer: Laura Boyle
Cover image: istock.com/D-Keine; mirror: istock.com/JNemchinova

Library and Archives Canada Cataloguing in Publication

Title: Blood atonement / S.M. Freedman.
Names: Freedman, S. M., author.
Identifiers: Canadiana (print) 20220159815 | Canadiana (ebook) 20220159823 |
  ISBN 9781459750241 (softcover) | ISBN 9781459750258 (PDF) |
  ISBN 9781459750265 (EPUB)
Classification: Classification: LCC PS8611.R4355 B56 2022 | DDC C813/.6—dc23

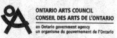

We acknowledge the support of the Canada Council for the Arts and the Ontario Arts Council for our publishing program. We also acknowledge the financial support of the Government of Ontario, through the Ontario Book Publishing Tax Credit and Ontario Creates, and the Government of Canada.

Care has been taken to trace the ownership of copyright material used in this book. The author and the publisher welcome any information enabling them to rectify any references or credits in subsequent editions.

The publisher is not responsible for websites or their content unless they are owned by the publisher.

Printed and bound in Canada.

Dundurn Press
1382 Queen Street East
Toronto, Ontario, Canada M4L 1C9
dundurn.com, @dundurnpress

*For the lost boys and girls of the FLDS: those who escaped,
those who survived, and those who were left behind.
For Clayne and Roy Jeffs, and all the other FLDS victims
who carried burdens too heavy to bear.*

PROLOGUE

Grace was cleaning blood from her thighs when the police raided Brigham for the last time.

At first she paid little attention to the shouting outside the trailer window. She needed to finish what she was doing before her husband came home demanding dinner. She'd propped herself over the toilet, one hip wedged into the side of the sink and her back pressed against the shower door. Her legs shook, her hands trembled. Her brain was hot with fever and her good ear buzzed.

Someone pounded on the side of the trailer, causing the walls to rattle. She lurched backward and grabbed the edge of the sink to keep from falling. Bloody rags splatted on the floor.

"Grace, hurry! The police are here," Desiree said.

The police. Now she heard the shouting. The crying. The chaos as children scattered into the forest.

"I'm here. I'm coming."

"Be quick."

Her dress hung from the hook by the sink, pale green with yellowed lace trim. But there was no time for her to get dressed. She grabbed a throw blanket from the foot of the bed and wrapped it around herself to cover her blood-soaked temple undergarments.

The world tipped sideways and slowly righted itself. Staggering forward, she somehow made it to the door and slammed a shoulder into it, unsticking the warped aluminum from its frame. She tumbled off balance down the outside stairs and would have fallen if her sister hadn't caught her.

"Come on." Desiree grabbed her arm and pulled.

They ran beneath a moon that was low and bright in the sky. Once Grace's eyes adjusted she could see perfectly well. Which meant she could also be seen perfectly well.

At the edge of the cornfield, reason or madness asserted itself.

"Wait."

Desiree spun to face her, eyes wide with panic. "What are you doing? We have to go."

Her sister's hair was pulled into a classic roll on top of her head and braided down her back. She panted, her bosom pressed against the cotton of her high-collared dress. Pimples dotted her chin.

How long until Uncle G had a revelation about Desiree's marriage? She was already a year older than Grace had been.

Desiree glanced toward the road. "Come on. They're catching up!"

This was true. The beams of their flashlights danced like fireflies as the police approached. Their voices grew louder.

She felt Desiree's panic, could feel it swell within her own chest. The urge to keep running was almost overwhelming. It's what they'd been taught to do. They needed to protect their way of life, their chance at heaven, and their prophet.

But blood trickled down her legs. Again. And more than anything, she wanted a better life for her sister. She grabbed Desiree's hands. Hers blazed with fever; Desiree's felt like ice.

"This is our chance."

Realization and fear blossomed in Desiree's eyes. She shook her head and tried to pull her hands free. "We shouldn't."

Grace squeezed. "We must."

"But what about Father and Mother?"

Grace's chest tightened with anxiety and guilt, but she shook her head. Too far down that path and she'd decide to stay. Then her only way out would be death. She opened her mouth, but nothing came out. Truth was so hard to speak. She'd been raised to be sweet, and the words burned like acid on her tongue. She almost gagged on the enormity of what escaped her lips.

"If I have to stay here any longer, I'll die. And so will you. How long until you're married?"

"Oh, Grace." Desiree's eyes swam with tears.

"You're fourteen. Your revelation is coming any day now."

"Maybe I'll be lucky, like our parents were."

"Until Mother Rebecca joined the family."

Desiree swallowed hard.

"Was it just a game to you?" Grace asked.

The police drew closer, the beams from their flashlights weaving and flickering.

"I know you're scared, but we can't waste this chance. The others will be waiting for us."

Desiree licked her lips, bobbing her head up and down. "All right. If they're really there, I'll do it."

She wrapped an arm around her sister's waist and together they ran along the edge of the cornfield. As Grace had predicted, the others were huddled beneath the scarecrow on the far end. But a quick head count told her only eight had made it. Grace rubbed a trembling hand across her brow. It came away wet. Her bones felt hollow, and she could barely hear over the ringing in her good ear.

"Where's Sariah?"

No answer, just eight sets of eyes begging for her leadership.

"Oh no! S-s—" Desiree's jaw tightened and spittle flew from her mouth. Her stammer always got worse under stress. "S-s—" She shook her head. "We need to go look for her."

The police lights grew distant, but somewhere nearby men shouted. It sounded like Uncle Redd and maybe Joseph Barlow. They'd be rounding up the children, herding them to the forest.

"There's no time! We have to go," Rulon said. He was Uncle G's sixth son, and her husband's half-brother. They had the same blond hair and pale eyes, but her husband was salt to Rulon's sugar.

Desiree spoke through her fingers. "We can't just leave her."

"It won't be for long," Rulon said. "Once we tell our story, they'll come back to rescue the rest."

"Maybe she's already waiting on the road?" Tabby said.

Joseph Barlow spotted them and strode across the cornfield in their direction. "What are you doing there? All of you, to the forest!"

"Hurry! Everyone buddy up," Grace said. "Stay with me."

"Hey!" Barlow called after them.

They rolled like thunder across the fields and gravel, linked hand to hand. Grace's legs trembled with exertion, threatening to collapse beneath her. But the others depended on her, so she pushed forward.

They made it to the main road with no sign of Sariah. Up close, the police looked terrifying. They moved in formation, wearing dark helmets and thick vests.

One by one she felt the others slow, paralyzed by the same fear that bloomed inside her own chest. This was their enemy in the flesh.

An officer stepped out of formation and pulled off his helmet. He had a shock of dark hair above a broad face. Their eyes met, and his arms opened as though in welcome.

She squeezed Desiree's hand and pulled Tabby close. The girls trembled against her side, thin as sparrows.

"Don't be afraid. God is with us."

She ran toward the officer's open arms, and the children followed.

ONE

The new goat had foot rot. Grace could smell it.

The local vet had brought the goat to her the day before. Some jackass in Arrowhead had bought her without any clue how to raise goats, and had kept her in a pen without fresh grass or even a rock to climb on. Hence the terrible state of her hooves. The poor thing had been abandoned at the clinic the previous week with a serious case of bloat, which was life-threatening if left untreated.

"C'mon." She tugged on the goat's lead. A good-sized young Saanen, she would make a nice addition to the flock if Grace could fix those hooves.

Her service dog, Bella, hauled herself upright and loped along beside them to the barn. The new goat wasn't producing yet, but the milking area was good for trimming hooves, as well.

"All right, dearie. Let's get those feet cleaned up."

The poor girl was understandably antsy, bucking and shaking. Bella drew closer, putting the pressure of her big body to use by leaning into the goat. It worked as well on the goat as it did on Grace.

She led the Saanen into the milking stall, closed the gate, and reached over to give Bella a grateful scratch behind the ears. Once the St. Bernard had received enough appreciation, she flopped onto a giant pillow and closed her eyes.

As Grace pulled on her gloves and sat on the bench beside the goat, she spoke in a gentle, conversational tone. She lifted the goat's left hind foot, gave it a wash, and used the orange-handled trimmers to slice away slivers of the hoof.

The rot didn't go too deep, thank goodness. She trimmed the side wall and levelled it so the goat would have an easier time walking, scrubbed it with udder wash and the Lavender Tea-Tree Power Combo, then moved on to the right rear foot, repeating the process. The front hooves were in better shape, requiring minimal trimming.

She released the goat back into the yard with a friendly pat on the rump. Buckeye bleated his way toward her, looking for treats, and allowed her to give him a quick pat on the head before bounding away.

The trees rustled with the promise of rain. She turned her face into the wind and breathed in the smell of lake and pine. She could also smell the metallic tang of an impending storm, and her brow creased with worry. Shelby was due in an hour. She hoped the storm held off until she'd arrived safely.

When another damp gust swept through the trees, several goats screeched their discontent. En masse, they moved toward her at the gate. They hated nothing more than getting wet.

"All right." She reached for her leads. "Let's get you guys inside."

Two at a time, she led them into the barn. Bella trotted contentedly at her side. A rumble of thunder set the goats bleating with renewed panic, and she led the last two into the warmth of the barn just as fat raindrops began to fall.

Bella whined and nudged Grace's hand with her nose, then issued a sharp bark. It was the signal of brewing trouble.

"It's all right, girl." She pulled the lead from Buckeye's neck and looped it over the hook by the door. "Let's head back to the house. Shelby will be here soon."

Bella whined again, nudged her in the ribs, and gave another sharp bark.

"No, I'm all right."

It was true. Her ear wasn't buzzing at all, and she felt clear-minded and present. Perhaps the storm was upsetting the dog. She patted Bella's massive flank. The dog's fur curled in the damp, white and auburn mixed with spots of black.

Bella came to an abrupt stop just outside the barn door, her body stiffening with alarm.

"What's up, girl?"

Bella's focus turned to the thick stand of cedar and hemlock near the cliff's edge. Her hackles rose and she issued a low, rumbling growl.

"Do you smell something?"

A lot of wildlife roamed the area: deer and raccoons and even the occasional caribou. But, given the dog's reaction, a grizzly bear was more likely. Grace cupped a hand over her eyes to keep out the rain and scanned the tree line. At a flash of movement to the left, Bella barked, deep and earth-shaking.

"Bella, quiet."

The dog was well trained. Her mouth snapped closed, but her body language didn't change.

"Let's get home."

The rain came down harder by the second. Despite her words, Grace paused to scan the trees again. Her instincts were nowhere near as fine-tuned as Bella's, but even her hackles were rising.

Someone's watching us.

Time to get inside. "Bella, heel."

Bella moved to her side. Heads bent against the rain, they slogged home. The side yard was already a boot-sucking swamp. Lightning flashed, immediately followed by the rumble of thunder. Through gaps in the trees, she saw Upper Arrow Lake madly frothing far below.

Hopefully Shelby had made it as far as Nakusp, where she could hole up until the storm passed.

She stomped up the porch stairs and Bella followed, giving a full-body shake that sprayed Grace with more water.

"Thanks, girl." She wiped rain from her eyes and froze.

A scrap of paper was pinned to the screen door. The corners curled inward with dampness, cocooning the message within.

At the sight of it, her head filled with cotton. The painless pressure set her eyes skittering from side to side. Her good ear buzzed. With fingers gone stiff, she plucked the note from the screen and unfurled the corners. Bella rumbled deep in her chest, in harmony with the storm.

The note was written in block letters with blood-red ink. It looked like a child's careful script, with the *R*s reversed. Red was a scary colour. It was forbidden.

SWEET SISTER WE MUST ATONE BY BLOOD BEFORE THE KINGDOM OF HEAVEN.

The wind gusted, stirring the hair from Grace's neck and tickling her exposed skin with icy fingers. She let go of the scrap of paper, watching as it fell to the plank flooring with a lifeless splat.

Bella issued a sharp bark.

"It's okay. We're okay."

She fumbled for the door handle. Her hands looked strange. They were too big, too old. She knew what that meant.

There was no time to close the door. In the kitchen, her boots slipped on the linoleum and she went down hard. A chair clattered and fell.

She moaned, closed her eyes. Bella whined and bumped her nose into Grace's side, pulling her from the fog and confusion.

She rolled over, climbed to her feet — why was she so heavy? — and stumbled to the living room. She needed to get to the phone.

Bella tried to push her toward the safety of the bedroom. She batted the dog away, picked up the phone's receiver, and hit the button to dial Shelby's cellphone.

"Grace?" Shelby's voice crackled on the other end of the line. "I'm almost there, but holy shit, this storm is exploding all around me."

"I'm sorry. They're coming."

The phone dropped from her hand and Shelby's voice grew tinny and distant. Thunder rumbled and Bella growled.

TWO

The storm gobbles the land behind me. It pummels the trees with sideways rain, and the lake far below rages like the belly of the beast.

I crouch beside the trunk of an enormous tree and pray for God's protection. A futile prayer. I am not yet worthy of Zion.

The dog barks from the porch. It is a behemoth of fur and teeth, which makes me nervous. It is so big and loud.

Headlights slice the yard, dance across the side of the barn, and come to a bouncing stop. It's the doctor. The psychologist. I recognize her Jeep.

The roof of the Jeep is dark and slick with rain. The headlights flick off, leaving the yard in shadow. As she opens the door, the interior light reveals a guitar case propped in the back seat. She wears a yellow raincoat. Not bright yellow, more like blighted sunshine. The hood covers her head and hides her face. She tucks her bag against her chest and runs for the porch. The doctor makes me nervous, too. But everything makes me nervous.

The dog wags a tail as thick as a tree branch, and the doctor pats its head. I imagine her asking about the dog's master. *Where is Grace? Is she all right?*

They go into the house, and the door closes. Soon they will be back. Soon they will begin to hunt.

It is time to run, but for a moment I stay still, yearning for the light and warmth. For safety.

The door slams open. The doctor steps onto the porch. Her dark curls swirl about her head like Medusa's snakes. She bends to retrieve the note I've left, unrolls it, reads it.

Her head snaps up, and she scans the trees at the edge of the property. Her gaze probes the darkness where I hide. She pulls up the hood of her coat and slaps a hand against her thigh, signalling for the dog.

I've stayed too long. Skittering backward along the sodden ground, I climb to my feet. I learned to be swift and sure-footed during the police raids — through the fence, across the field, into the forest. Protect the Family at all costs.

Now, I disappear into the belly of the storm. Lightning sizzles overhead and the angry crack of thunder shakes me to my bones. My feet slip on a sludge of wet leaves, and I stumble and fall. I land hard in the mud, and a thick tree root jabs into my ribs.

But the praying tree is just ahead. Sometimes God leaves messages in the little hole at the base of the tree, telling me what I need to do to earn my place in Zion. I need God's word today. I need to feel that connection, that hope.

I crawl toward the tree, through twigs and pine cones and mud and slugs. I dig into the dirt at the base of the tree, searching. There is no note.

Tipping my face toward the canopy of trees, I beg for God's forgiveness. What more can I do to earn my place in Zion? Raindrops hit my cheeks, as though even God is crying over the state of my soul.

THREE

S ince his wife's death, Beau's social life could be summed
up by the sparse call history on his personal cellphone.
The only number to show up with any frequency was
for Evergreen House, where Emily's mother was living out
the rest of her days. But this time when the phone rang, the
number on the display screen wasn't familiar.

"Yes?"

There was an electronic hiss of escaping breath. He pictured the phone pressed tightly against someone's mouth.

"Detective Brunelli?"

The list of people who would call him Detective on his
personal cellphone was extremely short. Beau's heart gave
a meaty *kathump* and he put the grocery basket down so
he could press the phone against his ear with both hands.

"Who is this?"

"Desiree DeRoche. I don't know if you remember
me —"

How could he ever forget? "Are you all right?"

"Is the line s-safe?" Her stammer brought back a flood of dead memories.

"Yes. What's going on?"

"S-something bad, I think. Can you come here? I know it's S-Sunday. I'm just really sc-scared." Her voice was tearful and shaky.

He was already moving, having abandoned his basket in the produce aisle. "Where are you?"

"Cordova and Jackson." She gave him the address.

"I'll be there in fifteen minutes."

The address Desiree had given was a three-level brick building spanning a whole block on the eastern edge of Vancouver's Downtown Eastside. In nearby Oppenheimer Park, drug addicts and transients sunned their sallow skin. A chill was in the air, and soon many would move on to shelters and doorways to survive the winter.

Desiree's apartment was on the third floor. On the way, Beau passed a clump of clothing and crumpled beer cans. The hallway carpet was stained with suspicious substances. A musty cat rubbed against his pants leg, the nubs of its spine clearly visible.

Desiree waited in the doorway. Her hair was short, in a style he believed they called a pixie cut. Her features were gaunt, her nose straight and red-tipped, her eyes puffy. If not for the eyes, he could have mistaken her for her sister Grace.

With a nod, she welcomed him inside. He closed the door behind him and looked around in surprise. The juxtaposition between the rest of the building and her apartment was startling.

The space was little more than a rectangle, with a living and dining room to the left and a wall of kitchen on the right. A hallway off the kitchen probably led to the bathroom and bedroom. The place was painted a sunny yellow with white trim. A loveseat and chair in matching blue denim sat in the living room, wedged around a block of pine serving as a coffee table. Freshly cut geraniums sat on the windowsill.

"Thank you for coming." Her voice broke on the last word. She took a breath and tried again. "I didn't know if your number would st-still be good. Or if you were st-still with the RCMP."

"I'm in the Serious Crime Section now."

"When I heard about your wife ..." Her left eyelid twitched. "I meant to s-send a card."

"What's going on, Desiree?"

"Is the case st-still active? I haven't heard anything for so long."

"There are no new leads."

Desiree nodded with easy acceptance, which gave him a flash of frustration. He wished she'd grown enough past her childhood to demand more of him, to question how hard the RCMP was working to find their bishop and bring him to justice. He wished she'd get angry for once.

Instead she bit a raw spot on her bottom lip. A trickle of blood ran down her chin, unnoticed. "I received a note in the mail."

A squeeze of adrenaline hit his veins. "From whom?"

She pulled a folded piece of newspaper out of the back pocket of her jeans. "I don't know."

He had her place it on the table, and used the tip of his pen to unfold it.

It was from the *Vancouver Sun*, dated the previous week. A man had jumped from the Lions Gate Bridge, a case that had barely crossed the periphery of his awareness. The deceased was listed as Stephen Bains, thirty-three years old, of no fixed address. He'd jumped during afternoon rush hour.

At the top of the article was a grainy photo of Stephen Bains. Above, written in red marker in shaky block letters, was:

REPENT
JDBY 4:219

"Repent. You received this in the mail?"

"Uh-huh."

"Any idea what *JDBY* and those numbers mean?'

"*Journal of Discourses*, Brigham Young. The text is 'When your brothers or s-sisters commit a s-sin that must be atoned by the shedding of their blood, will you love them well enough to shed their blood?'"

Desiree bit more deeply into her lip. Beau pulled a tissue out of his pocket and handed it to her. She dabbed at the blood, her eyes on the scrap of newspaper.

"Did you keep the envelope?"

"It's in my recycling bin, under the kitchen s-sink."

He grabbed a tissue from his pocket and lifted the envelope from the bin. Desiree's name and address had been scrawled in the same shaky block letters across the front of the envelope, the *R*s once again reversed. There was obviously no return address, but Canada Post could scan the barcode to see what part of the country it had been mailed from.

"I'm not sure how long it was in my mailbox. I don't check it very often, s-so I only s-saw it today."

"Do you recognize the handwriting?"

"No."

He scanned the article again, his eyes drawn to the red scrawl written across the top.

"You don't recognize him," she said.

The man's hair was a pale colour, either blond or light brown, and he had a long straight nose, high forehead, and a pointed chin with a visible cleft.

"It's Rulon." She burst into tears, as though saying his name cracked the dam holding her emotions in check. She dabbed her cheeks with the bloody tissue, catching the falling drops.

Rulon Smith. The boy had been named after former fundamentalist Mormon church prophet Rulon Jeffs, and had never been able to meet the high standard the name imposed upon him. He hadn't seen Rulon since he'd visited him in his foster home to tell him about his family's mass suicide. It was a particularly bad day.

"It's been a while. Are you sure it's him?"

"Of course I'm sure."

19

"May I keep this?"

Desiree dabbed at a fresh slew of tears. "What if s-someone convinced him to jump?"

Beau opened his mouth then closed it again, considering. It certainly wouldn't be the first time, but was there anyone left to do it? Brigham was a graveyard, its residents buried en masse behind the temple.

She seemed to read his thoughts. "You never found Uncle G."

His skin prickled with guilt. "No, we didn't."

Their bishop, Gideon Smith, had led the charge into fanatical martyrdom. They were under attack. Their kin in Bountiful were being persecuted. Their prophet, Warren Jeffs, had been arrested for arranging marriages between men and underage girls, and soon Smith would have stood trial on similar charges. Why? Because ten of their own children had escaped and co-operated with the police.

Brigham's Ten, set to blow the roof off the secrecy behind Brigham and the FLDS church. And Desiree DeRoche was one of them. At fourteen she'd escaped Brigham's shadow, only to be burned by the ensuing legal clusterfuck. Her bravery had earned her a spot in the foster care system and the hope of one day being forgotten. The fact that this seemed to be enough for her broke his heart.

She chewed on her lip again. "If Uncle G's st-still alive —"

Gideon Smith's body had not been found amongst the remains of Brigham's faithful. The RCMP had invested countless hours into tracking him down, and come up empty. But Beau would have laid a bet that the slimy son of a bitch was still out there somewhere.

"I'll look into it. Are you in contact with any of the others?"

"Just Grace, a little bit." Her cheeks flushed. "I'm st-still trying to make amends with her. I did a lot of bad st-stuff when I was on drugs."

"Where does she live?"

"Nakusp. She's got an acre of land in the hills outside town. She has goats, and she makes cheese and yogurt and s-soap. And she sells her pottery." Desiree spoke with a mixture of sisterly pride and bitterness.

"Sounds like she's doing well."

Her mouth tightened and fresh blood welled on her bottom lip. "Depends on your definition of *well*."

FOUR

"I'm glad you didn't call the cops," Grace said, easing into the deep armchair in her therapist's office without taking off her coat. The damp bit at her joints, and she couldn't get warm no matter what she did.

She'd developed Lyme disease as a child, and naturally it had gone untreated. Even now, with better medicine and nutritional supplements, she was subject to the occasional flare-up. The symptoms were similar to the body aches and fatigue of fibromyalgia, and usually brought about by periods of extreme stress.

Shelby leaned down to pat Bella's broad head. "How are you doing, girl?"

Bella rumbled a contented response and settled near the fireplace, exposing her belly to the heat produced by the flames.

Shelby took a piece of red licorice from the jar beside her on the table. The colour made Grace anxious.

"What do you remember?"

Grace shook her head. "There was something in the forest, a bear maybe. Bella didn't like it. I remember her barking."

She trailed off, stared at the merry crackle of the fire. She wished she could ease onto the floor next to Bella, curl up between the dog's heat and the fireplace, and sleep for about a month.

"Grace?"

She'd been working with Shelby three days a week for almost two years, since Dr. Goldberg had retired. The ink was barely dry on her diploma when Shelby took over his practice.

Although Grace had felt nervous entrusting her complicated mind to someone who looked like a teenager — a fact that wasn't helped by the sticks of licorice permanently jammed into the corner of her mouth — Shelby had proved easy to talk to. It didn't take long for her quirky charm to put Grace at ease, and Shelby's ability to sense when she needed a push and when she needed space had helped cement her trust in the new therapist.

She'd made more progress in the last two years than she had in all the years before that. The work was often painful and frequently terrifying, but as Shelby often said, there was only one way to go if she ever wanted to be whole, and that was through the thick of it.

"What happened before you called me?" Shelby said.

She turned her focus back to her therapist. The firelight danced across the tight coils of Shelby's hair, orange on black, and warmed the alabaster of her cheek. She could see her reflection in the dark of Shelby's eyes, and for a moment she didn't recognize herself.

Too old. And a girl.

"Can you check in? What was happening inside your body before you called me?"

Grace blinked, tried to focus. "Sorry."

"It's okay. Take your time."

"I was … scared. There was a fuzzy feeling in my head, like electricity, and that pressure that's not really a headache. My ear started ringing, and then my vision went dark."

"And what's the next thing you remember?"

"Seeing you. Bella licking my face."

"I read the note," Shelby said.

"Oh. What do you think?"

Shelby volleyed back. "What do *you* think?"

She chewed the skin beside her thumbnail. Shelby chewed her licorice.

"It could have been Harris."

Shelby said, "Then I'd like to talk to him."

Her gaze turned to the fireplace, drawn to the dancing flames. Bella was snoring, her hind legs twitching. She wondered what the dog was dreaming about.

Her eyes were heavy, her mind drowsy and slow. "We're really tired."

"Why don't you close your eyes, then?" Shelby's voice softened into the soothing tones she used to guide her into hypnosis.

She sank backward more quickly than usual. The sensation was similar to dunking her head in the bath. Her ears plugged, her pores opened to the warmth, and the world she was leaving became distant. The lamplight waited, and Mother's soft touch.

. . .

Mother Susan died on the temple steps, in hearing distance of her husband's Sunday sermon. Uncle G shouted about the sin that had been committed against their land of refuge, and against the children of God who lived within its borders. As his voice rose to preach the need for a blood atonement, his wife lay bleeding on the concrete landing outside the temple. The irony was lost on Grace until much later.

Just before Mother Susan collapsed, Grace stood waiting at the top of the stairs for her mother, who was slow and pendulous with her second pregnancy. Her feet had grown fat as sausages. She couldn't even stuff them into her own shoes anymore, so she was wearing Father's extra pair. They flopped around on her feet.

Grace was happy to wait for Mother. As far as she was concerned, Mother could take all day to get up those stairs. Although this one sounded more exciting than normal, Uncle G's sermons were so boring she usually had to fight her yawns.

Once the sermon was finished, they still had forever to go until it was time for cookies. The cookies and sweets were the best part of Sundays in Brigham. That and the free time that came after temple services were done. Most adults liked to nap on Sunday afternoons, which left the kids free to run amok — as long as they did so quietly.

It was pretty crowded at the top of the stairs, mainly with women and children. It was a good place to socialize and delay the necessary.

Clayne Johnson pulled away from his siblings to join her. He was a cousin, but they were all cousins in one way or another. It got very confusing, and eventually they all lost track.

Clayne's mother, Dinah, was her mother's younger sister. Or maybe half-sister. Dinah was Redd Johnson's second wife. She was nice and also quite pretty, so she was Redd's favourite. Or so Mother said.

Clayne was Dinah's second child, Boaz being the first, and she was pregnant with her third. She was almost as big as Mother and they were excited to have a second set of children so close in age, if the babies lived.

Clayne's hair was slicked down, but a chunk at the top had escaped to stick straight up in the air. His hair was white-blond and his skin and eyes were very pale. His fingernails were dirty and a smear of strawberry jam marked his neck.

"Keeping sweet, Gracey?"

She turned her good ear toward him. "Keeping quiet, Clayne?"

They made sure to keep several feet between them. The temple steps were no place to forget oneself.

The Johnsons lived next door and shared a large side yard. It was mainly dirt, with a woodshed on one side and some old play equipment at the back. At home, they were free to play together as much as they wanted. But they still had to be careful. Boys and girls weren't supposed to like each other until they got married.

Clayne was always getting into trouble. He couldn't keep still, his mouth often ran away from him, and he was generally infuriating. He was her best friend.

He ran a hand over his head, pressing the offending clump of hair back into place. It sprang back up a moment later. "Father says we've got to practise our drills again this afternoon."

This was bad news. They'd been running extra drills all week, and now they'd have to waste their Sunday on it, too. "All afternoon?"

"Until we can get to the forest more quickly." He leaned closer and spoke in a hush. "I think they're scared. I heard Mother saying that Dustyn must have called the police."

Dustyn Young had lost his priesthood over the winter. He'd cried and begged as they walked him to the gates protecting Brigham from the outside world. On the other side he'd fallen to his knees, begging to be let back in. His face had been covered in tears and mucus.

They'd heard him crying their whole way back up the road. At some point he started yelling he was going to tell on them. She'd had nightmares about it for days.

"Do you think he really went to the police?"

Clayne shrugged. "You heard him. Father says we should expect police raids like the ones they've had in Utah."

A chill rolled through her body at the thought, but excitement danced in Clayne's blue eyes. He liked danger, which she didn't understand one bit.

"God is testing us," she said.

"That's what my mother said." He nodded toward the stairs.

Dinah had met Mother halfway up, and they stood chatting with their bellies pressed close together. Mother Dinah wore a new dress. It was a pretty pale pink, and the lace ruffles at collar and hem were still clean and white. In comparison, Mother's faded grey dress looked like a sack.

Grace turned back to Clayne. "Maybe we can play Schoolhouse once the drills are done?"

"Or Attack of the Apostates?"

"We played that last week," she said. "Do you think —"

There was a chorus of gasps from those nearby, and suddenly everyone was moving. Caught in the crowd, she and Clayne surged forward. Everybody pushed against everyone else. A cacophony of voices rose skyward.

"Oh no!"

"What is it? What's happening?"

"God save her!"

"Step back! Give her some space!"

Inside the temple, Uncle G shouted about sin and hellfire.

Grace ended up with her face pressed into the folds of someone's skirt. She turned her head to the side and took in a gulp of air. Clayne was still next to her. His eyes were wide and his mouth hung open, revealing the gap where he'd lost a tooth. Crazily, her mind fixated on the dark hole in his mouth. The tooth had been there the previous evening. When had he lost it?

"Mother Susan!"

"Somebody help her!"

"Get Uncle G!"

Clayne grabbed Grace's hand. Tugged at her. "Come on."

With his help she yanked free. They squeezed through one tangle of skirts and then another. Moments later they stood in the empty space by Mother Susan's feet.

The feet were twitching.

Her skirt was made of thick blue cotton and embroidered with pretty white and yellow flowers. Above the skirt, her giant round belly shook with tremors. There was a miracle inside that belly, Uncle G had said. When she'd asked Mother what that meant, weren't all babies a miracle, Mother said it was extra miraculous because everyone had thought Mother Susan was too old to have more children.

One of Mother Susan's hands slapped against the concrete. Her head rolled to the side.

Then came the rush of blood, and everyone screamed. Inside the temple, Uncle G shouted about atonement. On the steps, blood pooled under Mother Susan's backside, a glistening red-black. It oozed toward where Grace and Clayne stood. They clutched hands, which at any other time would have netted them a correction. But in the chaos, no one noticed.

FIVE

Beau thought that if Judy Beers had a sense of humour, she kept it well hidden. But she was methodical in her investigations and unmoved by the ever-shifting political landscape, which made her his coroner of choice.

She was somewhere between the age of thirty-five and fifty-five — the startling combination of smooth skin and silver hair made it difficult to pin down. She spoke with the authority of long experience, moved with the straight-backed grace of a ballerina, and never cracked a smile.

"The body goes from roughly one hundred kilometres per hour to zero in a nanosecond." She pushed a pair of silver-rimmed reading glasses up the bridge of her nose and opened the file on the desk in front of her.

"If the body hits the water at some kind of horizontal angle, imagine a bellyflop, then death is almost instantaneous. But Mr. Bains wasn't quite so lucky."

"*That's* considered lucky?" Beau said.

"Indeed. Mr. Bains hit the water feet-first, which gives someone the optimal chance for survival, but in most cases just means they live long enough to suffer."

She scanned the page in front of her. "I haven't completed my report yet, you understand. I'm still waiting on toxicology, so anything I tell you today isn't official."

"Of course."

"When a body drops at that kind of speed and hits the water, it's like hitting concrete. There were multiple fractures in the lower extremities. Upon impact, inertia causes the internal organs to keep going in a downward trajectory. Consistent with this, Mr. Bains had lacerations to his aorta, liver, spleen, and heart. Essentially, his internal organs ripped free. His ribs, clavicle, and sternum were shattered, which sent shards of bone into his lungs and heart. His skull also had multiple fractures."

"Uh-huh. And you're saying he survived this?" Beau asked.

"Unfortunately for him, yes. He likely lived another three or four minutes after the impact. While there were some signs of vagal inhibition due to the temperature of the water, Mr. Bains had severe pulmonary edema and hypernatremia. Water gets drawn from the blood into the lung tissue to protect the lungs from the high salt content of the ocean water. Then, in an attempt to restore osmotic balance, salts from the lungs pass back into the bloodstream. The result is a slow death from asphyxia. The coast guard recovered the body thirty-two minutes after initial submersion. They had to pull crabs off his face." She slid a photo across the table.

Beau didn't look. "Are you ruling this a suicide?"

"That's likely," she said with a nod. "We have video from a traffic camera on the south side of the bridge that shows him walking alone toward midspan, which is where he jumped. Unfortunately, the camera covering the exact spot was broken. You can have a look at the video, if you'd like."

"Yes, please."

"Typically, the decedent's home would be searched, but Mr. Bains was homeless at the time of his death, and we haven't been able to track down any shelters where he might have had temporary accommodations. Considering the time of year, he might have been sleeping anywhere."

"Are you aware of his history?"

"Previously known as Rulon Smith, one of the ten children who escaped from that FLDS sect up in Bountiful —"

"Brigham."

"That was your case, wasn't it? Now I get why you're so interested." She looked back down at the file in front of her. "He went through a legal name change seven years ago, can't say that I blame him. Wasn't he the son of their prophet?"

"Their bishop. Their current prophet is Warren Jeffs."

"Still?"

He shrugged. "From what I hear, he's still running the FLDS from prison."

"What a creep," she said. "Do those folks up in Bountiful still follow him, too?"

"When Rulon Jeffs died and his son Warren took over, there was quite a dust-up within the sect. About half the

Bountiful folk split off — that's the Blackmore Group. The rest still follow Jeffs. And you may have seen it on the news recently, a couple of them are facing charges of bigamy."

"What a bunch of weirdos."

Beau shifted in his seat. "I don't like to paint them all with that brush."

Judy raised her eyebrows as though saying *whatever*. "I'll email you the traffic cam video."

"Thank you."

She stood, tucking her reading glasses into the pocket of her shirt. "Ten years ago the coroner's office made the recommendation that several bridges be retrofitted with higher barriers, to prevent suicides. Lions Gate was one of them."

"What happened?"

"I'm not quite sure. Something about wind load, I gather."

"It's a suspension bridge; maybe that's the problem?"

She shrugged. "The Second Narrows Bridge was done. But all they did with Lions Gate was install emergency phones. That's not a good enough deterrent. Obviously."

"I guess not. Thanks for your time, Judy. Will you let me know if anything new comes to light?"

"Certainly," she said.

The video was shaky, likely due to high winds on the bridge. The height of the camera angle made pedestrians appear stumped, their shadows stubby companions beside them. Cyclists passed with regularity, weaving around those who were walking or jogging.

There was a surprising amount of foot traffic on the east sidewalk, and a gridlock of cars stop-starting their way north, executives with expensive lives on the mountainous slopes of the North Shore. Whether it was skiing, hiking, tree-hugging, or ocean kayaking, suburban life in the midst of a rainforest offered a variety of ways to get in touch with nature. And to wear yoga pants.

The Lions Gate Bridge was built in the late 1930s, spanning the Burrard Inlet to connect North and West Vancouver to Stanley Park and Vancouver's downtown core. It comprised three narrow lanes, the centre lane switching direction depending on need. In recent years, as the Lower Mainland's population continued to boom, the bridge had become woefully insufficient.

He had to watch the video three times before he picked Stephen Bains, aka Rulon Smith, out of the crowd. He wore jeans and a dark-coloured hooded sweatshirt. Caught by the wind, his blond hair lifted and swirled around his head. His nose was sharp and his cheekbones were prominent. He was slender, his clothes baggy and flapping. He carried a small backpack strapped over his shoulders, and he walked with a noticeable hunch, bent against the wind.

He entered the frame from the south and left it thirty seconds later as he moved up the slope to the crest of the bridge. Beau replayed the video, this time taking note of the other pedestrians and nearby cyclists. Two cyclists passed going north, and then a trio going the other way. Four of the five weren't wearing helmets; apparently laws designed to protect fragile human skulls were just a suggestion.

Two joggers passed him going south, a man and woman who plugged along side by side. Rulon once again moved out of view. Almost two minutes passed. A burly man with a dark beard and an expensive-looking camera strapped around his neck ran from the south toward the centre of the bridge. Moments later a woman in a green jogging outfit followed, her hands raised. He imagined her shouting at Rulon not to jump.

The traffic ground to a halt, and several people exited their vehicles and moved swiftly out of view toward the centre of the bridge. They were all too late. At that point, Rulon's lungs would have been filling with sea water, his broken body on a swift descent into the icy depths of the Pacific.

He tried not to visualize what Judy Beers had so coolly described, her voice a careful monotone as she listed all manner of bodily horror. He tried not to picture the crabs.

Three minutes later, someone walked away from the crest of the bridge, moving swiftly south toward Stanley Park. He backed up the video and hit Play. When the person hit midframe he paused the video and squinted at the screen.

Beau couldn't even determine if it was a man or a woman. He or she wore a bulky grey winter coat extending beyond the knees, which did a nice job of masking the person's size and shape. Beneath it, the person wore dark pants and shoes.

That coat really bothered him. It was too bulky for Vancouver at any time of year, and definitely too much for early fall. The hood was pulled up so the face was lost in shadow.

He moved the video forward, frame by frame, and paused just before the figure stepped out of view. He couldn't be certain, but it looked like there was a backpack slung over one puffy grey shoulder. He put a call in to the coroner's office.

"Judy, it's Beau," he said when she answered. "Are there any other videos from that day?"

"Why? What do you see?"

"A figure in a grey winter coat with fur around the edge of the hood. Did you notice that?"

"Walking away from the scene, yes."

"See if you can track that person before and after the jump."

"Will do," she said, and he heard the scratch of pen against paper as she made a note.

"Did you speak to the man with the beard who ran toward the scene? He had a camera strapped around his neck."

"We did. No photos."

"Okay. Also, Rulon — Stephen — was wearing a small backpack. Was that recovered?"

"No," Judy said. "It's probably somewhere on the bottom of the ocean."

"Maybe not," Beau said. "That person in the grey coat looked like they were carrying a backpack. Might be worth a search of the bushes along the edge of the causeway, in case it was dumped."

"All right, I'm on it. Thanks, Detective."

SIX

Grace watched Shelby pull a piece of mangled licorice from her mouth, looking thoughtful. It was Friday, so they were at Grace's house.

"It might help to imagine a bunch of doors," Shelby said. "And each one leads to a different memory. All you have to do in order to explore that memory is find the right key to unlock the door."

"What kind of key?"

Shelby scrunched her eyebrows. "Well, I guess *you're* the key. Everything that's happened to you in your life, it's stored in these locked rooms inside your head. You can choose which doors to open *and* choose which ones you want to keep closed."

Grace stroked Bella's broad head as she gave the idea some thought. "So, I don't have to open doors I'm not ready for."

"Exactly."

"I like that. It makes me feel like I have more control."

"You do." Shelby sat forward. "You had so little control during your childhood. Everything they did to you, or taught you, or made you believe — you were at their mercy. You couldn't stop them, so all you could do was try to protect yourself. And you found some really creative ways to do that, I might add. You survived because of your own resilience."

"I guess."

"But when you chose to run toward the police? That's the moment you took control."

Grace shifted with discomfort. It was a memory fraught with guilt for those she'd left behind. Her family, her friends, and especially her youngest sister. Sariah was only eleven when she went to her grave, and Grace would never forgive herself for not saving her.

Shelby went on, waving the string of licorice in the air to punctuate her point. "And now you get to choose. You're completely in control. Everything they did to you is past. You steer the present. You choose your future. Do you want to be free of your past? Then open those doors and sift through the memories you find there. Take a look around, dust off the shelves, and decide which things to keep and which to throw away for good. Decluttering, in other words."

"Spring cleaning for my mind?"

"Without the farking garage sale."

Grace managed a smile. Shelby sat with her legs tucked under her and waited for her to speak.

"Have you ever done pottery?"

"No," Shelby replied.

"I could give you a lesson sometime. Working with clay can be so therapeutic."

"Can it?"

"It's cool and malleable. You can punch it and pull it and form it into any shape you like."

"I imagine there's satisfaction in creating something beautiful."

"And a lot of frustration when something doesn't work out as you'd planned. Especially when you can't figure out why your vase collapsed, or why something went into the kiln looking perfect and came out warped or blistered."

"Your mother taught you how to make pottery, didn't she?"

"That's right," Grace said. "She had a pottery shed behind our house, and Father built her a kiln. But she wouldn't make anything decorative. I once made a flowerpot and she told me to smash it."

"That must have been upsetting."

She shrugged. "A flowerpot was a waste of resources. The clay Father bought was intended to make things that were serviceable. Plates and bowls. But I wasn't always obedient. I couldn't bear to destroy it, so I hid it in the back of my closet."

Shelby pumped a fist in the air. "Good for you!"

"I wonder if it's still there."

"Have you given any more thought to going back there?"

Her ear began to buzz.

"I know it's frightening, but I'd be with you. I think it would be valuable to see the place again, maybe help you to unlock some of those extra-stubborn doors. And seeing the gravesite might help give you some closure."

Grace's voice became distant and high-pitched. "And now everything we make is a waste of resources. Pretty things that have no value."

"You're dissociating. Can you feel it?"

"Yes."

"Take some deep breaths," Shelby said. "Focus on me."

She tried, but it was too late. She sank backward, back through her mind and back through time, until her head found the groove of her pillow. It was made of feathers, and sometimes they poked through the linen pillowcase to jab her cheek.

Mother pulled the blankets over her shoulders, tucking them around her neck to keep the heat from escaping.

"Have you said your prayers, Gracey?"

"Yes, Mother."

There was a click as Mother turned off the lamp, shrouding her in darkness. Orange ghost-light danced across her eyelids. Mother's lips touched her forehead, soft and warm.

"God protect you," Mother said.

• • •

"That's good work, Grace," Mother said as she lifted the bowl to examine the underside.

"It's uneven around the edge," Grace said.

"It's still serviceable." Mother set the bowl aside and stroked the hair away from Grace's forehead. "I need to

40

start supper. You can go play once the goats have been milked."

Mother scooped Desiree from her cot and left the shed. After Desiree was born, Mother had handed over some of the household duties to Grace. It made her feel good to know Mother trusted her so much, and taking care of the goats was the chore she enjoyed the most. There were three of them, and Mother had let her choose their names.

As she left the goats' enclosure she saw Mother Dinah standing by the back fence, pulling clothes from the line. Tabitha was strapped to her chest, facing outward. She grabbed at dresses and shirts as Dinah pulled them off the line, clenching the fabric between chubby fists and chortling with laughter.

"Honestly!" Dinah said, freeing one of Redd's shirts from Tabby's grip.

"Do you want me to take her?" Grace asked.

Dinah spun to look at her. "Oh, hello, Grace. Would you? I'm getting nothing done."

Tabby was one of those babies who didn't like to be laid down or ignored. Mother Dinah looked exhausted. She pulled the wriggling baby free of the carrier and handed her over, taking a moment to tuck loose bits of hair back into the poof on top of her head before she resumed her work.

"Hello, Tabby," Grace said.

She bounced the baby up and down as best she could. At almost one year old, Tabby was getting heavy. But Grace was now six, and she was proud to be treated like a big girl. She and Clayne, who was only a month younger, had started taking lessons to prepare for their baptisms. This was very serious, but Clayne didn't seem to care. During class he wiggled in his seat and made jokes. His knuckles were permanently red from Uncle G's ruler.

Tabby curled her fingers into Grace's hair and pulled.

"Ouch!" She pried the strand out of Tabby's grip, which was surprisingly strong.

Tabby giggled and made another grab. She had a cap of blond hair that glowed in the late-day sun, and blue eyes just like Clayne's. She also had a dimple on her chin, like Uncle Redd.

As though her thought had summoned him, Uncle Redd came through the gate from the road and called out a greeting. Father was on the road not far behind him.

Tabby squealed, wiggling so much Grace almost lost her grip. Uncle Redd descended and lifted the baby into his arms, swinging her around until she shrieked with delight.

Free of the baby, Grace ran to meet her father at the gate. As though she weighed nothing, he scooped her into his arms and planted a kiss on the crown of her head.

"What's new, Gracey? Have you been keeping sweet?" He dug a finger into her side and wiggled it against her rib cage.

She giggled and squirmed. "Of course!"

"That's my girl. Let's see what Mother has for supper." He carried her up the steps and through the front door before dropping her to her feet so they could remove their shoes.

Mother emerged from the kitchen, wiping her hands on her apron. "How was it today?"

Father dropped his second shoe on the mat by the door. "Well enough. We got the roof on, just in time for the rain that's coming in tonight."

He moved toward her, wrapped burly arms around her waist, and lifted her from her feet. Mother laughed and planted a kiss on his forehead.

"You missed," he said. "Try again."

She swatted at him. "There will be no more of that until after you've cleaned up and had some supper. Now put me down."

He did as she'd asked, but said with mock sternness, "Are you disobeying your priesthood head?"

She smiled at him and rolled her eyes, but Grace knew that in other families this issue was much more serious. She'd witnessed enough in her six years to know that life in her family was much easier than with most others.

All she had to do was look at the Johnsons next door. Redd was as jolly as Father, but Mother Flora was a mean old buzzard with eyes that saw everything and hands that liked to hurt. As the first wife she had primacy over the rest of the family, including Mother Dinah and her children. She beat Boaz and Clayne for the slightest transgression, and Dinah couldn't do anything to stop her.

Flora had four living children, and they all had relation diseases. This was something that happened when cousins married. Three had breathing problems that made them turn blue, and the other had a cleft lip and palate. The ones who hadn't lived were buried in the baby cemetery behind the temple. There were a lot of tiny tombstones back there.

By the time Father was washed for supper, Desiree was scooping spoonfuls of cottage pie into her mouth and smearing it across her face and into her hair.

Father said grace and Mother served them each a wedge of pie.

Grace was chewing her first mouthful when someone knocked on the door. Mother raised her eyebrows, and Father scraped his chair back from the table and placed his napkin beside his plate.

"Might be Joseph with news on the tractor."

But it wasn't Joseph Barlow. It was Boydell, Uncle G's son with his third wife. Just the sight of him in the doorway was enough to put her off her supper. He was the meanest child in Brigham, and he got away with it because he had the face of an angel and his last name was Smith.

"Boydell," Father said. "Is everything all right?"

Boydell's chest puffed. He was clearly proud to have been charged with such an important duty. "Father requests that you attend him straight away."

"Oh? Just me, or the whole family?"

"Everyone."

Mother's fork dropped to her plate with a clatter, and Father turned to look at her. They held a frantic conversation with their eyes.

Grace had no clue what was happening. "Why?"

Boydell sneered in her direction, but didn't answer.

"Well." Father turned back to Boydell, trying to smile. He didn't do a good job of it. "Please tell the bishop we'll be right there."

Mother's face paled, and her lips pulled tight against her teeth. Even Desiree seemed to sense something was wrong. She paused with her spoon halfway to her mouth, her eyes wide.

After Boydell left, there was a breathless moment of silence.

Then Father said, "I suppose supper will wait."

"Patrick."

The way Mother's voice shook made Grace's heart squeeze into her throat. What in the world was happening?

"It's all right, Margaret." He stuffed his feet into his shoes. "Perhaps it's good news. Maybe Gideon has had a revelation."

Grace's heart dropped from her throat directly into the pit of her stomach. A revelation by the bishop could only mean one thing.

"You're going to get a second wife?" she asked.

"Perhaps." Father's cheeks were red. She wasn't sure if he was nervous or excited. "Wouldn't that be wonderful, Gracey?"

Mother's smile looked strange, but she wiped her napkin across her eyes and stood to follow him.

SEVEN

When Beau lifted the phone to his ear Judy Beers spoke without preamble.

"Good call on the backpack. It was dumped in the trees along the Stanley Park Causeway. It's being tested for prints and DNA as we speak."

"What was in it?"

"Clothing. Two shirts, some socks, and a pair of jeans. The Book of Mormon. And a note."

The Book of Mormon. That was interesting. "What kind of note?"

"A suicide note, it looks like. I'm sending you a photo. I'd like your opinion. I know you've become an expert on suicide notes …" Her voice trailed off.

Since Emily died. She didn't need to say it.

"All right. Thanks, Judy."

"Thank *you*," she said, and hung up without saying goodbye.

The photo waited in Beau's inbox. He clicked to open the image and studied it for several minutes in silence.

I cannot bear my guilt any longer.

I know I will never reach heaven, after everything
I did to bring shame to the Family. I hope my
death is a step toward making amends. This is
the only way. I've strayed from their teachings,
and I am ashamed and so very sorry.

Beau lifted the phone and dialed Desiree. When she answered, he asked if she'd be around later. They agreed that he would stop by on his way home.

He turned to his computer and searched for the rest of Brigham's Ten. He found addresses for several, including Grace DeRoche. Valor Johnson and Eliza Barlow were both dead. Valor had died three years before in Calgary, the cause of death listed as accidental carbon monoxide poisoning. Eliza Barlow had died the previous year in Abbotsford, by suicide.

Beau sent out requests for file copies to the RCMP detachments in Calgary and Abbotsford, and called for somebody to pull the Brigham files from storage. Then he went in search of his boss, Doug Delaney.

Doug was approaching retirement with all the excitement of one awaiting a colonoscopy. At first he'd lived in a state of denial and delay, but as his sixty-fifth birthday approached, he moved closer to grim acceptance. He was preparing for the inevitable by shouting orders, turning up the heat on cold investigations, and making jokes with large doses of gallows humour.

In Beau's eight years in the Serious Crime Section, he couldn't recall a time his boss's office door had been closed.

He knocked on the door frame. "Got a minute?"

Doug was bent over the desk, his head inches from the surface. This put the shiny crown of his head on full display. Sprouts of grey hair grew wild around his ears. He waved fingers as thick as sausages in Beau's direction, welcoming him into the inner sanctum.

He sat down and waited while Doug finished scribbling some notes. When his boss looked up, Beau grimaced.

"Jesus, Doug. Did Janice finally hit you with the pepper spray?"

Doug's wife of forty-odd years was looking forward to his retirement even less than he was.

"Grandkids stayed the weekend. Somehow we all ended up with pink eye."

"Did they fart on your pillows?"

"Who knows? Kids are monsters. Now we're on these antibiotic eye drops that burn like Satan's anus."

"Are you contagious?"

"I'll do my best not to rub my eyeballs on you."

"I appreciate it."

"Tell me you're not here on Betsy's orders."

Doug's office assistant was planning the largest and most lavish retirement party the RCMP had ever seen. Beau had been avoiding her in recent weeks, hoping not to get wrangled into picking table linens or lugging in boxes of champagne glasses from her car.

"Rulon Smith jumped off the Lions Gate Bridge last week."

Doug leaned back in his chair and steepled his hands over the slight rounding of his belly. "Go on."

When the Brigham case broke, Beau had been working on the Integrated Child Exploitation Team, and Doug had been his liaison in the SCS. After the Family's mass suicide, he'd moved over to Doug's team.

Sliding the plastic-wrapped newspaper article across the desk, he said, "Desiree DeRoche received this in her mailbox."

Doug bent low to examine it. "Damned eyes, everything's a blur. That's Rulon?"

"Yessir. He changed his name to Stephen Bains about seven years ago. Judy Beers is handling the coroner's investigation."

"She's a good one."

"She's waiting on toxicology, but is leaning toward ruling it a suicide."

"And you disagree?"

"It's not sitting well with me. First, there's this showing up in Desiree's mailbox. She says those numbers and the *JDBY* reference a quote from Brigham Young about sinners needing to atone by blood."

"So you're thinking it's from someone who knows their doctrine."

"I'm waiting to hear back from Canada Post on the origin of the acceptance scan. Traffic camera on the bridge caught someone in a puffy winter coat leaving the scene, carrying a bag that looked like the one Rulon carried onto the bridge. Judy's team found it in the bushes along the Stanley Park Causeway. Inside was the Book of Mormon, and this note." He opened the photo on his phone and slid it across the desk.

Doug squinted to read it. After a moment, he sat back and said, "All right. Go on."

"I'd lay a bet Rulon didn't write that note." Before Doug could say anything about Beau's obsession with proving Emily was murdered, he added, "There are several markers that indicate it's a fake."

"It's not signed," Doug said.

"Yep. And there's no neutral content, no instructions to those he's leaving behind. The apologetic tone is way too elaborate, and it's directed toward his dead family rather than those who might be hurt by his death."

"Maybe he didn't think anyone would mourn his loss?"

"Maybe." Beau shifted forward in his seat. "But I remember Rulon. He was angry, furious even. He felt betrayed by his father, by everyone in Brigham. You know how these lost boys of the FLDS are treated?"

"Refresh my memory."

"Girls are raised to be subservient plural wives. Seems like a good deal for the boys, right? They get multiple sexual partners who've been raised to be their servants. But you end up with too many males."

"Yeah, I can see that."

"As the son of their bishop, Rulon was raised to believe he was almost like royalty within the sect. But as he got closer to marriageable age, any errors he made or anything that showed less than perfect obedience cut his chances of getting a wife.

The elders kept the young and pretty wives for themselves, and the young men had little chance of getting even one wife, let alone the three they needed for their spot in heaven. So they'd become restless and angry, which would eventually lead to them being excommunicated for disobedience."

"Right. So, you doubt Rulon had a change of heart?" Doug said.

"The brainwashing runs deep, so I wouldn't discount it entirely. But my instinct says no. He was a very angry young man. And he had every right to be."

He leaned over and tapped his phone, which had gone dark. The note once again lit the screen. "Another thing. The note mentions the Family once by name, and references them twice more. This third-party mention is often a subconscious confession."

"You're saying someone from the Family killed him?"

"Gideon Smith's body was never found. I bet that evil bastard is still out there."

"I see your point. We'll reissue the BOLO so officers know to keep their eyes open."

"Thanks. And who knows, maybe there were others who didn't drink the Kool-Aid, so to speak. It's not like we had census information to use when we counted the bodies. I think that's worth looking into."

"Not much to go on, there."

"If we start shaking trees, maybe we'll knock something loose. I've been checking into the rest of Brigham's Ten. I've found a few of them scattered around BC and Alberta. Valor Johnson and Eliza Barlow are dead."

"Cause?"

"Eliza's is suicide. Valor's is accidental carbon monoxide poisoning. I've put in requests for their files."

Doug sat back in his chair and spun toward the window. Beyond was a grey slab of parking lot and the thousands of trees that made up Green Timbers Urban Forest.

Beau closed his mouth and waited.

"All right. Dig around."

He stood, slid his phone into his pocket, and picked up the plastic-wrapped newspaper.

"I'd love to end my career by hauling in that son of a bitch," Doug said.

"Amen," Beau said, although prison was far too light a punishment for the likes of Gideon Smith.

The alarm on Doug's phone jingled. He tapped the screen and grabbed the bottle of eye drops sitting on the corner of the desk. "Keep me posted."

Tipping back his head, he pushed his eyelid up with his fingers and squeezed the bottle. He hissed and smacked a hand against the desk. "*Goddamn* that burns."

Beau winced in sympathy and eased out before Doug could do the other eye.

A message waited when he returned to his desk. Desiree's newspaper article had been mailed from Cranbrook. Well, *that* got his heart pumping. Cranbrook was just a hop away from Fort Steele, and Fort Steele was the nearest town to the now dead-and-abandoned town of Brigham.

The sun was low in the sky when Beau left RCMP Headquarters. Due to an accident on the East-West

Connector, it took over an hour to make it to Desiree's apartment. Slow traffic allowed him plenty of time to note the lack of high barriers as he crossed the Alex Fraser Bridge. He kept a nervous eye on pedestrians in case one made a sudden move toward the railing and the Fraser River far below.

Desiree waited by the door. A stewpot bubbled on the stove, creating a heavenly smelling steam of meat, tomatoes, garlic, and onions. Beau's mouth filled with saliva. He couldn't remember the last time he'd had a home-cooked meal, but begging seemed unprofessional.

The bite mark on her lower lip had scabbed over, but her eyes were purple-rimmed with grief and exhaustion. She closed the door and moved into the living room, her slippers making a scuffing noise against the plank floor, and he followed.

"It was him?" she asked. "Rulon?"

"I'm sorry, Desiree."

She scratched at her forearms. She wore a long-sleeved shirt, and he wondered if it was hiding track marks. "I knew it."

"When did you last see him?"

She eased onto the denim couch and curled her legs under her. "About three months ago, I guess."

"Fill me in?" He sat in the adjoining chair and leaned forward, propping his elbows on his knees.

"He was angry. He was always s-so angry. He felt like he'd been cheated out of his rightful sp-spot within the Family."

"I remember."

"I don't think he ever got over it. We connected about four years ago, just by chance. I was in Gastown, heading home from work — I'm a s-server at The Flying Pig — and he was panhandling."

She sighed, rubbed her eyes. "I didn't recognize him until he called out. I invited him to come home with me. He s-slept on my couch for a few nights, but he was down the rabbit hole, and I just couldn't handle it. I'm in recovery myself, and I could feel the temptation building in me." She scratched at her arms again.

"S-so I asked him to leave." She pulled her sweater tight across her body, wrapping it around her guilt. "Maybe if I hadn't kicked him out …"

"You're not responsible for his actions, Desiree."

"But who else knows what he's been through? Maybe I could have gotten him s-some help. The last time I s-saw him, he was waiting outside my building. It was raining, and he didn't have an umbrella. He was s-soaked. He s-said he'd come to apologize. Make amends."

"He was in AA?"

She shrugged. "He s-seemed s-sober. I asked him if he wanted to come upstairs, get out of the rain. But he s-said that it was okay, he just wanted to talk to me for a minute. He apologized for taking advantage of me" — she gave him a nervous look — "I just mean when he st-stayed on my couch. I never did anything with him."

"I don't care if you did. You're free to have a relationship with whomever you choose."

She gave a short, bitter laugh. "That's hard to grasp." Tugging on her hair, she said, "Do you know how much anxiety I felt when I got my hair cut for the first time?"

"No."

"I was *terrified*. Women aren't s-supposed to cut their hair, *ever*. We're s-supposed to let it grow s-so we can wash our husband's feet with it in heaven. I went there at least twenty times before I had the guts to s-sit down in the chair. When she made the first cut, I sc-screamed. The poor hairdresser jumped out of her sk-skin. She thought she'd nicked my ear or s-something."

She ran her fingers through her tightly shorn locks. "I cried the whole time she was cutting it. Afterward, I had nightmares for weeks that I was going to hell. All because I cut my hair! That's what they do to you — they mess with your head s-so badly you can't even get a haircut like a normal person. And that's why I should have helped Rulon more than I did. Because I know … I *knew* what he was going through." So quietly he almost missed it, Desiree said, "S-sometimes I wish we'd never escaped. Then everyone would still be alive."

Beau sighed, scrubbed a hand over his face. "So, he apologized?"

She let out a shaky breath. "Yeah. He s-said he was s-sober for the first time in years. That he was in therapy, working on his anger. But I could s-see it festering in him. His jaw got tight when he mentioned the Family. I could s-see he s-still had a lot of work to do. Well, we all do. I'm s-sorry, I should have offered before. Would you like s-something to drink?"

"I'm fine. Go on."

"He wanted to find s-some of the lost boys, like Boaz and Clayne, to make amends."

"Those are the Johnson brothers?"

"Right. Boaz lost his priesthood first, and then Clayne …" She rubbed her hands together as though to warm them. "It happened just before the millennium, when all the end of days st-stuff was happening. Lots of boys were cast out around then. The st-story was Clayne lost his priesthood, but I'm not s-so s-sure. One day he was gone, and we weren't s-supposed to talk about it. Grace and Clayne were really close, and I know it has worried her ever s-since. It's horrible not knowing."

"Why did Rulon want to make amends with them?"

She shrugged. "He didn't say, but I think he felt responsible for what happened to Clayne."

"Do you know if he ever found them?"

She dabbed at her eyes with the soggy tissue. "I never heard from him again after that day."

"Have you ever heard from Boaz or Clayne?"

She shook her head. "Grace has looked for them over the years, but I don't think she ever found them."

Beau made a mental note to have a look for both the Johnson boys. "What else did Rulon say?"

"He asked what I thought might have happened in Brigham after we left. I guess he was trying to process why they did what they did." She covered her eyes with the tissue, took deep breaths. He waited, wishing he could reach over and offer her comfort, but knowing his touch would do the exact opposite.

"It wasn't your fault, you know," he said.

"We betrayed them. We went to the enemy —"

"The police, you mean."

She nodded. "They're all gone, my *whole* family is gone, because we followed Grace that night."

He pulled a fresh tissue from the box on the side table and handed it to her. "Do you think Rulon also felt guilty about what happened to the Family?"

She shrugged.

"All right. Have you been in touch with any of the others?"

"I've left a couple messages for Grace recently, but she's not very good about returning my calls."

"What about Eliza or Valor?" He was hoping she already knew they were dead so he wouldn't have to tell her, but no such luck.

She shook her head. "Not for years."

He took a breath and leaned forward. "Desiree, I'm afraid I have some bad news."

EIGHT

like the way the mud in the goat yard squishes between my toes. It oozes, cold and sloppy, around my feet. And when there's been rain, I sink right up to my ankles.

I also like the goats. They have big round bellies, and they are always nudging to get treats. Their mouths are warm and soft, tickling my hands. I feel safe around them. I don't need to play pretend. They never act like I'm strange.

The goats climb the rock, knock heads when they get mad, and go about their busy goat business, ignoring the dog's racket. The dog has been barking so long its voice is getting hoarse. But it is locked inside the house, so that is okay.

I squish mud between my toes and study the forest on the far side of the yard. Someone is out there. On my way to the praying tree the day before, I'd found a campsite. Tent and firepit and propane stove. There'd been no one around, but it all looked freshly used.

Someone is watching me. They know I've been bad.

I am scared to be in the forest now. But how can I receive the word of God if I can't get to the praying tree? I am trying so hard, doing everything that is asked of me. But still, it never seems to be enough to earn my spot in Zion.

The goats bleat, startling me out of my contemplation. The sun is almost at the treetops. I've stayed too long. It's time to go.

NINE

J ack Fletcher jumped out of his car and gave Grace a wave. "Morning!"

Jack was her distributor. A man of all trades, he took her goat milk products to local retailers and grocers, worked a side job as a mechanic, and also worked full-time as a welder. On top of that, he was a talented artist. He worked in oils and acrylics, and over the years he'd given her several lessons in colour composition in exchange for her knowledge of clay. She'd connected with him more than a decade ago at an art show, and in the years since he'd become the closest thing she had to a friend.

"Oh, Jack, I'm sorry! I'm running a bit behind. Let me go grab the stuff." Grace normally had the week's supplies organized and ready to go before he arrived, but time had gotten away from her this morning.

"I'll help."

"Thanks. There's an extra batch of lavender soap for the Kootenay Co-op this week. And Esther ordered another flat of the mixed yogurt."

They worked side by side, loading milk products into transport coolers and bars of soap into hard-sided boxes. As they loaded everything into his car, he told her about his latest series of paintings, about his desire to take some distance-ed courses over the summer, and about his plans to restore the 1965 Mustang he'd just bought at auction.

Jack was one of the few people Grace felt comfortable being around. He was easygoing and earnest, and he worked harder than just about anybody she knew. Plus, he never stopped talking — which meant she never had to start. It was a relief.

He slammed the back gate and moved over to her Subaru. "How's Baby Blue running?" He gave the side of her car an affectionate pat. A few years before he'd bought a newer model Subaru Forester in a darker shade of blue, and sold her his old one.

"Just great since you fixed that hiccup in the transmission."

"Time to change over to the winter tires," he said.

"Oh gosh, already?"

"Better early than late. I can come over Thursday evening, if that works for you?"

"That's perfect, thanks."

He had faded blue eyes and narrow features that reminded her of a fox, but when he smiled his face transformed into something warm and welcoming. Sometimes his gaze rested on her for too long, and it made her uncomfortable. This time it only lasted a few seconds before he tipped his fingers in a little salute and climbed into his car.

She turned her head so she could listen to the crunch of gravel under his tires as he made his way down the road. When silence descended, she realized the phone was ringing inside the house. It was probably Desiree, calling to lay some more guilt on her. She'd let it go to voice mail.

. . .

The DeRoche family settled into the Smiths' living room, waiting for Uncle G to finish his supper. Desiree was tired and grumpy, and Mother bounced her on her lap to no avail.

"Let me try," Father said.

She handed him the baby and he walked from the living room to the hallway and back again. Desiree's yowls eventually quieted to an occasional snuffle.

The Smith family was taking their meal in the dining room. They could hear the clatter of dishes and the scraping of chairs and the excited chatter of Uncle G's many wives and children.

Grace's stomach rumbled, and she wondered why they'd been called away from their own supper to sit and wait while Uncle G finished his. But eventually Uncle G's second wife — well, his first wife now that Mother Susan was dead — entered the living room to usher them up the stairs to the study.

"Grace can wait here," Mother Brinda said.

She didn't want to wait in the living room by herself. She wanted to be with her family to hear whatever news Uncle G shared. But she was a good priesthood girl, so she smiled the sweetest smile she could manage and sat back down on the couch. Father carried a sleeping Desiree up the stairs and Mother followed behind him, walking like there was a yardstick shoved down the back of her dress. Seeing her mother so tense made Grace's stomach quiver with nerves.

Footsteps thundered as the Smith family tromped down to the basement. They had a large room down there where they prayed and studied scripture, but she'd never seen it herself. Until this moment, she'd never even set foot inside the Smith house.

The living room was enormous, with four couches and many chairs. A giant fireplace sat at one end, with a framed painting of the prophet, Uncle Rulon, hanging above the mantle. He stared down at her with piercing eyes.

Because he lived on a big compound in Salt Lake City and didn't travel much, she'd never met him in person. But his son, Uncle Warren, had visited Brigham the previous year. Uncle G's sermons had seemed boring until she heard Uncle Warren's. But that wasn't a sweet thought, so she squelched it.

The house had grown quiet. No sounds came from upstairs in the study, but she could hear murmurs and the occasional exclamation coming from the basement.

She picked at the lace on her sleeve, wishing it hadn't turned so yellow. She fluffed the shoulders of her dress, making sure they were round and puffy. She tugged at her hair, trying to lift up the front as high as possible. The higher the hair, the closer she was to God.

Pulling her braid over her shoulder, she admired the way the lamplight made it shimmer with gold. Some hairs had come loose from the braid, though. She pulled out the ribbon and redid the braid, her fingers moving with slow, meticulous care.

"Doesn't matter how tidy you make yourself, you're still ugly."

She looked up. Boydell stood in the hallway. His smirk made her want to hit him. But of course she couldn't.

He moved into the living room and sat on the couch across from her. He leaned forward, studying her face, and then nodded as though confirming something for himself. "You're even uglier than your mother. At least both her eyes are the same colour."

She knew she shouldn't say anything in return. In fact, she couldn't think of a thing to say, so she lowered her head and fixed her gaze on her lap.

"Hey, you're not totally deaf, are you? Did you hear what I said?"

"Yes."

"Are you too stupid to answer, then?"

She shook her head.

He snorted. "You're as stupid as you are ugly. Well, at least now your father will have someone pretty to come home to."

She looked up, wondering what he was talking about.

"I doubt he'll want to have much to do with you or your mother once Rebecca's there to serve him properly."

"Rebecca?" There were two girls named Rebecca in Brigham. One was only three years old, but the other was fourteen or fifteen. Young, but not too young to marry. Her mind raced, processing what he was saying.

"You really are stupid, aren't you?"

She barely heard him. She thought about Rebecca Taylor, who led Sunday school and was one of the few people in Brigham with brown hair. It was light brown, but still. And she *was* pretty. She was one of the prettiest girls in all of Brigham. Was she really going to be Father's second wife?

"Hey," Boydell said. "*Hey.*" He snapped his fingers right in front of her nose, and she jumped. "I want a drink."

"What?"

"Lemonade. I want some lemonade."

She blinked at him. She couldn't process what he was saying because her mind was still racing a mile a minute. Her heart fluttered at a mad pace inside her rib cage.

"I. Want. Some. Lemonade."

Oh. She pushed to her feet. Her legs shook so badly she wasn't sure they would support her.

"What are you supposed to say to me?"

"I am-am here to do your will."

"Then do it so I can stop looking at your ugly face."

She moved toward the kitchen. It was huge. Staring at the massive row of cabinets, she wondered where she might find a glass. After opening one door after another with no luck, she figured they were probably in one of the top cabinets where she couldn't reach. She looked around for a stepstool but didn't see one.

Grabbing a chair from the dining room, she dragged it back into the kitchen. It wobbled when she stepped on it. One of the legs was shorter than the others. With care, she climbed onto the counter, hoping none of Uncle G's wives would come in and see her rubbing her dirty socks across the pristine white surface.

The counter was cold and slippery and so shiny she could see her reflection in it. She'd never seen anything like it before. The one in her house was a slab of stained and knife-scarred wood. Sliding along, she opened one cabinet at a time. She eased past the sink and a stack of dishes that were drying in a rack, and found the glasses in the last cupboard before the double-sized fridge. Now all she had to do was carry it back to the chair so she could climb down.

"What in the world are you doing?"

She jumped, and her feet slipped. One foot knocked the rack of dishes, and it tumbled into the sink with an uproarious crash of breaking ceramic. She flew backward and hit the floor, landing hard on her back. Suddenly she couldn't breathe.

Rulon bent over her, his fair brows creased with concern. "Are you okay?"

She couldn't answer. She couldn't get air into her lungs.

"Mother! Grace is hurt!"

A stampede rumbled up the stairs, but Boydell was closer so he got there first.

"What's going on?" he asked.

Rulon was younger than Boydell, but almost as tall and broader in the shoulders. When he spoke to his brother, it was clear he didn't have the same fear of him that Grace had. "I'm guessing this is somehow your fault?"

"She offered to get me a glass of lemonade," Boydell said.

Rulon rolled his eyes. "Since when do we have lemonade?"

Grace still couldn't breathe, so she was pretty sure she was going to die. And if she died without Father to bring her to heaven, she would end up in the lowest pits of hell forever and ever. All because of Boydell. In that moment, her dislike for him grew to utter hatred. How dare he steal her chance at Zion?

She finally managed to suck in a wheezing breath.

"See, she's okay," Boydell said.

The Smith family piled into the kitchen and crowded around her. Mother Brinda bent over and asked her what had happened, but Grace was completely incapable of answering.

Rulon stepped forward. "Boydell pushed her, and it knocked the dishes into the sink."

Boydell's mouth fell open. Before he could defend himself, Mother Brinda grabbed him by the ear and dragged him from the room.

The slap of the paddle against Boydell's backside was the most satisfying sound Grace had ever heard.

TEN

The Brigham files sat on the floor of Beau's office when he returned from lunch. Ten neatly stacked boxes labelled with the contents and the date they were sealed, triple-taped to prevent the influx of bugs and dust. He spent the next hour unsealing them and refreshing his memory on the case that had once been his obsession.

Over the years, many cases had been made or broken based on how officers stored their field notes. Missing or destroyed notebooks often led to dropped charges, and sometimes a retired officer produced key evidence in a cold case that made all the difference.

For that reason, he kept all his old field notes in a fireproof safe in his home office. He'd pulled the corresponding notebooks the previous night to reference as he went, fleshing out the details and giving him glimpses of the Beau that was: hair still dark, jawline still taut, heart still hopeful.

He'd had a horrible sinus infection during several of the interviews and the pain behind his eyes had made it nearly impossible to keep them open.

Emily lost her third late-term pregnancy on the same day charges were stayed against Gideon Smith for the second time. Beau had left the courtroom and driven straight to the hospital. He remembered the feel of his son's body in the cup of his hand, how the skin was soft and translucent, how the lashless eyelids covered eyes that would never open. He'd left his wife there, sedated against her grief, and gone home to an empty house and a nursery that would never see a child. He'd closed the door on that little room at the top of the stairs, and they'd never opened it again.

He swiped an arm across his eyes and took several deep breaths, stuffing the memories back into the space around his heart. Emily was ten years in her grave, and he could still close his eyes and feel the silk of her hair beneath his fingers or hear her raw, throaty laugh. His recollection was so clear it was as if she might have died just the day before.

At night he dreamed she walked with him through showers of cherry blossoms. Spring in Vancouver, her favourite time of year. Sometimes she held a baby in her arms, sometimes not. But when he asked her questions — *Should I keep searching for answers? Did you really do it? If you moved on so easily, then why can't I?* — all she gave him in reply was a smile.

He should have sold the house. It was far too large for a widowed cop. Instead, he'd moved a bed into the den beside the kitchen and let the top floor become a graveyard of dusty memories.

"Beau?" Betsy knocked on the frame of his office door.

He'd been sitting cross-legged on the floor in front of his desk for far too long. His right side from butt to foot had gone numb and tingly. He was risking another bout of sciatica. He shifted his weight onto the other butt cheek.

"Hey, Betsy. What can I do for you?"

"I haven't received your RSVP yet. You're coming to the retirement party, right?"

"Oh. Yeah, I'll be there."

"Good, because I've put you down to give a toast. Five minutes or less, okay?"

"I'm not much of a public speaker."

"You'll do fine." Betsy waved her hand and disappeared before he could argue.

He rolled over onto his hands and knees, moving slowly to bring feeling back to his lower extremities and hoping no one showed up in his office doorway while he was down on all fours. Several detectives would snap photos first and ask questions later.

Eventually, he made it to his feet. He took a walk down the hall to grab a cup of coffee, trying to get the blood flowing. When he returned to his office, he picked a file at random from the top of the stack and, like a grown-up, sat at his desk.

The file held a rundown on the history of the village of Brigham and its inhabitants. The Smiths were one of the families who had followed the Blackmores to Canada after the police raids on the polygamist sect in Short Creek, Arizona, in 1953. Fearing persecution, they'd made their way across the border to Lister, BC, and renamed the area Bountiful, although it wasn't listed as such on a map.

In 1962, Gerald Smith, with the financial help of then prophet Leroy Johnson, purchased fifty acres of land ninety minutes northeast of Bountiful. The land was fertile and ready to plant, tucked into the shadows of the Rocky Mountains, and the nearest civilization was the gold-rush town of Fort Steele, BC. Gerald died in 1970 and his son, Gideon, became the new bishop.

They first came to the attention of the RCMP thanks to a phone call placed by a fifteen-year-old boy who'd been excommunicated. Dustyn Young called the police from a pay phone in Fort Steele and in the coming days gave statements that implicated Gideon Smith and numerous others in everything from bigamy to child rape. But the boy died of meningitis three months later, long before he had the opportunity to testify in court. After that, it took the RCMP several years to gather enough evidence for a search warrant.

The first raid led to multiple arrests but no serious charges, as none of the minors in Brigham would admit to being abused, neglected, or forced to marry before the age of majority.

Beau wasn't involved at that point. He was a twenty-five-year-old newlywed still working patrol in Red Deer, Alberta. But he was there the following year for their second raid, and for each one that followed. By the last one, he was the lead detective.

As they moved in formation up the road toward the temple, people screamed and scattered, which was all par for the course. But one girl had come running down the road toward them, ushering a group of children along with her. He'd stepped out of formation and opened his arms. Not even slowing, Grace DeRoche had ploughed right into him.

And boy, did she have stories to tell. Multiple charges were laid against Gideon Smith and other members of the sect, ranging from polygamy to child endangerment, abuse, and rape.

On the charges of polygamy, they ended up facing a constitutional runaround as Canada's laws, specifically section 293 of the Criminal Code, were put into question, and Brigham's lawyers fought hard for their clients' religious freedom.

Three months before Gideon Smith was set to face trial on the other charges, and the day after their prophet Warren Jeffs was arrested in Las Vegas, the Family in Brigham drank a cyanide cocktail.

Their bodies were found two weeks later, piled in an open pit behind the temple. They'd dug a mass grave, but it seemed no one had been left alive to complete the burial. The bodies had been exposed to the elements, and the decomp process was well underway.

Coroner teams from nearby provinces were brought in to help sort through the rotting mess, and the work went on for weeks. One hundred and twenty-two bodies were categorized, but less than two dozen were positively identified. There were no records with which to make comparisons, and they didn't know who or how many people were actually living in Brigham. What became clear, however, was that Gideon Smith's body wasn't there.

The bodies were handed over to the FLDS in Bountiful, who buried them in a communal grave behind the temple in Brigham.

Over the next six months, Beau headed the search for Brigham's bishop, questioning folks in Bountiful and chasing down leads across the country. In the U.S., FBI agents questioned members of the FLDS in Utah and Arizona. They set up surveillance in Hildale, Colorado City, and the infamous YFZ Ranch in Texas that Warren Jeffs and his followers had constructed as a "land of refuge" where they could hide from the law. But all their searching for Gideon Smith amounted to nothing, and eventually the leads dried up.

The files went to storage and Beau moved on to other cases and other times in his life. He joined the Serious Crime Section, and when Emily died he became the resident expert in murders disguised as suicides. Not that it had done him any good.

His coffee had grown cold. A glance at the clock told him it was past four. His trip down memory lane was wasting time. With renewed determination, he dug through the files, searching for the statements.

He located them in a box near the bottom of the pile and searched for anything written by Rulon Smith. The best he was able to come up with was Rulon's signature at the bottom of his typed statement. He scanned a copy and sent it to Judy Beers, then repacked the boxes and stacked them in the corner of his office.

Picking up the phone, he dialed his boss. "I'm getting antsy."

"A day in the office will do that to you," Doug said.

"I'm waiting on those reports for Valor Johnson and Eliza Barlow, but I'd like to track down some of the remaining kids and speak to them in person."

"That sounds expensive. You can't use the phone?"

"I know these deaths may come back as unrelated," Beau said.

"Bet your ass they might."

"But I've got some threads to tug, and I'd like your blessing."

Beau closed his eyes and listened to his boss breathing on the other end of the line.

"Just tug on the cheapest threads, okay? I've got a budget to worry about."

"You got it." He hung up before Doug could get more specific.

Nakusp was at least eight hours non-stop by car from Vancouver. Beau started out at four in the morning and made good time with only the most minor slowdowns in Abbotsford and Chilliwack, despite some spats of rain.

The 97C, also known as the Okanagan Connector, wound through forest and mountain, with only one lane in either direction much of the time. He stopped in Vernon for a late breakfast before continuing onto the BC-6. The sun peeked through the clouds as he pulled up to the Needles cable ferry terminal. In front of him was a Ford with a truck bed full of tree trimmings. Three cars pulled in behind him before the cable ferry docked.

In due course, Beau drove onto the ferry's deck. He got out of the car to stretch his legs, admiring the view as the ferry made its five-minute trek across Lower Arrow Lake. The sun sparkled on the water, turning it blue and gold, and in every direction evergreen trees marched away on softly rolling hills. The drive into Nakusp was scenic, hugging the shores of the Arrow Lakes.

Feeling grubby and out of sorts, he checked into the K2 Rotor Lodge, an unassuming two-level building with a family dining restaurant on street level and a supermarket across the street. Two blocks away, the beach was visible through the trees.

He paid for a single room, filling out the appropriate forms and handing over his credit card. Within minutes, he pulled his wheeled bag down the hall, key card in hand. The room was simple, clean, and serviceable. He lifted his bag onto the rack in the closet and did a cursory inspection for bedbugs before unwrapping the bar of complimentary soap and hitting the shower.

Ten minutes later, Beau climbed back into his car, wearing fresh clothes and feeling much more alert. He stopped at What's Brewing on Broadway for a large coffee and a muffin, and fired up Google Maps on his phone, inputting Grace DeRoche's address. He sipped and munched on his way out of town, taking Highway 23 north, and turning right to follow the signs toward the hot springs.

From Hot Springs Road, he turned onto a gravel path that led up into the forest, with snow-capped mountain peaks visible above. He passed one home that was little more than a cabin, and continued up and around a switchback until the road abruptly ended. Google Maps piped up to let him know that he'd arrived. He looked around. Rock face and endless trees on the left. Gravel path on the right, barely wide enough to fit a car.

Taking a breath, he backed down the road and turned the wheel so he could approach at a better angle. He eased the nose of his car between thick rows of trees. The path dipped down at a sharp angle, and it was pockmarked by holes deep enough to swallow a tire. If he got stuck, it would be a long time before a tow truck found him.

Several bone-jarring seconds later, he came into a clearing. At the edge was a small, one-level home, painted a sunny yellow. The driveway angled around the right side of the house, ending in a parking pad wide enough for a car to turn around in. A blue Subaru Forester was parked near the stairs that led up to a screened-in side porch. He could see wicker furniture and a door that he guessed led to the kitchen.

Behind the house stood a barn, painted forest green, and a large fenced area in which goats munched grass and climbed a tumble of giant rocks in the shape of a mini Matterhorn. At the edge of the property the land fell away, and he caught blue glimpses of Upper Arrow Lake far below.

As he opened the car door he caught sight of the biggest bloody dog he'd ever seen tearing up the yard toward him. Beau promptly pulled his leg back inside the car and shut the door. The dog stopped a couple feet away, teeth bared, snarling and snapping and dripping drool. Its head was level with the car's wing mirror.

"Holy shit."

"Bella, heel!"

The dog closed its mouth and moved toward its master. Grace DeRoche stood by the corner of the house wearing jeans, knee-high rubber boots, and a heavy flannel jacket. Her blond hair was slicked back from her face into a tight ponytail, putting her angular features in sharp relief. She laid a hand on the dog's broad head, and the dog's tongue unfurled from the side of its mouth. It was as big as her hand.

He lowered his window and popped his head out the opening. He smelled forest and goat shit.

"Grace? It's Detective Brunelli."

She moved toward him, the dog at her side. "Is everything okay? Desiree —"

He caught the panic in her voice and quickly said, "Desiree's fine. I'm sorry to just show up like this, but —"

"You were in the neighborhood?" She moved a few steps closer. The dog remained pinned to her side, ready to pounce if she gave the word.

"Is it safe to get out of the car?"

She tipped her head to the side, and the dog did the same. "Go ahead, Detective."

Slowly, he opened the car door, prepared to retreat if the dog made any aggressive moves.

"You look a lot older," Grace said.

He ran a hand through his hair. "I *am* a lot older."

She raised her eyebrows, perhaps thinking he'd aged more than the years could account for.

The dog watched him attentively, lips pulled back in a show of teeth.

"When I was working in the Northwest Territories, they believed this myth about a giant wolf called a Waheela," he said as he eased out of the car. "It ripped people's heads off. There was even a place called the Valley of the Headless Men, where decapitated corpses would turn up every once in a while, supposedly victims of the beast."

"A perfect cover for some bloodthirsty psychopath," she said. "What's that quote? 'Man is the cruelest animal'?"

"That's Nietzsche, right?" he said. "I'd have to agree with the sentiment."

"So would I." She patted the dog's head. "This is Bella, my service dog. She's never decapitated anything larger than her stuffed bunny." Bella gave a mournful groan, and Grace added, "Sorry, girl. I know you're not ready to talk about that yet."

"Do you have a few minutes?" he asked.

Her eyes were wide set, and the right eye was a clear blue while the left was the dark brown of fine chocolate. They were just as startling to him now as when he'd first spoken to her in the East Kootenay Regional Hospital, but now faint lines creased the corners.

"Have you finally found Uncle G?"

"We're always on the lookout." He tried not to sound defensive. Grace turned her head when he spoke, and he remembered that she was deaf in her left ear.

"That's code for 'We're not doing a darn thing and we don't even care anymore.'"

"There have been some new developments. Can we go inside?"

She eyed him, and then turned to climb the stairs to the screened-in porch. Bella followed. He tucked in behind them, careful to give the dog space.

He removed his shoes and left them on the rubber mat beside her boots. The kitchen was plain and uncluttered. The wood cabinets gleamed with polish and the counters were wiped clean. A kettle sat on the gas stovetop, and she lit the fire underneath it as she passed.

She led him to a small living room at the front of the house. There was an apartment-size yellow couch and matching chair. A glass coffee table took up the centre of the room, covered in magazines about cheese-making and herbal remedies, and books about organic farming and PTSD.

She took the couch, gesturing for him to sit in the chair to her right.

"I'm afraid I have some bad news," he said.

Her fingers curled into fists, as though she were preparing for a painful blow. "Who died?"

He delivered the first blow, and then two more in quick succession. "Rulon. I'm sorry to say that Valor and Eliza are also gone, but you might have already known that."

Grace took the news in silence. Her skin paled, and red stress marks appeared below her eyes. Her expression went blank, and her breathing slowed and then seemed to stop. He watched her, growing alarmed as the silence stretched. Her eyes moved from side to side.

The dog jumped up and issued a sharp bark.

"Grace?"

She didn't respond.

He leaned forward, reaching toward her. "Are you okay?"

The dog growled at him, and he sat back with haste.

Her head snapped up so suddenly his heart rammed into his throat. "Who the fuck do you think you are?"

The voice that emerged from her throat was deep and full of venom. Her face had changed. It was broader, thick and masculine, and her jawbone jutted outward. Her pale brows drew down into a severe line and the eyes beneath them glared at him with such fury he instinctively pressed back into his seat, as though that might protect him from whatever damage was coming his way.

Bella turned on her owner, snarling and snapping.

"Shut the fuck up, you stupid mutt!"

Beau didn't dare move.

The kettle let out a high-pitched whistle from the kitchen. Grace blinked, and the colour faded from her cheeks. The dog went from snarling to whining. Grace's shoulders rolled forward, her back curved, and her forehead hit her knees. Her arms dropped, and she wrapped her hands around her ankles and rocked from side to side.

"I need Shelby," she said.

"Huh?"

"Phone. Shelby."

Beau looked around and saw the phone sitting in its cradle on a table beside the couch. To reach it, he'd have to pass by the dog. Bella whined, her entire focus on her master. Keeping a wary eye on both of them, he stood up. He shuffled around the coffee table on shaking legs. Bella gave him a cautious glance then turned back to Grace.

He lifted the phone's receiver, heard the buzz of a dial tone. It was one of those phones with ten programmable speed-dial buttons. Only one name was listed, written in heavy black marker on the line beside the top button: SHELBY. He pressed the button and listened to the ten beeps that indicated a number was being dialed. His hands trembled.

A woman answered on the fifth ring, just as he was expecting it to go to voice mail. "Grace, I'm here! Everything okay?"

"This is Detective Brunelli with the RCMP," he said.

"Is Grace okay?"

"She's okay. I think. I'm here with her right now. She asked me to call you. I'm afraid I had to give her some bad news, and she's … she's having a hard time processing it."

The woman on the other end of the phone took a deep breath, as though trying to calm herself. "Hang on, I'm driving. Let me pull over."

He waited.

"Okay. What kind of news?"

"Are you a friend of hers?"

"I'm her therapist."

"I had to inform her about the deaths of several people from her childhood. She's having a very strong reaction to the news. Are you anywhere nearby?"

"I'm near Castlegar about two hours south, on my way back to Nelson. Is she conscious? Is she able to talk?"

"Well, she's *conscious* …"

"Get her dog, Bella."

"The dog is with her."

"Okay, good. Now listen to me very carefully. I need you to give Grace the phone and then leave the house. I'm going to have to talk her down, and it will work best if you're not visible until she's calmer."

"All right."

"Wait on the porch. I'll have her bring you the phone once she's calm, so we can talk."

"Okay." Keeping a wary eye on Bella, he leaned over and held out the receiver. "Shelby's on the phone. Here you go."

She lifted a hand for the phone, not taking her head off her knees. He placed the phone in her palm and she pulled it in against her ear.

"Shelby?" Her voice was high-pitched and muffled against her legs.

Beau backed out of the room, stopped in the kitchen to turn off the flame beneath the whistling kettle, and let himself out onto the porch. He sat on a wicker couch with flower-covered outdoor cushions and dropped his head into his shaking hands. His belly rolled with nerves and his bowels felt dangerously loose.

Forty-five minutes passed before Grace came out onto the porch. Twilight was coming, and he was beginning to worry about making it back to the main road in the dark.

Her eyes were red-rimmed, her face mottled and puffy from tears, and her hair had pulled out of the tight ponytail, forming a knotted mess. Without a word she handed him the phone, re-entered the house, and locked the door behind her.

He put the phone against his ear. "Hello?"

"You sure walked into a steaming pile of shit, didn't you? And you set her back ten steps in the process."

"My apologies," he said.

"She's calm now, but she needs time to recuperate from her episode."

"Episode."

"I can rearrange my schedule for tomorrow. Can you come to Nelson? She's given me permission to discuss her situation with you."

"I can do that," he said. "But I still need to speak to her at some point, too."

"After we've spoken, okay? And it might be better if I'm with her the next time. Just in case."

Beau bit his tongue.

"Her situation is very fragile, Detective. Whatever this case is you're working on, I'm certain you don't want to damage a victim in the process."

"What's your address?" He reached into his pocket for a pencil and notepad.

She rattled it off, giving him her office phone number, as well. "Come around one. Oh, and she says you can leave the phone by the door." With that, she hung up.

Beau leaned the phone against the kitchen door and headed to his vehicle. As the car bounced up the driveway, he glanced in his rear-view mirror and caught sight of Grace. She stood on the porch, the light from the kitchen creating a halo around her. Bella was at her side. As he watched, the dog lifted her massive head as though she'd caught the scent of blood.

ELEVEN

After the detective left, Grace wrapped herself in a weighted blanket and curled up with Bella on the couch.

Rulon. Valor. And Eliza. How could they all be gone? Was that why Desiree had been calling her so frequently?

She reached over and pressed the speaker button on her phone, and then hit the speed-dial button to call her voice mail. There were three messages from her sister. The first was from the previous Sunday. Desiree's stammer was pronounced, and she sounded frightened. She asked Grace to call as soon as she could. The second message was similar. In the third, Desiree sobbed too hard to say anything other than Rulon's name, over and over again.

She lifted the receiver and dropped it back in its cradle, cutting off her sister mid-sob. The grief burned its way up her throat, a massive lump so painful it contorted her face into a silent scream. It was all her fault. If they hadn't followed her that night, they'd still be alive.

Bella cocked her head to the side, whining. She buried her face in the dog's furry neck and let the tears come. The grief tore her apart, ravaged her from the inside out. She clung to Bella, aching for the long-ago safety of her father's arms.

. . .

Though the house felt quiet and sombre, it was a day of celebration for the DeRoche family. Mother had made five blueberry pies for the communal meal that would follow Grace's baptism. Everyone agreed Mother made the best pie, with crusts that were flaky and delicate.

Mother Dinah was providing vanilla ice cream. Uncle Redd had lugged home a giant churn from a trip to Bountiful and given it to Dinah as a gift. She was clearly his favourite wife, which led to problems within the home and a lot of speculation from everyone else. Grace had heard other women debating what Dinah did to achieve preferred status. She was a poor housekeeper and her children were like wild things.

But Mother said there were many ways to gain favour with a husband, as Grace would learn when it was her time. Whatever Dinah had done, they were all grateful for it the day Redd brought home the churn. Besides, Mother Dinah was really nice, so Grace was happy to see her treated kindly by her husband. There were many wives in Brigham who weren't treated so nice.

Grace's father was kind like Uncle Redd. Mother was sixteen when she married him, and she often told the story of Uncle G's revelation and how fortunate she'd felt to be marrying Patrick DeRoche. To be a first wife was a special honour, and Patrick was young, handsome, and capable. It was a good match.

But a man needed at least three wives to be granted the highest levels of heaven, and women couldn't enter the heavenly realm at all unless brought by their husbands. So, Mother Rebecca joining the family should have been cause for celebration.

Certainly, Father found her charming. But Mother had to share the keeping of their home and didn't seem as enchanted. Her smile grew stiff and wrinkles sprouted around her eyes almost overnight.

Mother Rebecca's pale brown hair was an anomaly in Brigham. Grace found it fascinating; it was so different from her own straight blond locks. On a rare occasion, Mother Rebecca allowed her to brush it. It was a lovely blend of pale brown and dark gold that curled softly around her head and down her slender back. But in Grace's hands the hairbrush always caught in tangles, causing Mother Rebecca to cry out in pain. She'd grab the brush from Grace, eyes full of tears and accusation.

A second wife was meant to increase the love within a home. But something had gone wrong, and deep down Grace knew it was her own fault. For some reason, Mother Rebecca didn't like her. And no matter how sweet Grace tried to be and how fervently she prayed, she couldn't find the key to unlock her second mother's heart.

On the day of the baptism, Mother Rebecca stayed in bed. Grace swallowed back her hurt and followed Mother's lead. She brought her a bowl of soup and fresh crusty bread, and offered to brush the tangles from her hair. Mother Rebecca buried her head beneath the pillow and told her to leave.

When Mother saw the food-laden tray Grace carried back to the kitchen, her mouth pulled in like she'd tasted something sour.

"I'm going to say extra prayers before my baptism, that God help open Mother Rebecca's heart to our family." A prayer said before such a sacred ritual was sure to hold extra weight. She thought the idea would please her mother, but it didn't seem to.

Mother sighed as she scraped the soup back into the pot. "Pray instead for the next baby to take root."

"Root?"

"Never mind that now. Go clean up. You have to leave in ten minutes."

Mother had made a white gown for her baptism. The fabric was soft under her fingers, although the lace scratched at her neck. Under the gown she wore the cleanest pair of her temple undergarments. They covered her from elbows to knees, and she despised them — especially in the summertime, when the temperature soared and they had to work long hours farming the land under a brutal and unforgiving sun.

Her gown was supposed to reach her ankles, but she'd had an unexpected growth spurt and the hemline now reached her shins. Father said he was sure it would be fine, but the lines of worry creasing Mother's brow only deepened.

Once she was dressed, Mother came into the bedroom to do her hair. She pulled it into a high poof on the top of her head and braided the rest so it dangled to her thighs.

"Go scrub your hands. There's still clay beneath your fingernails."

When she emerged from the bathroom, everyone except Mother Rebecca waited in the kitchen. Father stood as she approached, his cheeks red with excitement. Mother's gaze travelled down to the bottom of her gown, fretting over the hemline.

"You look well," Father said with a smile, and folded her into his arms. He kissed the top of her head, careful to find a spot that wouldn't muss her hair. "How do you feel?"

"Nervous."

"I was nervous on my baptism day, too. You should be. It's a solemn occasion, Gracey."

"Yes, Father."

"But your grandfather told me something, and I'll repeat it to you for whatever worth it might have."

Father's father had died several years before, on his compound outside Salt Lake City. He'd had seven wives and twenty-eight children at the time of his death. In time, news had come to Brigham that the prophet had taken several of Grandfather's wives, including Father's mother. Father had been pleased that Grandmother would be well taken care of.

"What did he tell you?" she asked.

"He said, 'Patrick, today is the only time in your life you'll ever be given a fresh start. When you emerge from the water, all your sins will be wiped clean. And my son, this is something you sorely need, as you've been very, very wicked.'"

Father winked, and Grace giggled.

"But from this day forward" — he looked down at her with sudden seriousness — "you must make extra certain to keep sweet, for any sins you commit after today will be a black mark upon your soul, to be judged in heaven."

She swallowed hard, nodded her understanding.

"Don't look so worried, Gracey. It's just a little dip in the water — which I'll warn you is numbingly cold, but wc'll both survive it — and then we can join the celebration. I can already taste Mother's blueberry pie."

"Give me a kiss," Mother said, stepping forward.

She embraced her mother, accepted a kiss on the forehead, and bent to kiss the top of Desiree's head.

"We'll be waiting on the road." Mother handed her the bag with the dress she was supposed to change into after her baptism. It was yellow cotton topped with white lace, like lemon meringue.

"Go on, you don't want to keep Uncle G waiting."

Grace followed Father into the yard and turned back to wave at Mother and Desiree. Clayne emerged from the house next door and crossed the dirt of their joint yard. His breath fogged in the late afternoon air. He made sure to keep several feet between them.

"Good luck." His blue eyes were solemn. He had a new scrape on his chin, and a healing bruise near his right eye.

"Come on, Gracey," Father said.

The temple was at the top of the road, seated on a natural incline so it cast a shadow over the hearts of those who resided below. Behind the temple the first crags of the Rocky Mountains rose like fists trying to punch the sky. High above, clouds snagged against their sharp peaks. They dropped the first snow of the season up there, but above Brigham the sky was pale and clear.

As they moved up the road, she kicked at the dirt until Father pointed out that she was dirtying the bottom of her gown. People came out onto porches or stopped whatever they were doing in their yards to nod, smile, and wave. They passed Uncle G's massive house at the top of the hill.

Rather than climb the stairs to the temple's main entrance, they went in through the side door that led to the ritual bathing room in the basement. As she followed Father down the stairs, she tried to guess what was above them at each step. She figured the pulpit was right above the landing, but then the stairs doubled back on themselves and she lost her perspective.

The air was thin and cool, causing her to gasp and wheeze as she tried to take in enough oxygen to feed her racing heart. Candlelight flickered on the walls at the bottom of the stairs.

Father wrapped an arm around her shoulders and led her into a small, candlelit room to the left of the landing. His hand felt damp through the fabric of her gown.

Uncle G was there, with Uncle Redd and Joseph Barlow standing behind him. They were the three elders of the church. Uncle Redd gave her a friendly wink when no one was looking, but she was too nervous to acknowledge it.

Uncle G began the first prayer, his voice like the rumble of a tractor. A tractor had run over Bobby Taylor's leg last summer while he napped in the north field. Boydell said it served him right for resting when there was so much work to do. Bobby lost the leg, and now he could nap whenever he wanted.

"Grace DeRoche," Uncle G said, "you came here today to make a covenant with God. Have you prepared your mind and soul?"

She couldn't breathe. Her chest felt tight and heavy.

"Gracey," Father said, squeezing her shoulders.

She managed to give Uncle G a quick nod.

"Patrick DeRoche, do you present your daughter with a pure heart, to serve the bishop, the prophet in his eminent wisdom, and the Holy Spirit?"

"Yes," Father said.

"Grace?" Uncle G said.

Father pressed down on her shoulders, a silent reminder of what she was supposed to do next. She slumped to her knees and took in a gasping breath. The voice that emerged from her throat was little more than a squeak.

"I wish to be the humble servant of the bishop and our beloved prophet. I am here to do your will."

Uncle G wore denim pants held up by blue suspenders. His belly was huge but not jiggly. The buttons of his flannel shirt strained to hold everything together.

"Grace?"

She cleared her throat. "I will abide by the laws of our church, for all the days of my life. I make my covenant to you, our most respected bishop ..."

His boots were scuffed and mud-caked. Father squeezed her shoulders, urging her to continue.

"And I make my covenant to our beloved prophet Rulon Jeffs, and to God."

Her voice trailed off and her mind fixated on his boots. Father squeezed her shoulders again, and she closed her eyes.

"I will give myself, body and soul, to serve our church here on earth, and our God in heaven."

Was that everything she was supposed to say? Had she forgotten something?

Shakily, she said, "Amen?"

"Amen," the men repeated.

Uncle G signalled for her to stand, and with Father's help she did. They led her to a door marked Bath. When Uncle G opened the door she saw a rectangular pool of water, glistening and dark.

"Take off just your shoes and socks," Uncle G said.

While the men crowded beside the pool, Grace removed her shoes and placed her socks on top. She followed Father into the water. It was icy. She sucked in a breath, and decided the best thing to do was to get in quickly. She pushed forward, stifling the urge to yelp as the water hit her midsection.

Father hooked his hands under her armpits, and the next moment she was underwater. The icy shock took her breath away. He lifted her, dripping and gasping for breath, and said, "Twice more, Gracey."

Down and up and down and up. The water was biting agony. When he lifted her the third time she screeched from the pain of it.

The men cheered, and Joseph Barlow said something about the devil leaving her soul. They helped her from the water and wrapped a large towel around her shivering body.

Uncle G approached with a small glass bottle. He made the sign of the cross on her forehead, his finger firm and slick with oil. A violent wave of nausea rose within her. With no time to spare, she turned away from Uncle G and vomited on her father instead.

TWELVE

God must have left me a new message by now. I really need to get to the praying tree, and I've grown anxious enough to take the risk.

I wait until it is almost dark. To remain as far from the campsite I've seen as possible, I take the pathway closest to the cliff. Moving swiftly, I slip between trees and bushes, my senses on full alert.

When a twig snaps somewhere to my right, I dive behind a nearby cedar. Minutes pass before a raccoon lumbers through the bushes and continues deeper into the forest. I take in a lungful of moist air, watch the puff of my breath as I exhale, and then continue down the path.

The forest is deep in shadow by the time I make it to the praying tree, and the darkness makes me feel like I am being watched. I hunch down and scamper forward, half expecting someone to reach out and grab me at any moment. The fine hairs on my neck stand on end.

I reach into the hole at the base of the tree and pull out two items. The first, a note, will be my instructions. I set it aside and examine the other item. It is wrapped in thick plastic, but it looks like a piece of newspaper.

It has grown too dark to read, so I carefully stuff both items into my coat pocket and zip it closed. I say a prayer of thanksgiving that I am being given another chance, before moving back into the shadows of the forest.

Knowing God is still talking to me gives me renewed confidence. My curiosity wins out. Before I can think too much about it, I move off the path and slip toward the area where I've seen the campsite.

Up ahead, a faint orange glow flickers against the surrounding trees. A few more steps and I hear the snap and pop of a campfire, and smell a woodsy-smoky smell that reminds me of roasting hot dogs and marshmallows. I love marshmallows.

I slink forward, not daring to get too close. The dome of the tarp-covered tent comes into view. The tarp is blue, and tied down on four sides with yellow rope.

Keeping low, I circle to the left until the campfire comes into view.

A man sits beside the fire, his back turned toward me. The hood of his coat droops halfway down his back. His hair glows in the firelight, either light brown or blond. His shoulders are hunched, his head bowed as though deep in thought. After a moment, he leans forward and uses a stick to poke at the heart of the fire. Sparks rise like fireflies into the night, dying before they make it to the freedom beyond the treetops.

I watch him for a long time, but other than occasionally poking at the fire, he doesn't move. Eventually, I get cold and slip back into the gloom.

THIRTEEN

"Checking in, hope it's not too late. Are you doing okay?" Shelby asked.

"I think so," Grace said. She wiped a sleeve across her eyes. They felt swollen and raw, and the pressure from her clogged sinuses was making her head ache.

"Crying is good. It's a healthy way for the body to release tension. It doesn't mean you're losing control."

"I know. I hear you." She was bundled on the couch, a fire crackling in the fireplace. Despite this, her body was chilled, and her feet felt like blocks of ice. Bella lay across her legs and lower body, creating soothing warmth and pressure. She reached down and stroked the dog's fur. "Bella really came through for me today."

"She's good at her job," Shelby said.

"That she is." Tears burned her eyes. "Oh, God. I can't believe they're really gone. Three of them! I don't even know how to process the loss. It seems so unreal."

"Do you want to add an extra session this week? I can FaceTime you tomorrow evening."

"Yeah. That's a good idea."

"For tonight, are there any doors that need closing?"

Grace shut her eyes, doing a mental tally of her inner workings. "Yeah. Seeing that detective today, it blew a whole bunch of them wide open. Even without the uniform, even without the horrible news, just seeing him after all this time was so scary ..."

"I understand," Shelby said. "One of the hardest things to do is move past the fears that were instilled in us as children."

"Yeah."

"All right, get comfortable."

She pressed the speaker button on the phone and laid it on the coffee table, then pulled the weighted blanket up to her neck and settled back into the couch cushions. Bella readjusted her position, giving Grace more of her body weight.

She let out a deep breath and closed her eyes. "I'm ready."

"Good. We're going to go in and close every single one of those doors, all right? Let's start by taking a deep breath ... inhaling for four beats, and exhaling for four beats ..."

She followed her therapist's voice into hypnosis, as Bella's heated weight pinned her so she wouldn't get lost. Shelby's voice became a pleasant hum, background noise that accompanied her into the darkness of her mind. She roamed her inner hallways, shutting any open doors she found.

She passed a door with a thick padlock marked DESIREE. The next, a door that was partly open, had the name SARIAH written in ragged script. Her youngest sister. The one who, because of Grace's actions, never got the chance to grow up. She tugged on the door. It was heavy, and it took all her strength to close it. But once the latch clicked home, she turned the key to engage the lock.

· · ·

She was eleven and Desiree was six when Mother Rebecca birthed a child who lived. The baby came early one winter morning, while the snow was thick on the tree branches and the world was silent. The girls awoke to the weak sounds of the new baby trying to clear her lungs. She'd come four weeks early, and she was tiny as a doll.

When Mother Rebecca saw the girls hovering in her bedroom door, she smiled and beckoned them forward to meet their youngest sister. Grace was excited to meet the baby — she loved babies and one of her favourite duties was caring for the young ones in the basement of the temple while the adults prayed — and yet she hesitated.

She couldn't recall the last time she'd seen Mother Rebecca smile. It caught her by surprise, for it lit up Mother Rebecca's face and made her beauty almost too much to bear.

This made her heart ache for Mother, whose appearance was plain. Mother Rebecca was like a dove in a house full of hens, and despite the fact that Father and Mother had a connection of the mind and heart, Grace was old enough to understand that Father connected differently with Mother Rebecca. He shared Mother Rebecca's bedroom most nights, while Mother slept alone. She'd heard her mother crying when those other sounds started in Mother Rebecca's bedroom.

"Come in," Mother Rebecca said, motioning once again to the girls. Her sister had stayed back with her — Desiree would not make a move unless Grace made it first.

She walked over to the bed and gazed down at the bundle in Mother Rebecca's arms. The baby was nursing, and she stared in fascination at the tiny mouth clasped tight around the dark of Mother Rebecca's nipple.

"Does it hurt?" she asked.

Mother Rebecca grimaced. "Yes. But I'm told it's something I'll become accustomed to in time."

"I'll pray for God to ease your pain," Desiree piped up in her little bird voice.

"Thank you, child," Mother Rebecca said.

"What's her name?" Grace asked.

"Your father has named her Sariah."

Grace winced. How unfortunate for Desiree.

"S-s ..." Desiree's face turned red with effort. "S-sariah. She was the wife of Lehi."

"Very good, Desiree," Father said as he entered the room. His face glowed with excitement. He moved quickly to Mother Rebecca's side and gazed down in wonder at his third daughter.

"She's feeding well," he said.

"She is strong," Mother Rebecca said, stroking the fuzz on the baby's head.

"Girls, go help Mother in the kitchen. She is preparing the meal of celebration."

"Yes, Father," they said in unison.

As Grace left the room, she couldn't help but look back. Father gazed down on Mother Rebecca and baby Sariah, his expression soft and loving. The sight caused a stab of jealousy deep in her chest. They looked like a completed puzzle, one in which her own jagged piece didn't fit.

In the kitchen, Mother smiled and laughed as she brought out the good dishes, but her eyes were deep with pain. Grace thought Mother felt the shift within their family, too. Perhaps she also wondered if her puzzle piece still fit.

Once the meal was prepared and placed in the oven to keep warm, Grace and Desiree put on their coats and went outside. Desiree grabbed her sled and ran off to find Eliza Barlow. Grace waited in the side yard, throwing a soccer ball into a snowbank and waiting for Clayne to come outside.

Though she couldn't knock on his door and ask for him, their parents were accepting of them playing together as long as it occurred by happenstance. The trick was for both of them to appear only mildly interested in the other. In due course, Clayne came outside, as she knew he would.

"Mother Rebecca had her baby," she said by way of greeting.

"Did it live?"

It was a common question, asked even before asking if it was a boy or a girl. There were more tiny headstones stacked in rows behind the temple than there were children running around Brigham, and Mother Rebecca had lost six babies over the years.

Clayne said it was because Mother Rebecca and Father shared the same grandmother, and though she was uncertain what that had to do with anything, she tended to believe the things that Clayne told her. He was smart, and he was usually right.

"She lived. But she's very tiny. Father named her Sariah."

"A good name," Clayne said.

He kicked snow from a pile of stones as they spoke. He never could keep still. In order to focus on a conversation, he needed to move his body. Sitting in temple was the worst kind of torture for him, and he was always getting in trouble for his jittery legs, incessant jokes, and questioning nature.

Though she secretly admired his rebelliousness, she also wished that he was better at controlling himself so he'd get fewer corrections.

"Tabby has the croup," he said.

"I'm sorry to hear that." Tabby was one of her favourites. Grace always gave her an extra candy when it was her turn to hand them out after temple. The sugar on their tongues was meant as a reminder to keep sweet, but Tabby was born that way. "Is she all right?"

"I think so. But she passed it on to Valor and Patience. The whole house is in misery. Mother Flora asked Father to take Patience to the doctor in Bountiful before she gets any worse."

This was a good idea, considering Patience had almost died of an asthma attack the previous winter. Although all of Mother Flora's children were sickly, Patience was the sickliest.

He'd cleared the snow from the pile of rocks, and his kicking became something closer to stomping. "Mother Flora went after Tabby with the switch, and this time Father wasn't around to stop her. I ran from the back of the house when I heard what was happening, but I was too late to stop her from getting in a couple good licks."

"Oh, Clayne, I'm sorry. Is Tabby badly hurt?"

He wiped a sleeve across his eyes. "She'll do. I just …" He wiped his eyes again, and his voice lowered to a painful rumble. *"I hate Mother Flora so much!"*

"Shh." Grace looked around, hoping no one could hear him. "Sweeten your tongue."

He picked up a medium-size rock and, with a growl, hurled it at the back fence. It bounced off a wooden slat, leaving a dark mark on the white paint.

Grace's heart galloped into a panic. "Clayne, *don't*!"

He picked up and hurled another rock, and then another, his growls turning to shouts of rage. She could hear people running from as far away as the Barlows' house on the corner, from her own house, and worst of all, from the Johnsons'.

Mother Flora was the first to descend. As she hauled Clayne back into the house, Grace winced and covered her eyes. She didn't need to imagine what would happen next. She'd heard his screams enough times to know, and she'd seen the aftermath, too.

The Johnsons' kitchen door closed with a bang. Clayne screamed in pain.

Grace pressed her face into the cups of her hands. Her good ear buzzed, as it did when she was scared or upset.

"Come inside, Gracey." Mother's hands fell upon her shoulders, and she turned to bury her face in Mother's dress. Mother pulled her into their house and closed the door softly behind them. She pulled out a chair at the kitchen table and eased Grace into it.

Her head felt thick and foggy. She laid it against the table and covered her good ear, trying to block out the sound of Clayne's screams.

"Gracey, you need to calm down," Mother said. "Take some deep breaths, and think sweet thoughts."

She tried, but her breath came in hiccups and gasps. Mother sat next to her and held her hands, taking long slow breaths along with her. After several minutes, she felt calmer. The buzzing in her ear lessened.

"All right, now?" Mother held a wet cloth against her eyes. The cold was soothing.

"Yes, Mother."

"Good. Hold this against your eyes for another minute, and then go change into your yellow dress. It's almost time to go to temple."

FOURTEEN

t took Beau two hours to get from Nakusp to Nelson. Surrounded by the Selkirk Mountains, Nelson was tucked around the West Arm of Kootenay Lake.

According to the free brochure he picked up while filling his car with gas, the town had boomed in the late 1800s after the discovery of silver in the nearby mountains, then filled with draft dodgers, artists, musicians, organic food growers, and ski bums.

As he drove into town from the west, the sun sparkled on the lake and the leaves on the surrounding trees showed off vibrant shades of red, orange, and gold. Driving along Vernon Street with its low-level buildings, art galleries, and coffee shops, gave Beau an aching feeling in his chest. The town felt contained and calm, yet somehow still vibrant.

Shelby's office address corresponded to a beautifully restored craftsman-style home, painted a dark purple with white trim. In Vancouver, it would have already been torn down to build condos.

It was one o'clock on the dot when he exited his car. He moved past a Jeep Cherokee parked in the driveway with its nose pressed against the garage door and climbed the porch steps to ring the doorbell. To the left of the door was a porch swing, a plaid blanket neatly folded on one end.

In due course, a young girl opened the door. She had black curls pulled into a sprout on the top of her head, and she was wearing harem pants with an elephant design and a loose white shirt in some sort of natural material. He was opening his mouth to ask if her mother was home when she saved him from embarrassment.

"Detective Brunelli? You're right on time." She reached out a hand. "Shelby Jacobs."

His cheeks warmed. "Nice to meet you, Dr. Jacobs."

"Just Shelby," she said as he followed her inside.

"Then I'm Beau. Wow. This is a great house."

The hardwood floors were polished to a high shine and covered in colourful area rugs. The walls were painted a pale sunset orange framed by white wainscotting.

"It's a rental," she said. "I took over for a retiring psychologist a couple years ago, and renting his home was part of the deal. He gets to live by a beach in Israel and know that his house and practice are well taken care of, and I get to live above my means."

"Sounds like a good deal."

"For sure. The office is this way."

He could see part of a gleaming kitchen at the back of the house, and beyond a broad deck overlooking the lake.

"Would you like some coffee?"

"I'd love some."

She showed him into the office and left him there. Along one wall was a fireplace with a giant stone mantle. Rather than photographs or decorations, it was stacked with books. A fire crackled merrily, creating a cozy heat. A thick corduroy couch was covered in throw cushions, with a blanket neatly folded on the arm. Deep armchairs were stacked around it, and there was one high-backed chair next to a small table, where a notebook and pen sat waiting next to an old-fashioned candy jar filled with sticks of red licorice. No desk.

"Do you take cream or sugar?" she asked as she carried two thick ceramic mugs into the room.

"Black is fine."

She handed him a mug and motioned for him to sit in one of the armchairs. He did, and she sat down across from him.

"This is good, thank you."

"It's a San Francisco blend. I'm a bit of a coffee snob. I'm afraid I can't drink anything else."

"How'd you become a psychologist?"

She shrugged, giving him a dimpled smile. "The usual way. Dad ran off, Mom became an alcoholic. You know, your typical dysfunctional family. I started taking psychology classes in college in an attempt to figure out my own messed-up life, and got hooked."

He smiled. He knew a number of psychologists who could tell a similar story.

Shelby placed her mug on the table and said, "Grace tells me you were the lead detective on the investigation into the Family."

"That's right."

"Before I tell you anything, I want you to know that she gave her consent for me to discuss her case with you." Shelby lifted a document from the table on which he could see Grace's signature. "Just so we're clear that I'm not breaching my code of ethics."

"Understood," Beau replied.

She dropped the document back onto the table. "Grace is diagnosed with dissociative identity disorder, what used to be called multiple personality disorder back in the day."

Beau thought back to the day before in Grace's living room. How her features had thickened, how her gaze had hardened, how she'd sworn at him in a voice that was deep and raspy. Before that he probably would have treated the idea of multiple personalities with skepticism. But yesterday's experience had left him shaken.

"Okay. Go on."

"DID is a coping mechanism that typically begins in childhood, a way for a young mind to protect itself against severe and prolonged abuse. It's often linked to children who have been raised in cults."

"Well, that fits."

"Yes. Her mind is broken into fragments, and though she's been working very hard at reconnecting all the pieces, she's still a long way from being whole. Honestly, she may never get there."

"Can you walk me through this a bit? My knowledge doesn't extend much past seeing that movie with Joanne Woodward."

Shelby nodded. "*The Three Faces of Eve.* That's about as much as most people know, unless they have some personal experience. That story was both sensationalized *and* simplified, to make it palatable for Hollywood. Ever arrive home and realize you have no memory of the drive?"

"All the time," he said.

"That's a mild level of dissociation. It's completely normal and generally harmless. The mind removes itself from reality. On one level, it's continuing to function as required — in this case by driving a car — while another part of the mind is daydreaming, thinking about work, sex, whatever."

"But Grace goes beyond this?"

"Exactly. Her dissociation grew to the level of disorder. In order to protect herself, her mind fragmented so it could shield her from the trauma."

"The trauma of being abused by their bishop," he said.

"Yes. And from all the other abuse that was going on in Brigham. The Grace part of her mind is only aware of some of it — for example, the brainwashing and mental abuse that was inflicted on her by the sect. Women are considered priesthood property, and are meant to be subservient to their husbands. The psychological damage involved in being raised to 'keep sweet,' which doesn't just mean being subservient but also stuffing down any negative feelings. Disappointment, disagreement, displeasure — they weren't allowed to feel any of those feelings, so all the bitterness and anger simmered under the surface."

"Yes, that part I understand."

Shelby's skin was red and mottled with emotion. "Can you begin to imagine the psychological distress this causes?

Being taught to be pure and obedient so you can go to heaven on judgment day, which was always *just* around the corner."

"Yes, I know."

Her skin flamed a brighter red and she took a deep breath. "Right. I forgot you would know some of this."

He sensed she was embarrassed by the cracks she'd just shown in her professional detachment, but he understood the struggle between compassion and restraint all too well. He imagined psychologists went through the same internal battle that cops did. "She's lucky to have a therapist who cares so much."

"Well, I do." She shook her head and took another deep breath. "That sounded defensive. What I meant was thank you. I care about all my patients, of course, but Grace's case is unique. The damage caused by these fundamentalist Mormons is beyond comprehension. I've spoken to a couple psychologists in Salt Lake City. They're completely inundated with cases down there. The brainwashing alone can take a lifetime to get over, and that's before we delve into the other forms of abuse."

He placed his mug on the table. "Coming back to Grace, you're saying she doesn't remember most of the abuse?"

"That's right. But she remembers being forced to marry when she was thirteen. She remembers having countless miscarriages, and some of the abuse that took place in the marriage, but not all of it. There's so much more she needs to unearth and deal with."

"How does she do that?" Beau asked.

"Well, imagine that her mind is made up of thousands of fragments. Some are tiny and some are quite large. Some clump together to become a plural, an 'us' of sorts, and others remain separate. They all hold specific pieces of information or memories. For example, she has a section that deals only with pottery. She accesses it when needed and it gives her perfect recall of everything to do with pottery: clay, kiln, techniques, and what have you. The other fragments of her mind don't have a clue because they don't need to. For most of her life she wasn't even aware this was what she was doing."

"Interesting," he said.

"Fascinating, but it leads to enormous complications. She has trouble reading. So many different sections of her mind are always firing, taking her in different directions, that it makes it hard for her to concentrate. She has to read out loud to retain the information, but then she's able to tuck it away in one of her fragments and access it later with perfect recall. It's quite brilliant, actually."

"You're describing fragments, but does she have different personalities that take over?"

"She has that, too. Some fragments have grown big enough to take on their own names and personalities. Harris is the one I know best."

"Harris," he said. "I wonder if that's who I met. He seemed very angry."

"Protective."

"Are there others?"

"Oh, yes. But I've only caught glimpses of them. Harris has grown to trust me, so he comes out frequently. I'm working with him to understand that Grace is getting stronger and can handle more. This is a first step in getting more of her fragments to fuse together."

Shelby sipped her coffee, her forehead creased in thought. "DID is a useful tool to protect the mind against something that would otherwise destroy it. But once the abuse is over, it becomes a barrier to leading a normal life. Triggers are everywhere, like landmines. They pop up out of nowhere and she can't protect herself because the part of her that's Grace doesn't know everything that's happened to her. That's where her service dog comes in handy. Bella can warn Grace when she's beginning to dissociate, and she's able to give her some protection when she does. She is trained to get her to a 'safe zone' whenever possible. In her home it's the bedroom closet. Outside the home, it can get a bit more tricky."

"So, yesterday I triggered her."

"Just seeing you again after all those years would do it. Add in the news of several deaths ..."

"Right."

Shelby sat back in her chair. "Were they suicides?"

"That question is currently on the table."

"It's common amongst people who have experienced prolonged trauma and abuse. So is drug and alcohol abuse, promiscuity — addictions of any kind, really. Her sister Desiree is a perfect example of that. I don't know anything about these people or their lives. But considering where they came from, suicide wouldn't surprise me. Sometimes the damage runs too deep, and death is the only respite."

He rubbed a hand across his eyes.

"Are you all right? You've gone pale."

"Sure, fine," he said, shaking off the ghost of his wife. "I still need to speak to Grace."

"What for?"

"Among other things, to find out if she's been in touch with any of the others she escaped with."

"Not that I'm aware of."

"I'd like to hear that from her. And I also want to know if she's had contact with any other members of the Family."

"Aren't they all dead?" she said.

"I'm just gathering information."

"Okay. But I should be there."

After what he'd experienced and what she'd told him, he wasn't about to argue. "All right."

"Can it wait until Friday? We could meet there at ten o'clock. Then I can help her work through whatever comes up, afterward."

It was only Wednesday afternoon, which left him with a lot of hours to kill. But it seemed like a reasonable course of action, so he agreed.

He drained his coffee and stood up. "Thanks for your time today."

She stood and took the cup from him. "Of course."

As she followed him down the hall to the front door, she asked, "Are you staying in Nelson tonight?"

"I hadn't thought."

"Come down to Spencer's Tavern for supper. They make an excellent beetroot burger, and the in-house blues band is amazing. Especially their lead singer." Her dimples were endearing, and her eyes were a really nice chocolate brown.

"You?" he said.

"I'll even buy you a drink."

"Maybe I will, then. But I'll pass on that burger."

"Oh, Detective. That would be a mistake."

After she closed the door, Beau stood on the porch for a moment, feeling slightly bewildered. In the car, he plugged in a Google search for local hotels before he could talk himself out of it.

FIFTEEN

t took Grace several tries before she was able to finish dialing Desiree's number. She kept having to hang up partway through because her ear would start to buzz. But eventually she managed it.

"Grace?" Desiree's voice shook on the other end of the line.

"It's me," she said, and then found she couldn't say anything more.

She listened to Desiree breathing on the other end and imagined the miles of phone lines that linked them. Such a tenuous connection, so easily brought down by wind and storms.

There'd been a time when she knew her sister's every movement, her every thought, her every desire. A time when she could close her eyes and count every freckle on Desiree's nose. Now she couldn't even picture her. Was she as thin as she'd been the last time Grace saw her? Did she have lines around her eyes, as Grace now did? Was her hair also showing the first signs of grey?

Memory was a funny thing. She realized she was picturing Desiree as she'd been at fourteen, pimpled and sparrow-thin, with her hair rolled up at the sides and pinned high on top. The higher the hair, the closer she was to heaven.

"What's your hair like, now?"

"What?" Desiree said.

"Your hair? Did you ever cut it?"

"Really short. Like a boy."

A wave of pride rolled through her. "Good for you."

"Is that really what you called to talk about?"

Grace closed her eyes. Dug the fingers of her free hand into Bella's fur. "No, of course not."

"I've been calling you for days." The accusation in Desiree's voice was clear.

"I know."

"I needed you. I'm s-so sc-scared."

Her sister's stammer brought an immediate guilty ache to her heart. "I'm sorry."

"Do you know about Rulon?"

"Yes. Detective Brunelli —"

"I called him. He came and took the note. S-said he'd look into it."

Grace sat up straight, and Bella lifted her head from her front paws and whined. "What note?"

"The newspaper article. But I just don't believe he killed himself. Or maybe he did, but I think s-someone convinced him to do it. And then they s-sent that note to me. To let me know."

116

"What newspaper article? What are you talking about?"

"About Rulon's death. And it's not just him. Eliza and Valor are gone, too. Did he tell you that?" Her sister went on in a whispered rush. "I think it's Uncle G. I think he's coming for us."

Her good ear screeched and she shook her head, trying to stay present. Bella sat up and nudged her in the ribs.

"And I don't think he's alone. I was coming home from work last night, and I s-swear s-someone was following me. I ducked into a convenience st-store and called a taxi. I waited inside until the taxi got there, but by then he'd disappeared."

"Oh, Desiree, I'm sure —"

"I never s-saw him up close. But the way he walked, kind of hunched over and leaning forward, you know? It reminded me of …"

"Of whom?"

Desiree took in a gasping breath. "He looked like your husband."

Grace's heart rammed into her throat, and she dropped the phone. It fell to the floor with a clatter.

You are my property. Consecrated to me for time and all eternity. I'll never let you go.

Desiree's voice continued from a muffled distance, "What if I'm next? Please, Grace, you have to help me!"

She rolled forward until her forehead touched her knees.

"Grace? Are you there?"

Her body shook as though with fever. Her head bounced against her legs. "Oh no, I don't believe it."

"Hello?"

"He's dead. He's got to be."

"Are you there?"

She lifted her head from her knees. "I said he's dead."

"I can barely hear you."

She scooped up the phone and rammed it against her good ear. "If he was still alive, he would have come for me a long time ago."

Desiree snuffled, then let out a deep breath. "Maybe you're right. Maybe I'm just being paranoid. But s-someone did s-send me that article. That's for sure."

She rubbed her eyes, pressed until she saw spots of light. "What was it about?"

"It was about Rulon, about how he jumped off the Lions Gate Bridge."

"Oh my God. He did?"

"Didn't Detective Brunelli tell you that?"

"No. Oh God. No, he didn't get the chance to tell me."

"The article, s-someone wrote across the top of it. A quote from the *Journal of Discourses*."

"Which one?"

"4:219."

It took Grace a moment to think of it. "About shedding the blood of sinners?"

"That's got to be from s-someone in the Family, don't you think? Or at least s-someone who knows our sc-scripture."

"Or knows how to use Google."

Desiree's breath hissed through the receiver. "You think I'm being paranoid."

She sat back and stroked Bella's fur, seeking comfort. Tears burned trails down her cheeks. "No. I don't. I don't know what to think."

"You didn't get anything in the mail?"

"No."

"Are you being careful? You're so isolated up there —"

"I'm fine. I've got Bella, don't forget." Still, she couldn't help but look around, as though making sure she was still alone in the house. How quickly Desiree's fear had spread.

"Maybe I should get a dog," Desiree said.

"It's a big responsibility."

"What are you s-saying?"

She heard the tone in her sister's voice and knew better than to rise to the bait, but she did so anyway. "Are you still going to your meetings?"

Sniff. "I'm fine."

"Desiree," she said.

"I said I'm fine. Don't worry about me."

"I'll always worry about you."

"That's why it takes a week to return my phone calls. Because you're s-so worried about me."

She sighed. "I'm sorry if the boundaries I had to set for myself have hurt you."

"Uh-huh. *Boundaries.* That's one word for it."

"Desiree, let's not do this again. Please, not now."

"Fine. I'll s-save it for the next time we have a s-sisterly chat."

"You can't spend your life blaming me —"

Desiree let out a barking sob. Between shaky breaths, she said, "I don't blame you. I take full responsibility for my decisions. And I've apologized a million times for the things I've done. But you just won't ever let it go, will you?"

"You blame me for taking you out of Brigham."

There was a pause. Not very convincingly, Desiree said, "No, I don't."

"If we hadn't escaped, everyone would still be alive. Mother, Father, Sariah —"

"I don't —"

"And Rulon and Eliza and Valor. Do you blame me for their deaths, too?"

"What's happening to your voice?" Desiree asked.

It was deepening, thickening, dripping with venom. Bella sat up and growled at her. With the last of her strength, she pulled the phone from her ear. "I'll call you later."

"Grace! Are you —"

She dropped the phone in its cradle and tumbled back into the darkness and the lamplight beyond.

SIXTEEN

don't want to be here. It feels wrong. I'd hoped the door would be locked, but it opens easily.

A lamp is on in the living room, but that's okay. I know no one is home. And the light helps. I don't like the dark.

There are three doors in the hallway, and they are all closed. Dripping water comes from the room on the left, so I know it's a bathroom. I open the second one on the right. It's a bedroom. It smells of girl stuff, like moisturizing cream and hairspray and maybe some kind of perfume or a scented candle. But beneath that, there is a familiar smell. It is one I can't place, but it reminds me of home.

I move quickly, careful to follow my instructions word for word: Lift the edge of the blanket. Wedge the piece of newspaper between the mattress and the box spring. Smooth out the blanket. Leave everything exactly as it was.

I close the bedroom door and move quietly down the hall. I even remember to lock the door as I leave.

I feel proud of myself. I've been brave. I've behaved like a good priesthood child, so perhaps now I'll be worthy of Zion.

SEVENTEEN

"Yay! I knew you'd come," Shelby said.

She jumped off the stage where the band was setting up their equipment and moved toward Beau, grinning. Her hair bounced around her shoulders. She was dressed all in black, from her jeans to her high-heeled boots to her V-neck shirt.

"Hi!" she said when she reached him.

He smiled at her enthusiasm. "Hi."

"I've got thirty minutes until we start, and I promised you a drink. What's your poison?"

"You don't need to —"

"One strawberry daiquiri coming up," she said, turning toward the bar.

"A beer!"

Beau took a booth in the back corner, giving himself an unrestricted view of the room. Cop habits were ingrained for life. Shelby carried a pitcher of beer and two glasses to their table, and slid into the seat across from him.

"Did you get a room for the night?"

"Comfort Inn."

"Walking distance. Excellent."

"I'm not much of a drinker."

She poured them both a beer, angling the glass to allow for a nice head of foam on the top. "Neither am I. But I need a little something to ease my nerves, or I get up on stage and freeze." She imitated a deer caught in headlights.

He took a sip and wiped the foam from his upper lip with a napkin. "You don't seem like the shy type."

"That's my mask."

"Your mask?"

She shrugged. "Everyone has them. You showed up today wearing your 'serious cop' mask. I'm guessing that's one you rarely take off. Right now you're sitting here with a beer in hand, feeling uncertain. You keep trying on different masks, wondering which one is appropriate for the circumstances. The 'serious cop' doesn't quite work. But the 'young bachelor' is pretty rusty, and the 'grieving widower' is a bore."

"How do you know I'm a widower?"

"I have amazing powers of observation. Or maybe Grace told me."

"Ah."

"I'm sorry you lost your wife. She must have been very young."

"She was," he said. "What are *your* masks?"

"I note that you're changing the subject, but I'm choosing to go with it. I have all the usual. 'Smiley face' to cover anxiety, 'extrovert' to cover the fact that I'd pretty much always prefer to be at home with a tub of ice cream. And my go-to all-time favourite is 'you're so fascinating.' I use this one to cover the fact that I think most people are morons."

"That doesn't sound like something a therapist should say."

"Hence the mask. It saves me from losing clients or getting punched in the face."

He laughed, and after a moment she joined in. Her laugh was deep and melodic.

She glanced at her watch. "Not much time. Give me the rundown."

"On what?"

"On you. Where you grew up, your family, your hopes and dreams and dirty little secrets."

"I'll skip the last one," he said. "But I grew up in Rosemont, in the Italian section of Montreal. Large Catholic family, I'm the youngest of eight."

"The baby? I had you pegged as an oldest child."

"Nope. By the time I came around my parents were so worn out they either spoiled me rotten or completely neglected me. I could get away with pretty much anything. My brothers were always getting into trouble. I learned from their mistakes so I wouldn't get caught."

When she smiled, the tightness he always carried in his chest eased just a little bit.

"I guess I saw my career choices as pretty limited. Cop or criminal."

"Your parents must have been pleased with your choice."

"A life of crime pays more. And now it's your turn."

Her cheeks flushed. "I prefer to dig into someone else's life rather than rehash my own."

"Me, too. But fair is fair."

"I've already told you my family is seriously messed up, and that's what led me into the glamorous field of psychology." She drained her glass and poured another.

"That's it?"

Shelby smiled and shrugged, seeming nervous.

"Special interests?" he asked, trying to help her out.

"Well, singing, obviously. Eating, as long as I don't have to cook it first."

"This is like pulling teeth."

"I'm not good at talking about myself."

"What about religion? Morals?"

She grinned. "Don't have either of those."

"All right, then. Here's an easy one. Where'd you grow up?"

She pumped a fist in the air. "Vancouver girl, born and raised. I'd say, 'Go, Canucks, go,' but they suck so hard right now it's embarrassing."

"I live just off Victoria Drive," Beau said.

"Oh, yeah?" she said. "Not too far from where I grew up."

"What —" He was interrupted by a high-pitched whine as the speakers beside the stage turned on.

Adopting a smarmy game-show-host voice, Shelby said, "*Ooooh*, I'm sorry. Your time is up. But look what you've won! A deeeeee-licious beetroot burger!"

He looked up and saw a waiter approaching.

She slid out of the booth. "Seriously, you should try it. You won't be disappointed." She gave him a finger wave and worked her way through the crowd toward the stage.

He ate several french fries, and then lifted the edge of the hamburger bun to take a look. There was a thick layer of Brie, tomato, pickle, and red onion. Heartened, he took a bite. She was right; it was delicious.

He was halfway through his burger when the band started to play, but once Shelby stepped up to the microphone he forgot about his food. Her voice was as melodic as her laugh: low and sultry; sad and enchanting.

"Oh shit."

It had been a lifetime since he'd felt that quickening inside him, but he recognized it for what it was. He put down a tip large enough to cover the meal and left before the band finished the first set.

EIGHTEEN

Jack Fletcher stood in the driveway beside his Subaru, waving at Grace as she pulled up.

"There you are! I was just about to leave."

"Jack!" She slid out of her car and waited for Bella to jump out before slamming the door. "It's not Sunday, what are you doing here? Oh no! *Is* it Sunday?"

He laughed, an easy sound that broke the stillness of the surrounding forest. "You asked me to come by after work to put on your winter tires."

"Oh, right. But that's not until tomorrow."

"Thursday," he said.

"Exactly. Thursday. I put it in my calendar." She looked at her cellphone. "Crap, today *is* Thursday."

"The last I checked."

"I'm so sorry! It's really late, I hope you haven't been waiting long."

"No worries," he said, although he must have been waiting for at least an hour. "Are the tires in the back shed?"

"Yes. Let me just put my purse down and I'll come help you."

He gave a three-fingered salute and moved off toward the back of the property. She unlocked the kitchen door and turned on the security floodlights in the side yard so they would be able to see what they were doing. She dumped her purse and keys on the counter and trotted back down the stairs to join him. Jack was a couple inches shorter than she was, but she'd learned not to underestimate his wiry strength.

He was already rolling the first winter tire toward the driveway. Grace pulled the second tire out of the shed and rolled it across a marshy patch of grass to the gravel, laying it down by the side of her car.

"Were you in town?" Jack asked as they rolled the last two tires across the grass.

She hesitated a moment, trying to remember. "Yeah."

"Did you see the banners they put up for Harvest Fest? I designed them."

"You did? That's amazing," she said. "I'll have to look the next time I'm in town."

He gave her an embarrassed smile. "It's no big deal."

"It's a huge big deal. It's about time someone other than me saw your artwork."

He lifted his hydraulic hoist out of the back of his car and set it down on the gravel.

"Wait a minute. Did you get paid for your design?"

His lank blond hair fell across his face as he bent to set the hoist in place, but she was pretty sure she saw his cheeks flush with pleasure. "Fifty bucks."

She whooped, clapping her hands together. "You're a *paid* artist! That is way more than a big deal! Congratulations."

"Thanks."

As he worked, he told her how he'd done several different renditions of the same fall theme, and of course they chose the one he liked the least.

"There's no accounting for taste," he said, then turned the conversation to a welding job he'd just completed for the city works department in Revelstoke. As they rolled the all-season tires into the shed, he told her of his plan to travel Italy in the fall. All she had to do was listen and ask the occasional question to keep him going.

"Well," he said as he lifted the hydraulic hoist back into his trunk. "You're all set for winter now."

"I still hope the snow holds off a while longer."

"It will, now that you've got your winter tires on. If we hadn't changed them, it would have started snowing tomorrow and never let up. Murphy's Law."

She smiled. "How much do I owe you? And please include however long you were waiting for me."

"Well, I was thinking."

He looked down at his feet in a nervous way that made her stomach flip with sudden anxiety. She sensed what was coming, had sensed it coming for quite a while if she was honest with herself, and fervently wished she could stop him before he said anything more.

"Maybe I could take you for a drink, or even supper, to celebrate my artistic debut?"

"Oh, Jack."

He looked so nervous. "I mean, I'll buy. I just thought it might be nice to have a night out on the town, but if you don't want to …"

Her good ear buzzed, and her head filled with cotton. Sensing the danger, Bella jumped to her side and issued a sharp bark. He stepped back, looking startled.

She needed to get inside the house. Quickly. She backed away from him, tugging on Bella's collar.

"We're so sorry. We have to …" Her heel hit the first stair and she stumbled backward, catching herself against the railing.

"Grace? Are you okay?"

She barely heard him over the screeching in her good ear. "We're so sorry."

She bounded up the stairs and stumbled into the kitchen, where she slammed the door closed. With shaking fingers, she turned the lock and ran toward the bedroom. They were coming, pushing her toward the back of her mind, to where Mother waited to tuck her in.

Bella herded her into the bedroom, where the closet door stood open and waiting. Her shoulder banged against the door frame hard enough to leave a bruise. Dropping onto the blankets and pillows laid out on the closet floor, she covered her head with both hands. Her body shook so hard, she thought she might break into a million pieces.

Bella squeezed in behind her and bit down on the strap attached to the handle, pulling the door closed. Darkness enveloped them. Bella lay down on top of her, pinning her with weighted heat.

And then Mother was there, pulling the blankets up to her neck and turning off the bedside lamp.

"Go with God, Gracey."

. . .

"Clayne Johnson, that's not how you're supposed to play the game!" She fisted her hands against her sides and scowled.

Clayne scampered off in the other direction, giggling madly, with the soccer ball tucked against his chest. Sometimes he was so immature.

"Fine!" Stomping her foot in frustration, Grace turned for home. She kicked at the dirt, making clouds of dust puff up around her feet. Everything was turning to dust. It had been hot and dry for several weeks, and more and more often she saw the adults looking up in hopes of rain.

"Grace!" Clayne came running after her, as she knew he would.

The Johnson house was full to the brim. Mother Flora's children all required special care and attention, Mother Dinah was pregnant again, and Uncle Redd had just been given a third wife. There was little attention to spare for healthy children like Clayne, so someone turning their back on him was a natural challenge.

He was beside her before she'd taken ten steps. "Okay, okay!" He pushed the ball into her arms. "Here, have it back. I was just joking."

"You're not funny."

"Come on, let's keep playing." He grabbed her arm to slow her down. "Please."

She hesitated because she really didn't want to go home. Mother Rebecca would give her surly looks and demand things of her. Plus, as hot as it was outside, it was ten times worse inside.

"Come on, Gracey." He used her nickname in an attempt to gain favour. He smiled at her, charming her as he always did, and squeezed her hand. "You know you can't resist this stupid face."

She sighed. "Do you want to play Cowboys and Indians instead?"

"Yeah!" He loved chasing her across fields and trails, using a stick as a pretend gun.

"Hey!"

Boydell stood by the front gate. His cheeks were red with indignation, and his nose was crusted with mucus.

"Hey, *what*?"

Just the sight of him was enough to make her angry. He'd become a constant challenge to her duty to keep sweet. He was small for his age, and weak. He could barely last a day on farming duty without falling into a dead faint. As a result, the other kids gave him less respect than he thought he deserved.

"You're not supposed to do that!" Boydell said.

"Do what?" Clayne asked.

Boydell pointed at them. "*That!*"

In unison, they looked down at their joined hands. She tugged her hand free, a rush of shame heating her cheeks.

"I'm telling my father." Boydell ran off before they could plead their case.

Clayne looked at her, his eyes wide with panic. He'd been in trouble so many times recently his backside was probably still tender and bruised.

"Go home," she said. "I'll go after Boydell."

He shook his head and tried to argue, but she pushed him toward his home and took off after Boydell. She expected to catch him quickly, but he had the advantage of not wearing a long dress. It tangled around her legs as she ran.

He was already a hundred yards up the road, kicking up clouds of dirt as he ran. She wasn't going to reach him before he made it home.

"Boydell, stop! Please!"

He didn't even slow down. Within moments, he disappeared into his shadowy front yard and ran around the side of the house toward the kitchen door. She'd only been in the bishop's home the once, but she'd seen the mudroom from outside. It was as big as her bedroom, and coats and shoes and boots were lined up on hooks and racks, neatly labelled for each member of the household.

She froze in the middle of the road, riddled with indecision. Should she wait for Uncle G to come out or should she go home and start praying? Her heartbeat pounded in her ear and her breath came in ragged gasps. Sweat dripped into her eyes, causing them to sting and blur.

The front door opened and there stood Uncle G. He stepped out onto the front porch and smiled at her. It was a disarming kind of smile, both warm and kind, but she knew from experience that the smile didn't make it to his eyes. He beckoned her forward.

Grace couldn't feel her feet, but they must have been down there somewhere. They moved obediently in his direction. She opened the gate, crossed the yard, and climbed the steps into the shade of the front porch.

Stopping in front of the bishop, she clutched her hands in front of her and bent her head. Uncle G was barefoot. His feet looked huge. His toenails were yellow and cracked, and tufts of grey hair grew on his toes.

"Are you supposed to touch boys?"

"N-no, Uncle G."

"How should you view them?"

"Like they're poisonous snakes," she said.

"Would you hold hands with a poisonous snake, Grace?"

"No."

He shifted forward, his giant belly taking the lead. She forced herself to stay still.

"Were you holding hands with Clayne Johnson?"

She nodded.

"So, you're in need of a correction?"

Tears leaked from her eyes, making rivers on her cheeks. She nodded.

"Is Clayne in need of a correction?"

"N-no, Uncle G. I'm the one who grabbed his hand."

"Is that so?" The bishop's voice was soft and slow.

"He tried to pull away, but I held on to it."

If God was going to strike her down for the lie she'd just told, she hoped He'd do it soon.

"Come inside."

"Okay."

His voice boomed, making her jump. "How should you respond to a priesthood command?"

Her mind went blank, and she looked up at him in panic. He loomed above her, red-faced and sweating. He had thick grey hair and a long grey beard. He wore jeans and a blue plaid shirt, and the metal on his suspenders gleamed as though freshly polished.

His mouth twisted with disapproval, and he shook his head. "You need a lesson along with your correction."

Grace followed him into the house. Boydell waited just inside the door with a smile on his face that made her want to punch him. She looked down and bit into her lip, praying for the strength to keep sweet.

"Take off your shoes," Uncle G said.

She removed her shoes and placed them on the rubber mat by the door. As she straightened, her foot caught on the lace edging of her skirt. It tore, and Boydell snickered.

Uncle G moved toward the stairs. "Follow me. Boydell — you, too. You'll bear witness."

Boydell went pale and his mouth fell open. Uncle G climbed the stairs, leaving them in the entryway.

She straightened her dress, wiped an arm across her wet cheeks, and walked past Boydell without looking at him. Grasping the railing, she moved unsteadily up the stairs.

Boydell followed her. She kept her back straight so he wouldn't see how afraid she was. She could smell his fear, sour and tangy like warm yogurt. Mother always said she had a nose like a truffle pig, whatever that meant.

Uncle G waited at the top of the stairs, a hard smile on his face. He motioned her into a room on the right, his study. It was dim, lit only by a lamp in the corner. Shelves lined the walls, filled with leather-bound books. She'd never seen so many books. Within this room she might find the answers to all her asked and unasked questions, if she only knew how to read.

A large desk made of dark wood took up the middle of the room. It was covered with papers, handwritten notes, and a bowl half filled with almonds.

Chairs surrounded the desk, and off to the right was a wide couch covered in dark green fabric. The couch's arms were threadbare, the seat cushions worn and stained. She wondered if Uncle G took naps there. Boydell stood in the corner of the room, breathing in great big gasps.

Uncle G moved around the desk and took a seat. He pointed at a chair. "Sit down."

Her feet didn't quite reach the floor. She pressed her hands into her lap as a reminder not to swing her legs. She crossed her ankles and looked down at her lap. Her dress was pale blue with tiny pink flowers. The lace trim was grey with dirt and age.

"When speaking to an elder, how should you address them?"

"With respect?"

"Yes," he said. "But what words should you use? If a man of the priesthood asks you to do something, how should you answer?"

"I should bow and say, 'I am here to do your will.'"

"And what if nothing was asked of you. How should you make yourself useful?"

"By saying, 'How may I serve you?'"

"I see Patrick hasn't been completely negligent in your raising," Uncle G said.

Warmth spread outward from her chest. She was getting the answers right.

"As a priesthood girl, what words should be utmost in your thoughts?"

She almost sighed with relief. She knew this answer, as well. "I want to be the humble servant of the prophet."

"Good." Uncle G leaned back in his chair.

She bit her lip and remained still.

"Everything you do is a direct reflection on your father. Do you understand that?"

"Yes, Uncle G."

"If you are sweet and obedient, it means your father is raising you well."

She nodded.

"And if you are not, it reflects poorly on him. What happens if your father loses control of his family?"

Her voice shook as she answered. "He loses his place in the priesthood."

"That's right. He loses his family, and he has to leave Brigham and repent his lost ways."

Tears burned her eyes and stung her cheeks, which were already puffy and raw. She'd seen this happen to other families. The father was suddenly gone, and the women and children were reassigned to other priesthood elders. The thought of this happening to her family, happening because of *her*, was horrifying.

"I can see that you understand the seriousness of this," Uncle G said.

"Y-yes."

"And that you do not wish to bring shame upon your family."

"No."

"Then you will come to me for extra study on Tuesdays and Thursdays, and we will continue your education."

"I-I am grateful for your w-wisdom."

"Good. Now stand up."

She pushed herself forward until her feet could touch the ground. Shakily, she stood.

"I just asked you to do something. What should you say?"

She wiped an arm across her eyes, kept her gaze on the floor. "I am here to do your will."

His chair scraped. He moved around the desk and stood before her. She stared at his feet, at his hairy toes and yellowed toenails.

"Go sit on the couch, Grace."

Boydell wheezed in the corner.

She moved over to the couch and sat down. Her heart lodged in her throat, a panicked bird trying to escape. Her good ear buzzed. Her head grew foggy.

"What should you say, Grace?"

Boydell made mewling noises, like a hurt cat.

When she spoke, her voice sounded very far away. "I am h-here to do your w-w-will."

When Uncle G's shadow fell upon her, her mind unlocked from its moorings and floated free. She escaped into the shadows, seeking the warm protection of her mother.

Ahead she saw her bedroom, the comforting yellow glow of her bedside lamp. And there was her bed. The blanket was pulled aside, awaiting her body. She lay down and pressed her face into the pillow. It was both scratchy and soft against her cheek.

Mother pulled the blanket up to her shoulders and tucked it around her neck, locking in the heat from her body.

"Have you said your prayers?"

"Yes, Mother."

"Then you will be safe. Go with God, Gracey."

Mother stroked the hair from her forehead, then reached over and turned off the lamp.

NINETEEN

Beau drove back to Nakusp on Thursday and spent the rest of the day in his hotel room, doing what work he could manage from his laptop.

The coroners' reports had come through for Valor Johnson and Eliza Barlow.

Eliza's death eight months prior was from asphyxia caused by hanging. Abbotsford police were called for a well-being check after she didn't show up for work for several days. They found her lying on the floor beside her bed. She'd fashioned a slip-knot noose out of bedsheets, tied them to a high post on her bed, and used the weight of her body to cut off her supply of oxygen.

Because her body hadn't been discovered for six days, it was bloated to almost double in size. The Abbotsford coroner's office had included photos taken at the scene, which he skimmed through. There was mention of a suicide note, but the note's contents were missing from the coroner's report. He grunted in frustration and typed a quick email, requesting the missing information.

Valor Johnson's death in Calgary three years prior was from hypoxia due to carbon monoxide poisoning. He'd been living in a small cabin on the back end of an acre of land owned by a local rancher, caring for the horses in exchange for room and board. He'd used a gas-powered generator to power his cooktop, fridge, and several portable heaters. Because the cabin had poor insulation, he was known to stuff newspaper along the windows and door frames during the winter.

Hundreds of pages filled with his scrawl were found inside the cabin, but none stood out as a suicide note. He'd apparently been writing a book about growing up in Brigham. Much of the story centred on his brothers Boaz and Clayne.

Beau had already put out a BOLO for the missing Johnson brothers. He'd had no luck a decade before, but occasionally the passage of time unearthed bones instead of burying them deeper.

Valor's landlord found the body after Valor didn't emerge to feed the horses that morning. Toxicology revealed a lethal carboxyhemoglobin blood level. In other words, he'd suffered carbon monoxide poisoning from the gas generator's exhaust fumes. In the absence of a suicide note or any known suicidal tendencies, the death was ruled accidental.

Beau closed his laptop and lay back on the bed, thinking it through. So far, nothing linked their deaths aside from the obvious, but his gut rolled with unease. He needed to track down the rest of Brigham's Ten, along with any of the other boys who'd been excommunicated. He wasn't sure if he was looking for more victims, possible suspects, or just digging up proof that abused children grew up to commit suicide at a higher rate than the national average. Big duh.

To help him see things more concretely, he scribbled a list of Brigham's Ten, along with a brief description of what he knew of them:

1. Grace DeRoche — Nakusp
2. Desiree DeRoche — Vancouver
3. Rulon Smith — Deceased by jumping from Lions Gate Bridge
4. Shilo Smith — Whereabouts unknown
5. Shareen Smith — Whereabouts unknown
6. Valor Johnson — Deceased by carbon monoxide poisoning in Calgary
7. Tabitha Johnson — Kelowna
8. Eliza Barlow — Deceased by hanging in Abbotsford
9. Danielle Taylor — Edmonton
10. Ernest Young — Whereabouts unknown

Only four of the ten had been confirmed as alive. This added to Beau's unease. He made a note to visit Tabitha Johnson once he'd interviewed Grace DeRoche. Kelowna was a reasonable detour for him to make on his way back to Vancouver.

But Doug wouldn't approve a trip to Edmonton based on the current evidence, so he filed a request with the

Edmonton RCMP for a well-being check on Danielle Taylor, and asked them to question her about any contact she'd had with former members of the Family.

He left a message for Desiree, asking her to call him, and another for Judy Beers, requesting an update on Rulon's case. Perhaps the forensics had come back on the backpack they'd found along the Stanley Park Causeway.

After that, he couldn't think of another thing to do from his current location, so he stuck two pillows under his head, pulled up the covers, and took a nap. Emily waited for him in the sunshine, cherry blossoms dancing around her head.

Shelby drove into Grace's driveway just ahead of Beau the next morning. As he pulled to a stop she jumped out of her vehicle and trotted toward him, giving him a perky wave. She wore jeans and a neon green ski jacket. Her smile exposed dimples.

"Shit."

"What happened to you the other night? Was the burger that bad?"

He climbed out of his car. "I'm an old man. I'm on a curfew."

"You're not *that* old," she said with a wave of her hand.

"Might have sounded better without the '*that*.'"

She laughed in acknowledgement, and then turned serious. "I hope it wasn't the music?"

"Not at all," he said. "You sing like an angel."

Dimple flash. "That was just the compliment I was digging for. Shall we?"

He followed her up the stairs to the porch and waited while she knocked. A minute passed, and she knocked again. She turned to survey the property behind them.

"Bella would be yammering by now if they were home. Maybe they're in the barn."

He followed Shelby down the stairs and they crossed the property side by side. Mud sucked at his shoes. The goat yard was empty save for the smell of shit. It seared his nostril hairs.

"It's a sunny day. The goats should be outside. Something's not right." Shelby's brow furrowed.

Beau surreptitiously unlocked the harness over his gun.

When she pushed open the barn door, a group of goats tumbled forward, bleating complaints. She stepped back and the heel of her boot ground painfully against his toes. Wincing, he caught her by the arms and nudged her forward so he could close the door behind them before any animals escaped.

Grace was in a stall on the far side, red-faced and flustered, her hair a tangle of sweat and grime. She wiped her brow with her left hand while her right continued to pull at the teat of the goat standing before her.

"Sorry! I slept in. They're ticked."

"I can see that," he said.

The goats swarmed around him, voicing complaints in their strangely expressive language. Their bodies knocked into him, warm and heavy and pungent. He pushed them back, feeling coarse hair and the sharp ridges of their spines.

Shelby slipped to the side and pressed against the wall, holding up her hands as though someone pointed a gun in her face. "Stop crowding me. I'm not food."

He moved through the throng. "Can I help?"

"Ever milk a goat?" Grace asked.

"No. But I'm willing to learn."

"Then pull up a stool, Detective."

Once he was settled, Grace led a round-bellied goat onto the stand in front of him. "This is Gertrude. She's a pacifist."

She placed a bucket of food in front of the goat, and Gertrude buried her face in it.

"Give your hands a wash with this, and then use the cloth to clean the udder."

He followed her instructions. The teat felt soft and strange in his hands, and he quelled the urge to apologize to Gertrude for the intrusion.

"That's good," Grace said. "But move your hands up a smidge. You want to grasp right near the top of the udder to stop the milk from going back up."

"Like this?"

"Yep. But pulling down on her teat hurts. You have to press inward like this, drawing the milk down and out. There, you've got it."

The sound of milk hitting the metal pail was oddly satisfying. "Hey, Shelby, want to get in on this?"

"I'll pass." Shelby moved to a bench near the door. Bella followed and laid her head in Shelby's lap.

"She doesn't believe in manual labour," Grace said.

Shelby smiled, stroking the fur on Bella's massive head. "It's true."

"Is it okay if we talk now? Or would you rather wait?"

"We can try now. I'll do my best to stay with you." She gave him a nervous look. "Shelby explained my condition?"

"She did. I understand that something I say might trigger you to … what do you call it?"

"To dissociate."

"Right," he said. "I'm sorry for the way I upset you the other day."

"Not your fault. Unless you're the one who pushed Rulon off the bridge."

"I never said how he died."

Her cheeks went pink. "Desiree told me."

"Well, the jury's still out on his cause of death."

"Hold that thought. These girls are done."

She stood and took the milk pails over to a large metal cooler, where she poured the milk and closed the lid. Then she brought over two new goats.

He watched her from the corner of his eye. "In regard to Eliza's and Valor's deaths —"

Grace's hands trembled on the teat, and the goat bleated a complaint. "Are they really gone?"

"Yes."

She sighed, patting the disgruntled goat's side in apology. "I haven't seen either of them in more than a decade. It shouldn't hurt so badly."

"There's no such thing as time when it comes to people you love," Shelby said.

"I guess you're right."

"I usually am."

Grace gave her a small smile. "And modest."

147

"One of my best qualities," Shelby said.

"May I ask how they died?"

"Eliza's death was ruled a suicide."

Grace closed her eyes and let out a sharp breath, like she'd been hit in the gizzards.

"Valor's was ruled accidental. Carbon monoxide poisoning from a gas generator."

"Oh, that's awful." She took several shaky breaths. He guessed she was trying to stay present, so he shut his mouth and waited.

"All right," she finally said with a nod. "Go on."

"I'm tracking down the others who escaped with you that day. I'd also like to talk to Boaz and Clayne Johnson."

Grace jerked as though hit by an electric current.

"Any idea where they are?"

She shook her head, her hair falling across her face like a shield.

"Have you heard from them since they left Brigham?"

"Why would I?" Her voice sounded deeper, rougher.

"Grace," Shelby said. "Take a breath."

She did as instructed, and then shook her hair back from her face so she could look at him. Her eyes — one brown and one blue — were wide with pain. "I try not to think about them. Clayne especially."

"Why?"

"Because what happened to him was my fault."

"What happened to him?"

Instead of answering she went through the same procedure of emptying the milk pails, releasing the milked goats, and leading two more onto the milking stand.

"This is Brownie. Watch her hind legs. She'll step in the milk pail if you're not paying attention."

He took a shot in the dark. "Was he your boyfriend?"

Her lips curled in a sad smile. "If only I'd been so brave."

"I hear he was a bit rebellious."

"By Brigham standards. He got lots of corrections because he never learned how to keep his mouth closed."

"Is that why he was excommunicated?"

"No." She looked down, hair covering her face. Bella gave a sharp bark. Shelby stood up and moved toward them.

Beau said, "What happened to Clayne?"

Grace's head snapped up, and she glowered at him. Her face had broadened and somehow become more masculine.

Beau went still, trying to ignore the fact that his heart had set up residence in his throat. He saw Shelby approaching from the corner of his eye. Bella whined and pressed into Grace from the side.

"Stupid kid thought it was safe to trust Grace." Her voice was a thick growl.

Shelby leaned down and touched her shoulder. "Hey, it's okay."

She swung toward her therapist, her eyes like dual-coloured daggers. "What's okay, *Doc*?"

Still lodged in his throat, Beau's heart gave a meaty *kathump*.

"Grace is safe," Shelby said. "She doesn't need you right now."

"Really? And *you* know what she needs?"

"Grace," Shelby said, raising her voice. "Come on back. Everything's okay."

"Nothing will be okay until you stop fucking with her head."

Shelby recoiled as though she'd been slapped. Then she took a breath and tried again. "Grace, you're safe. You don't need to hide right now."

"You're wrong. I'm the one who keeps her safe. And what do *you* do, *Doc*?"

"Grace?" Beau said.

She looked up at him with someone else's eyes.

It made his skin prickle. He coughed, trying to get his heart out of the way so he could talk. "I'm Beau. What's your name?"

"I know who you are, Detective Brunelli." Spit flew from her mouth and hit his cheek. He didn't wipe it away.

"Then why don't you tell me who *you* are?"

Her mouth stretched into something not at all resembling a smile.

"Let Grace come back," Shelby said. "The detective wants to talk to her."

At the moment Beau was more interested in talking to whoever this was. He leaned closer. "Why does Grace feel guilty about Clayne?"

Grace's mouth stretched even more, becoming a snarl.

"Detective," Shelby said, "let me handle this."

"Yeah, Detective. Let her handle it. She's really good at handling things."

"What's making you so angry?" he asked.

Shelby leaned toward him, her face flushed. "That's enough."

He nodded in Grace's direction. "But maybe they have something to say. And I know I'd like to hear it."

"You don't understand the damage —"

"Do you have something you want to tell me?" he asked the person behind Grace's eyes.

Grace's mouth twisted as though she found him amusing. "Oh, there's all kinds of things I could tell you, Detective."

"I'm all ears."

"He was unworthy of the priesthood. He went astray."

"Astray? How so?"

"He ignored the teachings of the prophet."

"What teachings did he ignore?"

"Everything!" More spittle flew, hitting Beau on the cheek and forehead. "He had no respect for the elders. He questioned the word of our bishop. He dishonoured Grace's marriage."

Oh. That was interesting. "How did he do that?"

"Celestial marriages are sealed in the highest realms of heaven. No man can break that bond, and to try is the highest insult to both God and our prophet."

"What did Clayne do that was so insulting?"

She opened her mouth as though to answer, but then shook her head. "I've told you enough."

A brief stare down ensued, and then Grace's body shook like she'd been jolted with an electrical current. Her feet kicked out, almost toppling the pail of milk in front of her. Her chin dropped to her chest, and her head rolled from side to side.

Bella leaned against her, whining. Grace's hand flopped around like a fish on a riverbank, until it found Bella's neck. Her fingers dug into the fur.

"I'm sorry," Grace said. "Ooh, I think I'm going to be sick." She leaned over, retching.

Shelby stroked her back. "It's okay. You're okay, take some deep breaths." Her voice was soft and gentle, but the look she gave Beau was hot enough to leave blisters. She jerked her head toward the door, signalling for him to leave.

He decided he'd pushed his luck far enough. He left the barn and made his way across the muddy yard. Gravel crunched under his shoes as he crossed the driveway. He settled into the wicker couch on the porch to wait.

Eventually they emerged from the barn, the dog trucking along behind them. Shelby had an arm wrapped protectively around Grace's waist.

Where Grace was tall and lanky, Shelby was shorter and rounded at hip and chest. Grace's blond hair was stick-straight, Shelby's an unruly mass of dark curls. Despite these differences, they moved as one across the grass and gravel, as though linked by steel cables invisible to the naked eye.

As they climbed the stairs to the porch, Shelby said, "I think you'd better leave."

Grace's eyes were swollen and her cheeks were mottled and raw-looking, but she straightened with determination. "It's okay. Come inside."

Beau jumped up, ignoring Shelby's gaze. He followed Grace into the living room and sat in the same chair he'd previously sat in. Grace took the couch, and Bella lay down across the top of her feet. Shelby leaned against the doorway and crossed her arms over her chest.

"She's a great dog," he said.

"I don't know what I'd do without her." Grace gazed down at the dog with affection. "When I have an episode it's like I go to sleep, and someone else takes over. It can be pretty scary. Like one time I woke up near the edge of the cliff over there." She nodded toward where the property overlooked Upper Arrow Lake.

"But most of the time it's just inconvenient. Like this morning, I didn't actually oversleep. One of my alters over-stayed their welcome. Sometimes I wake up to a huge mess in the kitchen. Or the gate to the goat pen will be open, and they've all escaped."

She stroked the dog's head. "Bella's trained to pick up on changes in me. She can sense when one of my alters is taking over and she warns me. She uses her body weight to ease my anxiety and she tries to keep me safe when someone else takes a turn at the wheel."

"Do you know your alters? Do you talk to them or anything?"

"It's not like we're all hanging out at this pub inside my mind," she said with a smile. "When I was young I heard a lot of different voices, often contradicting each other. Like one would be telling me to argue with something I felt was un-just, while another was warning me to keep sweet. At times so many voices would talk at once, I'd basically just freeze."

"I can't imagine."

"And I can't imagine having a quiet mind. Must be lonely. But to answer your question, I don't really know my alters. They're like strangers I pass in a dark alley. I might catch a glimpse of them on my way by, but I couldn't pick them out of a lineup later."

"Grace, I'd like to ask you some questions now."

She stroked the fur on Bella's broad back. "Okay."

"Have you kept in contact with anyone since the escape?"

"In the beginning, I kept in touch with all of them. The social workers made sure the lines stayed open. I visited Tabby and Rulon in their foster homes a few times. And of course I saw Desiree. But after the Family —" she paused, blinked back sudden tears "— after there was no more case for the police to pursue, we all slowly lost touch. Desiree got into drugs. I spent years trying to save her, hauling her into one rehab after another. Worrying, crying, chasing her down." She shrugged. "None of it did any good. She'd be clean for a while, and then she'd slip. When she stole money from me that was the last straw. I cut ties."

"She seems to be doing well, now."

"Yes. She's been clean for a few years. This time."

His phone buzzed against his thigh with an incoming text message. "What about the others? Any contact with them?"

"Not in a long time."

His phone buzzed again, and he pulled it out of his pocket and hit the button to silence it. "What about the boys who were excommunicated? Boaz? Clayne?"

Shelby stepped into the room, ready to run interference.

Grace shook her head in her therapist's direction. "I've tried to find Clayne a few times. A few years ago, I hired a private investigator. But I couldn't afford to pay him for more than ten hours of work, and it didn't amount to much. I just wanted to know if he was …"

"All right?"

"Alive," she said.

Beau's phone buzzed a third time, vibrating against the palm of his hand. He looked down and read the message. "I'm sorry, but something's come up. I have to cut this short."

"Of course."

"Thanks for your time today. I'll probably need to come back."

"Okay," she said.

"Call me first." Shelby seemed poised to follow him to the door.

"I'll see myself out." He had neither the time nor the desire for a browbeating. He trotted down the stairs and jumped into his car. His adrenaline was pumping, his heart hammering in the base of his throat.

He called his boss's cell, pressing the phone against his ear while he yanked the seat belt across his chest and rammed it home.

"Doug? It's Beau."

"Get over there," Doug said. "The coroner's office is still on the scene. I've let them know you're on your way."

"It's going to take about three and a half hours to get there."

"Shit. All right, I'll call them back. But get going."

"Already gone," he said, and rammed the car into reverse.

TWENTY

The sound of gravel spinning under Detective Brunelli's tires relayed the urgency of the situation, and Grace's stomach tightened with anxiety.

"I wonder what that was about?"

Shelby shrugged. "You did well today."

"Yeah? I felt pretty steady, except for that episode in the barn."

Shelby waved a hand. "You're definitely getting stronger. You're needing the others less and less often."

"I don't know about that. I was gone all night."

"What was the trigger?"

"Jack Fletcher. He asked me out. On a date."

"Really." Shelby sat back, a frown creasing her brow. "How do you feel about that?"

"Well, obviously it triggered me at the time. But this morning I started thinking about it."

"Oh?"

Her cheeks prickled with warmth. "I like him. I mean, I'm not sure if I like him in *that* way. I don't even know what it feels like, to have romantic feelings for someone …"

Of course that wasn't true, but she shied away from the memory of her first and only love. If she spent too much time thinking about him, her grief would crush her. She shook her head, turning her thoughts back to Jack Fletcher. He was kind, thoughtful, and dependable. He was exactly the kind of man she'd encourage a friend to date, if she had any friends, so why shouldn't she want the same for herself?

"I enjoy his company. And I feel comfortable around him, which is rare in and of itself. So, maybe I should say yes?"

Shelby leaned forward and propped her elbows on her legs. "You haven't gone on a date since you escaped from Brigham —"

"I've never gone on a date."

"Right. And at some point, if you want to have a fulfilling life, you'll have to let other people in."

"I sense a *but*."

Shelby shook her head. "No, there's no *but*. From what you've told me, he sounds like a good man."

"It's not him you're worried about. You think I'm not strong enough? Or that I'll hurt him somehow?"

"I think you're projecting your own fears on to me," Shelby said, although her brow was creased with concern. "It's not up to me to decide what you're ready for."

Grace rubbed her forehead, trying to ease the ache between her eyebrows. "When I came around this morning, I had this feeling … it was weird. I didn't recognize it at first."

"What was it?"

"I think it was hope."

They sat in silence for a minute. Grace continued to rub her aching forehead.

"Have you told him anything about your past? Or your DID?" Shelby asked.

"No."

"That would be an important conversation to have."

Grace rubbed her forehead more vigorously. "Wouldn't that scare him off?"

"Perhaps. But wouldn't that be worth knowing sooner rather than later?"

She sighed. "My head hurts."

"Should we drop the subject for now?" Shelby said.

"Yeah."

"I'd like to know more about your dissociation. When did you wake up?"

"Around nine thirty this morning."

"Where?"

"On the porch. I was wearing different clothes, and my winter coat." She hesitated, and then pulled the note from her pocket. "This was beside me."

Shelby took the note from her and examined it. The lettering was childlike, with the *R*s reversed. Grace reread it upside down.

SWEET SISTER, THE PROPHET CALLS
ON US TO ATONE BY BLOOD FOR OUR
WRONGDOINGS

"Would you like me to speak to Harris?"

She thought about it for a minute. "All right."

"Get comfortable."

Grace untucked her feet from under Bella's body and lay down on the couch with a cushion under her head. The dog curled around her, supplying her with heated comfort.

As Shelby took her through the breathing ritual to begin her hypnosis — breathe in for a count of four, breathe out for a count of four — she eased into the darkness of her mind. She moved down the hallway, noting the doors that had been left open but not pausing to shut them. Someone moved past her, but she didn't try to see who it was. Instead, she moved toward the dim lamplight of her childhood bedroom, where Mother waited to tuck her in.

• • •

She spun clay on Mother's wheel, trying to make a water pitcher for the spring fair. The clay kept falling in on itself, and she had to keep punching it back into shape over and over again.

"Grace, wake up!"

The clay fell in again, a spinning blob of frustration.

"Grace! You must wake up now." Someone shook her hard.

She punched at the clay, trying to make it respond. It was drying out, and cracks were forming. She needed to add water, but she kept punching at it instead, her anger mounting.

Someone grabbed her hands. "Grace, stop!"

Mother. It was Mother's voice, and she sounded frantic. Grace opened her eyes and saw her darkened bedroom.

Mother pulled her to her feet. "You must get going!"

"What?"

When Mother let her go, Grace's legs gave way. She sat on the bed, blinking and trying to clear her head. It was nighttime. She was sick again. Her fever had peaked at one hundred and four. She'd been put to bed right after supper, delirious and dehydrated. Mother had placed a pitcher of water by her bedside and ordered her to drink as much of it as she could manage.

Now Mother shook her until her teeth clattered against each other. "The police are here!"

This brought her out of her fever fog. "What? Oh no!"

She grabbed Mother's nightgown, pressed her face into the rough cotton. What if they took Mother and Father away? What if they didn't come home?

Mother batted at her hands. "You must see your sisters safe. Do you hear me?"

"Oh, Mother!"

"Look at me, child." Mother grabbed the sides of her face. "Take Desiree and Sariah to the forest. Just like we've practised. Do you understand?"

"Y-yes." Just like they'd practised. But the police had never come before, so Grace had never taken their drills seriously.

"You are a brave girl." Mother stroked the sweat-soaked hair from her forehead. "God will be with you."

Mother shoved boots on her feet and helped her to stand. They went into the hallway, where Desiree wailed as Father helped her on with her shoes.

Her eyes wide and spilling tears, Mother Rebecca shoved baby Sariah into Grace's arms. "P-please take care of her."

"I promise." The weight of the responsibility was so much heavier than the blanket-wrapped babe in her arms. She pulled the blanket up to protect Sariah's head.

She took a deep breath, tried to calm her racing heart. "Come on, Desiree. Remember, you must be quiet as a mouse now."

Her sister snuffled back tears and nodded.

"Go with God." Father touched each girl on the head in farewell and opened the rear door of the house.

The icy wind took her breath away. She'd forgotten her coat, but it was too late. Mother pushed them out the door, and the girls were on their own.

They ran across the backyard. Desiree lifted the trick fence post and Grace ducked to climb through, a protective hand cupped over Sariah's head. Desiree followed and pushed the fence post back into place.

A few houses down the road, Emma Barlow screamed.

"Stay close beside me."

Desiree nodded.

They had to cross the pumpkin field and then another field that had gone fallow for winter before they reached the safety of the forest. The moon was high and full, and it lit their path well enough to weave around the pumpkins without tripping. But the moonlight also made her feel exposed.

She ducked low, keeping one hand on Sariah's head, and prayed to God and the prophet for protection. Sariah whimpered and kicked her legs in distress, rooting at Grace's chest for milk she couldn't provide.

Her nightgown was thin and threadbare, and soaked with fever sweat. The temperature wasn't far above freezing, and the wind whipping down from the ice-capped mountains slapped her cheeks and bit at her eyes. By the time they reached the end of the pumpkin field, she trembled with cold and fatigue. She tightened her grip on Sariah, frightened she'd drop her in the dirt.

Halfway across the second field, the world tilted sideways and began to spin. Grace cried out in fear. The moon rotated above her in maddening circles and she stumbled and swayed, trying to stay on her feet.

"Grace!"

Desiree's voice sounded like Father's records when she stuck a finger on the edge of the vinyl to slow their spin. It made Father so angry when she did that. She turned and stumbled, lost in the moonlight.

Desiree grabbed her by the sleeve to pull her along. Sariah wailed. She was probably squeezing too hard, but she was so afraid of dropping her.

"Hurry! They're coming!"

The trees rose around them, tucking the girls into the shelter of their darkness.

Everything spun. The ground shifted beneath her, and she stumbled sideways and fell. Sariah flew from her arms, baby blankets fluttering outward like wings.

"No!"

Grace hit the ground so hard the breath was knocked from her lungs. She couldn't move. She couldn't breathe.

She lay like a bag of aching bones, an empty cocoon. Where was Sariah? She couldn't hear anything. Her good ear was stuffed with cotton.

Above her, beams of light sliced the darkness. They danced and jittered, highlighting tree bark and spiny winter branches.

Oh, that was good. God was coming to lift them to heaven, just as promised. What prayer was she supposed to recite?

Her ear unplugged, and she heard men's voices. They were shouting. Closer, she heard children screaming. Not in rapture, but in fear.

So, it wasn't the time of judgment, after all. Desiree was right. The police were coming.

TWENTY-ONE

By the time Beau made it to Kelowna, the body had been removed to the morgue. The coroner waited for him by the glass doors of the apartment building, which was just down the street from the University of British Columbia's Okanagan Campus.

"Detective Brunelli?" she said as he approached. "Jessica Chambers, Kelowna Coroner's Office."

"Thanks for waiting for me." The late afternoon sun was already getting low in the sky.

"We're still processing the scene." She opened the door to lead him inside.

The apartment building was a modern three-level, the lobby floor covered in grey tile and the walls painted a stark white. They were covered with oversize black-and-white photographs, all depicting beach scenes in close-up: a towel laid out on the sand, an abandoned bucket and shovel, a sandcastle falling into the water. They passed a row of mailboxes and stopped by the elevator, where she hit the Up button.

"The body is on the way to the coroner's office," Jessica said. "Autopsy has been scheduled for tomorrow afternoon."

"That's quick," he said.

The elevator opened, and he followed her inside. She hit the button for the third floor, and the doors closed.

"Small town. And the sooner we get tissue samples, the better."

The car hummed upward, and the doors opened to reveal a long, dim hallway. Halfway down, crime-scene tape covered an apartment door. A uniformed officer was stationed out front, speaking in quiet tones to a group of curious neighbours.

The officer stepped aside to allow them to pass, and Beau paused to put on the booties and gloves waiting just inside the entrance. The walls and surfaces were grimy with fingerprint dust, and a man in coveralls was meticulously making his way along the hallway.

"All right, walk me through it."

"The decedent is Tabitha Johnson, twenty-nine. We're still looking for next of kin."

"You're going to have trouble finding any. She's a foster kid."

"Her roommate, Christy Seacrest, found the body. She came home this morning after spending the night with her boyfriend, and found Tabitha in the bathroom. No signs of forced entry, and Christy says the front door was locked when she came home."

Beau examined the door, the frame, and the locking mechanism. It didn't look like it had been tampered with. Jessica led him past a small galley kitchen, which was tidy aside from a bowl and spoon sitting on the strainer beside the sink, and into a combination living room-dining room.

"They're both students at UBC. Tabitha was working toward a degree in social work, and Christy is younger and doing her bachelor's. When Christy left for her boyfriend's last night, Tabitha was studying in the living room. We found several textbooks on the coffee table, along with a laptop and a notepad with handwritten notes. They're on their way to forensics for further testing."

"What did the notes say?"

"They look like notes for a research paper. Nothing that stuck out as suicide talk."

Beau pointed to a glass door that led from the living room to a small balcony overlooking the street. The balcony was just wide enough for two chairs and a small table. "The sliding door?"

"Two locks, one at the handle and one that goes into the floor. Both were engaged. And being on the third floor overlooking a residential street, it seems an unlikely point of entry. We've gathered prints and fibres, so we'll see. This way, Detective."

He followed Jessica down the hall, and they stopped by the bathroom door.

"Christy says when she came home, Tabitha's bedroom door was closed. She assumed she was still asleep. Christy went straight to the bathroom to take a shower. When she saw Tabitha in the bathtub, she called 911. She says she didn't touch the body. She took one look and understood there was nothing she could do."

She flipped open a notepad. "Her call came through at nine oh four. Officers arrived at nine twelve. They confirmed the presence of a body, secured the scene, and called us. We arrived at nine twenty-eight."

She pointed to the tub and turned back to her notes. "With the body in place, the tub was full to one inch below the top rim. The decedent was clothed in pyjama bottoms and a T-shirt, underwear but no bra. The head was submerged in the water. A small amount of white foam was observed around the mouth, which is consistent with drowning, and lividity was observed in the head, neck, and upper chest. There were no obvious signs of a struggle, but of course the autopsy will tell us more."

She flipped a page in her notebook. "No illegal drugs or prescription medications were found in the apartment. According to the roommate, Tabitha didn't drink, do drugs, or take any kind of prescription medication. Half a case of beer was found in the fridge, but Christy says it belongs to her. Obviously the viscera will be preserved for chemical analysis."

"Have the neighbours been questioned?"

"Still in the process, but so far we're coming up blank. No one heard or saw anything unusual."

"Where's the roommate now?"

"I believe she's still at the police station, but if not, she said she would be staying at her boyfriend's home until further notice. I'll give you her number."

"Has Tabitha's bedroom been processed yet?"

"They're in there now."

They moved down the hall to the last door on the right. Two techs were at work in the room, one going through the closet and the other running a UV light along the bed.

When the one at the bed saw them standing in the doorway, he moved in their direction. "Found this between the mattress and box spring."

He held up a scrap of newspaper, sealed in a plastic evidence bag. Even from a distance, Beau recognized the *Vancouver Sun* article about Stephen Bains's, aka Rulon Smith's, plunge off the Lions Gate Bridge.

"Can I see that?"

The tech handed it over. It was the same as the one Desiree had received in the mail, with the word *repent* and *JDBY 4:219* scrawled in red marker along the top.

He motioned for Jessica Chambers to follow him back to the semi-privacy of the living room. Once there, he scrolled through the photos on his cellphone. Without a word, he held up the phone and the scrap of newspaper so she could see them side by side.

"That's interesting."

"Do you remember the polygamist sect from Brigham? There was a mass suicide after their prophet, Warren Jeffs, was arrested in Las Vegas."

"I do," she said.

"During a police raid, ten children escaped and worked with the police to build a case against their elders."

"Brigham's Ten. I remember that."

"Tabitha Johnson was one of them."

"Well. You've got my attention."

He waved his phone. "This was sent to another one of them last week. And the jumper's real name was Rulon Smith. He's another of the ten."

She frowned. "Any of the others wind up dead?"

"Two that I know of so far."

"Then you'd better get some protection on the rest."

"Yep."

He called Doug to have officers dispatched on protection details.

"We can't do this indefinitely," Doug said, and Beau knew his boss was getting heartburn over the cost.

"I know."

"Did Grace DeRoche receive one of these newspaper articles?" Doug asked.

"I don't believe so." Beau sidestepped the fact that he hadn't actually asked her that question. He planned to rectify that at the first opportunity.

"I'm on my way to speak to Tabitha's roommate, but I'll give Grace a call to warn her. In the meantime, could you get someone to do a deep dive on finding the rest of the ten? That's Ernest Young and the twins, Shilo and Shareen Smith. I'd also love to get a line on Boaz and Clayne Johnson. I've put out the BOLO, but I'd love someone to dig a little deeper."

"Those are Tabitha's brothers?"

"That's right. Boaz was excommunicated sometime in the early to midnineties. There's some question about whether Clayne is alive, but whatever happened to him was right before the millennium."

"We'll get on it."

He hung up and was about to dial Grace's number when he thought better of it. Hearing his voice might trigger her. He called Shelby instead and left a message on her voice mail. Then he called Desiree, reached *her* voice mail, and left a similar message.

Tabitha's roommate offered to meet him at her boyfriend's apartment. By the time Beau pulled up, twilight had given way to darkness. The air was crisp and his breath was visible as he exited the car and made his way up the path. The smell of snow was in the air. He hoped it held off.

He pressed the intercom button and in due course was buzzed through. The apartment was on the first floor at the end of the hallway. Christy Seacrest waited in the doorway.

She wore sweatpants and a rugby shirt, and she had a tattered plaid blanket pulled over her shoulders. She dabbed at her dripping nose with a crumpled tissue.

"Christy? Thank you for seeing me. I'm so sorry for your loss."

She nodded, her eyes filling with tears. She motioned for him to come in, and moved back into the apartment. He followed, closing the door behind him.

"This is my boyfriend, Seth." She motioned toward an acne-faced young man with a puff of bleached blond hair. He sat on a dingy-looking couch in the living room, a game controller in his hands.

"Hey," Seth said, barely taking his eyes off the TV screen in front of him.

Christy dabbed at her nose. "Is there any word on what happened?"

"The autopsy is scheduled for tomorrow. We'll know more after that."

Her eyes squeezed shut at the word *autopsy*, and she shook her head. From the TV came the sounds of gunfire and people dying. It sounded like Seth was on a winning streak.

"Christy, I know you've already answered about a million questions today."

"It's okay," she said, hugging the blanket more tightly around her. "I want to do whatever I can to help. Tabby ..." She swallowed hard, and fresh tears leaked from her eyes. "She was my best friend, almost like a mentor to me. I can't believe she's gone."

"Do you know much about her background?"

"About that cult she grew up in? Yeah, she told me about it. But that was in the past, you know? She wanted to move on. She was so grateful for everything she had. So excited to become a social worker. I used to joke that I'd never seen anyone love studying so much. I mean I work hard, but she was just so *grateful* for every course she took, every bit of knowledge she received. It gave me a whole new perspective, you know? You don't realize what a blessing it is to be able to go to school. I always took it for granted until I met her."

"Anything change in her life, recently? Anyone from her past make contact?"

"She was upset that someone she knew had died, one of the kids who escaped with her. She said she read that he'd killed himself."

"Someone sent her that newspaper article. Did she show it to you?"

She shook her head. "She read it online. She subscribed to the *Vancouver Sun* and other papers, too. She liked to stay informed."

"When was this?"

"A couple weeks ago? Probably the same day the article came out or maybe the day after."

"Did she keep in contact with anyone else from that time in her life?"

Christy shrugged. "I don't think she wanted much to do with them, even though when she talked about them — I mean the ones who escaped with her — it was obvious she cared about them. But she needed to keep them at a distance. Kind of like an ex, you know? You want to know they're doing okay, but you don't want to actually see them or talk to them. Stalking them online once in a while is about as far as you want to go. But …"

Christy hesitated, looking toward Seth as though making sure he wasn't listening. He remained engrossed in his game.

"She'd get letters every once in a while. No return address. She'd get really excited, practically run to her bedroom to read them in private. I kept asking her who the letters were from. I'd tease her, joking that she must have had a secret boyfriend who was a time traveller. I mean, who writes actual letters anymore?"

"What did she say?"

"She'd usually just laugh it off. But then, one of the letters she got really upset her. I mean, she was really shook. And that's when she told me who they were from. She said it was from a brother who'd been kicked out of their cult."

"Did she tell you his name?"

"No, she never said. But she kept the letters in a jewellery box in the bottom drawer of her dresser."

"Ever read one?"

"Of course not!"

"All right. Can you describe her mood in recent days? Did you notice any changes in her?"

She honked into a tissue. "I've been asking myself that question all day. I can't believe she killed herself. She wasn't depressed."

Beau refrained from mentioning how common it was for friends and family not to see it coming. Those who were suicidal usually spent a lot of time quietly contemplating the act, but actually doing it was often a snap decision. He'd had one case where a woman stuck supper in the oven before slitting her wrists. Her husband came home to a perfectly cooked pot roast and a dead wife.

"Chris, grab me a beer, would ya?" Seth said from his place on the couch.

She went into the kitchen and opened the fridge. She popped the lid on a can of Kokanee and placed it on the table in front of him. He was too engrossed in his game to acknowledge her. It sounded like the death toll was nearing the thousands.

"When you came home," Beau said, "did anything seem out of place?"

"Not that I noticed. I've been trying to think back to every move I made when I got there."

"Sure."

"I unlocked the door, at least I think I did … but I keep going back over it, wondering. I stuck the key in the lock and turned it like I always do, but was the door actually locked?" She shrugged.

"The lamp was on in the living room. When I left the night before, Tabby was sitting on the floor with her back against the couch, using the coffee table in front of her as a desk. That's how she liked to work."

She dabbed at her eyes, took a trembling breath. "She was always leaving the lights on, and it drove me nuts. We're not exactly rich. She never admitted it, but I think she was scared of the dark."

Seth grunted and turned up the volume on the TV. Apparently their conversation was distracting him.

Christy sniffled and moved toward the kitchen, indicating that Beau should follow. Takeout boxes cluttered the counter and crusty dishes swam in filmy water in the sink. Cleaning probably didn't get done unless Christy came over.

"I turned off the lamp, closed her laptop. Then I went to take a shower." She buried her face in her hands and took several shaky breaths.

"There's no need to tell me the rest," he said.

She looked up at him, her eyes frantic. "Do you really think she killed herself?"

"I don't know."

"It's so horrible! I mean, it's bad enough if she had some kind of freak accident, but if she did it to herself …" She let out a great, gusty sob. "How could I not know she was that sad?"

In the living room, Seth turned up the volume.

"Christy," Beau said, taking her gently by the shoulders. He could feel her bones beneath his hands, as delicate as the wings of a bird. "We'll know more soon. But if it does turn out she committed suicide, I want you to know that it's not your fault."

"Thank you for saying that, but —"

"Ten years ago," he said, before he could stop himself, "I came home, much like you did this morning, and found my wife on our bed. I thought she was sleeping until I saw the empty pill container on the bedside table."

She looked up at him, aghast. "She killed herself?"

He couldn't admit to it, even now, so he shrugged instead.

"How do you live with it?" she asked.

Beau scrubbed a hand over his eyes, over the rough skin on his cheek. "Well, the truth is, I *haven't* been living. But I hope you'll find better ways to cope."

"I'm really sorry about your wife."

"I'm really sorry about your friend." They both dabbed at their eyes. "Do you have family around, anyone who can support you through this?"

Christy shook her head. "Just Seth. My parents are in Calgary."

He refrained from commenting on her choice of boyfriend, and said instead, "Maybe you should go home for a bit. Can you take a leave of absence from school?"

She gave a slow nod. "Maybe," she said. "I'll look into it."

"Good." Beau pulled a business card out of his wallet and scribbled his cellphone number on the back. "Call me if there's anything you need."

"Thank you."

He left her there, amid the sounds of battle.

TWENTY-TWO

Saturday was Grace and Bella's day to go into town. It was a routine they followed every week, weather permitting.

Bella wore her service vest on such outings, giving Grace the necessary barrier between her and the rest of humanity. She was well known around town for her pottery and goat milk products, not to mention her unenviable past. But the residents of Nakusp, Canadians through and through, treated her with polite smiles and respectful distance. Which was exactly what Grace wanted.

After her conversation with Desiree the other day, she paid particular attention to her surroundings. She looked around nervously as she exited the car, but saw no one suspicious. She owed Desiree a call back, and she vowed to do it as soon as she got home.

Their first stop was the post office to pick up her mail. Nothing but a few bills and the latest IKEA catalogue.

Despite never having been in an IKEA in her life, she loved to flip through the glossy pages of their catalogues. They were full of enticing displays of colour and organization, and the dream of it all made her happy.

After dropping off her prescriptions at the pharmacy, they went next door to What's Brewing on Broadway where she bought a chai tea and maple scone for herself, and a croissant for Bella. She tucked into her favourite armchair and flipped through the catalogue while dipping pieces of scone into her tea. Bella gulped her treat whole and settled by Grace's feet. Grace purposely kept her head down, enjoying the bustle and noise of the coffee shop. Her mind was quiet, and Bella snored softly.

As she drained her cup, she thought she saw someone watching her through the window. She caught the quick impression of blond hair and slumped shoulders. In response, her heart kicked into high gear. Her view was blocked as a group of women wearing yoga gear entered the shop, and when they moved out of the way, whomever she'd seen was no longer there.

But her good ear crackled like an amp turned up to ten, and the voices started screaming in her head.

They've come for us.

They know we haven't been sweet.

We need a correction.

Bella startled upright and barked, sensing the change in her master. She nudged Grace with her nose.

"It's okay, girl."

When she patted the dog's head, her hand looked too big. She closed her eyes and took deep breaths, trying to resist the pull of the darkness at the back of her head where Mother was waiting to tuck her in.

After several minutes, she felt more present. Her legs shook when she stood. She gathered their garbage and deposited it in the receptacle by the door. Bella stayed close as they left the shop. She scanned the sidewalk in both directions, but saw no one suspicious.

They picked up her prescriptions at the pharmacy. As they waited to cross the street to the Overwaitea Foods, Jack Fletcher came out of the hardware store. He caught sight of Grace and smiled, but kept moving in the other direction. She smiled back and watched him go, a wave of guilt and yearning washing over her. She felt the urge to chase after him, to apologize and maybe see if his offer was still good. Instead, she watched him until he was out of sight. With a sigh, she crossed the street and ducked through the automatic doors into the grocery store.

She and Bella cruised the aisles and picked up fruit, eggs, and bread. She grabbed a roasted chicken and some coleslaw for supper, and was on her way to the checkout when she caught another flash of blond hair, golden-white at the crown and darker near the tips. It struck a chord of recognition within her, a deep twang that began in her stomach and reverberated out to her extremities, causing an ache in her joints.

Adrenaline rolled through her veins like thunder on the lake, and a high-pitched whine filled her good ear. Someone shoved her out of the frontspace in her mind, and she hurtled back toward lamplight and feather pillows and Mother's soothing touch.

· · ·

The day began like most days in Brigham, with chores and farming and scripture. But it ended very differently. It ended with a march to the gates that separated Brigham from the outside world. It ended with saying goodbye to one of their own. And this time, the loss hit close to Grace's heart and home.

Late that afternoon, she sat on the stairs by the side of her house. Her chores were finished, and she had time to play before supper. She normally would have kicked a ball around in the yard, making enough noise to draw Clayne out of his house. Today, she felt too tired to do anything but sit.

There was something going on inside her head, and whatever it was seemed to be getting worse. More and more often, other voices were crowding for space and attention. More and more often, there were parts of her day that she didn't remember. It was like trying to look at something after staring too long at the sun. There were black spots everywhere.

She remembered what it was like to have a quiet mind. She'd had that when she was younger. Now she worried that her brain was very sick, and she was too scared to tell anyone about it.

She'd worked up the courage to ask Mother, as casually as she could, about the symptoms of Waardenburg Syndrome, which she'd been born with, and about Lyme disease, which she'd developed more recently. Mother said the first caused her hearing loss and dual-coloured eyes, and the second caused the aching in her joints, the fatigue, and the fevers. There was no mention of either causing strange things to happen to her mind, so she dropped the subject.

Behind her, from inside the house, Sariah's soft cries indicated she was awakening from her nap. Across the yard, from inside the Johnsons' house, Mother Flora's voice rose in anger. Neither Sariah's cries nor Mother Flora's shouting were unusual, so at first Grace barely paid any attention. It was nothing but background noise for her churning thoughts.

Behind her, Mother Rebecca moved through the house, cooing to her daughter. Sariah's cries gave way to a happy babble. Across the way, Mother Flora's voice grew louder. Now Boaz's and Clayne's voices rose to join hers. It sounded like they were arguing with her, which was always a bad idea.

Grace stood to go into her house. She didn't want to be in earshot when the beatings started. She was opening the screen door when a fourth voice joined the racket. It made her pause and turn her head, angling her good ear toward the Johnsons' house. Surely what she thought she'd heard was a mistake. But no. Mother Dinah shouted even louder than the rest. She'd never heard Mother Dinah raise her voice beyond the level required for cheerful gossip.

Grace closed the screen door and stood listening with an awe that quickly turned to anxiety. She only caught a word here and there, so she couldn't determine what the argument was about. But whatever it was, it was serious. It was the tone of Mother Dinah's voice that caused her stomach to clench with nerves. For as loud as Dinah shouted, she didn't sound angry. She sounded terrified.

The Johnsons' kitchen door slammed open, causing Grace to jump and bite down on her tongue. Later that night, she'd notice that one side of her tongue was painful and swollen to twice its normal size, and she'd have no memory of injuring it.

Mother Flora flew through the door and stormed down the stairs, shouting that she was going to see the bishop. Mother Dinah stumbled after her, grabbing on to the back of Flora's dress.

"Please, Flora! I beg of you!"

An assortment of Johnson children scrambled out to the yard, including Boaz, Clayne, and Tabby. Dinah's children shared their mother's stunned and terrified expressions. Tabby's cheeks were streaked with tears. Boaz and Clayne stood with their fists clenched, looking like boxers who were too scared to fight.

No one noticed Grace standing on her porch.

Mother Flora was in a proper snit. "He's dishonoured God, in my house! In *my* house! He's brought eternal shame upon this family."

"Please, Flora. Please, my sister." Dinah kept clutching at different parts of Mother Flora's dress, and Mother Flora kept spinning out of her grasp. "Please, let our husband handle this."

"Our husband has worked hard to earn a place of respect within the church. And this son of yours" — she pointed to Boaz — "has not only put Redd's place in the priesthood at risk, he's put the *entire family's* place in heaven in jeopardy!

No, Dinah. There is only one path toward salvation, and I must follow it. For all of our sakes."

"Flora," Dinah said, "I beg of you, please don't do this. I know Boaz has gone astray, but he can repent. I know he can make this right. Please! Give him a chance."

Flora scoffed at her. "He feels no guilt for what he's done."

Boaz stepped forward. His cheeks were so pale he looked like he might pass out or vomit, or perhaps both. "I *am* sorry, Mother Flora."

"You're only sorry you were caught."

Boaz opened his mouth as though to argue, but no words came out.

Mother Flora spun on her heels and bustled across the yard toward the gate. She was on the road and heading up the hill toward Uncle G's house before anyone could even think to follow.

Mother Dinah let out an inhuman wail, lifted her skirt, and took off after Mother Flora at a run. Boaz, Clayne, and Tabby followed along behind her. The other Johnson children stood, stunned and silent, in the dirt yard.

Behind Grace, the screen door creaked open.

Mother Rebecca came out onto the porch with Sariah cradled against her shoulder. "What on earth was that about?"

No one answered. They simply stood there, struck dumb.

Patience was the first to move. Slowly, as though she walked through a dream, she turned and went back into their house. Justice followed, and then Noble.

"Well, I never heard such a racket." The screen door creaked and banged closed as Mother Rebecca retreated into the house.

Valor stood by himself in the yard, his face blank with shock. Grace climbed down the steps and moved toward him. He didn't seem to notice she was there.

"Valor?"

He didn't even blink.

"Valor? What happened?"

Finally he looked at her. His eyes were wide, shock giving away to something that looked like fear mixed with guilt.

"It's my fault," he said.

"What is? What happened?"

"I saw them in the pantry. And they were kissing."

"Who was?"

"Boaz and ZoAnne."

Her mouth fell open with shock. *What?*

ZoAnne was Uncle G's daughter with his third wife. She was fourteen and about to be sealed in marriage. The wedding was in two days.

"They were *kissing*?"

"He says he loves her. That they love each other."

"But … she's to be *married*."

Valor ran a shaky hand through his hair. "I shouldn't have done it. I wasn't thinking. I was just so shocked."

"What did you do?"

"I told Mother. Oh, God. I shouldn't have. Now Boaz will be …"

"What?"

He looked at her, shrugged his shoulders.

"Maybe it won't be that bad," she said. "Maybe Uncle G will just give him a correction."

"Are you kidding? Boaz was kissing Uncle G's *daughter*. Two days before her wedding." Tears welled in his eyes. "I shouldn't have told Mother."

"What do you think will happen to him?"

Valor wiped an arm across his eyes. "He's either going to be asked to atone by blood, or he's going to lose his priesthood."

It turned out to be the latter.

No one in the DeRoche house slept that night, too overwrought with shock and grief. But even if they hadn't been, Mother Dinah's keening from next door would surely have kept them awake.

TWENTY-THREE

Danielle Taylor was alive and well, according to the Edmonton RCMP. And it looked like Ernest Young had gone back to his religious roots.

Beau scanned the documents Doug had sent over. Ernest had married in Creston, BC, several years back. Since it was a legally filed marriage, he guessed it was Ernest's first. There were no records for him beyond that, but chances were good he'd find Ernest living in or near Bountiful.

Doug gave Beau approval to make the trip, so he left Kelowna at ten in the morning, which would put him near Bountiful that evening.

Several years back, the FLDS in Bountiful had split into two sects. One stayed loyal to Winston Blackmore after his excommunication, while the rest followed their new bishop, James Oler. This group still considered Warren Jeffs to be their prophet, even from his Texas prison cell.

In recent years, Winston Blackmore's son Brandon and James Oler had been charged with removing girls under the age of sixteen from Canada for sexual purposes. As the courts sorted out the issue of religious freedom, both Winston Blackmore and James Oler had also been convicted of polygamy. With all their legal troubles, Beau doubted he'd be a welcome presence in the community.

It was dark and spitting snow when he pulled into Creston, the nearest town to Bountiful. He checked into a Ramada Inn and was asleep before he could give more than a fleeting thought to grabbing some supper.

Beau awoke before five the next morning, took a shower, drank hotel room coffee, and waited until it was a reasonable hour to head into Bountiful. He hoped to reconnect with a family who had been friendly to him during the Brigham investigation.

The Bartletts lived on a small farm in the town of Lister. As Beau pulled into the gravel driveway, he could see not much had changed. The rambling two-storey farmhouse was large enough to accommodate James and his wife Samantha, along with any other wives he wouldn't admit to having, and their gaggle of children.

The house had been freshly painted, and at the rear of the property the barn had been rebuilt. A heavy-duty Ford truck sat next to two beat-up minivans in the driveway. He hoped this meant James was home. Otherwise his knock would go unanswered.

Gravel and snow crunched underfoot. He made his way up the steps to the broad front porch, and the door opened before he could knock.

"Detective." James Bartlett hooked his thumbs into the straps of his suspenders and gave him a serious once-over.

"Mr. Bartlett." He reached out to shake hands, and after a moment of consideration, Bartlett acquiesced. His hand was warm and rough-skinned, with hard ridges of calluses on the fingertips.

"I'm not here to stir up any trouble for you, but I have a few questions."

"Uh-huh."

Beau thought an extra bit of reassurance was in order, considering the look of caution on the other man's face. "I have nothing to do with your legal issues, and I don't care how many wives you have, or if you owe back taxes, or anything else. I'm over in Serious Crime now. So, as long as you're not hiding any bodies around here, we're good."

He knew better than to ask to come inside, so he motioned to the plastic chairs scattered across the front porch, requesting permission to sit. Bartlett closed the door and eased into the nearest chair, placing his hands on his knees.

Beau sat across from him. "I'm looking for Ernest Young, one of the kids who left Brigham back when all the legal trouble started. I'm wondering if he lives around here?"

"Why are you looking for him?" Bartlett's expression was neutral.

"I'm concerned for his safety. Some of the others have met unfortunate ends."

"I'm sorry to hear that."

"I'm wondering if you can help me understand — what is the Mormon belief about suicide?"

"Someone committed suicide?" Emotion showed in the reddening of the skin on his neck beneath his heavy beard. Beau guessed he was thinking about the loss of his brethren in Brigham.

"We're still trying to determine that."

Bartlett sighed. "I can't say that's a surprise."

"No?"

"We've lost a lot of young ones since the … incident, in Brigham. It's become an epidemic. Seems like there's more each year." Bartlett wiped a hand across his mouth. "I lost my oldest son last year."

"I'm very sorry."

"He had a rebellious spirit. The end of days is near, and not all are pure enough to withstand the final tests."

During the Blackmore split, the Bartlett family had remained faithful to Warren Jeffs before his imprisonment. Beau wasn't certain if the Bartlett family had remained loyal to Jeffs as he continued to tighten the noose from his prison cell, or if they'd been cast adrift in the turmoil like so many others. But Bartlett wasn't about to share personal information with him.

A mass excommunication of men from the FLDS community in Short Creek, Arizona, had the wives and children reassigned to more "worthy" men. There'd been a complete shutdown of social gatherings, and husbands were banned from having sex with their wives. Instead, higher-ups in the priesthood were now charged with "planting the seed" for new generations of children.

"Do you know Ernest?"

"I do," Bartlett said. "He found his way back to the church. He and his family were living on the east side of Lister, and he was working in timber for the Blackmores. But they moved to Hildale a couple years ago."

"Any other folks from Brigham around?"

"A few of the lost boys have come around, here and there. Mostly looking for handouts or a road to redemption. Their families are gone, so we're the closest they can get to home. We'll take them in for a short time, in hopes of steering them in a positive direction."

"You've personally taken them in? Or the community?"

"Bit of both," Bartlett said. "Though it's frowned upon and could lead us to trouble. So, it's not something we talk about."

"Were Boaz or Clayne Johnson taken in?"

"Boaz lived with us for several years after he left Brigham. He was trying to repent. He even joined the reform program for kids shipped up from the States."

"The work camp, you mean."

Bartlett's mouth turned down with displeasure, letting him know he'd crossed a line.

Trying to get back on track, he asked, "When was this?"

"Midnineties. He was gone before the millennium. He knew he hadn't found his way back to a spot in heaven, and we believed at the time that the world was about to end."

"And then it didn't."

Bartlett gave a flat smile. "God gave us the gift of more time to perfect ourselves."

"So, Boaz left before the new year?"

"Late fall, if I had to guess. Maybe the beginning of December. Said he was heading east."

"Did you ever meet his younger brother Clayne?"

"No."

"This would have been late in 1999."

"There was a lot of movement at that time."

"The righteous preparing for the end of the world by kicking the not-so-righteous out of their communities?"

Bartlett's mouth turned down and he shook his head, as though Beau couldn't possibly understand.

"Father?" A young girl in a drab prairie-style dress stood in the open doorway, holding two glasses of what looked like lemonade.

Bartlett sprang to his feet, his cheeks red with anger. "Didn't your mother tell you to stay inside?"

"I thought you and your guest might be thirsty." She bowed her head, her eyes welling with tears.

"We don't serve gentiles. Get back inside. Now."

The girl did a clumsy curtsy and disappeared into the shadows of the house.

"Mr. Bartlett —"

"It's time for you to leave, Detective. The more the outside world intrudes, the more our children slip through our fingers. Don't come here again unless you have a warrant."

Beau was on the stairs when Bartlett called out to him. "Are you still looking for Brigham's false bishop?"

He turned. "Gideon Smith? Absolutely."

Bartlett's expression was dour. "I've heard he's got a small compound north of Medicine Hat, with maybe twenty followers."

"Where'd you hear this?"

"I'm not going to tell you that."

"Have you seen him for yourself?"

Bartlett shook his head. His eyes were glassy with tears. "If I had, I would have put a bullet through his skull. I hope you find him, Detective."

Beau sent Doug a text with the information about a possible compound outside Medicine Hat, along with Ernest Young's relocation to Hildale, Utah. Doug replied that he'd get the Alberta RCMP on the Medicine Hat lead right away, and touch base with local law enforcement in Utah to see if Ernest Young's whereabouts could be confirmed.

As he drove through Bountiful and Lister, the snow hit his windshield and blew in drifts to the side of the road. He saw no one. Snow fell softly on empty yards and driveways, on houses that were shuttered and dark. But he could feel people watching him.

Without giving it much thought, Beau turned east on BC-3. Brigham was only ninety minutes away. He had a sudden urge to place his feet on its abandoned soil, as though it might give him some grounding in the investigation.

As he cut north, he left the snow behind, though the heavy clouds above him continued to threaten. He stopped for a late breakfast in Cranbrook, taking the time while he waited for his food to call Jessica Chambers at the coroner's office in Kelowna.

"I just emailed you the initial autopsy results," she said. "Waiting on toxicology, but at the moment, we're looking at death by asphyxiation due to drowning. There were no grip marks on the body consistent with forcible immersion, and no contusions on the head to indicate an accidental slip and fall. No signs of a struggle."

"Accidental drowning or suicide?"

"I'm not ticking any boxes yet," Jessica said. "Not without toxicology. And I'm still waiting on the forensics from her apartment. But the techs found a possible suicide note on her computer."

"Can you email it to me?"

"Already have. No fingerprints on the keyboard, before you ask. The whole laptop was wiped clean with one of those alcohol wipes. Seems suspicious to me. Also, you were right about the jewellery box in her dresser. It held a stack of handwritten letters. They're full of cryptic references that I'm sure Tabitha understood, but they make no sense to me. Maybe you'll understand them better. I'll scan them when I get a moment and email them to you. I found the last few particularly concerning. Each of them is signed 'your loving brother,' but no actual name. Oh, I've got to go, but I'll call you when more results come in."

He logged into the restaurant's free Wi-Fi and checked his email. While ploughing through his food, he read the pathologist report. It was a dry read, broken into a series of weights, measures, and clinical observations — skillfully masking the bodily desecration involved in the procedure.

Beau wiped grease from his fingers, then pulled out a pen, and opened the second document. He scribbled on a fresh napkin, noting the similarities between this note and the one found in Rulon's backpack. This note spoke of the excessive guilt Tabitha felt for abandoning the Family and mentioned how she couldn't find any other way to make amends for the terrible wrong she'd done when she betrayed the people of Brigham. The Family was mentioned twice, and was referenced once more. There were no instructions or apologies to those she'd left behind. Both notes had the same language and phrasing and could have been written by the same person.

Beau left a twenty on the table and went back to his car, where he turned on the engine and pushed the heat dial up to full blast. He'd spent too many years in Vancouver's temperate climate, and the exposed skin on his face and hands was already feeling dry. He scrolled through the contact list on his phone until he found the number for Judy Beers in the Vancouver coroner's office.

"Judy, Beau Brunelli," he said when she answered the phone. "Anything new on Rulon Smith's death?"

"All evidence points to suicide, but I haven't made it official yet," she said.

"How did the handwriting on the note compare to Rulon's signature?"

"Inconclusive. It wasn't enough to do a good comparison."

He let out a frustrated breath. "What about the person in the grey coat?"

"We picked him or her up on the traffic cam near Denman and Georgia, walking east. And that's it. From there, they could have gone in numerous directions."

"Or dropped the trail by tossing the coat in a nearby garbage bin."

"True. And if so, the coat would be long gone in the city dump."

"Were you able to get a better look at the face?"

"It's not enough to pick someone out of the crowd, but it might help us do a side-by-side comparison if we ever have a suspect in custody. Want me to send it to you?"

"Yes, please."

"You never gave me your opinion on the suicide note," she said.

"I'd lay a bet it's a fake. In genuine suicide notes, you usually find instructions or neutral content to those left behind, which is missing from this one. Instead it's an elaborate apology to the Family, and it mentions or references them several times in one short paragraph. This is something you often see in fake notes. The perpetrator references themselves within the note, as strange as that may sound. I also don't buy that Rulon had such a huge change of heart. He was pretty bitter and angry about them."

"You never know with these cult types, though. Maybe he had a religious awakening."

"Anything's possible, but I know where I'd lay my bet. There's been another apparent suicide in Kelowna. Tabitha Johnson, another of Brigham's Ten. The note is very similar to Rulon's."

"Hmm."

"That's what I thought." With renewed promises to keep each other informed, they hung up.

Fort Steele was twenty minutes east of Cranbrook, and the ghost town of Brigham was another ten minutes southeast along Wardner Road.

As he pulled onto the unmarked gravel lane, the sun found its way out of the clouds to light the jagged, snow-covered peaks of the Rocky Mountains. Around him were evergreens as far as the eye could see. Past a broken gate, he drove due east toward the mountains. The forest closed in behind him as he emerged into fallow farmland. The mountains towered above the crumbling town.

Houses lined the main road leading up an incline to the temple at the top. Beau parked and climbed out of the car. Dirt and gravel crunched under his feet. Weeds tangled around children's toys and play equipment in front yards. Porches fell in, and doors hung open to expose dust and debris and rotting furniture.

The DeRoche house was on the left, a plain clapboard structure with peeling paint and broken front steps. Cautiously, he climbed to the porch and peered through the shattered front window. Inside were the remnants of a kitchen, cupboard doors open to expose rotting boxes of cereal that had long been picked over by creatures large and small.

He stepped back and continued up the hill. The silence was peaceful, nothing but the sound of birds chirping and small creatures nesting. His mind travelled back to the night a young woman ran toward him out of the moonlight, begging for his protection. He could feel the weight of her body as she clung to him, like a starling in winter. It felt like both yesterday and a million years ago.

The wind kicked up from the northeast, clearing the fog of dead memories from his mind. His nose caught the brown smell of Brigham's rot and decay, clear mountain air, snow and pine and growing things.

At the top of the hill sat the largest house in Brigham. It had once belonged to their bishop, Gideon Smith — adored leader, polygamist fanatic, and child molester. The house sprawled grandly in every direction. It had clearly been built to a higher standard, and it had fared better over the years.

The house style coordinated with the temple beside it. Built of white stone, the temple was a three-level structure with spires reaching toward heaven. It was no larger than a Vancouver special, but with the Rocky Mountains in the background, it looked quite imposing.

Beau stopped in front, taking in the heart of Brigham's evil. Nothing but a secondary tumour metastasized from the red rock regions of Utah, Colorado, and Arizona.

A flagpole stood beside the temple, the flag at half-mast. He pictured them standing there solemnly, the men in their suspenders and the women in their prairie-style dresses, as the flag was lowered. He pictured them walking around to the back, climbing one by one into the giant hole they'd dug for their mass grave, and passing out cups of cyanide-laced fruit juice. He pictured the parents lifting cups to their children's lips, encouraging them to take a sip. *We'll move on to heaven together.*

And what of Gideon Smith? Did he stand there watching his congregants take their last agonizing breaths? Did he then move east into the mountains, without even giving the bodies of his faithful a proper burial? Beau would have bet that was exactly what he'd done.

Damn him.

He crossed to the flagpole, grasped the cold metal in his hands. The chill made his joints stiffen and ache. With furious determination, he tugged at the knots in the halyard. The fibres were ragged and swollen. Eventually the first knot loosened enough for him to undo the loop. He undid the next knot, and then the next. He unwrapped the halyard from the hook and gave it a good pull, craning his neck to watch the flag make its way up the pole. When it reached the top, he wrapped the halyard around the metal hook and reknotted it, making sure to tie it tight enough to hold against winds and winters to come.

His anger left as quickly as it had come. Feeling strangely forlorn, he headed back to the car. As he drove away, he took one last look in the rearview mirror. The Canadian flag, now in its rightful position, danced strong and free on the breath of the wind.

TWENTY-FOUR

Grace was thirteen when her courses began. She'd felt ill for a couple of days, with a low-grade fever and flu-like symptoms. Her chest felt sore, rubbed raw by her undergarments, and her nipples were so sensitive they drove her crazy. Mother said maybe her Lyme disease was acting up.

She went to bed early on Saturday night, carrying the hot water bottle with her. Her lower back and abdomen hurt and her stomach had been upset all evening. But the next morning she awoke feeling well enough to attend temple services. She helped Mother prepare breakfast for the family, cleaned up after, and dressed in her temple dress.

Father went on ahead, and the women and children followed twenty minutes later. At the age of two, Sariah no longer wanted to be carried. She toddled up the road, stopping frequently to examine pebbles and fallen leaves. Everything she saw was funny, and when she laughed her voice rose to the heavens and her blue eyes twinkled. They paused and waited, nodding and exchanging pleasantries with passing families. Grace felt weak and a little woozy. She was grateful for their slower pace.

The Johnsons approached, Mother Flora and her children in the lead. Behind them, Mother Dinah walked with Mother Naomi, who was huge with her first pregnancy. Grace and Desiree fell into step with Clayne and Tabitha, who were at the rear.

"Shareen says they're bringing chocolate cake today." Tabby wore a new dress. It was pale yellow with white lace trim, and she kept looking down to admire the skirt as she walked. It rested just above her heels, and she picked it up a little so the hem wouldn't drag in the dirt. Sariah, who loved Tabby more than just about anyone, toddled up to her and insisted on holding the older girl's hand.

"We made sn-snickerdoodles," Desiree said. "Mother let me add a s-secret ingredient."

"What is it?" Tabby asked.

"It's a *s-secret*."

"Grace." Mother's voice was unusually sharp. She'd been uptight all week, and Grace wasn't sure why.

"Yes, Mother?"

"Come up here. Walk with the women."

Grace widened her eyes at Desiree, who shrugged.

"Yes, Mother."

With regret, she moved toward the grown-ups and their boring conversation. She turned her good ear toward the debate going on behind her. Which was better, chocolate cake or vanilla? Grace wanted to jump in and mention the spice cake with maple frosting Mother had made for her last birthday. She was certain it was the best cake anyone had ever tasted.

"It's almost Grace's time." Mother spoke in a hushed tone like she was imparting a secret, and Grace immediately lost any interest in cake. Her mother's mouth was pinched into a thin line, her eyes tight with worry.

Dinah gave a slow nod. "I've been wondering."

"Wondering what?" Grace asked.

Mother's gaze lingered on her, mixing pride with something deeper. Sadness, perhaps.

Unrest stirred within Grace's abdomen.

Behind her, Clayne was being accused of breaking the rules during a stickball game, and he heatedly defended his honour.

"Hush," Dinah said as they neared the temple. "Sweeten your tongues."

The pain in her abdomen was grinding, making her legs feel weak and her head feel light. She followed Mother toward their usual seats halfway toward the front, and squeezed in between her and Desiree. Mother Rebecca joined them after dropping off Sariah in the daycare program.

She couldn't concentrate on the prayers, and Uncle G's sermon was as grim as usual. He'd heard from Uncle Warren, who spoke on behalf of his father, the prophet.

The prophet had been given another sign that the end of days was near. They needed to ensure their purity of heart and soul if they were to be lifted from the coming destruction of the world. The congregation stirred. She could taste their fear like metal on her tongue. Desiree slipped a hand into hers, seeking comfort.

The voices rose inside her head, drowning out the rest of Uncle G's sermon. The wooden bench beneath her was hard and unforgiving. It always gave her a sore bottom, but today she felt damp and sticky, as well, and she kept shifting with discomfort. Mother pressed a warning elbow into her side.

After what felt like hours, they moved into the final prayers of the service. She'd never been more eager to stand up and escape the temple. She no longer cared if there was chocolate cake. As she moved into the centre aisle, her lower abdomen cramped with grinding pain, making her want to curl in on herself and groan.

"I'm not feeling well. May I please be excused to go home?"

Mother spoke to Alta Barlow as they moved toward the door, and didn't hear her plea. It had started raining while they were inside and people grouped near the doorway, complaining about having left their coats at home. Women flocked together like chattering birds, and men stood around with their thumbs hooked through the straps of their suspenders.

"Grace, you're bleeding!" Desiree said.

People turned to look.

"What?"

"The whole back of your sk-skirt is covered in blood." Desiree's voice was so loud that it silenced everyone around them.

"What?" She turned like a dog chasing its tail.

"Are you hurt?" Clayne stepped forward. His pale brows were drawn down with concern. His hair was in need of a cut; it hung into his eyes. Underneath his fingernails were half moons of dirt. He risked a correction for stepping too close to her.

"Let's go, Grace." Mother grabbed her arm and steered her out the door into the rain. They clattered down the steps of the temple and Mother dragged her, half running, down the hill toward home.

As she stumbled along she tugged at the end of her skirt, twisting it around until she saw the blood. There was so much of it! But where was it coming from?

We must be dying. We're dying just like Mother Susan did.

Over the years, Grace had pieced together what had happened to Mother Susan. She hadn't been growing a baby, after all. She'd had "The C Word." It made her hemorrhage, which was the word for losing so much blood.

"Am I having a hemorrhage?"

"What? Don't be ridiculous." It would have been reassuring if Mother hadn't sounded so scared.

"Do I have 'The C Word'?"

"What are you talking about, Grace?" Mother dragged her up the stairs and through the front door of their home.

"Like Mother Susan!"

Her fear was a great swelling beast within her, and her ear buzzed in response. She could feel her mind fading, and this caused even more panic. What if instead of sleeping for a while, she actually died?

"You're hyperventilating. Calm down or you'll faint."

"I don't want to die!"

Mother grabbed her by the shoulders. "What makes you think you're dying?"

"There's so much blood!"

Mother's eyebrows sprang up toward her hairline, and then something strange happened. Mother laughed.

"Oh, Lord," Mother said eventually, wiping at her eyes. "You're not dying. You've just started your courses."

"My courses?"

"Undress and clean yourself up. We'll need to soak your clothing before the blood sets in. I'll bring a rag to put between your legs."

"What for?"

"To protect your clothing from the blood, of course."

"But ..." She felt completely lost. "But where is the blood coming from?"

"From your womb. It means you're ready to have a child."

"I'm going to have a *baby*?"

"Not until you have a husband. But you will bleed like this every month, and when you do it's your body telling you that you *don't* have a baby growing inside you."

"Oh. Well, that's good, then." But a new thought occurred to her, one that caused a fresh wave of panic. "A husband. So, now I can be married?"

"Yes." Though Mother's lips smiled, she saw her own fear reflected in Mother's eyes.

"Then that's ..." She searched her mind for one of the negative words, something that was not sweet on her tongue. "That's *terrible*."

"Grace," Mother said.

"I don't want to be a wife."

"I wouldn't worry," Mother said. "I'm sure it will be some time before Uncle G has a revelation about your marriage."

Mother was wrong. It only took eight days.

. . .

Grace stood in front of the hall mirror, her hands cupped over her breasts. Her face looked odd, older and broader than she remembered. Her breasts felt soft beneath the stiff fabric of her shirt. She let her hands drop, and continued to stare at herself in the mirror, trying to find herself in the reflection. Her eyes were the feature that usually brought her home. One blue, one brown. A duality that seemed fitting.

The doorbell rang. The receiver was on the wall in the hallway directly above her, and the chiming hurt her ear and made her jump. She pulled away from the mirror, smoothed her hair, and moved toward the front door.

A uniformed RCMP officer stood on the stoop. Alarms went off in her head, and the voices started screaming.

Police!

We're in danger!

"Grace DeRoche?"

"No."

"Is Grace home?" the officer asked.

"What? No, we're Grace."

He blinked. His eyes were so dark she couldn't tell pupil from iris. "You're Grace DeRoche?"

"What's wrong? Why are you here?"

"I'm Officer James Fellner with the Nakusp RCMP. Ma'am, a protection detail has been ordered for you, just as a precaution."

Grace's hands went to her chest, as though trying to stop her heart from breaking free of her rib cage. "Protection detail?"

He pulled a notepad from his pocket. "It was ordered by RCMP Headquarters in Vancouver."

"Why?"

"Weren't you informed? I was told to head on up here, introduce myself, and set up a perimeter surveillance."

"No."

"Ma'am?"

"No. We can't have you here."

When the police come, we must run for the forest.

She shook from head to toe, her ear buzzed, and the familiar fog settled over her mind.

We must hide.

"Shut up!"

The officer stepped back, his expression hardening. "I didn't say anything."

"Sorry," she said.

Just get him away from us.

"I'm sorry, but I don't need you here. I'm fine, okay?"

"Are you refusing protection?"

"Yes. I'm sorry. I don't need it."

He backed away from her, one hand on his gun belt. She could feel her eyeballs skittering from side to side. She knew how crazy it made her look.

"You're sure?"

"Yes! But thank you." She closed the door and listened to the sound of gravel crunching under tires as the officer left. Once he was gone, she ran to the phone, intent on calling Shelby, but saw from the call display that her therapist had already called.

TWENTY-FIVE

Beau didn't have any cell service until he was almost back in Cranbrook. On the outskirts of town, his phone chimed with incoming emails and text messages. But wet snow was falling, and the highway was slushy and treacherous.

He resolutely kept his eyes on the road and his hands on the steering wheel until he could pull into a local gas station. It was full serve only, likely in an attempt to increase local jobs. He handed his credit card to the gas attendant and went inside to use the facilities. On his way out, he purchased a large cup of coffee and a bag of almonds.

He steered the car over to the edge of the gas station property so he wasn't in the way, and checked his phone. Several text messages were from Doug.

Eliza Barlow's suicide note had come in. The content was similar to the other two. Doug would scan and forward it when he got the chance.

A partial fingerprint found on the newspaper article sent to Desiree DeRoche did not match the ones they had on file.

Shareen and Shilo Smith were living in Regina under assumed names.

No news yet on the possibility of Gideon Smith living near Medicine Hat, but Ernest Young had applied for and received a Utah driver's licence, and he was listed at an address in Hildale.

Next, he checked his email. Judy Beers had sent him several photos of the person seen carrying Rulon Smith's backpack toward the Stanley Park Causeway. The thick grey coat did a great job of masking body shape and size, but the height estimate was somewhere between five foot six and eight.

The camera angle was bad, and the photos were grainy. He got the impression of a straight nose and rounded chin. The forehead and sides of the face were masked by the coat's heavy hood. Judy was right, the video might prove beneficial if a suspect came to light, but otherwise it was pretty useless.

He scanned his other new emails, replying to those that were important and ignoring those that could wait, and opened Shelby's last. She'd received his message about the protection detail for Grace, and promised to call her to let her know. She signed off by inviting him to join her at the Nelson Wine and Beer Festival and Artisan Show, if he was in the area. She had an extra ticket to that evening's food and wine tasting.

Ignoring the flutter that started in his chest, Beau pulled up Google Maps. Nelson was two and a half hours west of where he sat, and it made sense to head in that direction. It was closer to Nakusp and Kelowna.

His weather app decided it for him, although he never would have admitted to becoming such a Vancouverite that driving in inclement weather made him nervous. Heavy snow was forecast for Cranbrook and areas north, but the southern route to Nelson looked pretty clear. He sent her a quick email to let her know he'd be in town later that afternoon, and got back on the road.

He was pulling into Nelson when Doug phoned with the news that they were having trouble locating Desiree DeRoche. She hadn't been showing up for work, and no one seemed to know where she'd gone. The assumption from her boss was that she'd relapsed.

"Her photo's gone out to the VPD, but there's not much else to be done at the moment. Also" — he could hear Doug moving papers around on his desk — "Grace DeRoche refused protection."

"She did?"

"Sent the officer packing. According to the officer's report, she was acting erratic and paranoid, and she shouted at him to shut up when he wasn't talking. He thinks she was under the influence of medication or narcotics."

He sighed. "I doubt that, but she *is* mentally ill."

"How so?" Doug asked.

"She's been diagnosed with dissociative identity disorder."

"As in multiple personalities?"

"That's right." Feeling defensive on her behalf, he added, "From what I understand, it's a creative way for a child's brain to cope with persistent abuse and trauma."

"Well," Doug said, "there's certainly been that."

"I'm back in Nelson, where her therapist lives. I'll see if she can convince her to accept the protection."

"All right. Let me know," Doug said, and clicked off.

Beau watched Shelby hang up the phone.

"She's probably gone into town. She goes twice a week to run errands and stuff."

Shelby left a message asking Grace to call back when she got the chance. "We've been playing telephone tag. I left her a message about the protection detail, but she didn't get it before an officer showed up at her door. It triggered her, obviously. She's still working to get past her childhood conditioning that police equals danger."

"You think she's okay?"

Shelby shrugged. "She left a message after the officer left, but I was with another patient and didn't get it for another hour or so. By that time, she'd left a second message. She sounded much calmer."

"What did she say?"

"She asked me to call her back later, if I was able, because she was going to her pottery shed. You know she's quite famous around here for her pottery, right?"

"I know she makes pottery, but I don't know much beyond that."

"You can't go anywhere in the Okanagan or the Kootenays without seeing Grace Pottery. She makes amazing vases and bowls, and I love her Animals of the Forest series. But the most popular ones are her figurative sculptures. People can't get enough of them."

Shelby lifted a tiny figurine off the mantle and brought it to him. Dropping it into the cup of his open palm, her fingers brushed his, on purpose he suspected. He ignored the stirring in his belly.

The figurine was of a woman, her face and arms lifted triumphantly heavenward. Her golden hair rippled down to her waist. Her dress was painted a glossy red.

Beau smiled. "This is great."

"It's called *Courage*."

"It looks like courage." He handed it back to her.

Shelby cradled it in her hand, running a delicate finger over the figurine's cheek. "Did you know the FLDS aren't allowed to wear red?"

"No, I didn't. Why is that?"

"It's the colour Jesus will wear when he returns to earth during the end of days."

"You seem to know a lot about them."

Shelby placed the figurine back on the mantle, next to a stack of books. "I can't help someone heal unless I understand what broke them in the first place. Should we get going?"

It was a ten-minute walk to the Prestige Lakeside Resort. Shelby filled the time with cheerful banter, to which Beau barely held his own. The Artisan Show was well underway when they arrived. One room had been divided with tables where local vendors sold their wares, the other was the dining room where they were holding wine and food tastings.

"Are you hungry?" Shelby asked, unwrapping her scarf from around her neck until it hung to her knees. It was a lovely pale green colour, made of some kind of silky material. Her cheeks were rosy from the walk, and he thought she looked exceptionally pretty. "Or do you want to check out the tables first?"

He shrugged.

"Let's shop first, then." She grabbed his hand to tug him forward, but dropped it almost immediately.

They moved through the rows of tables, side by side. He feigned interest in displays of silver jewellery and wooden carvings. She insisted he try on a sweater with a moose head on the front. After a bit of arguing, he removed his coat to comply.

"It looks great!"

"I'm not sure where I'd ever wear it." He spoke quietly, hoping the vendor wouldn't overhear.

"Where *couldn't* you wear it?"

He pulled it off and she refolded it and placed it back on the table. He smoothed the static from his hair and followed her farther into the room. They paused at each stall to examine the items on display.

Shelby bought a pair of earrings at one stall and a jar of honey at another. When they reached the far back corner, she nodded at a large table surrounded by shoppers. Though the vendor was a woman he didn't recognize, the name on the sign made it obvious whose items were on display.

"Grace's?" he asked with interest.

Shelby smiled proudly. "That's right. She doesn't do crowds, but her stuff is popular enough that local shops have no problem working the displays for her, for a commission."

They moved over to the table, and Beau examined the pottery on display. He was by no means an expert on anything artistic, but even he could see that Grace was talented. Her work evoked emotion, and people clearly responded with their wallets. A grey-haired woman tugged on Shelby's sleeve to say hello, and they moved away from the table, engrossed in friendly conversation.

He picked up one of the figurines, feeling drawn to it in particular. A woman was hugging a younger girl, her head tilted down as though whispering in the younger one's ear. They wore long blue dresses. Their golden hair blended together, unifying them as two halves of a whole. He put it down, but quickly plucked it back up. Before he could give it too much thought, he moved toward the woman working the table, pulling his wallet from his back pocket.

Shelby moved to his side as the woman handed him the figurine in a plastic bag. "What did you buy?"

Before he could chicken out, he held the bag out to her.

"For me?" Her eyebrows rose in surprise. "What is it?"

"Open it later."

Too late. She tore into the package with childish delight, coming up with the figurine.

"Oh, wow." She turned it in her hands, examining it from all angles.

Feeling like he needed to explain himself, he said, "It reminds me of you and Grace."

Her gaze jumped to his, a strange expression in her eyes.

"When you led her out of the barn the other day, the way you two walked back to the house side by side. You

213

seemed so connected. Like them." His cheeks grew warm. He was regretting his impulsivity.

"I mean, I know they're both blond and you've got dark hair, but …" He wasn't doing himself any favours, so he decided to shut up. What the hell was wrong with him, anyway?

She looked down at the figurine in her hand, turning it over to read the title underneath. "*Sisters*." Her voice was so soft he could barely hear her.

"If you don't want it …"

"No, I do." She wrapped it back in the tissue paper and put it into the plastic bag. Her eyes looked shiny. "Thank you, Beau. That was very sweet of you."

They stood there, smiling awkwardly at each other.

"Should we go eat?" he said.

She handed over their tickets, and they were ushered into a dimly lit dining room filled with brass shaded lamps and dark wood furniture. Shelby seemed to recover her composure and chatted cheerfully while they stood in line at the booze table. She chose a glass of red wine and Beau asked for their darkest beer.

They found a table, and a waiter brought them a cheese and fruit plate.

She pointed to a round of cranberry-drizzled goat cheese in the middle of the plate. Like a mother showing off her child's artwork, she said, "This one's Grace's."

He spread some on a cracker and munched appreciatively. "It's really good."

She smiled in acknowledgement and popped a grape into her mouth.

Beau's phone buzzed as they were sharing a mixed dessert platter. He glanced at the screen and stood up. "Would you excuse me?"

"Duty calls," she said with a shrug. "And now I don't have to share."

She dragged the plate toward her as he left the table.

"Brunelli."

"Hi, Detective," Jessica Chambers said. "Something interesting popped up in the forensics from Tabitha Johnson's bedroom. Thought I'd run it by you."

"Oh, yeah?"

"We pulled some unusual hair samples from her bedspread. White, about an inch and a half in length, coarse texture. They were cleaned and degreased in seventy percent ethanol, and analyzed under forty times magnification. Then the cuticle scales were investigated using the clear nail polish method, which is an interesting technique where we coat the shaft in a thin layer of nail polish —"

"What were the results?"

"Right. Well, the diameter was coarse, and the medulla was an unbroken lattice going up the entire width of the shaft. We were able to eliminate deer and antelope hair due to the absence of their characteristic scale pattern. The curved margin was oriented —"

He closed his eyes. "So, what are they from?"

"We're looking at the Bovidae family and the Caprinae subfamily."

"Help me out here. In layman's terms."

"It's goat hair. And as far as we know thus far, Tabitha hasn't visited any farms or petting zoos recently."

After a moment of silence, Jessica asked, "So, any thoughts?"

"Oh, plenty," he said. "I'll get back to you."

Shelby watched him walk back to the table, her forehead creased with tension. "Everything okay?"

"Fine. You didn't eat any of the dessert."

"A moment on the lips," she said.

"I doubt you need to worry about that." It might have been a compliment, but he didn't look at her as he said it.

"Aren't you going to sit down?"

"Do you mind if we cut this short?"

She pulled the napkin from her lap and laid it on the table. Standing up, she said, "You can't take the job out of the man, huh?"

"Sorry." He tried to smile but did a poor job of it.

"You don't need to walk me home. I'll be fine."

"My car is there," he said.

"Right. Well, I mean you can get going right now so I won't slow you down."

"No, it's fine." He waited while she did up her coat and wrapped her scarf around her neck.

"Is this about Grace?" she asked as they stepped outside. The air had grown chilly when the sun went down. She pulled her scarf up to her chin.

"No. A different case." He forced himself to match her slower pace, ignoring her searching look.

"Seriously, just go," she said. "I'll be fine."

He shook his head. "Tell me more about your music?"

"Like what?"

"I noticed the guitar case by your front door. But you didn't play it the night I was there."

"I don't always. In Nelson I have Gary, Finn, and Matheu. And sometimes we have a saxophonist, too. But I do solo gigs other places, and I play the guitar for those."

"Where do you go?"

"Oh, just about everywhere. I do monthly gigs in Kamloops, Vernon, Penticton, and sometimes in Revelstoke or Salmon Arm. I've gone as far as Calgary and Vancouver, but that's rare. I like to stay more local. Or maybe I'm not good enough to compete with the big-city scene."

"I doubt that. You have a beautiful voice," Beau said.

She shrugged, a small smile touching her lips. "I never trained professionally, which is one of my big regrets. I wish I'd had that opportunity."

"Self-made. I admire that."

"Yeah? Well, thanks."

"What kind of music do you play at your solo gigs? Still blues?"

"A mixture. Blues, folk, some classic rock. And some original stuff, too."

"Really?" He took her elbow to guide her around a pile of dog shit someone hadn't scooped. He let go, but a couple seconds later than was necessary. Some kind of electricity seemed to travel between them. It made his stomach do a weird wobbly thing.

"I'd like to hear you play sometime," he said before he could think too much. "I mean, again."

Her smile was shy and a little uncertain, which was endearing. "I'm in Kamloops next Saturday. Maybe we could go out for supper first. I mean, if that works for you."

"I'd like that. I'm not sure where I'll be, but …"

"Sure, I understand."

She paused on the sidewalk as though expecting to say goodbye near his car, but Beau continued up the path to her front door. He stood there while she unlocked the door.

"Thanks for walking me home." She raised the bag that held her new figurine. "And thank you for the gift. It means a lot to me."

It had been a strange night, and feelings were stirring within him that he wasn't comfortable with. "Thank you for the invite."

The wind shifted, blowing icy kisses against his cheeks and forehead. There was a scraping sound across the street, and they both turned to look. The street was dark. Footsteps swiftly moved away with the rustle and scrape of shoes kicking dead leaves.

He caught a glimpse of someone as they stepped through the puddle of light beneath the street lamp on the corner. It looked like a man. His shoulders were slumped, and his hair was either grey or blond. A split second later he disappeared into the darkness. Just someone out for an evening stroll, or had he been watching them?

Shelby placed a gentle hand on his chest, which refocused his attention in a hurry. In the porch light, her eyes were wide and dark. "Would you like to come in for a bit?"

Damn. It had been a long and lonely lifetime since any woman had looked at him with that seductive mixture of vulnerability and desire. Her hand was still on his chest, right over his heart. She tilted her head back, her lips parted to reveal the gleam of her teeth.

"I can't." His voice was hoarse, barely a whisper.

Her hand dropped and she turned away, reaching for the door handle.

"This case ..."

She nodded, but didn't look at him. Beau could still feel the warmth of her hand on his chest, like a ghost. "It's okay, I know. It was silly of me."

"I'm sorry," he said.

She shook her head. Even in the dim light, he could see how pink her cheeks had become. "No, *I'm* sorry. I'm so embarrassed. I know you've got work to do. I don't know what I was thinking. I've never done that before. Invited a man in, I mean. It's not —"

He couldn't stand it. Without thought, he bent down and stopped her words with his mouth. He buried his hands in the cloud of her hair, cupped his palms around the curve of her skull. Her lips were soft and plump against his, and they tasted like wine and chocolate. He could feel the heat of her body, just inches away, and he ached to close the gap.

But she'd frozen at his touch, her lips turning to marble against his.

He pulled back. Her eyes were wide and glassy, her body rigid with tension. He'd thought her request to come inside was pretty clear, but maybe he'd read her wrong. He was certainly out of practice. It had been a long time since he'd kissed a woman, and decades since he'd kissed anyone other than Emily.

He let her go and stepped back. "I'm sorry, I thought —"

Shelby didn't move. Her hands were up in a defensive posture, the bag with the figurine dangling from her wrist.

His brain was foggy with desire, so it took a moment to recognize her posture for what it was.

There were three common responses when faced with an intense threat: fight, flight, or freeze. What he was seeing here was tonic immobility, or the "freeze response." The body flooded with cortisol and other stress hormones, causing the victim quite literally to freeze. It was especially common in victims of sexual assault, and often cruelly turned against them in court. *Why didn't you say no? Why didn't you fight? Obviously, you must have wanted it.*

He took another step back, lifted his hands in front of him with his palms out. "I won't touch you. You're safe."

He stood still, waiting for her to make the next move. It took at least a minute before she blinked. Slowly, her hands dropped to her sides. She shook her head, blinked several more times.

"Oh," she said. "I'm sorry. I don't know what happened there."

"It's okay. I understand."

She looked up at him, her face tight with shame and fear.

"I've dealt with my share of survivors over the years." He purposely avoided using the word *victim*. "I really do understand."

She exhaled a long breath. Nodded. "Right."

"I won't ever touch you again without your consent."

The tension in her jaw seemed to lessen. "It's not that I didn't want you to. I just wasn't expecting it right then. The surprise …"

"It needs to be on your terms. I get it. You lead, I'll follow."

A small smile touched her lips. "Maybe next time?" She tipped her head to the side, looked up at him nervously. "If I haven't scared you off?"

He couldn't help but smile. "Not in the slightest."

She smiled in return, and reached for the door handle. "Good night, Beau."

She pushed open the door. There was a scrap of paper on the entryway mat. It caught against the bottom rim of the door, slid along the mat, and dropped onto the hardwood floor. She bent to pick it up, and he saw the quickscratch of a handwritten note. Messy printing, blue ink. She curled her hand around it before he could read it.

"Everything okay?" he asked.

"Fine. It's just a former patient of Dr. Goldberg's." She saw the look on his face. "Really, it's nothing to worry about. He's totally harmless."

"Do you want me to look around?"

"No, no. It's okay, really. He sticks a note through the mail slot sometimes. I'll give his new doctor a call."

"You sure?"

"Absolutely. And I've held you up long enough. Get to work, Detective. You're wasting my tax dollars." With that, Shelby shut the door in his face.

TWENTY-SIX

God is still not revealing Himself to me. I clearly haven't done enough yet to repent for my sins against the Family. I am thinking more and more that only a blood atonement will earn back my place in Zion.

It's like Uncle G said: Those of apostate influence, who have turned from Jesus Christ's Gospel, Church, and Kingdom, must repent in exile and atone by the spilling of blood.

Yet I keep turning away from His good word because I don't like hurting people. Just the thought of it makes my belly ache.

Even Grace, who has not only abandoned the Family, but also led nine other children astray. She betrayed God and her own kin by talking to the police and telling them the Family's secrets.

Yes, I know that Grace is the worst of all the apostates. But I still love her. And I want to hurt her least of all.

TWENTY-SEVEN

G race called her sister and left another message on her voice mail. The tables had turned, and now it was Desiree who wasn't returning her phone calls.

She tried to put her sister out of her mind and spent the morning packaging her latest pottery into bubble wrap and felt-lined boxes to protect them from damage during transport. Once a month, she drove her latest work to her distributor in Kamloops, and her next trip was scheduled for tomorrow.

Though she would never have admitted it, she always felt strangely forlorn as she emptied the shelves that lined her pottery shed. Over the years, she'd developed a private ritual. Before she wrapped each piece, she said goodbye to it by planting a kiss on the hardened clay, and saying, "May you give joy wherever you go, and may you know a long and unbroken life." It seemed a good wish to make for people as well as pottery.

Once everything was wrapped and the shelves were empty, she took loads to the car. She pulled the dolly slowly along the path and up the gravel driveway so that nothing jostled too badly.

Goats brayed in greeting as she passed the yard, and she paused on the way back to hand out treats and head scratches. The new Saanen was doing well. Her hooves were healing nicely and she was finding her place within the herd. Her playful personality was emerging as she got more comfortable. Grace gave her an extra treat, scratching her behind the ears affectionately.

It took several trips to load the Subaru, and lunchtime was approaching when she closed the trunk. Grace grabbed a plastic bag and opened the passenger door to clear out the miscellaneous junk and empty takeout coffee cups. While she kept her home meticulously tidy as she'd been taught as a child, the car didn't get the same attention. It was embarrassing.

She pulled out a slip of paper that had fallen into the well between the passenger seat and the door. It was from a free notepad advertising a local realtor, one she kept on her kitchen table to use for grocery lists. But this wasn't a grocery list, she saw when she unfolded the paper. The writing was childlike, familiar, with the *R*s reversed. It said *Tabitha Johnson*, with an address in Kelowna.

A flash of guilty heat rolled through her. She looked up and hastily scanned her surroundings, fearful that someone might see her holding this incriminating piece of evidence. Then she shook her head and let out a breathless laugh. How ridiculous! There was nothing wrong with having

Tabby's address. She already knew Tabby lived in Kelowna, although she hadn't known exactly where.

And yet she remained anxious. Her stomach churned, and her ear buzzed. She stuffed the note into the plastic bag, piled other garbage on top, and tied the handles closed. A wave of relief washed through her when the note was out of sight, and the buzzing in her ear eased. She deposited the bag in the garbage bin by the side of the house and went inside to lie down. She no longer felt like eating lunch.

. . .

Revelations about marriages and other important things were supposed to be given from God directly to the prophet. But most people in Brigham had never met Rulon Jeffs, who was advancing in years and didn't travel.

His son, Uncle Warren, had visited on a number of occasions to bring them the good word of the prophet and lift their spirits with his sermons. Or at least that's how others seemed to feel, but Grace found Uncle Warren's delivery bland and exceedingly boring.

He ran Alta Academy in Salt Lake City. In Brigham, learning happened at home or at temple, and Grace was awed by the idea of going to an actual school. She used to daydream about moving to the big city and attending Alta Academy, but her feet had never left Brigham's soil. The closest she got was a promise that Father would bring her on a supply run to Bountiful in the fall, but by that time much had changed.

In Salt Lake City, people could sometimes delay or even refuse a marriage. She'd heard a story about someone's sister worrying about her placement with a disliked first cousin. Uncle Rulon advised her to pray and then follow her heart, and when she did, she received her own revelation that her placement was indeed God's will. She went ahead with the marriage with a happy heart.

In Brigham, there was no such freedom. Due to their isolation, their bishop was allowed to make marriage placements for his people. And no one dared question a revelation given to Gideon Smith.

Uncle G was devoted to his community and hands-on in his teaching. At thirteen, Grace still took lessons with him several times a week. He took pride in making sure the girls were trained, knowledgeable, and obedient. Good priesthood wives were the backbone of the community.

He'd send one of his children to request her or Desiree's attendance. Whenever they heard that triple knock on the door, Desiree would run to her bedroom. Grace thought it was very childish of her to hide like that. Sure, Uncle G's lessons were boring. They were so boring, afterward she could rarely remember what she'd been taught. Nevertheless, Uncle G said she was an excellent student and he often told Father how pleased he was with her progress. Desiree never got the same praise, and this made Grace feel special.

When they heard a triple knock on the door just before suppertime, Desiree ran for her bedroom. Clearly thinking it was a game, Sariah squealed and toddled after her. Grace shook her head, feeling embarrassed for Father, but continued to lay the table for supper while Mother went to answer the door.

Rulon Smith entered the house and stood nervously by the coat tree. He was one of Uncle G's youngest, and one of the few she genuinely liked. He was shy and unassuming, he spoke carefully as though ensuring his words were kind, and when called upon during learning he always gave thoughtful answers. Plus he'd once lied on her behalf and gotten Boydell a whipping, a favour Grace had never forgotten.

"What can we do for you this evening?" Mother asked.

Rulon's cheeks reddened, and he stammered to get out his words. "Father has called for Grace to attend him."

"Does she have time for supper first?"

"He's asked for the whole family to come."

"Oh?" Mother's eyebrows went up to her hairline, and Grace felt the first chill of dread.

Father came down the hall and exchanged a hasty look with Mother. "Best not to delay, then." Usually Father's smile crinkled the skin around his eyes like a candy wrapper, but not this time.

Mother turned off the oven. "Grace, go put on your blue dress. Hurry up now!"

Numbly, Grace left the kitchen. In her bedroom, she pulled off her beige housedress and yanked the blue dress over her head. It was edged in a creamy lace that she and Mother had just finished sewing the previous week. She hadn't even worn the dress to temple yet. The fabric was stiff, scratching her skin even through her undergarments.

From the hallway, Mother called for Desiree and Sariah to clean up and come to the kitchen. Mother Rebecca called out from her bedroom to ask what was happening. Sariah started crying. Desiree remained silent.

With trembling fingers, she undid her hair and ran a brush through it. She rolled up the sides and pulled the front up in a poof, then tied the back in a quick braid. When she was done, it dangled past her bottom. She leaned close to the mirror, checking her face for dirt and making sure there was no food stuck in her teeth. Then she slipped on her good shoes, the heavy leather ones that didn't yet have any holes. She met Desiree in the hallway, and the girls automatically clasped hands and moved forward together.

They followed Rulon up the road, silent except for Sariah's sniffling. Mother and Desiree walked on either side of her, holding her hands. It had been forever since she'd held her mother's hand.

She thought of the funeral processions she'd witnessed for Brigham's many lost babies and children. The family of the deceased would crowd around the tiny casket as it was carried up the road to the graveyard, which was tucked behind the temple with an unrestricted view of the jagged peaks beyond.

At the top of the hill, the Smiths' house was brightly lit against the coming twilight, giving it a festive air.

As they climbed the porch steps, Mother squeezed her hand.

They shuffled inside and stood in a clump in the entranceway. Uncle G's second wife, Brinda, came from the back of the house to greet them. Mother and Father responded politely, but Grace could barely hear them above the buzzing in her good ear.

Brinda led them up the stairs to Uncle G's study. Father went in first, followed by his wives and daughters. Uncle G rose from behind his desk, smiling warmly. He motioned for them to sit. Father sat in a chair, and the rest of the family squeezed onto the large couch behind him.

Grace didn't like sitting on the couch. It made her feel anxious. Desiree squirmed, and Mother wrapped an arm around both daughters' shoulders. Sariah climbed into Mother Rebecca's lap and buried her face in the thick cotton of her dress. Mother Rebecca absent-mindedly stroked her daughter's hair.

"Thank you for coming so quickly." The smile on Uncle G's face was alarmingly broad. "I have some wonderful news! A placement has been revealed to me."

Grace sent up a silent prayer that it was for Father. He needed a third wife to secure his spot in the heavenly realm.

"Oh?" Father's voice cracked.

"A very fortuitous placement, I do believe. One that will bring together our two families."

Father's smile looked strange. "You know how highly we esteem your family."

"Yes, yes." Uncle G waved his hand. He looked like a toad.

She took a quick mental tally of Uncle G's daughters, wondering who might be a suitable match.

"Grace," Uncle G said.

Mother squeezed her hand so tightly she jumped. "Yes, Uncle G?"

"You have recently become a woman."

"Y-yes, Uncle G."

"How wonderful. Although I must admit, as selfish as it may be, that I will miss guiding you in your learning. I want you to know," Uncle G said, turning to Father. "Grace is one of my favourite students, always so quick to learn, so humble ... she will make a dutiful wife to my son."

"I'm so grateful to hear it," Father said. "Uh, which son?"

She knew before he said it, and bile rose up her throat.

"It is God's will that Grace be placed with Boydell. Which grants her the honourable status of a first wife, I might add."

Mother and Father both made exclamations of joy, but Mother's hand tightened as though anticipating the grief of letting her go.

"But," Grace said before she could help herself, "you know I'm only thirteen, right?"

Some girls were married at fourteen or fifteen, but she'd never heard of one being placed before that.

Uncle G laughed. "Yes, dear girl. I'm aware of your age, as is God. This is a great honour, one that is only bestowed upon the sweetest girls. You should feel proud to be singled out for your good service. He knows how pure your heart and spirit are, and He's chosen you for one of the noblest boys in the priesthood. One day, you might be the wife of the bishop."

"Isn't that wonderful?" Mother Rebecca's voice sounded flat.

"That is good fortune, indeed," Father said, turning to Grace with pride. "And an honour."

"But ..."

Mother squeezed her hand in warning, but she couldn't stop her mouth.

"But I *hate* Boydell!" The words tasted so bitter on her tongue.

A weighted hush fell over the room. Uncle G's cheeks turned red and his eyes bugged out. The buzzing in her ear grew to a ferocious roar.

"Well." Uncle G forced a smile. "Then I suggest you go home right now, and start praying."

Mother stood and pulled her to her feet. Grace tripped over Desiree, and both girls stumbled. Her body was going numb. She moved away, into the darkness at the back of her mind.

Father grabbed her around the waist and lifted her into his arms.

"Father, please," she said, clinging to his shirt. "I can't ... I can't."

Her father, her hero, her only chance at being saved from this fate, remained silent. He carried her from the room, but paused in the hallway when Uncle G called out to him.

"Patrick."

Uncle G moved around his desk and walked toward them. His feet were bare, as they always were when he was at home.

"The wedding will take place tomorrow evening, at sunset."

Father nodded.

Uncle G cupped a broad hand against Grace's cheek. It was warm and callused. "Welcome to the family, daughter."

TWENTY-EIGHT

I n his hotel room in Nelson, Beau propped his laptop on the bed and began his search. The British Columbia Ministry of Transportation and Infrastructure had traffic cameras set up at ferry crossings along BC-23 and BC-6 toward Nakusp. The videos livestreamed, and you could click a link to view the past twenty-four hours.

He watched the video from the camera situated above the Needles Ferry. It was difficult to see the licence plates from that angle, but it might give him an idea if Grace had travelled to Kelowna prior to Tabitha Johnson's death. That was if the video was saved beyond the initial twenty-four-hour loop.

As soon as it was nine in the morning, he snagged his cellphone and called the main number for the ministry. He waited on hold several times but was eventually put through to someone who had the authority to give him the information he required.

"Dan Wizen." The man's voice was gruff.

After explaining who he was and waiting while his credentials were checked, Beau said, "I'm investigating a crime that occurred in Kelowna, and we have a potential suspect who lives in the Needles area. I'm looking for the past week's video from the traffic cams along BC-6 and BC-23."

"Well, that might be tough," Wizen said.

"Why?"

"We have an internal website that saves display images for a month, after which they're overwritten."

"Okay, right. And the time frame I'm looking for is within the past month."

"Problem is, they're not surveillance cams. The resolution is very low, so you're likely to have a problem with accurate identification. And it's not video. They're still images taken at regular intervals, varying from two to thirty minutes, depending on available bandwidth at the location."

"Am I able to see them?"

"You understand it wouldn't be admissible in a court of law."

"That's fine, I'd just like to see."

"All right. Give me the locations again, and the time frame you're looking at. I'll get back to you."

"That's great, thank you."

"Might take me a bit, so be patient."

Next, Beau used Google Maps to search gas stations along both routes, and placed calls to each one to request security footage from the past week. It was slog work, but it might net him something. Over and over, he explained what he was looking for and asked for the owner or manager of the gas station to call him back.

This ate up much of his morning, and by the time he stood up his head was pounding and his sciatica was kicking in. He did a quick series of stretches before lying flat on the bed and stuffing both pillows under his head so he could stare at the smoke detector on the ceiling and ponder the situation.

He didn't have enough evidence to request a search warrant for Grace DeRoche's home, which is what he sorely wanted to do. But, as it stood, there wasn't even any evidence that crimes had been committed. Yes, the death ratio among Brigham's Ten was high. But none of the deaths had even been listed as suspicious.

Judy Beers was leaning toward calling Rulon Smith's death a suicide, and he doubted she would hang on much longer before clearing the file from her desk so she could move on to the others in her stack.

The newspaper articles with their childlike writing, the grainy video of someone leaving the bridge deck with Rulon's bag, the goat hair on Tabitha Johnson's bed — it all led Beau in a particular direction. He'd been a cop for a long time. Instinct told him to keep digging through this pile of sand until he unearthed something concrete.

But he'd never before worked a case where he didn't have some proof that a crime had been committed — well, except for Emily's death, but he'd done that without the support of the RCMP. It had gone nowhere and had caused him to lose years of his life obsessed with her death instead of trying to come to terms with the loss. At some point, he knew he'd have to deal with it in a healthier way. Not today, though.

If these deaths were not suicides, then who were his top suspects? Considering the goat hair found on Tabitha's bedspread, Grace DeRoche took a top spot. But he didn't have a clue what her motivation might be. The children who'd followed her out of Brigham were as much victims as she was. Victims didn't generally turn on other victims. He had a hard time imagining that Grace could harm them, but that didn't exonerate any of the alters living inside her head.

Of course, all of Brigham's Ten had a pretty obvious enemy in common. Anyone within the Family, from Gideon Smith on down, would feel like their lives had been ruined when their children escaped and betrayed the Family's secrets to the police.

The Alberta RCMP was still looking into the possibility that Smith was living somewhere outside Medicine Hat. If the lead checked out, Smith and any of his followers would make a quick leap to the top of Beau's suspect list. But until then, he was stuck with the information he could actually corroborate, and he was getting impatient.

He closed his laptop and tucked it into the protective sleeve, shoving a little too hard out of frustration. He hadn't heard from either Shelby or Grace regarding the protection detail, but he didn't feel like tracking either of them down. In his current mood, he was inclined to say that if Grace didn't want protection from the RCMP, it was her funeral.

There was no point in him hanging around any longer. It was a waste of resources and time. It took five minutes for him to pack his suitcase and hit the road. He felt guilty about leaving Nelson without saying goodbye to Shelby, but in his current frame of mind, he didn't think he'd do a good job of it anyway. Best to call her once he was in a better mood.

His cellphone rang as he approached Castlegar. A quick glance at the screen told him that it was Jessica Chambers calling from Kelowna, likely to tell him that she was ruling Tabitha Johnson's death as a suicide.

He hit the Bluetooth button to answer the phone. "Brunelli."

"Hi, Detective. Jessica Chambers from the Kelowna Coroner's Office. I just wanted to let you know, we're ruling Tabitha Johnson's death as suspicious."

"You're kidding. Did something show up on toxicology?"

"Not a thing," she said. "But the ME noted a mark on Tabitha's chest. It's about an inch wide, located halfway between her collarbone and her right breast. I've emailed you a picture."

"All right." Beau pulled onto the side of the road and checked his email. The picture waited in his inbox. He clicked on it and waited impatiently for the image to load.

"It looks like a bruise, but I've done some research, and I think it's a burn mark from a stun gun."

"Huh. So, what's your thinking?"

"It's possible she was stunned, which caused her to lose control of her body and essentially took the fight out of her. And then she was placed in the bathtub and held under water until she asphyxiated."

Holy shit. Now he was in business.

"Any leads on the goat hair? She didn't visit a petting zoo or anything in recent weeks?"

"Not as far as we know."

He leaned back in his seat and closed his eyes. "One of Brigham's Ten, Grace DeRoche, keeps goats at her place in Nakusp."

"That's not too far away."

It was time to get Crown counsel involved. "Email me a report so I can request a search warrant."

"Will do. Oh, I've also emailed you a copy of the letters we found in Tabitha's drawer. If you could take a look, maybe there's a clue in there that I'm missing."

Beau called Doug to get the search warrant process started, and asked him to send officers to Desiree's apartment to see if she'd returned home. Now that Tabitha's death had been ruled suspicious, Desiree's absence was making him uncomfortable.

He then left a message updating Judy Beers and asking if Rulon had been pulled from the water with any marks on his body consistent with the use of a stun gun, ignored a call from Shelby, and headed back to Nakusp.

He checked back into the K2 Rotor Lodge, brought back supper from the Overwaitea Foods across the street, and ate while flipping through Eliza Barlow's and Valor Johnson's autopsy reports.

Neither report mentioned finding goat hair at the scene. Eliza's body had decomposed too much to tell if markings from a stun gun existed. Valor's report made no mention of it, so he studied the photos carefully. There was a mark low down on Valor's back, just left of his spinal column, that might have been a bruise or a burn. It also might have been a birthmark or a smudge of dirt.

He turned to the letters they'd found in Tabitha Johnson's dresser drawer. Jessica Chambers was right. The letters were cryptic and coded. There were sixteen of them in total, dating back over the past three years. They were written in ballpoint pen, the handwriting a stocky scribble. He read through them several times, taking notes as he went.

There were twenty-three mentions of someone named "B." "B" had invested money in a wheat stock that went south, "B" was being argumentative and bossy, or "B" wasn't listening to ideas about how to better run the business.

Being the youngest in his own family, Beau was familiar with the tone. Nothing was more grating than an overbearing older sibling. Could this be Clayne writing about Boaz? There were numerous mentions of a joint business venture, which Beau surmised was probably agriculture-related.

"B" got married, and his new wife got pregnant soon after. The letter writer spoke of moving into a new apartment, and how strange it was to live alone. He mentioned having trouble sleeping due to the sounds of city life outside his windows.

The tone of the letters changed eighteen months ago, after a quick reference to being contacted by someone from "our family." Flipping from one letter to the next, Beau could see the downward spiral into worry and paranoia.

The updates on the writer's day-to-day life ceased. There were no further mentions of "B." The letters became shorter and more cryptic, and for the first time numbers started to appear. They reminded Beau of the numbers written at the top of the newspaper article about Rulon Smith's death.

> *Sister,*
> *Sleep eludes me tonight. I'm thinking about 17:159. I know you will understand. Out my window, I saw a ghost from our past. I don't know if it's real, or just my conscience playing tricks on me. But it gets me thinking. My head is not right. My soul is in exile.*
> *Your loving brother*

> *Sister,*
> *14:133 is on my mind lately. Do you think it's true? I'm thinking a lot about the others. I think it's time to keep my promises. I'll write again.*
> *Your loving brother*

Several more went on in a similar vein. The last two came within a week of each other, three months ago.

> *Sister,*
> *Please be careful. 4:220*
> *Your loving brother*

> *Sister,*
> *Things are happening now, and I need to go. Please be careful and keep to yourself. Don't go out alone. 1:83*

I'll write again, if I can.
Your loving brother

Beau sat back and tapped the end of his pen against his bottom lip, mulling it over. According to Desiree, the numbers written on the top of the newspaper article she'd been sent referenced a passage from Brigham Young's *Journal of Discourses.*

A quick check of his field notes refreshed his memory. She'd said the passage was "When your brothers or sisters commit a sin that must be atoned by the shedding of their blood, will you love them well enough to shed their blood?"

It stood to reason that the numbers written in these letters would also match up with Brigham Young's teachings. He did a quick Google search, and came up with several hits.

17:159 matched a passage in the *Journal of Discourses* that read: "There is not a man or woman who turn up their noses at the counsel that is given them from the First Presidency, who, unless they repent of and refrain from such conduct, will not eventually go out of the Church and go to hell, every one of them."

14:133, which he'd asked if Tabitha thought was true, corresponded to: "Who will be saved in the celestial kingdom, and go into the presence of the Father and Son? Those only who observe the whole law, who keep the commandments of God. Those who observe all his precepts and do his will."

Several others were similar, and made it clear that whoever wrote the letters was struggling with his faith.

But Beau couldn't find matches for six, including the last two where Tabitha was warned to be careful. He sent the scans to Doug and requested they do a deeper search than what Beau could manage from his hotel room, along with a search for any agriculture-based businesses run by two brothers in Saskatchewan, Alberta, or Manitoba, where the majority of the country's wheat was grown.

An hour later, the search warrant came in. It was issued for the following day at nine in the morning. Beau made contact with the Nakusp RCMP and arranged to meet two officers at the bottom of Hot Springs Road at a quarter to nine. The warrant gave him the right to search for and seize any conducted energy weapons found on the property and any other evidence pertaining to the death of Tabitha Johnson in Kelowna. It also gave him the right to remove hair samples from the goats located on the property to take for further analysis.

TWENTY-NINE

"**F**ather, please!" Grace was on the floor in their living room, in a puddle of grief and terror. "Please, don't make me do this!"

"Grace DeRoche, this is no way to behave." Father's words were kind rather than stern. "Stand up, daughter."

Rather than stand, she slid across the floor toward her father's shoes and curled around his feet. "Please, Father, I can't marry him. I hate him. And I'm too young to be married."

"Oh, Grace." He tried to move, but she firmed her grip on his ankles. "You're going to make me fall."

"Can't you speak to Uncle G? Ask him to show me mercy?"

"Mercy!" Mother Rebecca said. "You want to be absolved from your duty? From being a good priesthood girl? From going to heaven?"

"That's enough," Mother said.

Grace didn't need to glance up to see the scathing look that passed between her two mothers. She'd seen it many times before, brief moments where their true feelings emerged into the light of day.

"Grace," Father said, more sternly this time. "Stand up."

Somehow, she managed to find the strength to unwrap her body from around Father's feet. Her legs didn't want to support her, but Mother was there to prop her up.

"Please." She turned to bury her face in Mother's dress. "I can't do it."

"But you must," Mother said.

Those three words, spoken with quiet certainty, took the last of Grace's breath and strength away. Her legs gave out, and Mother was not strong enough to hold her. She fell and Desiree ran to her side. The sisters clung to each other, wailing. Sariah buried her face in Mother Rebecca's skirt and joined in.

"Desiree," Father said. "Take Sariah to play in your bedroom. We must speak to your sister."

"Please don't make Gracey go!" Desiree said.

"Desiree."

Whimpering, Desiree did as she was told. Grace slumped over and rested her cheek against the plank flooring. It felt rough and gritty against her skin.

"Oh, Grace." Father scooped her into his arms. She was getting big, but he was bigger and so very strong. He'd always been her North Star, her protector. She felt his strength and his love for her in everything he did. He was her hero, her champion, and her safe place to fall. But she was just beginning to understand that this time, he could not and would not be able to protect her.

When she married, Boydell would become her priest-hood head. A boy who chose cruelty over kindness and thought he was better than everyone else.

"I would rather die."

Father sat on the couch, and she curled in his lap like she'd done when she was little. He held her until her tears had quieted, and then mopped her face with a cold cloth. It soothed her swollen eyes, but did nothing to ease the ball of grief and terror lodged in her chest.

Mother Rebecca sat in the rocking chair by the door with a pile of knitting in her lap. *Click-click-click* went the knitting needles. She clucked her tongue. "Really, you do go on."

Father stroked her cheek. "We must trust in God, and do His will."

"But —" She knew her thoughts were blasphemous, but she couldn't help it. "What kind of God would do this to me?"

Mother buried her face in her hands, and Mother Rebecca gasped and dropped her knitting into her lap.

Father closed his eyes as though pained by her words. "Sweeten your tongue."

A wave of fear crested within her. She'd never had cause to question God before, but was it really Him she questioned? She'd always believed in His power and good-will, always felt His loving presence in the dawn light or the sound of her sisters' tinkling laughter or the feel of Mother's cool hand on her fevered forehead. No, it wasn't really God she questioned, and somehow that was more frightening.

"But what if Uncle G is ... *wrong*?"

The two women looked at her blankly.

Father shook his head. "Sometimes God's will is hard for us to understand. I suggest you pray for His guiding hand as you fulfill this most sacred duty."

Mother took her by the hand. "Your father is right. I know you feel young and unprepared for this new role, and that's my fault." Tears filled Mother's eyes, and she dabbed at them with her sleeve. "I always thought we'd have more time to prepare."

Fresh tears spilled hot down Grace's cheeks. "Mother, I'm so scared."

Mother Rebecca took up her needles. "Then you must pray."

"Yes," Father said. "You must pray."

"And prepare," Mother said. "We don't have enough time to make you a dress, but I could alter the one I was making for myself. Come. There's much work to be done."

"I don't care what I wear."

Mother Rebecca tsked.

Mother said, "I know you're frightened, but don't you want to be a beautiful bride?"

The answer was no.

Mother dragged Grace to the bedroom. The dress lay, half finished, on the chair beside the bed.

At Mother's urging, she undressed and pulled it over her head. It was the pale colour of the sky in August, or Clayne's eyes.

"This will do." Mother picked up her box of pins. "Hold still, Gracey, I don't want to poke you."

While her mother worked on the dress, Grace took deep breaths and focused on getting her emotions under control. Perhaps if she could speak calmly, Mother would actually hear her.

"Mother."

"Mm-hmm?" her mother said through a mouthful of pins.

"I really can't do this. There's nobody I'd rather marry less than Boydell."

"But Boydell is young and handsome. And he's a *Smith*. It's truly a fortunate match."

In that moment, Grace gave up. No one would listen to her; no one would stop this abomination from occurring.

She stood on the bed, her knees trembling, while Mother pinned up the hem of the dress. Mindful of the pins, she pulled it over her head. They stitched in silence and once that was done Mother pressed the wrinkles from the fabric.

It was their last night together as mother and child. Rather than tuck her in and leave the room as she would have normally done, Mother curled up beside her and stroked Grace's hair until she relaxed into a troubled sleep. At some point in the dark of night, she awoke to the sound of soft crying beside her.

"Are you all right?"

"Of course," Mother said. Her voice sounded thick and foggy. "Get some sleep."

Her eyes closed. Down the hall came the familiar sounds of Father taking his comfort from Mother Rebecca.

"Mother?"

"Shh." Mother stroked the hair from her forehead. "Go with God, Gracey."

Grace's wedding day arose warm and clear, and everyone agreed it was a good day to seal a marriage. Even Desiree grew excited as she helped decorate and cook the celebratory meal. Grace remained in her bedroom as much as possible. She had no interest in how she looked, what decorations were being strung in the yard, or what food would be served. As far as she was concerned, they were making her funeral meal.

She was supposed to fast all day to purify her body and soul for marriage. She was fine with that, having absolutely no desire to eat. But by the time the sun was on the west side of the sky, she felt weak from lack of food, dehydration, and fear.

She'd been fervently praying for the wedding to be cancelled, but late in the day, she turned her hope in a different direction. Uncle G could seal a marriage for time or for time and all eternity. If they were sealed only for time, her soul would be freed from Boydell's come Judgment Day. Knowing she'd be released from the marriage bond in a couple of years made the idea of marrying Boydell almost bearable.

As evening drew close, Mother and Desiree entered her bedroom to help her get dressed. Desiree took photos as Mother styled her hair in an elaborate braid and pinned in the tiny crown of pearls Mother had worn for her own wedding.

They oohed and aahed over how pretty she looked in her dress. Grace kept quiet — the only way she could keep sweet. The words she stopped on her tongue were burning and bitter.

"Twenty minutes." Mother tugged Desiree from the room, instructing Grace to rest with a cold cloth pressed to her face to reduce the redness and swelling.

Before she knew it, Mother was back to help her sit up and fix the mess she'd made of her hair. With shaky steps, she moved down the hall to the bathroom and locked herself in for some final minutes of privacy. Her hands shook against the sink, her ear buzzed, and her head felt foggy.

Her face was raw and puffy. Her eyes, one blue and one brown, were swollen almost shut. The lace collar of her dress was stiff and scratchy, and the skin at her throat looked red and irritated.

The buzzing in her ear grew louder, and her vision dimmed. She had the sensation of moving away into the darkness at the back of her head, but a knock on the door jolted her forward. It was Father, telling her it was time to go.

Her family waited in the living room, dressed in their Sunday best. Mother Rebecca stood near the door with Sariah tucked against her side. They looked like larger and smaller versions of angels, with their pale brown curls and cherubic features.

Desiree stepped forward and took Grace's hand, her eyes solemn and fearful. She was losing her oldest sister, and long before anyone had expected. Once Grace was sealed in marriage, it was only a few short years until Desiree might meet the same fate.

She squeezed Desiree's hand, though whether she was seeking or trying to give reassurance, she wasn't sure. Desiree's golden hair was pulled up in a poof and braided tightly in the back. She wore a pale pink dress with lace trim. Her face and hands were scrubbed clean for the occasion, her eyes glassy with unspilled tears.

Mother stepped forward to give her a hug. Her greying hair was pulled up and bedecked with flowers. The lines in her face were prominent, her skin drawn and eyes puffy and red. The skin on her hands felt coarse, her fingers callused from years of hard work.

Father stepped forward next, and Grace leaned into his embrace. He wrapped her in his warmth and tucked her face into his broad chest. She sent up a fervent prayer that the end of days would come right that instant, so she could follow her father up to whatever level of heaven he'd attained. She didn't even care if they ended up on one of the lowest levels, or even in hell. It would be better than whatever she faced in the coming hours.

"Come on, Gracey." Father led her to the door.

Outside, the residents of Brigham waited to cheer her toward the temple. She saw Mother Dinah first, standing near the garden gate that separated the DeRoches' front yard from the road. Next to Dinah stood Clayne and Tabitha. Though Grace had promised herself that she wouldn't look at Clayne, his gaze was the first she sought. But he looked at the ground, so all she saw was the crown of his head.

Father took one of her elbows and Mother took the other. It reminded her of when she was little and they used to lift her between them, swinging her so her feet never touched the ground.

People crowded behind them to follow them up the hill, the same way they followed a casket. The entire Smith family waited on the temple steps. When she saw Boydell, her legs shook. He was tall and slender, his blond hair slicked back. She hadn't noticed how much the rounded cheeks of youth had given way to more chiselled features. At some point, Boydell had become a man.

Uncle G stood behind him like an overinflated toad, his hand resting on Boydell's shoulder. Boydell's mother, Christina, stood on his other side. She was Uncle G's third wife, sealed at the age of fourteen. Boydell looked like her.

He didn't wait for Grace to climb the stairs. Instead, he trotted down to meet her, holding a small bouquet of flowers wrapped in blue ribbon. The women crowded close and sighed their approval. He smiled at her nervously and she stared at him blankly in return.

"May I?" He held up the bouquet of flowers.

"How nice." Mother prodded her forward.

As he pinned the flowers to her dress, his fingers grazed her neck. It made her skin crawl with revulsion and fear.

"Your mother told me your dress was blue, so I chose the ribbon to match. Do you like it?"

Mother elbowed her, and she bobbed her head yes.

Boydell took his place beside her, nudging Mother aside. Panic swelling within her, she reached for her mother. But Mother shook her head and stepped back. Father kissed her on the cheek, his beard pricking her tender skin. His eyes were full of tears as he moved to Mother's side. She had never felt so alone.

"You look just lovely, daughter." Uncle G leaned in to kiss her cheek. The touch of his lips made her sway with fear and revulsion.

Boydell tightened his grip on her hand, and they followed Uncle G through the doors and into the temple. Others crowded in behind them. It seemed the whole town was there to bear witness. After all, it wasn't every day that a member of Brigham's royalty was sealed in marriage.

At the front of the room, Uncle G waited to speak until everyone had found seats.

Grace barely listened to the service. Her hand was cold and sweaty inside Boydell's, but she realized he was shaking just as much as she was. She kept her eyes on their feet, pale slippers on hers and boat-size black leather on his.

When Boydell said, "I do," it startled her.

"And Grace, do you come here of your own free will, as a good priesthood girl, to seal yourself to Boydell?"

She opened her mouth, but no words came out. After a heavy silence, Uncle G repeated the question.

Boydell squeezed her hand.

"I d-do."

From the front row she heard Mother's sigh of relief, but she barely took notice. The next part of the service was the most important, and she sent up one last fervent prayer to be sealed only for time.

Uncle G gave his toad-like smile. "I seal you, Boydell Addicus Smith and Grace Harriet DeRoche, for time and all eternity."

Her good ear screeched along with the cheer of the crowd. Boydell kissed her, his lips soft and warm and strange. Her vision grew dark. She wanted to pull away, wipe a sleeve across her mouth. She couldn't seem to move.

Boydell let her go so he could shake hands, laugh, hug his father, and receive pats on the back from his older brothers. Surrounded by priesthood men, he moved down the aisle.

Mother nudged her to follow. She stumbled forward, following the crowd into the haze of twilight.

The celebratory meal traditionally took place in the bride's home. The DeRoches' house was too small to hold everyone, so they'd set up tables in the front yard and along the dirt patch that joined the DeRoche and Johnson properties.

Plastic tables and folding chairs had been laid out across the yard. Boydell found her a chair and went off to get them some food. He placed a warm hand on her back as he set the plate in front of her, squeezed her shoulder in a possessive way.

"You must be as hungry as I am," he said. "I haven't eaten a thing all day."

Neither had she, but the food was unappealing. With effort, she lifted a bite of chicken to her mouth, chewed, and swallowed.

He pressed a leg into hers under the table, a private message that they were now linked. Next his hand was on her thigh, squeezing. When she tried to pull free, he squeezed harder, giving her a smile that dared her to rebel. At that moment, he looked so much like his father.

Her ear buzzed, and darkness crept into the sides of her vision. She focused on taking small bites of food. Everything tasted like sawdust, and her mouth was so dry she could barely choke it down. She coughed and took a hasty sip of her drink. The fruit punch was cloyingly sweet, a reminder for her tongue. Mother had baked her favourite spice cake with maple frosting, but she gagged after just a mouthful.

A new thought occurred to her partway through the meal. She had no idea where they would live. She had a sudden, panicked thought that they would be ushered up the hill to Uncle G's house. She couldn't imagine living in the busy Smith house, sleeping steps away from Uncle G's study.

But after the meal wound down, they were led in the opposite direction. Grace breathed a sigh of relief when they turned right instead of left, moving away from the temple.

They stopped in front of a trailer on the outer edge of Claybourne Street, which was little more than a dirt track that ran along the edge of the cow pasture. Someone had decorated the yard with streamers and balloons and pinned a sign above the door that read HONEYMOON SUITE. The stench of cow manure was ripe in the air.

At the urging of those crowded around, Boydell lifted her into his arms. She wasn't expecting it, and she cupped her hands over her face and yelped in fear.

"Smile!" People shouted, and the flash of cameras almost blinded her when she removed her hands from her face. It felt so odd to be cradled in Boydell's arms, not twenty-four hours after her father had held her the same way. This felt very different, and not at all safe. She didn't know what to expect once they went inside, but she doubted she would like it.

Boydell carried her over the threshold, set her on her feet, and closed the door behind them. Outside the cheers turned to happy chatter as folks meandered away, leaving them in eventual silence.

The trailer smelled like dust and mildew. She preferred the smell of cow dung. But someone had been busy cleaning it up, and decorations were strung across the kitchen and living room. Streamers lined the hallway toward what was probably the bathroom and bedroom.

Boydell looked around with interest. When he spoke, his voice was soft. "I've never lived anywhere but my own house."

"Neither have I."

For a moment, she felt a tenuous connection form between them. They were both away from the only homes they'd ever known, and uncertain how to step into this new life that had been chosen for them. Since they were sealed for time and all eternity — just the thought made her chest burn — perhaps they could use that nervousness to lay the first brick in the foundation of their marriage.

Marriage. She was married. A fresh wave of shock rolled through her.

"Well." He laid his hands on her shoulders. She flinched, but took a breath and tried her best not to pull away. He pressed against her back, his body warm and wiry and strong. This time she pulled away. She couldn't help it.

Not knowing what else to do, she feigned interest in checking out the kitchen. She opened the cupboards and the fridge, and turned on the faucet so water ran, cool and clean, over her hands.

He played along, smiling, answering questions about his favourite foods, and suggesting she ask his mother for recipes. She pushed the moment as far as she could, but eventually he grew tired of it.

"Grace. Come here." He spoke plaintively, and she looked up to see him standing in the kitchen doorway.

"What?"

"Come here," he said more firmly, and reached a hand toward her.

She swallowed hard and moved in his direction, but she didn't take his hand. Instead, she stopped while she was still out of his reach. She bowed her head in what she hoped looked like submission. In reality she was trying to hide the tears welling in her eyes.

"Let's go see the bedroom."

"Why?"

He laughed as though she'd told a great joke. Grabbing her hand, he tugged her down the hallway to the bedroom. In the middle of the room stood a queen-size bed, like the ones in Mother's and Mother Rebecca's bedrooms. The bedspread had been covered in rose petals, which seemed like an awful waste of flowers.

At home, Father moved back and forth between their bedrooms. Something went on behind closed doors, but she wasn't sure what it was. When they'd start up with their grunts and moans and banging sounds, she would put a pillow over her head until it was over.

Grace eyed the bed nervously, wondering what caused her parents to make such noises. When Father shared Mother's bedroom, things were pretty quiet. She'd hear soft noises and whispers and sometimes even laughter. That didn't seem so bad.

But in Mother Rebecca's room, Father made a lot more noise. Sometimes Mother Rebecca would yell like she was being hurt. But she always seemed fine the next day, and Grace had a hard time imagining that her father could hurt anyone.

Boydell, on the other hand.

He pushed her toward the bed and told her to sit. She could barely hear him over the buzzing of her good ear. He sat next to her and placed a hand low down on her back. Her skin prickled with disgust.

"Will you undress for me, or should I do it?" He still sounded nervous, but she heard an excitement in his voice that she didn't quite understand.

"What?"

"All right, be that way."

Before she could think to stop him, he unzipped the back of her dress all the way down. She sprang to her feet and moved to the corner of the room, holding her dress so it wouldn't fall.

"What are you doing?" she said.

"My priesthood duty."

He stood and moved toward her. She wedged herself between the night table and the wall. Her good ear exploded with static, and her vision throbbed from black to red and back again.

"What's with this act? You know what we're supposed to do."

"No, I don't!"

He rolled his eyes. Quick as lightning he reached out and grabbed her wrist.

"Hey!"

He yanked her toward him and smashed his lips into hers, forcing her mouth open with his tongue. She gagged at the intrusion, trying to push him away.

He pulled his head back. "What's your problem?"

"I don't like what you're doing!"

"But —" He blinked at her, looking genuinely confused. "But you've been trained for this."

"No, I haven't! I don't even know what *this* is."

"Father said you're the most obedient girl he's ever trained."

Nausea burned its way up her throat. She slammed a hand across her mouth, hurting already-bruised lips, and shook her head.

Boydell's eyes were glassy with tears. "Is this some kind of game?"

"N-no," she said through her fingers.

They stared at each other in silence for several moments, and then he shook his head, and his lips curled into a smile.

"All right, if you want to pretend you're so innocent, I'll play along." He grabbed the shoulders of her dress and pulled them down to her waist, making her gasp. "It's really nice of you, to pretend this is your first time. It makes me feel …" He yanked at her temple undergarments. "Special."

"What are you doing?" She clutched at the thin fabric covering her chest, trying to hold it in place. She'd never felt so naked. So scared.

"I wouldn't have expected it from you. You've never struck me as particularly kind or thoughtful. I guess it makes up for being so ugly."

He gave a hard yank and her temple undergarments ripped, leaving her exposed. The buzzing panic welled inside her, and her vision grew dark. She stumbled sideways and caught herself on the edge of the bed, woozy with fear.

"I am now your priesthood head. Show me the respect I deserve."

He pushed her down. She sprawled across the bed, crushing rose petals beneath her. Their fragrance hit her nose, sharp and overwhelming. They stuck to her skin like soft fingers.

As he moved over her, her vision went dark. She flew toward the back of her mind, where soft lamplight glowed and Mother waited to tuck her in.

She awoke the next morning sticky with blood and other stuff. She rolled off the bed, crushing rose petals gone brown at the edges. They smelled like funerals.

Boydell lay in a sprawl across the bed, naked and snoring. She turned from the sight and hobbled toward the bathroom to clean herself up.

. . .

Grace heard the cars coming up the gravel road as she left the pottery shed. It sounded like there were two of them.

The police are coming.

She shook her head, trying to quiet the noise inside her head.

We must run for the forest.

"No. I'm not running anymore," she said out loud.

They'll take us away. We must hide!

"Stop it." She covered her ears, as though that were any protection against the voices speaking inside her head.

The first car to nose through the trees into the clearing was Detective Brunelli's. The second was, indeed, a police car. Her ear screeched, and darkness crept into the sides of her vision.

We told you it was the police.

Detective Brunelli exited his car. Two officers got out of the second one and followed him toward her. One officer was a woman. The other was the man who'd come to her house to offer police protection.

It's him again. Watch out for him. He's dangerous.

But it was too late to run. She was trapped.

Detective Brunelli said, "Hi, Grace."

THIRTY

Rain was coming down the next morning when Beau met the officers at the bottom of Hot Springs Road. The officer who had dealt with Grace on the protection detail, James Fellner, was a young man with less than five years on the force. His partner, Adeline Bouchard, was in her forties and had moved to BC from Quebec three years prior. She had a heavy Quebecois accent, though she spoke perfect English.

While they waited for nine o'clock, they hunched under the cover of trees on the side of the road so he could fill them in.

"She's quite the loon, eh?" Fellner said.

"She spooked him," Bouchard said with a grin. "He came back to the station with his knickers in a bunch."

Fellner gave her a look. "You're laughing now."

"You guys remember Brigham's Ten? The kids who escaped that FLDS compound?"

Fellner shook his head. "Before my time, I guess."

"I remember that," Bouchard said. "She's one of those poor kids?"

"She is." He went on to explain the circumstances and the reason for the warrant. By the time he finished it was almost nine, so they climbed back into their vehicles and he led them up the hill.

Grace had clearly heard them coming. She waited in the yard when they pulled to a stop in the driveway, arms wrapped around herself as though that might stop her body from shattering into a million tiny pieces.

"Hi, Grace," he said as he came toward her.

"We told *him* we don't want any protection." She eyed Officer Fellner fearfully. Her eyes were shifting from side to side. Something about the male officer was obviously triggering her.

"It's okay." Beau lifted his hands in a gesture of appeasement. He moved over to them and quietly said, "Officer Fellner, I need you to get back in the squad car."

The young officer looked at his partner with raised eyebrows, but did as requested. Beau moved back toward Grace with Officer Bouchard by his side.

"He's going to stay in the car. This is Officer Bouchard."

"Hello." Bouchard's expression was open and friendly, and after a moment Grace nodded.

"Grace," he said, "I have a search warrant to execute. I'd like you to take a look at it, okay?"

Grace's hand fluttered up to her neck. "Search warrant?"

"This allows us to search your house and property for weapons, in particular for conducted energy weapons, like a stun gun." He handed it over.

She glanced at the document, but he doubted she read it.

"It also allows us to take hair samples from your goats."

"What?" She shook her head.

"Please read it over carefully, take your time, and make sure it's accurate. Address, date, all of that."

"But I don't understand. What's this about?"

"Please look over the warrant."

Her hands trembled, and the paper rattled as she examined it. She looked up at him, her eyes skittering from side to side. Beside him, Detective Bouchard took a step back and placed a hand over the butt of her gun.

Grace's body shook as though a train rumbled through it, and the search warrant fluttered to the ground. He was no expert, but he thought an alter was on the way.

"We haven't done anything wrong."

"Then you have nothing to fear."

Her head rolled on her neck, and her eyelids fluttered. "I'm sorry."

"It's okay —"

"I've got to go." She staggered up the stairs to the porch.

"Grace?"

"Just do what you need to do, Detective!" She disappeared inside the house, the door closing behind her. Inside, Bella barked. Then all was silent.

"*Mon Dieu*," Bouchard said.

He climbed the stairs and eased the door open. He caught a flash of Grace's back as she disappeared into the back bedroom. Bella was on her heels. A door slammed closed, and then another.

He waited for half a minute, and then said, "Okay. Let's get started."

"You're not going to detain her? She's probably destroying evidence in there."

"She's already detained herself. Right now she's locked in her bedroom closet and guarded by a hundred-and-fifty-pound dog. We can search that area last. But if you'd rather try to detain her, be my guest."

"Never mind, then."

They went through the house inch by methodical inch. Grace didn't leave the confines of the bedroom closet, but Bella growled any time they got too close to the door.

The search of the rest of the house netted zero results, but their job was easier than Officer Fellner's. While they worked inside, he had the unenviable job of going through the garbage and recycling bins; searching the forest, barn, and pottery shed; and taking hair samples from twenty-five very curious goats — all in a steady downpour. By the time they reconvened in the afternoon, Fellner was in a notably bad mood.

"No weapons," he said as they moved toward him across the gravel driveway. The rain dripped from the edge of his hood, catching on his eyelashes and the tip of his nose. "But the good news is I've been violated by a herd of goats."

"We'll get you a rape kit," Bouchard said.

Ignoring her, Fellner said, "Looks like someone's been camping in the trees over there. Found remnants of a campfire, and there's a square of cleared ground where someone staked a tent." He handed over an evidence bag with a slip of crumpled paper inside. "I found a bag of trash that looks like it's from her vehicle: empty coffee cups and napkins and food wrappers. And this note."

Tabitha Johnson's address was written in an all-too-familiar childlike scrawl.

"Well, shit," Beau said. He turned to look back at the house, wondering what kind of damage a dog Bella's size could do to him. Quite a bit, probably.

"Detective?" Bouchard asked.

"Come with me. Let's see if she'll come in for questioning."

THIRTY-ONE

S ariah and Tabby Johnson were sprawled on the living room carpet, their dolls neatly lined up before them, when Grace entered the house.

They looked up as the door closed, and Tabby's face automatically lit up. Although Tabby was the same age as Desiree, she had a nurturing soul and she often played with younger children like Sariah.

"Gracey!" Tabby bounced up to give Grace a hug, while Sariah turned back to the dolls. "Have any candies?"

She searched her pockets and eventually came out with two foil-wrapped strawberry sweets. Deciding her eldest sister was interesting after all, Sariah came over with her hand outstretched and her eyes round and pleading. Not for the first time, she thought that Sariah's eyes were the sweetest blue she'd ever seen.

Handing over the candy, she asked, "Is my mother home?"

Sariah dropped the strawberry sweet onto her tongue. "Nuh-uh. She took Desi to Unca G. But my mama's here." She hooked a thumb toward the back of the house.

"That's all right, I'll wait."

"Read us a story?" Tabby said, her eyes full of hope.

Her Lyme disease was flaring, which was why she'd stopped by. She was shaky and weak, and her joints were aching and swollen. She hoped Mother still had some of her special tea left. It was a mixture of green tea, cat's claw, and goldenseal.

Though she didn't feel up to reading, it would give her an excuse to rest for a few minutes. She sat on the couch with her eyes closed while the girls went through a long debate on which book to choose. They finally plunked *The Three Little Pigs* on her lap, rousing her from a semi-conscious state. She flipped the book open and began to read, doing her best to infuse the wolf's huffing and puffing with the proper amount of bluster.

Mother returned near the end of the story, took one look at her eldest daughter, and went to put on the kettle. Once the story was finished, Grace kissed both girls on the top of their heads and followed her mother into the kitchen.

"How long?" Mother asked without preamble.

"It came on last night." She eased into a chair at the dining room table. Her knee joints throbbed with pain, making her feel like she was about a thousand years old.

Mother's brows furrowed with concern. "Why?"

Something usually triggered an outbreak, whether she was fighting a cold or flu or experiencing something particularly distressing. A cold or flu was less likely in the summer, hence Mother's concern.

She couldn't talk about the problems in her marriage, or how the blank spaces in her memory were growing increasingly large. She certainly couldn't talk about how she'd wake up in the morning covered in fresh bruises and dried blood, with no idea what had occurred the night before.

There was nothing Mother could do about it anyway, except worry. So, she shrugged. "I don't know."

The kettle whistled, and Mother pulled it from the stove and poured steaming water into the teapot. She closed the lid, covered it with a tea cozy, and came to sit beside her.

Mother laid a hand on her forehead and frowned, then pressed gently up and down her neck. Grace's glands felt painfully swollen.

"How are things with Boydell?"

She couldn't lie, but that didn't mean she had to tell the whole truth. "They could be better."

Mother's eyes narrowed. "Are you obeying him? Treating him as your priesthood head?"

"I'm trying to."

"Try harder, Gracey."

"Yes, Mother."

"The tea needs to steep for twenty minutes, and then you can drink a cup. I'll send you home with the rest. Four cups a day until you're better, all right?"

"Thank you."

"When did you have your last courses?"

The question surprised her. "I haven't had another since the first one."

"That was more than two months ago," Mother said.

"I guess so."

"Gracey. You must write it down on a calendar to keep track."

She frowned at her mother. "Write down when I have my courses?"

"Yes. It should happen once a month. If it doesn't, you might be pregnant."

Her entire body went white hot with shock. "Pregnant! How?"

Mother's cheeks flushed. "Marital relations cause pregnancy."

"Marital relations?"

Mother scrubbed a hand roughly across her forehead, looking as uncomfortable as she'd ever seen her look. "In the bedroom? When a husband and wife lay together?"

Now her body turned to ice. She shivered uncontrollably. "When we sleep, you mean?"

"Grace, seriously!"

"I *am* being serious! Would you stop speaking in codes and tell me what you mean?"

Mother looked like she wanted to sink through the floor and disappear. "Hasn't Boydell touched you? Without your clothes on?"

Grace thought of their wedding night, how he had yanked at her clothing and thrown her on the bed. But then she'd gone to sleep, as she had every night since. What did Boydell do to her while she was sleeping?

"Grace?"

"Huh?" She wanted to focus on Mother because she had a feeling this information was a big missing piece in her puzzle, and yet her ear buzzed and her head filled with cotton.

"Are you and Boydell having marital relations?"

"Probably."

Mother's eyebrows rose toward her hairline. She opened her mouth to say more, but at that moment the front door slammed open.

Desiree stumbled into the house, her hair mussed around her head and her face swollen from tears. Her dress was ripped along the bodice, her lip bloody. She stood swaying silently in the kitchen doorway and looked blankly from Mother to Grace and back again, as though she didn't recognize them. Her crashing entrance brought Sariah and Tabby running. They stood staring wide-eyed from the hallway.

Mother took one look at Desiree and sucked in a quick breath, as though someone had punched her in the stomach. Grace looked over in time to see the flash of anguish on Mother's face. But a moment later, a mask of calm denial wiped her brow smooth.

She recognized her mother's quick transition — storm to calm — all too well. For one brief moment she teetered on the verge of understanding. But the buzz grew louder and her vision dimmed. Her brain short-circuited, leaving her floundering in confusion.

"Desiree, go clean up for supper," Mother said. "I'm speaking with your sister."

"Mother," Grace said. Her voice sounded very far away. Desiree's shoes had blood on them.

Sariah moved toward her and her cherub face filled Grace's dimming vision from edge to edge.

"Oh, wook." Sariah's clear blue eyes examined Grace with interest. "They coming."

Grace's vision went dark.

• • •

"Grace."

It sounded like someone was knocking on a door. Bella rumbled a warning deep in her chest, and she unearthed an arm from under the dog's heated body and curled her fingers into Bella's fur.

The knock came again, this time more insistent. "Grace!"

It was a man's voice.

Lost in a fog of confusion, she said, "Father?"

"Grace DeRoche." His voice was full of authority, and she roused herself in response.

Bella rumbled, but rolled her weight off Grace's body.

"Hello?" she said. "Who's there?"

"It's Detective Brunelli," he said from the other side of the closet door. "Can you come out?"

"What are you doing here? Is everything okay?"

"It's fine. But I need you to come out, okay?"

"Oh. Okay."

She rolled to her feet and unlatched the closet door. She pushed it open, blinking as the light hit her eyes. Her mouth was dry and her heart thundered inside her chest, while her mind felt heavy and slow. "What's happening?"

Detective Brunelli stood before her, his features a neutral mask. Behind him, the female police officer — Grace had forgotten her name — stood with a hand near her gun.

The sight jogged her memory. They'd come with a search warrant, looking for weapons they wouldn't find. And for some reason they wanted hair samples from her goats. She wondered what they could have found that would make Detective Brunelli look at her like that.

"Am I in trouble?"

"I need to look in your closet now."

"Oh. Okay."

"Officer Bouchard is going to pat you down, and then I'd like you to wait with her while I have a look."

After the pat-down, Bouchard ushered her into the living room. When Brunelli came out, he handed Bouchard a plastic evidence bag. It looked like there was an electric razor inside.

"What's that?" Grace asked.

Instead of answering, Brunelli said, "Grace, I'd like you to come into the station to answer some questions."

"What?" Her ear buzzed so loudly she could barely hear him. Somewhere from behind, Bella issued a sharp, warning bark. "What's happening?"

"Are you listening?"

"Y-yeah. Yes."

"I'd like you to come in for questioning in the death of Tabitha Johnson."

"What!"

"I want you to understand you're not under arrest. But you're still welcome to call a lawyer before you come in."

"Oh my God. Tabby's dead?"

"Would you like to drive yourself down? Or I'm happy to drive you."

"Can I bring Bella?"

Brunelli gave the dog a wary look, but nodded. "Yes, no problem."

"Then you'd better drive. I'm a little …" Grace wiped a shaking hand across her brow.

They ushered her out of the house. The other officer stood watching from a distance.

When she went to climb into the back seat of Detective Brunelli's car, he said, "You can sit in the front, Grace. You're not under arrest."

"I'll sit with Bella."

"Okay, then."

They were halfway to Nakusp before she found the wherewithal to speak. "Can I call Shelby?"

He plucked his cellphone from the cupholder. "I'm putting it on speaker."

Shelby answered on the third ring. "Well, it's about time you called, Beau."

Grace blinked at the flirtatious tone in Shelby's voice, and the detective's ears went pink.

"Shelby," Brunelli said, "I'm bringing Grace in for questioning in the death of Tabitha Johnson. She'd like to speak to you. You're on speaker, so I can hear anything you or Grace say."

Silence.

"Shelby?" the detective said.

"Holy shit. What did you just say?"

"I'm bringing Grace —"

"Holy shit. Okay, yeah. I got it."

"Shelby?" Grace said.

"Grace! Oh my God, are you okay?"

"He says Tabby's dead." Tears blurred her vision and burned tracks down her cheeks. "And he thinks I did it!"

"I don't understand. What happened?"

"They came this morning with a search warrant, and now he's taking me into the station."

"They came this morning?"

"What? Yeah."

"What were they looking for?"

"A weapon. And for some reason they wanted samples of my goats' hair. Can you come? I'm so scared. What should I do?"

"Do you want me to find you a lawyer?"

Grace closed her eyes, fighting the buzzing panic that wanted to overcome her. The last thing she needed right now was for someone else to take over. "I guess that's a good idea."

"All right. Let me look into it."

"Can you come?" She tried and failed to keep the desperation out of her voice.

"I'm fully booked with appointments today. But I'll drive up tomorrow."

"Okay."

"It's going to be okay, Grace. I promise. This is obviously some kind of mistake." With that, Shelby clicked off.

The detective dropped his phone back into the cupholder. She pressed against Bella, and tried to hang on to the front part of her mind.

THIRTY-TWO

"Would you like some water?" Beau asked.

When Grace shook her head, he moved around the table and took the seat beside her. He sat facing her, but made sure to keep a bit of space between them. Bella curled beside Grace's feet and kept a wary eye on him.

"Okay. Grace, I'd like to remind you of your right to legal counsel."

"Why do we *need* a lawyer?" Her voice rose to a childlike pitch.

"Both the guilty and the innocent can benefit from legal counsel. Availing yourself of your right to counsel does not make you look guilty."

"Shelby's looking into it. She'll get us one."

"Would you like to wait until the lawyer arrives?"

Her eyes were round. "No. We haven't done anything wrong."

"Your presence here is voluntary. You can stop the interview at any time. You can also leave whenever you want. That door" — he pointed — "will remain unlocked."

"Okay."

"I also want you to be aware that there is a camera in the corner of the room." Beau pointed again. "It is recording this interview. You don't need to say anything. And anything you've already said, you don't need to repeat. But anything you do say may be used as evidence. Do you understand?"

"Okay. Yeah."

Usually he would have leaned forward, given her an earnest look, maybe touched her shoulder. The goal was to establish a connection, disarm the person he was questioning, and portray himself as a friendly guy just looking for answers. Then he'd ask some basic questions to establish a baseline for how a suspect responded when the questions were easy, so he could watch for changes when they got hard.

But in this case, he knew his usual tactics for disarmament would be seen as threats, and that might bring an alter forward before he was ready to talk to them. He leaned back and rested his hands on his lap. He decided to skip the usual baseline questions and jump right in.

"When did you last see Tabitha Johnson?"

"It's been years."

"Years?"

"Yeah. I think it was about a year after the Family ..." She made a motion with her hand so she wouldn't have to find the words.

"You haven't seen her since then?"

Grace shook her head. "She made it clear at that time that she didn't want to have any kind of relationship with us."

Beau kept his mouth closed, waited for his silence to lure her into saying more.

"You have to understand, it's not that she didn't care. She was trying to move on. We all were."

"But you knew she was living in Kelowna."

Her eyes skittered to the side. Her hands clenched and released. "Yes."

"How did you know that, without talking to her?"

"We tried to keep tabs on her. On all of them. We just …" Her gaze fixed on a spot over his right shoulder.

"You just?"

She shrugged. "Just wanted to know how they were doing."

He waited.

"I felt responsible for them. They followed me. They trusted me. If something happened to any of them …" She scrubbed a hand across her eyes, leaving a wet smear on her cheeks. "Everything that's happened is my fault."

"How so?"

A quick tremor went through her body. Her face pinched and her eyes tightened to slits. "Stop it."

"Stop what?"

She waved a hand. "No, not you."

Okay. "Would you like to continue?"

"Yeah. Fine."

"How is everything that's happened your fault?"

"We didn't kill her, if that's what you're thinking." She turned her head to the side. "I said stop it. Just shut up."

"Grace?"

"Sorry. Yes, I'm here."

"You seem angry."

Her head turned to the side again. The voice that emerged from her throat was gruff. Deep and broad. "Fuck. I'm fucking furious." And then in Grace's voice, she said, "I told you to shut up." Her body trembled, and her head turned from side to side. In a softer, whispering voice, she said, "Oh we're being so bad. We must keep sweet, or we'll get a correction." Her voice changed again. "Keep quiet. We mustn't talk to the police." And then the deeper voice emerged again. "Don't fucking tell me what to do."

Beau took a long, slow breath, wondering who would win the battle for her mind, and wondering how he should proceed. This was nuts, but he was in it now. And it wasn't just Tabitha who had died. He owed it to the rest of them to get to the truth, if he could.

"Hi. I don't think we've met."

Grace's body shook like there was an electric current running through it. When she looked at him, he was once again struck by the strangeness of her dual-coloured eyes. But her features had settled back into those he was most familiar with.

"What are you talking about?" she asked.

"Grace?"

"Yeah?"

His head spun. As he watched, he could almost see different people surfacing behind her eyes, like they were coming out of the depths of a murky lake. They'd take a quick breath, look around, and then sink back into the darkness before he could catch more than a glimpse.

All right. Just keep going. "So, you knew Tabby lived in Kelowna."

"I knew she went to school there."

He remained silent, watched her discomfort grow. But this time he wasn't able to lure her into speaking. She firmed her lips and watched him with wary eyes.

"Do you have her address?"

Her eyes skittered to the side again. "No."

"No?"

She shook her head.

"I thought you were keeping tabs on her."

She did a quick neck roll and her vertebrae made a popping sound.

Beau decided to drop that for a moment. "So, you did that with all of them. Because you felt responsible for them."

"Yeah."

"If I were you, I would have also wanted to maintain a connection with something from my past. Something familiar."

Her shoulders slumped. "That's true."

"People I cared about."

"Yes."

"Perfectly understandable, not wanting to lose that connection."

Her eyes grew damp. "No, I didn't."

"How did the rest of them respond to your attempts to keep in touch?"

Her gaze dropped to her lap and she shrugged.

"Did they feel the same way Tabby did?"

"I guess."

"How about Valor?" he asked.

"We lost touch."

"Eliza?"

She shrugged. "She stopped answering my calls."

"Rulon?"

"We see where you're going with this." Her voice deepened again. Her eyes tightened.

"Rulon changed his name, didn't he? Do you think he did that to get away from you?"

"Don't be ridiculous." Her voice grew deeper still. It was almost a snarl.

"None of them wanted anything to do with you, did they?"

She huffed out a breath, but kept silent.

"After all you'd done for them. Helping them escape, watching over them, sending them money. And they all turned their backs on you, didn't they?"

"No. It wasn't like that."

"What was it like, then?"

She kept her gaze on her lap, but her breath came in shallow gasps. He got the impression she was trying to stay in the driver's seat of her mind.

"They rejected you. Didn't they? The only people you really knew, the only people who could possibly understand you and understand where you came from and what you were going through. But they wanted nothing to do with you."

Her head dropped toward her lap. Bella, who'd been watching their interaction with increasing doggy concern, now stood up and whined at Grace.

"Stop. Please, just stop."

Bella nudged Grace with her nose, and Grace wrapped a trembling arm around the dog's neck. She buried her face in Bella's shoulder.

"If it were me, I would have felt so hurt by that. Did it make you angry, how ungrateful they all were?"

Grace moaned into the dog's thick fur and Bella whined, as though pleading for Beau to stop talking. His heart *kathumped* and anxiety burned a hole in his stomach, but he knew he couldn't back down. Not now.

"Let's talk about Tabby."

No answer.

"She didn't want anything to do with you, either, did she?"

Her fingers tightened in the dog's fur.

"Did you call her? Send emails?"

No answer.

"Did you drive down to Kelowna? Pay her a visit?"

"No."

"She didn't want to see you, did she?"

"I never …"

"But you did. Grace, you did. Or one of your alters did."

That got her to look up.

"They found goat hair in her bedroom."

He might as well have shot her. The words left his mouth and hit her right in the gut. He saw their impact.

Her body curled around the injury he'd inflicted, and her face went through an extraordinarily quick transformation, like she was flipping through a deck of cards: confusion, shock, horror, denial, and finally guilt. Her eyes skittered to the side. "What?"

"How do you think it got there?"

"I don't …" She shook her head. "I don't understand."

"How did she get goat hair in her bedroom, Grace?"

Her head turned to the side. "Shut up. Just shut up."

"Her roommate found her. In the bathtub."

"No. Oh no."

There she went. He could almost see the Grace part of her mind retreat. There was a heartbeat of utter blankness, and then her face broadened, her cheekbones jutted out, and her eyes turned to slits.

"Why are you doing this to her?" The voice that emerged from her throat was barrel deep and spitting venom.

Bella's hackles rose and she growled at her owner.

"Shut up, dog."

Whining, Bella backed away and lowered herself to the ground.

This must be Harris. He sure was angry. Beau had no trouble believing this one could commit murder, all in the name of protecting Grace.

"Hello again," Beau said.

She turned to him, her eyes brown and blue slits of utter fury. "You're not playing nice, *Detective*."

"Where's Grace?"

"With Mother. You're not allowed to talk to her like that."

"I'm happy to talk to you instead."

She snorted. "Oh, I bet you are."

"You do a good job of protecting her, don't you?"

"Spare me your sweet talk. I'm not buying it."

"All right. Then let's talk about Tabby."

Her eyes narrowed so much he couldn't see her irises anymore. "I have nothing to say about that."

"She hurt Grace, didn't she?"

"You think you've got this all figured out."

"She used her and then ignored her, just like the rest of them."

"But you don't know a damn thing, *Detective*."

"Then tell me where I'm wrong."

She snorted. "As if. I'm not telling you shit."

"Why not?"

She crossed her arms over her chest and slumped down in her chair. Her legs spread as though making room for an imaginary ball sack. "Why would I trust you, man in blue?"

He was getting a picture of who this Harris was. He pictured a teenaged boy, maybe seventeen or eighteen years old, stuffed full of hormones, anger, and defiance. He'd dealt with many just like this in his career.

"The police are the ones that got you out of Brigham," he said.

Snarl. "Sure. Into a better life."

"Isn't it better to be free?"

"Our soul's not free. It's eternally damned."

"Because you're an apostate?"

She rolled her eyes as though saying, *Well, duh*.

"And you blame the police for that?"

She sat forward, got right in his face. "No. I blame Grace."

Okay. What should he do with that information? "Because it was Grace's idea to escape?"

"It sure as shit wasn't mine. We were doing okay, thanks to me. Still earning our place in heaven, trying to be a good priesthood wife. Trying to be sweet. But then Clayne got into her head."

"What did he do?"

She snorted. "What didn't he do? He was always a bad influence. Always leading her astray."

"How did he lead her astray?"

"He opened her eyes."

"How?" Beau leaned forward.

She shrugged, and her mouth pinched into a tight line. "It doesn't matter. He got what was coming to him, in the end."

His scalp prickled. "What happened to him?"

"Christ atoned for our sins when he died on the cross. But there are some sins that even Christ's sacrifice can't wipe clean. Theft. Fornication. Adultery. Apostasy. For those, a blood atonement is required."

Beau scrubbed a hand across his cheek, felt the rough scratch of stubble. "Did you hurt Clayne?"

She looked up at him with her strange, dual-coloured eyes. "Not me."

"Then who?"

"I wasn't there. How should I know?"

"Is Clayne still alive?"

She shook her head. "If he was, he would have come after Grace a long time ago."

"I don't understand. Why would he come after Grace?"

"It was her fault, what happened to him. Everything is her fault."

"So, you're angry with Grace?"

She leaned back in the chair, assuming the same spread-legged position as before. "Nah. We're cool."

"You said one of the sins requiring a blood atonement is apostasy. Isn't that what Grace did to you when she escaped Brigham? Isn't your soul damned to hell because of her?"

"Probably would have been damned no matter what. We weren't so good at keeping sweet."

"I thought you said you were doing okay?"

Shrug.

"What about the others? Rulon and Eliza and Valor. What about Tabby? Would they have been damned before, too?"

"Who knows?"

"But when they escaped Brigham they damned their own souls, just like Grace did?"

"You've got it."

"Don't you blame Grace for *that*?"

Her lip curled up in a snarl. "Why should I care about any of them?"

Interesting. "Because Grace does."

She snorted, turned her head to the side.

"Don't you care about the same things as her? Aren't you her protector?"

"Grace is a child. She doesn't know what's best for her."

"And you do."

She gave him a hard, wolfish smile. Her teeth were shiny with saliva.

"Listen. If you really do care about Grace, you should help me get to the truth. Because things aren't looking good for her right now. Of the nine children who escaped with her that day, four are dead."

She shook her head as though amazed by his stupidity. "Are you accusing Grace of something, here? Because she couldn't hurt a fly."

"Then who did?"

"How should I know?"

"I think you know a lot. I think you know way more than Grace about pretty much everything. Don't you?"

She shrugged.

"Is it you who came forward to protect her from Gideon Smith?"

Another shrug, then a curt nod of acknowledgement.

"You're the strong one."

"I've had to be strong."

"Of course. And you've done a good job of keeping Grace safe."

She snorted. Shifted in her seat.

"So, do your job. Keep her safe. I know you don't want her to go to jail. She doesn't deserve to be there. So tell me, what happened to Tabby?"

She met his gaze. Stared him down. "I don't know."

"Why did you go to her apartment? Did you want to talk to her?"

She shook her head.

"Maybe you didn't mean to hurt her. But she made you angry, didn't she?"

Her mouth tightened.

"Grace can't go to jail for something you did." He was speaking out of his ass on that one. He honestly had no idea how a court system would ever figure out this mess. But what he said might have been the truth.

"I was never there. I didn't do anything to her."

"How come they found goat hair in her bedroom?"

"How the fuck should I know?"

"Harris, listen —"

"That's not my name."

Beau sat back, blinking. He could almost hear Doug saying to him, "Never assume anything. When you assume you make an ass out of u and me."

"My apologies. Who are you, then?"

Her mouth closed tight.

"What's your name?"

She let out a deep breath, cocked her head to the side. Beau got the impression she was debating whether to trust him with the name, so he kept his mouth closed and waited. Just as he was about to move on, she spoke.

"Xander. It's short for Alexander. It means saviour."

"Well. Nice to meet you, Xander."

The anger was visible, bubbling beneath the surface, but she spoke calmly. "I didn't do anything to Tabby. Or the others."

"Then who did?"

A shrug.

"What about Harris?"

"No way."

"Could I speak to him?"

She shook her head. "Harris doesn't talk to people he doesn't know."

"I'd like to try."

She shrugged. Sat up in her seat. Her features softened, and her eyes went blank.

He waited.

After several moments, she blinked. Her whole body shook with a tremor that seemed to roll through her from her feet all the way to her head.

"Oh. Sorry." She shook her head, looked around. Bella stood up, approached her cautiously. "Think I went away for a minute there. What were you saying?"

"Grace?"

"Yeah?"

He sat back in his chair, realizing how much tension he'd been holding in his body. He felt limp and damp. Letting out a breath, he said, "I think we need a break. Are you sure I can't get you something?"

THIRTY-THREE

When Detective Brunelli left the room, Grace rolled forward until her head touched her knees and took long, slow breaths. She wondered which of her alters had come forward, and what they had said. Whatever had happened, it had made the detective look like he'd run a marathon and followed it up by going three nights without sleep.

Bella laid her head against her side, and she stroked the dog's fur. Her mind was surprisingly quiet, but rather than feeling relief she felt alone and abandoned.

She wondered how much longer she'd have to wait for Shelby's lawyer to show up. Maybe she should just shut up and wait, after all.

· · ·

"You're going to get in trouble, Clayne Johnson! Because

I'm going to tell on you!" Sariah shouted through the doorway of the DeRoche house.

"Tell about *what*?" Clayne shouted in return.

"I *saw* what you was doing!"

"Get back inside, Sariah, and mind your own business." To allay the harshness of her words, Grace kissed the crown of Sariah's head before shutting the door in her face. Sariah continued to scream threats for several minutes, but Grace ignored her sister and turned back to Clayne.

At the end of the day, she knew that the bitterness and anger churning inside her had nothing to do with her sister, no matter how annoying she might sometimes be, and had everything to do with the fact that she was trapped in a marriage and a life that felt like eternal hell.

"I was just trying to *talk* to you," Clayne said in defence of his virtue. "I didn't even get closer than five feet. I made sure."

"It's all right," she said. "I know."

"Well, then, tell that to your brat of a sister!"

"Clayne, sweeten your tongue." Grace said it without her usual fervour. She was tired, aching in every muscle and joint. Her pregnancy had weakened her immune system, or at least that's what Mother told her, and she was having a terrible time of it. First she'd had a reoccurrence of the symptoms of her Lyme disease, and that had led to an endless series of colds and flus. Add to that the nausea, and she was truly in a miserable state. She sat on the stairs leading up to her family home and leaned against a wooden post. Her head had gained weight, she was certain of it.

"You don't look well," Clayne said.

"Mother says I should feel better in a few weeks, once I'm into the second trimester."

"My mother threw up into her ninth month with Tabby."

"That's not at all helpful," she said.

Clayne stood awkwardly at the foot of the stairs, kicking dirt beneath the toes of his leather shoes. "I worry for you, Gracey." His voice was so soft it was hard to hear him.

"I worry for *you*, too," she said. "You're more angry every time I see you."

He shrugged. "The bishop doesn't see fit to give me a wife. Not that I blame him, I'm not deserving of one. And I'm not sure I even want one. I'd hate to boss her around the way we're supposed to."

An ache blossomed around her heart. "No, you wouldn't be much good at that."

"Another failing to add to the list."

"That's the opposite of a failing."

"I'll work the fields and come home to an empty house until the day I die. Or I'll become an apostate like Boaz."

"Don't say that! You are worthy of so much more than that."

"Am I?" His blue eyes flashed with anger, but he couldn't seem to sustain the emotion. He had grown tall in recent months, and his shoulders had broadened. There was even a bit of hair dusting his upper lip with golden fuzz.

She loved him deeply. Not for the first time, she thought how sad it was that she could never tell him so. It might have helped him to see his own worth.

Instead, she said, "I should go inside. It's almost supper-time, but I need to see Mother before I go home."

He gave her an oddly formal bow, and moved toward his own kitchen door. His shoulders slumped, and dirt and stones kicked out before his feet.

Grace sighed and pulled herself upright, using the post as leverage. She entered the kitchen into a familiar scene. Mother was cooking stew in a large pot, her back turned as she added seasonings. She had an overwhelming urge to bury her face in her mother's skirts, the way she used to do not so many years ago.

Without turning, Mother said, "Gracey, there's tea on the table for you. How is your stomach today?"

She dropped onto a chair. "Queasy."

"It's ginger tea. It should help."

"Thank you."

Mother stuck the lid on the pot and moved toward her, wiping her hands on her apron. Her hands were red and calloused from a lifetime of hard work, the knuckles swollen with arthritis. She looked older than thirty-four.

"What were you and Clayne speaking about?"

"Nothing important. He was asking after my health."

"And complaining about his lot in life?" With a groan of relief, Mother eased into the chair across from her.

Grace raised her eyebrows in acknowledgement and took a small sip of her tea.

"I fear that boy will never find his way to heaven," Mother said.

"I fear that, too."

"You must be mindful not to let him drag you down."

"Clayne wouldn't do that."

"He would. He already does. Your care and worry for him creases your brow. I can see it when I look at you. But he is not your husband, and you must remember that at all times."

"How could I possibly forget?"

Mother's mouth turned down with disapproval. "Sweeten your tongue, daughter, and hold true to the prophet's teachings. Clayne has no place in your life or in your heart. Spending time with him reflects badly on you. It puts your morals into question."

"I've done nothing wrong."

"But how might it look to your husband? To your *father-in-law*?"

Grace swallowed back a mixture of bitterness and anxiety. It burned her throat with fresh nausea. "Thank you for your wisdom, Mother. I'll do better. I promise."

The front door crashed open, causing both of them to jump. Mother Rebecca stormed into the kitchen. Sariah's pale face peeked out from the folds of her mother's skirt, her eyes wide and full of tears.

Mother Rebecca's cheeks flushed a pretty pink. Her eyes flashed with something that looked like satisfaction. "Your father-in-law wishes to have a word with you."

Grace's ear gave a warning screech. "What? Why?"

"It's not our place to question," Mother Rebecca said.

Grace reached across the table, automatically seeking the comfort of her mother's touch.

But Mother pulled her hand away from her. Shaking her head, she said, "Go on, Gracey. Swiftly."

She stood up on legs that felt wooden, and moved toward the door.

Mother Rebecca unearthed her mewling daughter from the safety of her skirt and pushed her forward. "You're to take Sariah."

"What?"

"She's to bear witness."

Oh. This was very bad, indeed.

She took a steadying breath, trying to calm the buzzing in her ear. "Come along, Sariah."

She grabbed her sister by the hand and tugged her out the door and across the yard. "Sweeten yourself. Nothing will happen to *you*."

Sariah's sobs turned to hiccups as they moved up the road toward the temple. "But ... but what will happen to you?"

"I'll receive a correction."

"But what does that mean?"

What *did* that mean? Though she'd had numerous corrections over the years, she didn't recall much of her time in Uncle G's study. It was strange how little she remembered. "I suppose I'm in for a lecture."

"Is that all?" Sariah wiped an arm across her eyes. "Tabby told me ..."

"Told you what?"

Sariah shook her head. Her hair stuck to the wetness on her cheeks. "Other stuff."

"Well, maybe I'll get the strap, too."

Her comment had the desired effect. Sariah burst into immediate tears, which made her feel bad. But not too bad.

"You told Uncle G that you saw me alone with Clayne, didn't you?"

Sariah let out a great, whooping wail. Mucus flowed in a slimy trail from her nostrils to the bow of her mouth.

She shook her sister's arm. "Hush, child! They'll hear you all over Brigham."

"I'm s-s-sorry."

"Yes, well, it's too late now, isn't it?"

Mother would have said this was an opportunity to lay a foundation of kindness under her sister's feet, but she didn't feel kind. She was both furious and terrified, and no amount of positive thinking could sweeten her mind or tongue.

"Come along, then."

She tugged Sariah up the steps to Uncle G's large front porch. Sariah looked around fearfully.

We weren't that much older than her when we got our first correction.

She remembered being led to Uncle G's study. She remembered the books, stacked on shelves and side tables and the corner of the desk. She remembered thinking that all the knowledge in the world was within reach, if only she knew how to read.

The door opened, and Uncle G stood before them. He wore faded blue jeans and a checkered shirt. His belly was like a beach ball. The metal on his suspenders gleamed.

"Daughter," he said without preamble. "Have you been untrue to my son?"

"Of course not." She heard the temper in her voice and winced. This was not the way to speak to the bishop.

Uncle G's mouth turned down with displeasure, and the buzzing in her ear grew louder.

"Come inside."

Clutching hands, they followed him up the stairs to his study. Sariah's hand trembled, but she remained silent. She stepped inside the study and stood beside Grace with her head bowed, like a good priesthood girl.

Uncle G leaned on the desk. The buttons on his shirt strained, exposing hairy white skin.

"Your sister tells me she saw you kissing Clayne Johnson."

"What?" She snuck a quick look at Sariah, but all she could see was the top of her sister's head.

Uncle G's face was an unhealthy, furious red.

This time he might kill us.

She fought against her narrowing vision, determined to stay present, and frantically calculated the risks. Admitting to something so serious could lead to her excommunication, and that was a best-case scenario. Women were beaten for smaller transgressions than this. Disfigured. Sometimes even worse.

But if she exposed her sister as a liar, Sariah would face a correction.

She tucked her chin into her chest, looked down at the floor, and tempered her voice with sugar. "I think she misunderstood what she was seeing. I *did* speak to Clayne without my priesthood head's permission, and I'm very sorry. I will take whatever correction you or my h-husband sees fit to give me. But I did not kiss him."

"Hmm," Uncle G said. "Sariah, did you see them kissing?"

"I'm sure that's what she thought she saw."

"Do not speak for your sister. Sariah, look at me."

Sariah looked up. Her cheeks were mottled and shiny with tears.

"Did you lie to me?"

Say no.

She opened her mouth, but no sound came out.

"Did you *lie* to me?"

Please say no, Sariah.

"I …"

We must stop this. We know what will happen if we don't.

Grace stepped forward, ready to admit to kissing Clayne, but she was too late.

Sariah nodded, fresh tears spilling from her eyes. "I-I'm s-s-sorry."

Uncle G sighed. "You stood here before God and lied to your bishop."

She snuffled. "Uh-huh."

"Then you are in need of a correction."

No.

Sariah went still and silent, her eyes wide with terror.

"And your sister will bear witness."

Grace shook her head. "Oh, please no, Uncle G."

"Sariah," Uncle G said. "Sit down on the couch over there."

"I kissed him! I'm sorry I lied. Sariah was telling the truth. Please, Uncle G!"

Ignoring Grace, he said to Sariah, "What should you say when an elder asks something of you?"

"I-I am here to do your w-i-ill," Sariah said.

"No!"

"Very good, Sariah," Uncle G said. "Now go on."

Sariah moved toward the couch.

"Oh, please no."

As Sariah climbed onto the couch and primly pulled her lace-trimmed skirt down to cover her knees, something deep inside Grace's abdomen let go. It started as a breathless squeezing pain and built into a grinding rolling cramping. Warmth flooded the area between her legs.

The darkness rushed toward her. It crackled behind her eyes, buzzed around inside her good ear, and set her brain on fire.

Go on! Get out of here!

She was shoved violently out of the frontspace and sent hurtling back toward lamplight and linen pillows and warm blankets.

Mother waited to tuck her in and tell her to go with God. And she knew that everything was going to be okay.

THIRTY-FOUR

Beau was splashing cold water on his face in the men's room of the Nakusp RCMP station when his cellphone rang. He grabbed a clump of paper towels and patted the moisture from his face and hands before digging his phone out of his pocket. It was his boss calling.

"Hey, Doug. Even if we get enough evidence to lay charges, I doubt she'll be found competent to stand trial. It's been bonkers."

"Beau," Doug said. "Desiree DeRoche is in the ICU at Vancouver General Hospital. No word on her status yet, or on what happened to her. She was brought in early this morning, unconscious."

The paper towels dropped to the floor.

"Can you hear me? I'm getting an echo."

"Yeah, I'm here."

"Once you've wrapped up over there, you might want to come home."

"Will you okay a flight for me?"

"Not yet. I'll let you know when I hear more."

"Okay, thanks, boss." Beau hung up and stood staring at his reflection in the mirror for a moment, trying to figure out the best way to proceed.

He couldn't hold or charge Grace with anything, based on the evidence currently in his possession, so he was going to have to release her. But he didn't feel comfortable with her roaming around free, after what he'd just witnessed in there. This Xander alter had quickly risen to the top of his suspect list. He could only think of one thing to do.

Shelby answered the phone on the second ring. "How is she?"

"She's … interesting. Listen, Shelby —"

"Did any of her alters come through?"

"Oh yeah, you could say that."

"What did they say?"

"Listen, I need your help. Grace's sister was just taken to the hospital in Vancouver. I need to get down there."

There was a beat of silence. "Desiree? Is she okay?"

"I don't know —"

"But she's alive?"

"Yes, she's alive, but I don't know how serious her situation is yet. I need to go, but I'm concerned about leaving Grace on her own. Especially once she knows about her sister."

"Uh-huh."

"I know you have other patients and this is a big ask, but I think she needs the support of someone she trusts right now."

He waited, listening to her breathe into the phone.

"Okay," she said. "I'll clear my schedule, but I won't be able to make it to Nakusp until late this evening."

"Understood. Thanks, Shelby. I appreciate it."

"I'm not doing it for you — I'm doing it for Grace." She hung up without saying goodbye.

THIRTY-FIVE

G race awoke on the couch in her parents' living room. Mother, Father, and Desiree stood over her, their foreheads creased with worry.

"Mother?"

"How are you feeling, Gracey?"

"I don't know. What's happening?"

Mother took her hand, patted it gently. "I'm afraid you've lost the baby."

Desiree slapped her hands over her eyes and burst into tears.

Grace reached for her sister. "Hush. Don't cry. It'll be okay."

Desiree sobbed harder. "But the baby died! I'm s-so s-sorry, Gracey."

"Oh." Grace closed her eyes, trying to process what she'd been told. Her mind was fuzzy and far away. She felt so tired, like she could just go to sleep and maybe never wake up.

The baby had died.

Her abdomen felt cramped and swollen, like one big mound of bruised flesh. And her head hurt. Had she fallen? What had happened?

You are in need of a correction. And your sister will bear witness.

Her eyes sprang open. "Sariah! Where is she?"

Mother pushed her back down. "Don't try to sit up."

"Is she okay?"

Mother Rebecca spoke from her chair in the corner. "Sariah's in her bedroom, resting. It was very upsetting for her, seeing you fall over like that. And you ruined the carpet in the bishop's study. I doubt they'll be able to get all the blood out of it."

The way she spoke made Grace feel like she was being accused of something. Being unmannerly, perhaps.

"Did Uncle G ... is Sariah okay?"

Click-click-click went Mother Rebecca's knitting needles. "She'll do."

Grace closed her eyes. If she'd had to lose the baby, at least maybe she'd saved her youngest sister from ...

From what? She frowned, trying to think.

From the bad stuff that happens on the big green couch.

Well, no matter. She could figure it out later. At the moment, she just felt so tired.

"Gracey?" Desiree touched her arm. "Can I make you some tea?"

"That's a good idea," Mother said. "Yarrow and red raspberry leaf, Desiree. And black cohosh, if we have any left."

After her tea, Grace dozed off. The next time she awoke, it was dark outside the windows and Boydell sat in Mother

Rebecca's chair. The lamp was turned on so he could read, but he flipped through the pages too quickly to be paying much attention.

"Hi," she said.

He looked up. His eyes were tight with grief, and her heart flipped at the sight. She didn't think Boydell felt many emotions, unless they were mean ones.

"Are you okay?" she asked.

His eyes filled with tears. He thumbed them away before they could fall and flipped the pages of the book on his lap. He pressed his fingers against a page to hold his spot. His voice shook as he spoke. "And God commanded Abraham, and Sarah gave Hagar to Abraham to wife, and from Hagar sprang forth a nation."

"Boydell?"

He snapped the book closed. "And from *Hagar* sprang forth a nation."

"Yes," she said. "I know the verse."

His voice rose with emotion. "Are you my Sarah?"

"What?"

"You lost my baby."

As though she'd accidentally dropped it somewhere and couldn't remember where she'd left it. She almost smiled at the absurdity. "Boydell, I don't —"

"*My* baby. *My* seed. How could you be so careless?"

"I wasn't!"

"You didn't want this baby."

That's true, we didn't.

"I saw it in your eyes, every time I looked at you. So, I want to know. What did you do?"

"Don't be ridiculous," she said.

He sprang to his feet. "Ridiculous? Is that how you speak to your priesthood head?"

"I'm sorry." She tried to sit up, but everything from her waist down felt like dead weight.

"That was *my* seed you were carrying. You should have taken better care. A good priesthood wife —"

"Would what? What could I have done?"

He snarled. "You are impudent and disrespectful."

"Those two words mean the same thing," she said.

She expected it, but the blow shocked her, nonetheless. She screamed and flopped backward on the couch cushions, blood spurting from her nose.

"What's going on in here?" Father thundered into the room, tugging his bathrobe over his shoulders. Mother followed close behind him.

"Grace!" Mother ran forward. "What happened?" She pulled a handkerchief from her robe pocket and pressed it against Grace's nose. It hurt.

When she spoke she sounded like a honking goose. "Boydell hit me."

Father turned on Boydell. "That's not how a man of the priesthood should behave."

Boydell pointed an accusatory finger at her. "She disrespects me at every turn! She's rude and thoughtless and selfish! Speak to *her* about her duties as my wife."

Father shook his head. "She's still young. She needs time to learn how to be a wife to you. But with patience and kindness from her priesthood head —"

"You didn't train her well enough," Boydell said.

Mother gasped. Father went still.

After a moment, Father said, "Perhaps that's true. But now that's your job. And treating your wife with kindness will work much better."

"She's my property. I'll treat her however I want."

Father took a deep breath. Grace knew he was trying to control his temper. "And owning property, whether it's a house or livestock or a wife, is a responsibility as well as a privilege."

Boydell scowled. "Come on, Grace. We're going home."

Mother stepped forward. "She shouldn't be moved yet. Please let her stay the night, so I can see to her needs."

"No. I need her at home, so she can see to mine."

Mother waved an arm in Grace's direction. "She's in no position —"

"I can see where she gets her impudence from. Come on, Grace."

She expected Father to step in, to continue trying to talk some sense into Boydell, but he didn't. He shook his head and his lips curled down with disapproval, but he moved out of the way.

Boydell shoved Mother aside and grabbed Grace by the arm. He yanked her from the couch. She didn't get her feet underneath her fast enough, so she tumbled to the floor. She felt a gush of warmth between her legs, and her vision went fuzzy and dark.

He grabbed her under both arms and dragged her out the door. She cried out in pain, but Mother and Father remained silent. They did not follow.

Clayne stood in the yard, his hands clenched into fists. "I heard Grace scream. What's going on?"

"I'm taking my wife home."

"Oh no, you're not." Clayne moved toward Boydell, his face twisted with fury.

Boydell dropped Grace on the dirt and lifted his fists in the air. "Go on, hit me. I'd just love to see you lose your priesthood."

"It would be worth it, to see you laid out on the dirt."

"Clayne, don't." Grace rolled to her side, struggling to get to her feet. "I'm okay, see? I'm going with you, Boydell."

"Look at her. She's bleeding out. She needs a hospital!"

She'd managed to get to her feet and stood there swaying. "She doesn't."

"Do you see the blood? How much more do you think she can lose?"

Boydell looked over at her.

"She could die," Clayne said.

Boydell shrugged. "If it's God's will."

Clayne struck so quickly, she doubted Boydell even saw the fist coming toward his face. He certainly didn't have time to react to it. One moment he was standing there sneering, and the next he was on the ground, bleeding and unconscious.

"Clayne, no!" She seemed to fall forever, but he caught her just before she hit the ground.

Her head was so foggy, she could barely see. "You stupid, stupid boy. Why did you do that?"

He helped her to a sitting position, leaned her up against the stairs that led to her childhood home. "Are you all right?"

She was too loopy from blood loss to be anything but honest. "I won't be if I lose you, you moron."

"That felt good. I've been wanting to hit him my whole life." He looked at his hand. A gash marked his knuckle.

"You could lose your priesthood."

"I'm going to lose it eventually. Might as well be for a good reason."

"Oh, Clayne."

"Can you walk, or should I carry you? We only have to go as far as Father's garage."

"Why?"

"So I can take you to the hospital."

"You better go ask Uncle G for permission, then."

Clayne gave her a sideways look. "Or we could just leave."

She thought she'd misheard him. "What?"

"Leave. And never come back."

She opened her mouth to tell him he was crazy, but she didn't get the chance. The door opened behind them and Mother and Father came out onto the porch. Clayne closed his eyes and sighed.

"Let's get her inside," Mother said.

Father helped her to her feet and kept a steady arm around her waist as she walked up the stairs. Clayne stood and followed.

Once she was back on the couch in the living room, Father tucked an arm over Clayne's shoulders and said, "Clayne, you shouldn't have done that. But God forgive me, I'm glad you did."

• • •

When Detective Brunelli entered the room, Grace saw the look on his face and knew right away that something was wrong. Her ear gave a warning buzz.

"Grace." He moved around the table and sat down. "Desiree was taken to the hospital this morning in Vancouver. I don't have any word on what happened to her or how she's doing, but I'll —"

She stood up so abruptly her chair fell behind her with a clatter.

"What are you doing?" he asked.

"I need to go."

"Grace, I don't —"

"You said I'm free to leave. I need to go to my sister."

"I understand, but whatever happened to Desi—"

"I need to go to Vancouver. Will you drive me home, now?"

"Of course. Shelby is coming down to be with you. She said she'll be at your place later this evening. Why don't you wait until she gets there and we have a better idea of Desiree's status, and then you can head down if it still seems like the right way to go."

"You don't trust me around my sister. You think I might hurt her."

"I think you need support right now. Also, this may not have occurred to you, but it's possible you're in danger."

"*I'm* in danger?"

Brunelli leaned forward, crowding her space, but thankfully kept his hands away from her. "Grace, if some or all of these deaths are related, then you and the others who escaped Brigham that day could be targets."

She blew out a breath. "Okay. I'll wait for Shelby."

"Thank you." He pulled his cellphone from his pocket and scrolled through the call list until he found the right number. He pushed the phone across the table toward her. "That's the main number for VGH, if you want to call. Since you're a family member, they should be able to give you an update."

THIRTY-SIX

A s he drove Grace home, Beau went back and forth between imagining her as a suspect or as a potential victim. He decided it was best to treat her as cautiously as he would treat a suspect, but also to give her the respect he would give a victim. After all, no matter what came of this, she'd been a victim first.

"Is there someone I can call to come stay with you until Shelby arrives?"

She turned her head to look out the window. "I don't exactly have a lot of friends."

"Were you aware of someone camping in the woods beside your house?"

She turned toward him. "There is?"

"Well, there was. We found the remains of a campsite." He glanced at her in the rear-view mirror.

Grace's eyes did that weird moving-from-side-to-side

thing. When she spoke, her voice had raised an octave. "Maybe someone's been watching us."

"Or maybe someone's just camping in the woods nearby," he said. "But I'd like you to reconsider the protection detail. I can see about getting Officer Bouchard, if that would make you more comfortable."

"I'll think about it."

There was a second Subaru waiting in the clearing beside her house when he pulled into the driveway. Hers was a pale sky blue colour, and this one looked like a newer model in a darker shade of blue.

"Who's that?" he asked.

"Oh no. Is it Sunday?"

"It's Tuesday."

"Okay, good. That's Jack Fletcher. He's my distributor; he picks up my goat milk and yogurt and stuff. But that's on Sundays. I wonder why he's here?"

A man with dirty-blond hair exited his vehicle as they pulled to a stop behind him. He lifted a hand and gave an uncertain wave.

As Beau got out of the car, Fletcher took a step back and his face did a quick transition from uncertain to dismayed to carefully neutral. He wondered if Fletcher smelled the cop on him, or if he thought Beau was competition for Grace's affection.

"Hi, Grace." Fletcher glanced at her, but then turned his gaze back to Beau. "I got worried when your car was here but there was no sign of you or Bella. Is everything okay?"

"What are you doing here?" she said.

Bella sat down beside her master and pinned Fletcher with an unwavering gaze. Fletcher shoved his hands into his jeans pockets and glanced from Bella to Grace to Beau and back again. "I felt bad about the way we left off the other day. I just wanted to make sure we're still cool."

"I'm sorry. I've been meaning to call you. I owe you an explanation." Now it was her turn to glance at Beau.

This was getting awkward, which of course made it even more interesting. He stepped forward and held out his hand. "Hi. I'm Beau."

After a moment of hesitation Fletcher shook his hand. "Jack. Good to meet you." His hand was slick with sweat, but he had a strong grip. Beau wondered if he was purposely squeezing extra hard.

Grace shifted her feet. "I'm sorry, I should have introduced you. Jack, this is Detective Brunelli. He's the one who helped me after ... well, after I left home."

Fletcher's fair eyebrows went up toward his hairline. "You're the one who handled the Brigham stuff?"

"I am."

"I didn't know you knew about that." Grace had gone pale. Her dual-coloured eyes grew wide and nervous.

Fletcher gave her a bashful look. "Everyone knows about that around here. I just don't bring it up, because it's obvious you don't want to talk about it."

"Oh."

There was a moment of uncomfortable silence.

Fletcher dug his hands even deeper into his pockets and rocked back and forth on his feet. "Well."

"My sister's in the hospital." Grace spoke in a rush.

Fletcher blinked at her, and Beau had a feeling that this was the first time she'd ever told him something personal. "I'm sorry to hear that. What happened?"

"I don't know yet. They said she's stable, but she's still unconscious. She has been since this morning. That's not good, is it?"

Fletcher shrugged. "Is she nearby?"

"In Vancouver. I think I should go down there."

Fletcher pulled his keys out of his pocket. "Do you want me to drive you?"

It was Grace's turn to blink.

Beau stepped in. "Grace is waiting for —" He almost said she was waiting for her therapist, but then he thought better of it. She might prefer if this guy didn't know that much about her. "Her friend Shelby to come."

"You mean her therapist?"

Grace gave Fletcher a sharp look.

"That's right. She's coming over to give Grace some support."

"Oh," Fletcher said. "Okay, well, in that case I guess … do you want me to stay until she gets here?"

He'd put the question to Beau, but Beau turned to Grace to see how she felt. He couldn't quite get a fix on what was going on between the two of them, and as much as he wanted Grace to have someone around, he wasn't sure this was the guy for the job. Grace was giving all kinds of mixed signals.

Her eyes flicked from side to side, and the voice that emerged was higher in pitch than her normal voice. "No. It wouldn't be proper."

Fletcher took a step back and raised his hands in the air. "Right. Got it."

Without delay, he moved toward his vehicle. He opened the driver's side door, and turned back to them.

"But call me if you need anything. Okay? The offer stands to drive you down to Vancouver. And, well, whatever else you need … I'm here."

They watched him do a three-point turn, angling around Beau's car, and head up the driveway out of sight.

"He seems nice," Beau said.

She gave him the side-eye. He wasn't sure who he was looking at, but he didn't think it was Grace.

"What are you accusing us of, Detective? We're a married woman."

THIRTY-SEVEN

I run through the trees to the edge of the road so I can watch the detective's car until it's out of sight. The dog is locked inside the house, but I can still hear it barking.

The detective's car kicks up a cloud of dust in its wake. The road is dry. It hasn't rained since the day of that big storm, when the doctor came looking for me.

When had that been? I can't remember.

Once I'm sure the detective is gone, I move deeper into the forest. Anxiety stirs inside me. From the house, the dog won't stop barking. It is enough to drive me crazy. It makes it hard to think, and I *really* need to think. My mind spins with questions and confusion and worry.

I need to think about the Family. About *my* family. I promised them protection, and time and again I've failed. I've brought them nothing but death and destruction.

Stopping to lean against a giant hemlock tree, I think about the prophet's good word, and about the sermons of my youth.

There are two ways to merit a return to God's good graces. One is by exile, and the other is by the spilling of blood.

I've been in exile for many years, and yet I still walk alone in the wilderness. The opportunity to atone by blood is so tempting, and yet so terrifying. But is that really what God wants of me?

For the first time, it occurs to me that God might be testing my faith. Maybe the notes I found at the base of the praying tree aren't actually from Him. Maybe they are the words of a false prophet, like Uncle G. Maybe God wants to see if I can be led astray.

I press on through the trees, trying to sort it all out. I find it all so confusing. I'd always been a good priesthood child. I'd minded my lessons well. But it was so easy for those lessons to be twisted. I need to dig back into the truth. I need to pray.

I move quietly as I approach the campsite, but the area has been cleared. There is nothing left but a pile of ash where the campfire had been. The ghost of a tent lies next to it, the ground smoothed away in a perfect square. I kick at the ground, scuffing up the dirt and burying the bits of charcoal.

Once that is done, I continue my walk. I have so much to figure out.

THIRTY-EIGHT

The year 2000 was coming, and with it the end of days. They would soon be lifted to heaven to avoid the coming destruction, and then they would be placed back on earth to build Zion. There they would reside peacefully with God for a thousand years.

Excitement built, and preparations ramped up. Grace was still recovering from her miscarriage, so she missed several of the planning meetings. But she felt well enough to help by the time they were packing away the food, which they stored in large airtight containers in the basement of the temple.

When they were brought back to earth, it would be some time before they could grow new crops. They needed enough food to get them through the transition, and there'd been many arguments over the logistics. How long would it be until they could rely on their new crops? How much food did they need to store?

They'd all been asked to tighten their belts by eating half as much as they would normally eat, and storing away the extra for later. The building of Zion, it was argued, would require a lot of energy. In the meantime, the Family went to bed every night with sore muscles and rumbling bellies.

In the final weeks of the year, many of the young men were particularly on edge. Several had already lost their priesthood and been shown through Brigham's gates.

Thus far, Clayne had managed to avoid the same fate, but every time Grace saw him she noted the tense set of his shoulders and the creases that seemed to have permanently formed in his brow.

It had taken some time for her to piece together what had happened after she lost the baby, but while Mother fed her another cup of tea and Boydell still lay unconscious in the dirt, Father had ushered Clayne home and gone to see Uncle G. When the bishop came to the door, Father told a hastily revised tale in which he was the one who punched Boydell, and then he dropped to his knees and begged for forgiveness. At the moment, Father was not in Uncle G's good books. But at least he'd maintained his priesthood.

As for Boydell, he seemed content to go along with the story, enjoying the strain it caused between Uncle G and Father. Grace suspected it also allowed him to plot a more private revenge against Clayne.

When Mother heard that Father had lied to the bishop, she became terrified that he'd just damned the whole family to hell. She'd been fervently praying for his soul ever since, and Mother Rebecca was angry for reasons that weren't clear. Grace had been trying to avoid the whole lot of them.

As grateful as she was that he'd saved Clayne from losing his priesthood, she couldn't erase the memory of Father stepping back and letting Boydell drag her from the house. Nor could she forget the fact that neither of her parents had followed them out the door.

That moment had opened her eyes, and set her to exploring questions she'd never thought of before. Questions like, why would her parents allow her to be forced into a marriage she didn't want? Why would they not defend the needs of their child above all else?

The juxtaposition between that and the way Clayne had stepped forward, prepared to defend her at any cost … it was both eating away at her, and opening her heart in new and unexpected ways.

She found herself seeking out Clayne in every group. Her spirits would lift when their eyes met, which they did with increasing frequency. She felt like someone had flicked a switch inside her soul, and now everything felt different.

She'd loved Clayne since they'd toddled around in diapers. He'd always been part cousin, part brother, and part friend. But she'd been so focused on keeping him at the prescribed distance that she'd never allowed herself to see him.

She saw him now. It should have scared her, but instead she felt exhilarated.

Thoughts of Clayne filled her days and made them bearable. She endured Boydell's aggression and advances with a calm she'd never felt before. Mentally, she'd removed herself from her own life, and in so doing she'd started to see that she might be able to have a life that was entirely different.

We could just leave, Clayne had said. *We could leave, and never come back.*

Was there really a world beyond Brigham's gates in which she could be free? Even if it were only for a few weeks, it would be worth it. If she escaped with Clayne before the end of days, she would surely damn her soul to hell. So when Boydell was lifted to heaven, she could be free. Of course, she'd also be in hell. But that seemed a better option than spending time and all eternity with her husband.

. . .

Shelby didn't arrive until well past nine that evening. Grace heard the rumble of her Jeep coming up the gravel road and went to the back door to flip on the exterior lights. They were floodlights, and they lit up the property like a baseball diamond.

She happened to be looking in just the right direction when the yard lit up. For just a second, she met the eyes of a man standing at the edge of the trees. And then he disappeared back into the shadows of the forest, and she disappeared back into the shadows of her mind.

THIRTY-NINE

eau stood up to greet the doctor as she approached. He handed over his credentials and waited while she gave them the once-over.

Seemingly satisfied, she said, "Ms. DeRoche was brought in yesterday morning with a fentanyl overdose. She's got track marks on both arms, and she tested positive for heroin. A jogger found her in MacLean Park. No idea how long she'd been there, but she was unconscious and barely breathing. We got her stabilized and administered Naloxone. There's still brain activity, so now we need to wait and see how she is when she wakes up."

"You think there's brain damage?" he asked.

"Most likely, but as for the severity ..." She shrugged. "She's lucky she was found when she was. She was on her way out. You're welcome to go in and see her, if you'd like. Second room on the right."

The doctor moved away, but stopped when he called out to her. "Any sign she was hit with a stun gun? It would leave a mark maybe an inch wide that looks like a bruise or a burn."

The doctor raised her eyebrows, but shook her head. "Not that I noticed."

There weren't any that he could see, either, but his view only consisted of everything above her collarbone. Desiree looked shrunken under the weight of wires and the breathing apparatus. Her body looked childlike beneath the pale blue hospital blanket. Her skin was sallow, the area under her eyes bruised dark purple. Her hair was a dirty tangle on the pillow. Without makeup, he could see several telltale scabs on her cheeks and chin.

Had the stress of Rulon's death and the note she'd received in her mailbox caused her to relapse? It was quite possible.

He sighed, and gave her hand a gentle squeeze. "You hang in there, kiddo. I'll be back soon."

Beau found his car in the large parking complex across from the hospital, and sat there for several minutes without turning on the engine. What now? He knew he should go home and get some sleep. He'd driven back to Vancouver overnight, and had only stopped by home for a quick shower. His eyes were tight and blurry with exhaustion, and his mind felt foggy.

There were loose ends he was anxious to deal with, but he doubted he'd do much good in his current condition. So, home it was. After he called Grace to update her on her sister's condition. His cellphone rang as he was pulling it from his pocket.

"Hey, Doug. Just leaving the hospital. No change in Desiree DeRoche's condition, but I've —"

Doug cut him off. "Beau, we've found Boaz and Clayne Johnson."

Beau sat up straighter in his seat. "Yeah? Shit, both of them?"

"Yep. Clayne's definitely alive, or at least he was a few months ago. They both went through legal name changes, and you were right about the agriculture angle. They bought some farmland outside Saskatoon. Started Lost Boys Organics, which grows and sells beans, chickpeas, and lentils. Apparently Boaz, who now goes by the name Stuart Redden, got married a year or so ago and started a family. He bought out Clayne's shares a few months back, and says he hasn't seen his brother since. He said Clayne's 'troubled.'"

Beau scrubbed a hand across his eyes. "Troubled?"

"Well, what he actually said is he's paranoid and delusional, possibly schizophrenic. But that seemed like his own opinion rather than a professional diagnosis."

"Does he have any idea where Clayne is now?"

"He says no. Clayne now goes by David Redden. I've run it. He's clean. Not even a parking ticket. I've also added the new name to his BOLO."

"I'd like to talk to Boaz."

"Of course you would. He's amenable. We'll set up a Skype call for later today or tomorrow."

"That's great. Thanks, boss."

"I let him know about his sister's death. He took it hard."

"I'd imagine."

"Says he hasn't seen Tabitha since he lost his priest-hood, I guess that's what they call it when they're excommunicated —"

"Yes, that's right."

"I gave him the contact info for the coroner in Kelowna. He said he'd get in touch to make arrangements."

"Good."

"He's going to email me some business docs Clayne wrote so we can have our techs compare the handwriting to the letters they found in Tabitha's drawer. And speaking of, we got some hits on those scripture numbers. They're all from Brigham Young. Most are sermons, and one is from an article he wrote for a newspaper. A lot of the same theme, about sin and following God's orders to get to heaven."

"What about the last two, where he warns Tabitha to be careful?"

"Right. The first one, 4:220, is 'I have known a great many men who have left this Church for whom there is no chance whatever for exaltation. If their blood had been spilled, it would have been better for them.'"

"Huh. And the last one?"

He heard Doug shifting papers around. "Here it is. It's from a sermon. 'I say, rather than that apostates should flourish here, I will unsheath my bowie knife, and conquer or die. Now, you nasty apostates, clear out, or judgment will be put on the line, and righteousness to the plummet.'"

Beau scrubbed a hand across his forehead. "So, what's he warning her about? Or is that a threat?"

"Not sure. Get some rest, Beau. You're gonna need it." There was a click, and Doug was gone.

Clayne Johnson was alive. Beau pumped his fist in the air like a quarterback who'd just made a sixty-yard throw for a touchdown, and then turned back to his phone to call Grace.

FORTY

"What's out there that's so interesting?" Shelby asked.

Grace turned her gaze from the window that looked out on the back and side of her property, giving her therapist a sheepish smile. She didn't dare talk about the person she thought she'd seen the previous night when she turned on the floodlights. "Just watching the new goat."

She wasn't used to sharing her space with anyone other than Bella, and having her therapist on hand hour after hour stretched the boundaries of both their comfort zones. Shelby had stayed the night in the spare bedroom, but the house was small and there was only one bathroom. Although she didn't say as much, she bet Shelby was dying to go home.

For her part, Grace felt trapped and unable to do either of the things she was itching to do. On the one hand, she was desperate to explore the forest that edged her property, to see if the person she thought she'd seen the previous night was really there. On the other, she was anxious to get to Vancouver and see Desiree as soon as possible. But thanks to Detective Brunelli, she was basically under house arrest.

Shelby filled the kettle and set it on the stove. "Tea?"

"I should have left for Vancouver last night," Grace said.

"Best not to do that drive in the dark. And you were dissociating when I arrived. Do you remember?"

"Being here, I'm not getting any information from the hospital."

"Maybe that's because there's not much information to give?"

"But if I were there, I could see her for myself. And maybe track down a doctor to talk to, instead of whoever's at the nursing station repeating the same bits of nothing."

"They said it was an overdose, right?"

"She's been clean for so many years."

"An addict is always an addict, no matter how many years they're clean. There's always a risk."

"I know. You're right. It just doesn't sit well with me."

"Why don't we go to the living room and talk it through?"

Grace's cellphone rang as Shelby was pouring the tea. She recognized the detective's phone number, and her heart gave a galloping triple beat.

She pressed the phone to her ear. "Is she okay?"

"No change," Brunelli said. "She's still unconscious."

Grace squeezed her eyes closed. "Still?"

"I spoke to her doctor. She said Desiree was using heroin laced with fentanyl, and she overdosed."

"Right, I know."

"She was found in a local park, unconscious and barely breathing. They stabilized her and gave her a drug meant to reverse the effect of an opioid overdose. She's stable, and they expect her to wake up. But there is the chance of brain damage. They just won't know until she's awake."

Grace fisted a hand against her mouth, tears burning her eyes.

"Grace? Are you still there?"

She dropped her hand. "Yes, sorry. I'm here. Thank you for calling me."

"I have some other news."

She really didn't think she could take any more, but she sat down at the kitchen table and dug her fingers into her thigh. "Okay. What is it?"

"We've found Boaz and Clayne Johnson. They're alive."

Her ear buzzed like a swarm of bees had suddenly awoken inside her head. "What?"

"Clayne's alive, Grace."

"He's … oh my … are you sure? Really?"

"Yes. But listen. According to Boaz, Clayne isn't well. He disappeared a few months back —"

"He's alive? For real?"

"Yes. But we don't know where he is. And if he's mentally disturbed, as Boaz claims, then there's a chance he's dangerous. I want you to be extra cautious —"

"Clayne would never hurt me. That's ridiculous!"

Shelby spun to look at her, her eyes wide and questioning.

She pulled the phone away from her mouth and said, "It's Clayne! They've found him. He's alive!"

"Grace, listen," Detective Brunelli said.

Her vision had blurred with tears. She wiped at her eyes, but the tears just kept coming. "I can't believe it! Oh my goodness, this is the best news. Thank you so much, Detective."

"I know this is good news, Grace, but I have to warn you … the man Clayne is now may be very different than the boy you used to know. Do you hear me?"

"Yes, yes," she said.

"I want you to be careful, Grace. And if Clayne approaches you, I want you to call the police. Do you understand?"

"Yes, sure," she said.

He sighed. "Let me speak to Shelby."

She sniffled back tears and mucus. "All right."

She handed over the phone, and Shelby listened in silence for several moments.

"Uh-huh. Okay, I hear you. Just hang on a sec." Shelby placed a hand over the mouthpiece and gave her an apologetic look. "Do you mind giving me a minute?"

"Oh. Yeah, sure. I'll give Bella a quick walk."

"Thanks." Shelby waited, watching as she slid her feet into rubber boots and pulled on her jacket, and then gave her a finger wave as she and Bella clattered out the door.

"Come on, girl. Let's go explore the forest."

She trudged quickly across the mud and grass toward the thick stand of cedar and hemlock trees. A tight achiness had formed beneath her breastbone. It was a feeling she hadn't experienced much in her life, so it took her a moment to recognize it for what it was.

It was hope.

. . .

Grace's heart thundered inside her chest as she approached him. She placed the rubber storage container on the ground and whispered, "We need to talk."

Clayne leaned a sack of cornmeal against the pile waiting to be carried down the stairs to the temple's basement and wiped sweat from his brow. "All right. Pass me the duct tape and scissors, will you?"

She did, using it as an excuse to move closer to him. The people around them were focused on their work — stacking crates of food, labelling boxes, or carrying things down to the basement for storage — but in Brigham, there was always someone watching.

"No, in private," she said. "Can you meet me by the Indian tree in an hour?"

Without missing a beat, he said, "I'll see you there."

The tree was the safe zone they'd created as kids when playing Cowboys and Indians. If you were an Indian being chased by one of the Cowboys, all you had to do was keep a hand on that tree and nobody could touch you.

Grace placed a hand against its rough bark, remembering the innocent times not so many years before when the only thing she'd had to worry about was being a good priesthood girl and keeping sweet. That had seemed challenging at the time, but as it turned out, it was so much more difficult to be a good priesthood woman. Especially when you were only fourteen.

"Game over. I declare the Indian team the winner," Clayne said from behind her.

She smiled but didn't look at him. "I could never win when I was playing against you."

"That's because I was so good." He reached out and touched the tree, a foot higher than where she could reach. "But we always won when we were on the same team, didn't we?"

She turned to look at him, but out of habit she kept her hand on the tree. Still playing safe, but not for much longer. He stood closer than the five feet they normally had to keep between them, and she almost moved away. But she caught herself and held firm.

From this close she could see how broad his cheekbones were becoming, the pimple on his chin, and the fuzz of hair growing on his upper lip. "And you always helped me. Even when we were on the opposite team, you'd distract the others before they could catch me."

He shrugged. "You couldn't hear them coming as well as I could."

"You've been protecting me my whole life, Clayne."

He turned to look down at her. His eyes were so blue, so familiar. "We've always protected each other. Remember that time Boydell caught us holding hands in the yard?"

Grace's ear gave a warning screech at the memory, and she shook her head to clear it.

He must have thought she was saying she didn't remember. "You chased him up the road and took the correction for me. I never forgot that."

"Clayne." She paused, took a deep breath. "The night you punched Boydell, you said something ..."

"Yes."

"About leaving." Her voice had quieted to a hush.

He turned, leaned his back against the tree's broad trunk. "I think about that all the time. I know where Father keeps his keys. I'd wait until the middle of the night, then push the car out of the garage and down the road until I was far enough away that no one could hear the engine. And then I'd just keep driving."

"How would you get through the gates?"

His smile was wistful. "I have bolt cutters. It wouldn't be that tough."

The thought of it was both terrifying and exhilarating. "Would you really do it?"

He turned his blue-eyed gaze in her direction. "Not alone, I wouldn't."

Her heart jumped into her throat. "What if I came with you?"

"Are you serious, Gracey?" His smile lit up his whole face.

Pressing her fingers into the bark so hard her knuckles turned white, she said, "I'm thinking about it."

He took her hand, causing her to gasp. His hand felt broad and strong.

"You said something that night, too. Something I keep thinking about. When I asked if you were all right, you said you wouldn't be if you ever lost me." He squeezed her hand, setting off a butterfly flutter in her stomach. "Did you mean that?"

"Yes." And then more firmly, she said, "Yes, Clayne. I did."

"Then we feel the same way because I won't *ever* be okay without you. Will you come with me?"

Before she could think too much and let her fear take over, she said, "Can we leave tonight?"

He leaned down, and before she could even comprehend what he was doing, his lips touched hers. It didn't hurt like it did when Boydell mashed his mouth against hers. Instead his lips felt warm and soft, like he was asking her a question. And after a moment, she answered.

Before Grace was ready, Clayne pulled away. "Meet me at three in the morning, by Father's garage."

She nodded her agreement. He gave her another quick kiss, even sweeter than the last, and left before she could say a word.

She stayed there for a while after he left, her hand pressed to her lips, paying little attention to the rustle and shift in the forest around her. For the moment she'd forgotten that, in Brigham, there was always someone watching.

FORTY-ONE

’ve been praying a lot, and I’ve finally gained the clarity I’ve been seeking. It has not come in the form of a note hidden beneath the praying tree, or from a booming voice in the sky. Instead, it has come from a quiet voice in my own mind, a voice that speaks with both certainty and strength.

It tells me that I’ve been misled and lied to. That the things I’ve done are wrong. God doesn’t want me to hurt the people I love, or for anyone else to die. It is such a relief.

But how can I stop it? There isn’t much time, so I need to be very brave and very, very smart. If I do everything right, I may walk with the righteous in Zion after all.

Confess my sins.

That is the first step. But I have to do more than that. I have to tell someone about the false prophet. About the notes and the praying tree. The idea of calling the police is oh-so scary. But I can talk to the detective. He is scary, too, but Grace trusts him, at least a little. Maybe he will understand. Maybe he will help.

And I know how to find him. All I need to do is get Grace's phone.

FORTY-TWO

When Grace approached the garage with a small bag of clothing and family photos tucked against her chest, it wasn't Clayne waiting for her, but Boydell.

"What are you doing here?" she asked.

In the sliver of moonlight coming through the trees, his face looked like thunder. "No, Grace. What are *you* doing here?"

He knows what we planned. And he's going to kill us for it.

They watched each other, a hunter and his half-tame beast, each waiting for the other to make the next move. Maybe he was waiting for her to speak, to explain, to beg for forgiveness. And she decided, right then and there, that she would never ask him for forgiveness ever again. No matter how much he hurt her, she would hold on to that bit of herself.

Her first thought was to run, but her feet wouldn't move. Then she thought maybe if she called out for

Clayne — Where was he? Had he fallen asleep? — he'd come charging out to save her once again.

"You've been unfaithful." Not a question. A statement.

She opened her mouth, not sure if she would agree or deny.

"You've betrayed me."

Her ear buzzed, and her vision grew dim.

No. Let me handle this.

The buzzing lessened to the sound of a faraway wasps' nest.

Her voice was little more than a croak. "How did you know?"

"Rulon saw you in the forest. He's a loyal brother. He came and told me what you were doing." He looked at her with a mixture of hurt and incredulousness. "Don't you know you're risking your soul? You could be sent into exile for doing something like that."

He didn't understand that that was precisely what she'd been trying to do. Willful exile was a concept beyond his comprehension. It had been beyond hers until Clayne had planted that seed in her mind.

She bowed her head in the posture of a good priesthood wife, and tried to think of what to do. Run? Call for Clayne? Where in the world was he?

"Don't you love me?" Boydell asked.

Her head snapped up, and a bubble of surprised humour made its way up her throat. But no, she could see by the look on his face that he was serious. He actually thought she might love him.

For the first and only time in her life, she felt a stab of pity for him. He didn't know the difference between love and cruelty. And being raised by Uncle G, how could he? The big house on the hill might have been beautiful, but filled with love and compassion it was not.

And Grace, for all the tension and division within her home, had always known that she was loved. Maybe not enough, or in the right way. After all, they hadn't protected her from Uncle G's cruelty, or from marrying someone she hated. But her roots were firmly planted in the love of her little family. Mother and Father and Desiree, and even Mother Rebecca and Sariah. There was complication, but there was also love.

"You're my wife." Boydell's voice shook with emotion. Moonlight shone on eyes gone glassy with tears. "You're *my wife*, Grace. Why do you treat me with so little respect?"

"Because I didn't want to marry you, Boydell. And you didn't want to marry me, either."

"That's not true," he said.

"You think I'm ugly. Ungrateful and impudent. Is that what you wanted in a wife?"

He scrubbed a hand across his eyes. "God's wisdom isn't ours to question."

"I'm not questioning *God's* wisdom, Boydell." Oh, just saying it out loud made her tongue taste so bitter.

She could read the thought in his head, *Then whose wisdom are you questioning?*

"Just let me go," she said. "You'll be given more wives, ones who will respect you and love you the way you want me to. But I can't, Boydell. I can't be that wife to you."

He bowed his head, seemed to be giving it some thought. Hope bubbled within her.

"Is it because of Clayne? Is that why you don't love me?"

"No, it's because of me. It's my fault."

"But you *do* love him."

It wasn't a question, so she decided she didn't need to answer. "Just let me go. Please."

He huffed out a breath, turned and walked away from her, leaned a hand on the door of the Johnsons' garage.

"Please, Boydell."

"You'd rather go to hell than live in Zion with me."

She bowed her head rather than answer.

"You are my property. Consecrated to me for time and all eternity. I'll never let you go." With an inhuman bellow, he punched the garage door. It buckled inward. He punched it again, and then again.

Lights clicked on in the Johnsons' home, and then the DeRoches'. Grace heard the thunder of feet, the exclamations of surprise and concern.

"What's going on?"

"Grace? What's happening?"

They spilled out into the yard, the men and boys in their pyjamas and the women and girls in long cotton nightgowns. But no Clayne. Where was Clayne?

Boydell kept punching. Blood sprayed from his hand. The garage door caved in.

"Boydell, stop it!" Grace said.

He spun on his heels and thundered toward her, his face twisted with fury. The women screamed and backed away. Grace stood rooted to the spot, too shocked to move.

"Don't you *ever* tell me what to do!" He grabbed her by the hair, yanked her off her feet. "Don't you ever!"

He dragged her across the dirt toward the road. Her feet stumbled along behind her, trying to find purchase and failing.

"Boydell!" Father moved toward them, Uncle Redd at his side. "Let her go."

Boydell shoved her away, and she stumbled and fell against the fence. He collapsed to his knees, pressed his fists against his face, and howled like a wounded animal.

This was her chance. She stood up, slipped through the gate, and ran. Her feet pounded against gravel, and her heart pounded a painful rhythm inside her chest.

Where oh where was Clayne?

Boydell caught her before she'd even made it to the edge of town. He grabbed the back of her dress and slammed her down. She slid, face first, along the road. Gravel sliced her palms, her face. It cut into her gums and crunched against her teeth.

He jumped on top of her, pushing all the air out of her lungs in one mighty rush. Hot breath tickled her neck, puffed against her good ear. "Where do you think you're going, *wife*?"

She would have sobbed, but she didn't have the breath. Her ear screeched, and her mind faded away. He lifted off her enough that she could catch a breath. She wheezed and spat rocks and blood and possibly some of her teeth onto the road.

There was only one thing left she cared about. She needed to know, before she died. "Where's Clayne?"

He pressed her down, breathed into her good ear. "Your boyfriend is gone."

Gone.

It took her a moment to process what he'd said. He hadn't said that Clayne lost his priesthood. He'd said that Clayne was *gone*. Deep inside her chest, something tore free. The pain ripped through her, an avalanche of grief and shock and fury.

"Oh my God, what did you do to him?"

"You should be more worried about what I'll do to you, *dear wife*."

She pressed her face into the ground and gravel bit into her cheeks and nose and forehead. If Clayne was gone, what else mattered?

"You will be obedient." He hit her in the back of her head, pushing her face into the road. Her nose broke with blinding pain and a spurt of hot blood.

"You will be a good priesthood wife." He punched her in the side, and she felt the crack of her ribs. "And you will carry my seed. You will give me my son."

He lifted the back of her dress and kicked her legs apart. As he pressed himself down on top of her, her ear roared to life and her vision went black.

No. Not this time. Let me take it.

She heard them approaching — her family, the Johnsons, and probably others who'd been awoken by their racket. She heard the crunch of their footsteps on gravel, she heard their murmurs of dismay and confusion, and then she heard them retreat. This was business between a man and his wife, and his wife was his property. No one would step in.

From the opposite direction, from the road that led to the gates at the edge of her world, came the sound of many footsteps fast approaching.

"The police!" someone whisper-screeched.

People scattered, running back to their homes to awaken children and send them running for the forest.

Boydell's weight lifted from her body. For a moment she wondered if he would abandon her there, but he yanked her up by the back of her dress. It tore from shoulder to waist. He hoisted her bloody and broken body over his shoulder and staggered back toward Brigham.

· · ·

When she came back to herself, she was in the forest beside her house. The edge of the cliff was about twenty feet away. She could see blue patches of Upper Arrow Lake far below. Bella nudged her nose into Grace's thigh, whining.

"Hey, girl." She rubbed a hand over the dog's broad head. Her hand looked too big, too old.

"I'm okay. What happened?"

Well, she knew what had happened. She just didn't remember what had triggered it. But when the wind blew cool against her cheek, she caught the sweet smell of roses. She hated that smell, it reminded her of her wedding night. Maybe that had been the trigger.

Bella whined again.

"No, I'm okay." She was. Her hand began to look like her hand again. The fog cleared from her head. She'd wanted to search the forest, she remembered. But if someone was still out there, she hadn't found them.

"Grace!"

It was Shelby, calling from somewhere behind her. Searching for her. She wondered how long she'd been gone if Shelby had come out looking for her.

"Shelby!"

"Grace? Oh, thank goodness."

"Sorry! I'm okay. Head back toward the yard, and I'll meet you there!"

They met on the gravel driveway.

"Are you okay?" Shelby asked.

Grace dug her fingers into Bella's fur, seeking comfort. "Yeah. Sorry to scare you."

"No need to apologize. You're handling all this stress amazingly well. I'm proud of you."

"I'm not handling anything well right now. I feel like I'm losing it." Tears burned her eyes, and she blinked them back.

"Let's go inside. Have some tea. I think you could use an extra session today."

"I need to go see my sister. I'll call Jack to take care of the goats. I want to head down to Vancouver right away."

Shelby took a deep breath. Then she reached out and took Grace's hand, giving it a gentle squeeze. "Then I'll come with you."

"You don't need to do that. I'll be fine."

"I'm not coming as your therapist, Grace. I'm coming as your friend."

A flood of warmth filled her chest, and the tears started to fall. "Okay. Thank you."

"Come on, let's go inside. You call Jack, and I'll make you a fresh cup of tea for the road."

FORTY-THREE

The phone woke Beau from a troubled sleep. He rolled over and grabbed it from his night table, sticking it against his ear without opening his eyes.

"Brunelli."

It was Doug. "There is indeed a compound north of Medicine Hat. Way north and way off the grid. The property was purchased by WSJ Industrial Holdings two years after the folks in Brigham drank their cocktail. It's twenty acres of farmland, and they've got twelve-foot-high solid concrete walls around the entire thing, plus cameras, security lights, you name it. I've sent you some initial surveillance photos. From what we can see, it sure has the makings of an FLDS compound. Aerial photos show several large bunkers, along with the expected farming equipment, silos, etc."

"WSJ Industrial Holdings," Beau said. "As in Warren Steed Jeffs?"

"Could be. It's a Canadian shell corporation that was started about six months before the property was purchased. The funds to buy the property were transferred in from several U.S. accounts, including Spitfire Precision, which is owned by a top church leader, and several construction companies based out of Hildale and Salt Lake City. There's been a steady stream of transfers in over the years, adding up to hundreds of thousands of dollars."

"Okay. What's next?"

"More surveillance. We've got drones flying over at regular intervals. Hopefully we'll get lucky and Gideon Smith will show his face. In the meantime, Boaz Johnson is waiting for your call, if you're ready to talk to him?"

"I need five minutes."

"Sure." Doug gave him the number and signed off.

Beau made hasty work of washing up and getting dressed, before settling in front of his laptop to place the call.

A man with short silver hair and a thin grey moustache popped onto the screen. It looked like he was in an office. Behind him were several posters advertising Lost Boys Organics. One had a wholesome-looking child spooning beans toward her smiling mouth. The other was a close-up of a heaping pile of lentils cupped in a woman's hands. Beneath the posters was a wide row of steel grey file cabinets.

"Boaz? Beau Brunelli. Thanks for speaking with me."

"I go by Stuart now." His voice was soft and low-pitched. His cheeks and nose were ruddy with rosacea, and his eyes were an icy pale blue.

"Of course. My apologies."

"You're looking for my brother."

"That's right. When did you last have contact with Clayne? Sorry. I mean David."

"About three months ago, when I bought out his shares."

"Can you walk me through it?"

Boaz leaned back in his chair. "Sure. Like I told that other officer, my brother is very troubled. He's been in and out of counselling over the years, but he never sticks with anything long enough to make an actual difference. Don't get me wrong; my brother is brilliant. He's the true brains behind our company, which we started from scratch with literally nothing. I'm more of the big ideas man, and he's the one who figures out how to actually make them work."

"How did the two of you reconnect? I understand you were the first to lose your priesthood."

"That's right. I was living in Bountiful when he showed up. Boydell Smith beat him to a pulp and dumped him over the gate. He managed to walk to Fort Steele, and somehow made his way to Bountiful from there."

"Boydell. That was Grace DeRoche's husband, right?"

"Apparently. But they weren't married when I left."

"Any idea why Boydell did that?"

He shook his head. "My brother never talked about it, but I'd bet Boydell caught him and Grace in a compromising position. They were inseparable from the time they were born, practically, and our parents never did anything to stop it."

"So Clayne — *David* — showed up in Bountiful just before the millennium?"

He nodded. "We left the area not long after, made our way east. Changed our names, started a new life."

"Ever connect with others who'd been kicked out of Brigham? Or the kids who escaped?"

His lip curled into a bitter smile. "I wasn't interested in rehashing the past. But I guess I missed my opportunity, didn't I?"

"I'm very sorry about your sister."

Boaz blinked several times in a row, and pulled his shoulders up toward his ears. "I bought her a burial plot at the cemetery out here. I hope that's what she would have wanted."

Beau's throat closed over, and he coughed to clear it. "I'm sure that's perfect." Before Boaz could ask him questions about Tabby's death that he didn't want to answer, he moved on. "Ever hear your brother mention connecting with others from Brigham?"

Boaz sighed. "I told you, my brother isn't well. I tried to get him help, but he wouldn't listen."

"Is that a yes?"

"He thought someone from the Family was watching him, following him. I'm telling you he was paranoid, completely delusional. When he'd talk to me, his eyes would kind of bounce around, like he couldn't get them to focus on any one thing. I kept reminding him that everyone in the Family was dead and gone, but ..." Boaz shrugged. "When it became clear he wasn't going to get help, I asked him to stop coming to work. He was scaring our employees. Frankly, he was scaring me. I convinced him to take a leave of absence. Paid, of course."

Boaz leaned forward, ran his hands over his tightly cropped hair. "He came by my house late at night a couple weeks later. I sent my wife upstairs with our baby — I have a five-month-old son — but he was pretty calm. Said he'd cleared out his apartment and turned it over to his landlord, and that he was going away for a while. He asked me to buy out his shares so the business wouldn't suffer. I told him that wasn't necessary, but he insisted. Said he wasn't sure how long he'd be away, or if he'd ever come back."

"Did he say where he was going?"

"He didn't, and I didn't ask."

"You just let him go?"

Boaz shrugged his shoulders. "I know it seems heartless on my part. But I was tired of dealing with his drama. And I was worried about protecting my family."

"Do you think he's capable of harming anyone?"

Boaz's lips turned down. "Other than himself? No."

"You think he's suicidal?"

A sigh. "No. Well, I don't know." He shook his head. "I don't think so. Are we through? I've got a meeting in ten minutes."

"Okay. Yes, thanks for taking the time to talk to me."

"Sure." Boaz swiped an arm across his eyes and clicked off without saying goodbye.

Beau laid his head on his arms and took several long, slow breaths. Boaz was convinced Clayne was delusional and paranoid. But considering their sister had wound up dead in a bathtub, Beau wasn't so sure.

———

He must have dozed off. He awoke some unknown time later with pins and needles in his arms and a crick in his neck. He wiped drool from his cheek and blinked blearily at the clock. It was one in the afternoon. He hadn't slept so late since his early days as a patrol officer, when he was working nights. He didn't remember feeling quite so rough at the time, but he'd been much younger then. Now he felt like he was recovering from a two-day bender without the prior enjoyment of having committed the crime.

He stood up, stretched, and then opened his inbox to check his emails.

"Well, hot damn."

Dan Wizen from the British Columbia Ministry of Transportation and Infrastructure had sent over a Dropbox link to the photos covering the two Arrow Lakes ferry crossings. He'd asked for images from both ferry crossings for the seventy-two hours around Tabitha Johnson's death. Wizen had sent him more than seventeen hundred low-resolution images.

Beau went to make some coffee.

Properly armed, he searched the lineups for a blue Subaru that would match Grace's. Wizen wasn't kidding about the challenge of identifying a specific vehicle. The photos captured random moments in time, with many gaps in between. The ferry lineups were only one lane wide, but any vehicle not at the back of the line when the image was captured was partially or fully blocked by the traffic behind it.

After an hour he scrubbed his eyes, took a pee break, and got himself another cup of coffee. An hour after that, he started to seriously consider taking early retirement. By the evening, his back screamed, his head pounded, and he'd come up with a couple dozen Subaru station wagons that were debatably blue in colour. He sent the images to Doug, hoping they could be digitally enhanced. With any luck, one of them would actually place Grace DeRoche on a ferry heading to or from Kelowna.

He did some stretching in the kitchen while he waited for a can of soup to heat up, and ate while reading the newspaper. He was back in bed by eight that evening, scrolling through Netflix in search of comedic relief.

The phone rang as he was dozing off, and he grabbed it from his night table and propped it against his ear. "Brunelli."

"This is Janis calling from the ICU at VGH. There's a note in Desiree DeRoche's file to call you with any updates?"

He bolted upright in bed, his heart slamming into his throat. "Yes?"

"She regained consciousness for about five minutes this evening, and asked for water."

"Oh, that's good news. Any idea about brain damage?"

"Still too soon to tell, she'll need to be conscious for extended periods before we can do the proper neurological testing. But this is progress."

"When can I visit?"

"Anytime that's not a shift change, which is between seven and eight thirty in both the morning and the evening."

Beau checked his watch. "Great. I'm on my way."

It was late, and the hospital was quiet. But the ICU was brightly lit, creating a permanent daytime for those most at risk of slipping from this world.

Desiree was sleeping or unconscious, her head turned to the side, her hair matted and greasy against the pillow. Monitors beeped, keeping track of her heart rate and blood pressure and whatever else they kept track of. Her breath fogged against the inside of the oxygen mask.

Beau took the only seat in the room and settled in to wait.

Hours later, he startled from a doze. She shifted in the bed, her legs moving back and forth under the covers.

"Desiree?" He stood up and approached the head of the bed. Her eyes were open, shifting from side to side in a way that reminded him of her older sister.

"Hey, you're okay." He placed his hand over hers and leaned forward, hoping to catch her attention. "You're okay, Desiree. You're in the hospital, and they're taking good care of you, and you're going to be okay."

Her gaze caught his and held. She whimpered, her eyes filling with tears.

"It's okay, sweetheart. You're going to be okay."

"S-s—" She shook her head, squeezed her eyes closed. Tears leaked down to her temples.

"It's okay, just relax."

Her eyes opened, widened with urgency. When she spoke the mask muffled her voice. "No."

"What is it? Do you need something?"

"No." She shook her head and her eyes flicked from side to side again, like she was searching out danger.

"Desiree," he said. "Did somebody do this to you?"

Her eyes found his again. They were wide and blue with fear. "S-s—"

He leaned closer. "What?"

"My ... s-s— s-s—"

His heart caught in his throat. "Your sister?"

Her eyes squeezed shut, and she nodded, tears leaking toward her temples. One hand fluttered up and tugged down the neck of her hospital gown, revealing a burn mark on the upper part of her arm. It was about an inch long.

Beau scrubbed a hand across his face, over rough stubble and a jawline loosened with age. "You're safe now, okay? I'll get some security outside your door. Don't you worry about anything, except getting better."

But she'd already lost consciousness.

He exited through Emergency and pulled his phone from his pocket as soon as he was outside. The sky brightened toward dawn. First he called in a protection detail for Desiree's hospital room, and then he called Doug at home.

His boss answered on the third ring, his voice like sandpaper. "Yeah?"

"Doug, Desiree just accused Grace DeRoche of attempted murder. I've already called in protection for her, but can you get a forensics team over here ASAP? She showed me a mark on her arm that looks consistent with a stun gun."

"You got it."

"We're still waiting on the forensics from the weapon we removed from Grace's closet, and the comparison report to see if it matches the mark on Tabitha Johnson's chest.

But if it matches, and those goat hair samples also match the hairs found on Tabitha's bed, I think we've got enough for murder one. As soon as Desiree is able to give a statement, we'll have enough for another charge of attempted."

"I'll call Crown counsel as soon as it hits nine."

"Any chance you'll okay a flight? I'd like to be on the scene when it comes time to make the arrest."

"You know the answer to that. Get driving."

FORTY-FOUR

Shelby's Jeep was warm and cozy, and Grace was so tired. Her body felt like it was weighed down, pinned to the passenger seat. Bella snored peacefully from the back seat.

She forced her eyes open, stared blearily at the passing greenery. "I'm sorry."

"For what?"

"I'm not much company, am I?" Her voice was slurred.

Shelby chuckled. "How much sleep have you gotten lately? Don't worry about it."

"Then wake me up if you get too bored."

"I like driving. Get some rest."

• • •

When news came of the prophet's death, Grace was in the bathroom cleaning up from her fourth miscarriage. She'd hidden the last two from Boydell to avoid his fury and accusations. He was certain she was losing the babies on purpose, and no amount of reasoning could convince him otherwise.

As she stuffed the clump of bloody towels into the wash, someone pounded on the door.

"Coming!" Grace said.

"Grace!" It was Mother, and her voice was high with panic.

Her first thought was that something had happened to Father. He'd been ill for several weeks, running a fever and coughing so hard he occasionally spat up blood. She'd begged Mother to take him to a doctor. But no one was leaving Brigham anymore, not for any reason. After the police raid two years before, the Family had gone into what Uncle G liked to call "lockdown."

She yanked open the door to see Mother and Desiree standing outside. "What's happened? Is it Father?"

Mother's eyes spilled tears, but Desiree's were wide and dry.

"No, no," Mother said, waving a hand. "Word's come from our kin in Bountiful. The prophet has made his transition to the heavenly realm. We must go to temple and pray."

"Oh. All right, then. Let me put on my shoes."

Mother stood on the stoop, sobbing into a handkerchief while Grace slipped on her coat and shoes. She caught Desiree's eye and raised her eyebrows. Her younger sister shrugged.

"Come on, Mother." Desiree took their mother's arm and they moved up the road, joining the crowd moving toward the temple.

Grace was slow and shaky, her legs weak. "You go on ahead, I'm right behind you."

Tabby and Sariah caught up with her partway up the hill. Sariah was six years old, and her eyes were wide with fear and worry. She clutched Tabby's hand.

Grace dropped a kiss on each of their heads. Sariah's curls tickled her cheeks. "Are you girls all right?"

"What's going to happen now that the prophet went to heaven without us?" Sariah asked.

Grace put an arm over her youngest sister's shoulders. "A new prophet will be named."

"So, we won't wander around lost forever and end up in hell?" Tabby asked.

"Who in the world told you that?" Grace shook her head. "No. We'll say lots of prayers to lift the prophet's soul in heaven. And we'll get a new prophet to guide us here on earth."

"Until the end of days comes," Sariah said.

"That's right," she said, although she'd lost faith in the notion that they'd be lifted up to heaven and then dropped back to earth to build Zion. After the new millennium came and went and the world went on as it always had, she'd started to doubt. One day while helping carry up boxes of food and supplies from the temple's basement, she'd overheard Uncle G saying they'd been blessed with extra time to perfect their souls, and she'd stopped believing all together.

It was at that point that she'd started making plans to escape in earnest. But at the same time she set her sights on escape, the Family tightened security around Brigham.

The old gates were replaced with electronic ones that would sound an alarm if triggered, and loudspeakers had been installed around town. Testing the system had sent people running and screaming. The alarm was very loud, which made the elders feel much more secure.

She bet the police had some way of dismantling the alarm before they entered Brigham, but she kept this thought to herself. Along with the alarm, security cameras had been installed around the perimeter of town and up the main road toward the temple.

No, escape was no longer so easy, and she'd pondered the problem for days. It was bitter irony that escaping would have been so easy all the years she'd never considered doing it, and only now had it become next to impossible.

The solution came to her one night as she walked home from temple, and like all good ideas it seemed to come out of nowhere. It was so simple, and all it required was patience. Well, patience and a complete rewiring of the mental programming that said police were dangerous, which was probably why it took her so long to think of it in the first place.

Several weeks went by until it occurred to her that she could take other children with her. It started with Desiree, who struggled more and more to follow the rules and keep sweet. Desiree had a free and rebellious spirit, and the older she got, the more Grace worried for her future. She wished desperately to spare Desiree from the kind of hellish marriage she was enduring.

One sweet spring evening, she'd asked Desiree to go for a walk with her through the fields. She'd sworn her to secrecy and told her of the plan. At first Desiree seemed as shocked as she'd felt when Clayne first brought it up, but her sister's eyes soon lit up with possibility. The idea of being free was intoxicating.

It went on from there. Rulon came next, even though he was the one who'd told Boydell about seeing her and Clayne in the forest. He'd come to her not long after that night, begging for her forgiveness. And because she'd never forgotten the time in his kitchen when he'd lied to protect her, and because she knew he'd acted out of loyalty to his brother with no real understanding of what the consequences might be, eventually she did forgive him. Rulon was a good one, despite his last name.

The official word on Clayne was that he'd lost his priesthood. Although Grace no longer prayed very often, she did so with fervent frequency for this to be the truth. She imagined Clayne trying to find his way in a world she could barely fathom, perhaps even finding his older brother Boaz. She imagined him safe and alive and free. She hoped he didn't blame her for what had happened. She hoped someday she'd join him.

With the younger children like Sariah, who couldn't be trusted to keep such a big secret, they'd made it into a game. When one of the older children gave them the signal by calling "Ollie ollie oxen free," they would all run to meet under the scarecrow at the far edge of the fields. From there they would follow Grace through whatever obstacles they'd set up for that day. Over time, the game progressed to pretending that the police had arrived, and soon the call of "Police!" became the first part of the signal.

She planted another kiss on top of Sariah's and Tabby's heads, and shuffled them up the stairs to the temple. The girls went to sit with their families while she moved to her assigned seat beside Boydell. As much as she hated every aspect of it, she was now part of Brigham's royal family. She was a Smith, and Smiths sat in the front.

Boydell smelled nauseatingly of sweat and grease. He'd come straight from the fields, as had many of the others, and hadn't washed. She tried not to breathe through her nose.

When everyone was seated, Uncle G moved to the front of the room. His face was fat and solemn, his cheeks red with exertion. His belly had grown to the size of a giant pumpkin, and she doubted he could even see his feet anymore.

"My friends. This is a sad day for our community. Our most esteemed prophet, Rulon Timpson Jeffs, has left this earth."

Around the room, women sobbed and men sniffled and someone got into it enough to wail. Since Grace couldn't work up any tears, she bowed her head and stared at her lap.

"We've received word that his son, Warren Steed Jeffs, will soon succeed him as President and Prophet, Seer and Revelator. And now, let us pray for the soul of our beloved prophet, that he may be elevated to the highest level of heaven."

They shifted in their seats and bowed their heads in prayer, and there they stayed for the next three hours.

When Uncle G was finally satisfied that they'd done their part to elevate Rulon Jeffs's soul, he launched into his sermon. Grace's bottom had gone painfully numb, and she kept shifting uncomfortably in her seat. She wasn't the only one.

The children's choir was called to the front to sing some hymns.

Sariah's birdsong voice rose above the rest, and she smiled at Grace as she sang, "Amazing grace, how sweet the sound, that saved a wretch like me ..."

Grace returned Sariah's smile.

Then Uncle G read through an excruciatingly long list of Rulon Jeffs's virtues. Her stomach rumbled, and Boydell dug a sharp elbow into her side. Behind them, someone's breathing deepened to a gentle snore.

Uncle G wound his way from topic to topic, building up a head of steam over the persecution their brethren to the south were facing. Always, the police were on their doorsteps. Always, they were trying to take their children and rip families apart. It was never-ending, the trials they all had to face to stay true to their God and be worthy of Zion.

She yawned. Boydell gave her another elbow in the side.

"But God has seen fit to reveal this truth to me, and, my brethren, I am humbled by this honour. I do not take His trust in me for granted."

"Amen," someone said.

"Yes, amen. I see the path before us so clearly. The path of righteousness that will lead us to Zion."

"Yes!" someone else said.

"And I see a fork in the road up ahead, my brethren, a moment when we may need to choose which way to go. I see more persecution ahead for all of us. We will be tested to the very far reaches of our faith. I see — God has revealed this to me in His most infinite wisdom — that a time may come when He will call upon us to ascend to heaven, even before the end of days, to stand beside Him in His glory."

People shifted in their seats. Someone cleared his throat.

"Yes, He has revealed this plan to me. And I am so grateful for His eternal wisdom and for His guidance through these challenging times."

"Amen," someone said.

"Yes, amen. Let us pray."

FORTY-FIVE

Beau's phone dinged with incoming messages his whole way back to Nakusp. Every time he went through an area with cell signal, his phone lit up with new information. The avalanche had begun, and it was burying Grace DeRoche. He wished he felt better about it. He wished he could reach Shelby to make sure she was okay, but she wasn't answering her phone. As he passed through Kamloops, he called Doug for an update.

"Good news, bad news," Doug said without preamble. "The stun gun you found in Grace's closet doesn't have any usable fingerprints or DNA. But the make and model do match the marks on Tabitha Johnson's chest. Also, there were latent prints found in Tabitha's bedroom that don't match Tabitha or her roommate. We'll compare them to Grace DeRoche's fingerprints once we've got them. We've also got some hair pulled from Rulon Smith's backpack, so we'll have that for a DNA comparison. Where are you?"

"Kamloops."

"Right. Keep in touch."

He tried Shelby again. Still no answer.

By the time he reached Revelstoke, the arrest warrant had been issued and RCMP officers were en route to set up a perimeter surveillance.

"Now I would have authorized a flight," Doug said. "How's your ass?"

Beau snorted and hung up. His ass was screaming, and sciatica sizzled down the side of his leg.

He called in again as he stood stretching at the Shelter Bay ferry terminal, waiting to cross Upper Arrow Lake.

"Perimeter's been established. Grace's vehicle is parked in the driveway," Doug said.

"Just the one vehicle? There should also be a Jeep Cherokee belonging to her therapist."

"Let me double-check." Doug clicked off and came back a minute later. "Nope. Just the one vehicle."

Damn. Where had Shelby gone? He dialed her number yet again. This time, it went straight to voice mail without even ringing. If something had happened to her, he'd never forgive himself.

He met Officers Fellner and Bouchard at the bottom of Hot Springs Road. As he stepped out of the vehicle, Bouchard nodded.

"Perimeter was established almost two hours ago. The forest surrounding the house is clear."

Fellner jumped in. "Someone's kicked dirt over the campsite since we were there."

Bouchard said, "There's been no movement from the house since we arrived, except for Fellner's goats."

Officer Fellner rolled his eyes.

"All right. Officer Bouchard, will you back me on the arrest? Officer Fellner —"

"Yep. I'll join the perimeter team."

Bouchard said, "We've got another female officer up there right now who can assist with the arrest."

"Good. Let's get moving."

With teams in place, Beau moved in on Grace's home with Officer Bouchard and Officer Westlake, who looked like she was in her early twenties at most.

There was no answer to his knock. No dog barking.

He rang the doorbell again, hammered his fist against the door. "Grace DeRoche? It's Detective Brunelli. There's been a warrant issued for your arrest. Open the door, please."

He went through the whole thing again, with the same results.

"We have an officer standing by with a Halligan bar," Bouchard said.

"Yep. Let's do it."

He stepped back while the officer popped open the door, and then moved into the kitchen with Bouchard and Westlake behind him. They cleared each room. The house was empty.

As they exited the house, Bouchard's radio crackled to life.

"Blue Subaru turning into the driveway."

Officers swarmed, surrounding the vehicle as it pulled into the clearing. It skidded to a stop, and the driver's hands lifted into the air. One officer stepped forward, gun raised, and ordered the driver out of the vehicle.

Jack Fletcher climbed out and lifted his hands above his head. The officer stepped forward and gave him a pat-down.

"He's clear," the officer said as Beau approached.

"Hi, Jack. What are you doing here?"

Jack turned to him with wide eyes. "Grace asked me to take care of the goats."

"You can put your hands down now. Why does she need your help with the goats?"

"She called me this morning and asked if I could take care of them for a few days. I've done that for her before, when she's away."

"Do you know where she went?"

"To Vancouver. To see her sister."

"Her car's still here. Did she fly?"

"She said her therapist was going with her." Fletcher shrugged. "I guess they took her car."

Beau moved away and tried Shelby's cell. Once again, it went straight to voice mail.

"Hey, what's going on? Is Grace in trouble?" Fletcher asked.

Ignoring the question, he placed a call to Doug so he could issue a BOLO for Shelby's vehicle.

Moving back to Fletcher, he said, "Jack, could you come into the station to answer some questions?"

Fletcher placed a hand against his chest. "Am *I* in trouble?"

"Not at all," Beau said. "But you might have information that can help."

Fletcher agreed to head down to the station after he'd fed the goats, and the officers cleared off.

As Bouchard drove him down the hill to his car, he scrolled through his inbox. Maybe Shelby had sent him an email.

She hadn't, but Grace had sent him a video.

When Bouchard pulled over in front of his car, he said, "Will you hold tight for a minute?"

"Sure thing."

Beau hopped out and climbed into his own car. The video image was an upward shot of trees and slivers of blue sky. He tapped play. The wheel spun and spun as the video loaded.

The camera panned down, and Grace's face filled the frame. Her eyes were wide and round, her face somehow plump and youthful.

She was no longer Grace. She was a young child. "Detective? Hi. I'm Harris."

She turned her head to the side as though checking her surroundings. Turning back to the camera, she said, "I did something really, really bad. And I need your help."

He played the video twice before forwarding it to Doug along with several requests. Within a minute, he received a thumbs-up emoji in return.

He stepped out of his car and moved toward Bouchard's. "Can you take lead on questioning Jack Fletcher when he comes in?" He laid out the questions he wanted her to cover.

"You've got it. Where are you running off to?"

"Nelson, for starters."

FORTY-SIX

The pregnancy seemed to be sticking this time, and Grace had never felt so nauseous in all her life. She hadn't yet told Boydell, but she could see from the way he kept examining her from the corner of his eye, and from the gentleness with which he was currently treating her, that he suspected she was once again with child.

He didn't argue when she told him she was going up the road to visit her mother, and even that was unusual. She hoped Mother had brewed the ginger tea she'd promised after temple. Hopefully she'd stuck it in the fridge to chill, as well.

The day was stifling and humid, and even the mosquitos moved slowly. She swatted them away as she lumbered up the road, smashing one against the back of a hand beaded with sweat. Her temple undergarments clung damply to her, making her itch. What she wouldn't have given to strip down and jump into a tub of cool water.

She could hear them yelling inside the house while she was still on the road. It was Sariah and Mother Rebecca for the most part, but Mother's and Father's voices joined in occasionally, as well. Tabby sat curled on the porch stairs, her hands pressed against her face.

She placed a hand on Tabby's shoulder. "Hey. What's going on?"

Tabby looked up, her cheeks streaked with tears. "Sariah told them."

Inside the house, Mother Rebecca screamed something unintelligible, and Sariah wailed.

"Told them what?"

Tabby wiped away a fresh slew of tears and mucus. "About Uncle G."

"I don't understand. *What* about Uncle G?"

Tabby gave her a disbelieving look. "You know. How he touches us."

Her legs grew weak, and she flopped down on the stairs beside Tabby. Her good ear buzzed. "What?"

"I told her she shouldn't tell. Now she'll get even more corrections." Tabby sobbed into her hands.

Grace sat beside Tabby for several minutes, listening to her cry while she took deep breaths and fought with her own mind to stay present. The yelling continued inside the house, but with the buzzing in her ear she couldn't pick up enough of what they were saying for it to make sense.

When she felt calmer, she pulled herself to her feet and entered the house. Sariah and Desiree huddled together on the couch, their arms wrapped around each other and their faces mottled with tears.

"This is outrageous! It's blasphemous!" Mother Rebecca paced back and forth, her broad skirt swishing from side to side. Her cheeks were bright red with indignation, and even her hair seemed angry. It bounced free of its pins as though electrified.

Sariah wailed, and Desiree's arms tightened around her. Desiree was the first to spot Grace standing by the door, and she motioned for her to come over.

She moved past Mother Rebecca and sat beside Sariah. Her youngest sister flung herself on top of her and sobbed into the folds of her dress.

"Grace," Father said, "now's not the best time."

"I'm still part of this family, aren't I?"

Desiree said, "Father, she's telling the truth. Grace, tell them."

All three adults turned to look at her. Grace opened her mouth, but nothing came out.

Desiree gave her a desperate look. "Go on, Grace. Tell them what Uncle G does. Tell them how he touches us."

She shook her head. "I'm sorry, I don't —"

Sariah looked up. "She doesn't remember. She always goes away when it happens."

"What do you mean?" Mother said.

Sariah wiped an arm across her nose and shrugged.

Desiree leaned forward. "It doesn't matter. She's st-still telling the truth. I sw-swear. I sw-swear on the life of the prophet. May God st-strike him down if I'm lying."

Mother gasped. Mother Rebecca's mouth fell open with shock.

"Desiree!" Father shouted.

Rather than looking chastened, Desiree lifted her chin defiantly into the air as though sure that such a bold statement would convince them she was telling the truth.

Grace's mind spun in turmoil. She looked from one mother to the other.

Mother Rebecca was red as a tomato, her hands pressed against her hips. She looked furious, but she didn't look disbelieving. And Mother stood there with an expression on her face that was all too familiar. Her skin was pale, her jaw was tight, and her eyes were glassy with denial.

The truth hit her in the gut like one of Boydell's fists.

"He's done it to both of you, too."

All eyes turned to her.

"You both knew. You've always known. Because he touched you, too."

Mother put a hand across her mouth, shaking her head.

Mother Rebecca snorted. "Don't be ridiculous."

"It's not ridiculous." Grace unearthed herself from under her sister and stood up. At eighteen she was taller than Mother Rebecca and the same height as her mother. She stared them down, woman to women. "It's not ridiculous *at all*. You sent us to him for lessons, for corrections, even though you *knew* what he was doing to us. You knew because he'd done it to you, too. And yet you still sent us."

There was a deep well of silence, and then Father stepped forward.

"These accusations are ... *horrid*. I just don't believe it." He shook his head. "No. He is our bishop. He is a holy man, a man God entrusts with His good word."

Grace reached for him, the man who for thirteen years had been her hero, her safety net, and her priesthood head. "Father, please —"

"No, Grace. We will not speak of this again. Not in this house, not anywhere. Do you understand?" He pointed a finger at each of his daughters in turn, and then at both his wives. "Mother Rebecca is right. This is blasphemy. Our good bishop says we'll face enormous tests to our faith. And maybe this is one of mine."

Desiree stood up. "But Father —"

"No, Desiree. Not ever again." Father turned and stomped out of the house, slamming the door behind him.

In the wake of his departure, nobody spoke. After several moments, Mother pressed a handkerchief to her mouth and went back to the kitchen. Mother Rebecca walked stiffly from the room, and her bedroom door closed with a soft click.

"But I told the truth." Sariah's voice wobbled with tears. "Why didn't they believe me?"

Desiree pulled Sariah to her feet. "Come on, let's get out of here."

When they left the house, Tabby was gone.

"Let's go to the fields," Grace said.

They walked slowly, their arms around each other. The fields were the only place in Brigham with enough privacy to talk freely. No one could sneak up on them, unlike the forest where people could hide amongst the trees. Grace had learned that lesson well enough.

They settled under the scarecrow. It provided only a sliver of shade, not enough to stop them from baking in the late afternoon sun.

"I think she's old enough to be trusted," Desiree said.

"Yes." Grace took one of Sariah's hands, and Desiree took the other. "Sariah, I'm going to tell you something really important, but you have to swear that you'll keep it a secret."

. . .

The car rattled and bumped, jostling her back and forth in the seat. Grace moaned and turned her head. She tried to pry her eyes open, to see where they were, but she was just so tired. Sleep was a weight, it seemed, and she was pinned underneath it.

The tires spun against gravel. She could hear the ping and clank of tiny rocks hitting the undercarriage.

Where were they? She tried to ask the question out loud, but her mouth wouldn't move.

She sank beneath the surface, and there was no lamplight or Mother waiting to tuck her in. There was nothing but darkness.

FORTY-SEVEN

Beau pulled into Nelson as the sun hit that late afternoon angle meant to blind unsuspecting drivers. He slowed down, squinting as he adjusted the visor.

He pulled to a stop across the street from Shelby's house. The windows looked dark, and her Jeep Cherokee was missing from the driveway. Nevertheless, he climbed the steps and rang the doorbell. He turned the handle and gave a hard pull, but the door was locked. Well, it was worth a try.

He edged around the side of the house to the backyard, which fronted onto the lake. The deck overlooking the water was up a floor. He saw wicker furniture and colourful cushions. He craned his neck, trying to get a peek into the kitchen windows. He could see the corner of the fridge. Everything else was dark. And there were no easy points of entry for him to entertain, either. Damn.

Moving back around the front of the house, he stood in the driveway and debated what to do. The garage door was an old roll-up. He could jam a crowbar under it and give a good yank, and he'd be in business. Instead, he crossed the street and slid behind the wheel of his car.

Doug called as he was buckling his seat belt. "You in Nelson?"

"Yeah, boss."

"We've got Shelby Jacobs."

"Is she with Grace?"

"No, no, sorry. The BOLO's out, but no word yet. I meant we've got her records. Born at BC Children's May 10, 1990. Mother father older brother, blah blah blah, not important right now. Did an undergrad at Capilano University, got her degree in psychology from UBC. Moved up to Nelson to take over the practice of a Dr. Goldberg —"

"Yeah, okay. That all sounds right."

"Right. Here's where it gets interesting. I spoke to the brother, and man, did he have a lot to say. But the gist of it is this: The entire family is pretty messed up. Dad ran off and shacked up with someone new, and naturally wanted nothing to do with any of them anymore. Mom took to drink."

"That computes. She said her family had issues."

"The brother says he hasn't heard from his sister in over two years, and as far as he knows Mom and Dad haven't, either. He didn't seem too concerned, but when I pressed he did say it's not typical of her. Apparently she's the peacekeeper of the bunch."

"Hmm."

"On a hunch, I asked him to email me a recent photo. It should be sitting in your inbox."

"Hang on, I'm putting you on speaker. Still with me?"

"Yep."

"All right, it's downloading." He tapped his fingers against his thigh and listened to Doug breathing on the other end of the line. "Oh shit. Who's that?"

"Shelby Jacobs."

The girl in the photo had a cloud of red hair and a broad, freckled face.

"That's not the Shelby Jacobs I know."

"Hot damn, I knew it."

Beau scrubbed a hand across his stubble. "So, who the hell did I meet?"

"I'm not sure. But I suspect Shelby Jacobs — the *real* Shelby Jacobs, that is — might have met a bad end."

"Holy mother of — hang on." He opened the car door.

"What are you doing?" Doug asked.

"Satisfying my curiosity. I'll be right back."

He pulled the crowbar from the trunk of his car and moved down the driveway. He jammed it under the garage door and gave a hard push. The lock popped, and he rolled up the door. A blue Subaru Forester exactly like Grace's sat in the garage.

He snagged his phone from the seat. "Doug? Still with me?"

"Still here."

"Can you get me a search warrant?" He told him what he'd found and rattled off the address.

Doug clicked off and Beau sat chewing his nails for thirty-five minutes until his boss called back.

"You're a go on the search warrant. Your team is on the way."

FORTY-EIGHT

race's head pounded as though someone had driven a nail through the top of her skull. She groaned and pried her eyes open. Her lashes were crusted together like that time she'd had an eye infection. She blinked to clear her vision. Wherever she was, it was dark and it smelled of mould and rat droppings.

She lay flat on her back on a soft surface, maybe a bed.

No. Wait. She couldn't move. Her heart kicked up to a roar, pumping blood and adrenaline through her system. She tried to sit up, and when that didn't work, she twisted from side to side.

She was strapped down. Wide bands of fabric pressed across her chest, torso, and hips. Metal flanked her wrists and ankles.

Oh my God, we're shackled.

Where was she? And what in the world was going on?

She turned her head to the side, searching the darkness. There was a door to the right. It was open a crack, and dim light came from the other side. It shone just enough to reveal a bedside table and the curved edge of a knotted rug on the floor.

We're home.

It couldn't be true, could it? She closed her eyes, whimpering. Her ear buzzed. She opened her eyes and once again saw the bedside table and the knotted rug. To the left was a window. The curtain had fallen down on one side to reveal a triangle of darkness beyond.

There was no denying it. She was in her childhood bedroom. She was in her childhood home.

She was in Brigham.

Her ear crackled with electricity, and she was shoved from the frontspace. She flew back toward Mother and the lamplight. But this time she dug in imaginary fingernails. *No. I need to stay.*

It's okay. We will protect you.

Once again, she was knocked back into the darkness. Ahead she saw the lamplight. *No. No! Not this time.*

She skidded to a stop, turned toward the front, and pulled herself forward. *This is my head. I'm staying.*

This is our head, too. You are not you without we.

But after a moment the *we* part of her mind stepped aside, allowing Grace to move into the driver's seat. *Thank you.*

We are here.

All right. She took a deep breath, and then another. How was it possible that she was here? What had happened?

Her mind was so fuzzy, like it was stuffed with cotton balls. She remembered being in the forest with Bella. And then Shelby called out, looking for her.

We wanted to go to Desiree. And Shelby said she would come with us.

Right. She'd called Jack to take care of the goats and packed a bag for her and Bella, while Shelby made tea.

She insisted on making us that tea before we left.

And she'd insisted on driving.

Yes. In case we wanted to rest.

She'd put the travel mug of tea in Grace's cupholder, and she'd said …

Drink up, buttercup.

But why? Why would her therapist do this to her?

Bella barked somewhere outside. Grace craned her neck, turning her good ear toward the window. She knew her dog well enough to decipher different tones in her bark. This one was higher-pitched and desperate. It meant she was trapped somewhere — the goat shed, if it was still standing? — and wanted to get out.

She dropped her head back, her eyes filling with tears. Poor Bella must have been so scared.

"Oh, good, you're up. I thought I heard you whimpering in here."

Shelby pushed open the bedroom door. She held a propane lantern that lit her face from underneath, like a child about to tell a ghost story. She plunked the lantern on the bedside table and turned the dial to light up the room. Grace squinted.

"That's better." Shelby dragged in a kitchen chair, dusted it off with a tissue, and sat down. "Well, hi."

She waited as if she expected Grace to answer. When she didn't, Shelby waved her arms around and said, "And here we are."

Outside, the dog barked and howled.

"Bella?"

"She's fine. But it's nice to see you caring about something other than yourself. That's progress."

"What are we doing here?"

"Oh, yeah." Shelby looked around, wrinkled her nose. "Gross. This place is ready for the blowtorch, don't you think?"

"But why are we here?"

"Still haven't figured it out, huh?" Shelby shook her head. "Always caught up in that party going on inside your head. All those people pushing around in there trying to find some space, it must be distracting. But it's also made you unobservant, Gracey."

It had been many years since someone had called her by her childhood nickname, and the way it rolled off Shelby's lips sent a thrill of fear from her scalp to her toes. "Okay. What did I miss?"

Shelby laughed. "What *didn't* you miss? That would be a shorter list. And it's funny. It's *really* funny. I always expected you to figure it out at some point. I kept waiting for it. Every day, every session, I'd be thinking, is today the day she finally sees?"

"Sees what?"

Shelby blinked. Looked at her. "Sees *me*, of course."

"You?"

Her cheeks went pink and she slammed a fist against her thigh. "Me! Me-me-*me*."

"I'm sorry," Grace said.

Shelby let out a great gust of air. "You still don't see, do you? Even now, even *here*, you don't see me. You never did. It was always Father this and Mother that and oh, poor Desiree with her stupid little stutter. But you never saw me." She banged her hands against her chest. "Hair dye and coloured contacts. I couldn't believe that's all it took."

She pulled up each eyelid and plucked out her contacts. She flicked them into the air, two glistening brown circles that caught for a moment in the lamplight. She stood up and bent close, shoving her face right in front of Grace's. Her eyes were now blue, the sweetest blue Grace had ever seen.

"Now do you see?"

"Oh my God."

Her round cherub features had chiselled with age, and her curls were black instead of pale brown. But the blue of her eyes and the pink bow of her lips ... those were still the same.

"Amazing grace," she sang, "how sweet the sound, that saved a wretch like me."

Her voice still reminded Grace of birdsong. She remembered how it had risen above the choir's as though winning the race to heaven.

She hadn't seen what was right in front of her eyes. It was true. Maybe she *was* distracted and selfish. Or maybe it was because the last time Grace saw her, she was only nine years old. And she'd died with the rest of Brigham at the age of eleven. Or so Grace had thought.

"I once was lost, but now I'm found. Was blind, but now I see."

"Sariah," Grace said.

She grinned. "Surprise, my sweet sister."

FORTY-NINE

Beau worked through the night with the forensics team and came away with a lot of circumstantial evidence but no clearer idea of who the imposter pretending to be Shelby Jacobs might be.

The most interesting thing they found were several handwritten notes in her office. It reminded him of the night he'd walked her home, after he'd kissed her. There'd been a note waiting on the mat inside the front door, which she'd told him was from a former patient of Dr. Goldberg's.

To his untrained eye, the handwriting looked similar to that of the letters they'd found in Tabitha Johnson's dresser.

I see you, said one. The next said *I'm watching you*, and the third said *I know who you are.*

He waited until seven to call his boss, but Doug sounded like he'd been awake for hours. He filled him in on what they'd found, then asked, "Any hits on the BOLO?"

"Not a one," Doug said. "The hospital is on high alert, but so far Desiree hasn't had any visitors."

"How's she doing?"

"Status quo. She woke up just long enough to give the forensics team the okay, so they were able to do their thing. Haven't heard anything more about the mark on her arm yet, but I'll let you know."

Beau rubbed his eyes, which were gritty and dry. "They should have made it to Vancouver long before now."

"Yep."

"So, where the hell are they?"

"Hang tight, Beau. This one's coming together."

"Hopefully it does before someone else dies."

"Update on the compound outside Medicine Hat," Doug said. "The drones have captured photos of women wearing prairie dresses, so we're pretty certain we're dealing with FLDS."

"I sense a 'but.'"

"Could be. There's new intel from the FBI. They believe these folks escaped the YFZ Ranch after Jeffs was arrested, and made their way across the border with financial help from family in Hildale and Colorado City. But it's still possible Gideon Smith is there, too."

"Hmm."

"Get some rest. I'll call you the moment there's a new development."

Beau checked into the same hotel he'd stayed in on his previous trip to Nelson, closed the blackout curtains, and was asleep before his head hit the pillow. Emily waited for him in the sunshine, the cherry blossoms dancing around her head.

The phone startled him upright some unknown time later. His heart gave a sickening squeeze inside his chest. "Yeah?"

"Rise and shine," Doug said. "You awake? I'm patching someone through to you, but make it quick. You're getting the helicopter for this one."

"What?"

Doug was gone. There were several beeps, followed by a screech of interference that made him wince and pull the phone away from his ear.

He heard the sound of traffic, and a car horn beeping. And then a man said, "Hello?"

"Yeah, hi. Detective Brunelli with the RCMP. Who's this?"

"This is Clayne. Clayne Johnson? I'm one of the kids from Brigham —"

Holy shit. "I know who you are."

"Oh. Okay, good. You know Grace? Grace DeRoche?"

"Yeah, I do. What's going on, Clayne?"

"I think she's going to kill her. She's killed others, too. I think. I mean, I don't know for sure —"

"Who, Grace?"

"No, no. Not Grace. Her sister."

Desiree? But that made no sense, Desiree was currently unconscious in the ICU at VGH, and ...

He thought back to her hospital room, to how hard Desiree had been trying to communicate with him. To how she'd struggled over her *S* sound. He'd filled it in for her, asking if she was trying to say the word *sister*. And she'd nodded, but she'd never actually said Grace's name, a name that was much easier for her to say. He'd just assumed he understood, and he knew what Doug would say about that.

"Are you talking about Sariah? Are you saying she's alive?"

"Pretty sure it's her. I've been watching her for a few months now. And Grace, too. I mean, it started with Grace. I wanted to make sure she was okay. I was working up my nerve to go talk to her, but then I saw this woman with her, and I knew something wasn't right. So, I started following *her*, watching where she went —"

"Clayne. Where are you?"

"Fort Steele. I followed them. But I don't have a cell. That's how people track you, you know. So I had to come back here to find a pay phone so I could let someone know. I'm heading back there now, but I just —"

He knew the answer, but he asked anyway. "Where did Sariah take her?"

"To Brigham. She brought her home."

FIFTY

"You left me."

"Oh, Sariah, no —"

Tears streamed down Sariah's cheeks. "You left me. All of you did. After you promised. After you sat under the scarecrow with me and we made a pact."

"We couldn't find you."

"I was right behind you! You didn't even look. I got to the scarecrow late, because Father left the house with me and took me partway across the field. He was watching, so I had to keep going all the way to the forest and then sneak back from a different direction. I could see you all up ahead of me. Running. Holding hands. I kept screaming for you to wait up, but you just —" She waved an arm. "Kept going. Buh-bye, sis. Probably won't write."

Tears burned in Grace's eyes. "I'm sorry."

Sariah snorted. "Yeah. You're sorry. Do you have any idea what it was like around here after you guys escaped?"

She could only imagine. She'd *tried* to imagine. But whatever she'd come up with probably fell way short of reality.

"For two years I waited for you to come get me. Every day and every night for *two years*." She wiped a hand across her eyes, giving a humourless laugh. "I was so stupid! I believed that you would come. I believed that you'd find a way to rescue me. I believed that you *cared*."

"I did care," Grace said.

"No. No! Don't you say that to me. Don't you lie to me. Did you ever even *try* to save me? Or did you just go on with your life, never giving me a thought?"

"We were waiting for the trial. For the legal —"

"Two years, Grace. *Two years* of Uncle G's corrections. *Two years* of watching him get crazier and crazier because of what you did, *two years* of him shouting about the 'investigation' and the 'police scrutiny' and the 'persecution.' *Two years* in this fanatical hellhole."

Sariah pointed in the direction of the temple at the top of the hill, her face twisted with fury and grief. "We had to pray for eight or ten or sometimes even twelve hours a day. He'd go on for hours about taking us all to heaven before the police came to get us. And did you think everyone died that one day, when we got word that the prophet was arrested?"

Of course, she *had* thought that.

"He sent 'scouts' ahead of us. Time after time, he stood up there on the pulpit and said he'd had yet another revelation. God needed another man up there to help him prepare for the end of days. And then he'd point to someone."

"Oh my God."

"There is no God, Gracey. If there was, He would have stopped it."

"I'm so sorry —"

Sariah scrubbed a hand across her wet cheek. She looked out the window in the direction of the temple, but Grace thought she saw something far more distant.

"The elders went first. Uncle Redd. Joseph Barlow. Father."

"No."

"Uncle G promised he would take care of their families and bring us with him up to heaven. He made them bear witness while he 'took ownership' of their wives. He took our mothers, too. And the men consented. They kissed his hand. They drank the poison he gave them."

"Father?"

She turned back to Grace. "He *smiled* at us as he lifted the bottle to his lips."

Tears blinded her, and her chest ached so much she couldn't catch a breath. "Oh, Sariah."

"But really, Father was already gone. We lost him the same day we lost you and Desiree and all the rest. It just took longer for his body to catch up."

"What about our mothers?"

Sariah's voice was soft with grief. "They died as Smiths. Most of the women did."

"I'm so sorry," Grace said.

"You're sorry. Yeah. I dug my *own grave*." Sariah bowed forward until her forehead touched her knees and she keened against the denim.

Tears burned rivers down Grace's temples to her hairline, and filled her nose with so much mucus she had to open her mouth to gasp for breath. The grief was a weight on her chest, so heavy she expected it to push her straight through the bed and the floorboards below until it buried her in the dirt. And surely that's where she belonged.

They stayed that way for hours or minutes, lost in their grief. Eventually Sariah pulled herself upright. She wiped her eyes and blew her nose with a tissue she pulled from her pocket.

"How did you escape?" Grace asked.

Sariah shrugged. "I just didn't drink it. I took my cup like all the rest. I climbed down into the hole and sat beside my mother. But when the time came, I only pretended to drink."

"Uncle G," Grace said. "They didn't find his body."

Sariah's mouth twisted with bitterness. "Apparently he had the same idea I did. I lay there with my eyes closed, waiting, listening as everyone …" She cleared her throat. "I waited until everything was quiet. And I was just about to sit up when I heard this grunting noise. I opened one eye and saw him climbing out of the hole. You know, he didn't even look back down at us. He just left."

"So, he's still alive."

Sariah smiled. "Oh, no. He didn't make it another forty-eight hours."

"What did you do?"

"I followed him into the mountains. He was old. Clumsy. And the ground was icy and slippery. All I had to do was wait until he was beside a really steep drop-off. I snuck up behind him and screamed." She snorted a laugh. "You should have seen the look on his face as he fell. It was amazing. But you know what? It wasn't enough. I hope he's burning in hell when I get there, so I can stick a pitchfork in his fat, lying face."

"My God."

"I already told you, there is no God. If there were, He would have taken mercy on me long ago."

Sariah leaned forward in the chair, wedging her elbows against her thighs. Her voice went as sweet as syrup. "But after that everything got better. This really nice family adopted me. They gave me all the love and nurturing I deserved —"

"Really?"

Sariah walloped Grace across the face so hard her vision went temporarily white.

"Hell, no! I only made it two weeks before I got picked up by some pedo outside Calgary and forced into his sex-trafficking ring. And thanks to Uncle G, I was what they call a *skilled recruit*. I was with them for nine years before I stabbed the guy in the neck and made my escape, and I swear, the only thing that kept me alive was thinking about what I'd do to the ten of you once I got free. I mean, I planned this whole thing *for years*. I played the long game. Hunted each of you down, learned about your lives. But I couldn't figure out how to get close enough to that freaky little brain of yours. I knew all those people you had hiding inside you were the key to everything. And then your therapist hired a replacement so he could retire, and poof! I got my opportunity."

Sariah scrubbed a hand across her cheek and laughed. "I studied so much psychology I practically earned my own doctorate. But it was worth it." She leaned close and gazed into Grace's eyes, allowing Grace to see the monster she'd become. "It was all worth it."

"Did you kill the others? Rulon and Eliza and Valor? Did you kill Tabby?"

"Not all of them. I didn't have to. Once we'd talked, once they truly understood what they'd done" — she shrugged — "they made their own choices."

"They killed themselves. I have trouble believing that."

Sariah shook her head. "Valor and Tabby needed an extra ... push. But Eliza and Rulon understood. They knew there was only one way to atone for what they'd done to me."

"And Desiree?"

She sighed. "I didn't do such a good job there, I guess. But yeah, Desiree wasn't so convinced." She leaned forward and stroked the hair back from Grace's forehead. Her hand smelled like dirt. "I'm hoping you'll do better."

"If you think I'm going to help you murder me, you're crazy."

Sariah cocked her head to the side, continued to stroke Grace's hair. "But you've already been so helpful, haven't you, Harris?"

"What?"

"Such a good priesthood child, such a good little helper."

Her ear buzzed. "I don't understand, what did he ... what did *we* do?"

She smiled. "Oh, nothing too much. Just wrote some notes for me, put your DNA a couple places, stuff like that."

"But why?"

"Why did he help me?" Sariah shrugged. "Guess he wanted to help a sister out. Or do you mean, why did I use him? That's pretty obvious, don't you think?"

"To set us up."

"Well done, Gracey. That whole murder-suicide thing is very on trend at the moment."

"You're completely crazy."

Sariah laughed. "More ironic words were never spoken, dear sister, but I accept your accusation. After all, if you don't know crazy, then who does? Wow, just digging around in that wackadoodle head of yours was quite the thrill ride. And it's funny, I think I helped you." She shrugged. "Turns out I'm a pretty good therapist. It's just too bad I had to speed things up because I was actually starting to enjoy myself."

"What do you mean?"

"That detective made me nervous." Sariah waved a hand in dismissal. "But it's all right. Four out of ten ain't bad. And you'll bring it up to an even half. I think I can live with that."

Sariah stood up and stretched. Her vertebrae popped and she gave a satisfied moan. "Well, good talk, sweet sister. I've got some more digging to do before I'm ready for you" — she turned back in the doorway — "and I know you're a bit out of practice, but I'd imagine you've got some praying to do? You know, atoning for your sins, getting right with God, all that good stuff. I'll leave you to it." She blew Grace a kiss as she left.

The light shone through the triangle of window when Sariah came back. Grace thought it was maybe midafternoon.

She pushed a wheelchair through the door and wrinkled her nose. "Whew! It smells like pee in here. I guess I forgot to give you a potty break, didn't I?"

"Sariah, please don't —"

"Nope. Don't bother trying, Gracey. I'm not in a listening mood." Sariah ripped off the three straps holding her to the bed, and then pulled a small black object out of her pocket. "All right, this might hurt. But only a little bit, so don't be scared."

"What —"

Sariah held the thing to her chest, and all coherent thought ceased. Every muscle and tendon in her body convulsed, squeezed, shook, and then went flaccid and useless.

"Four ... five ... six. That should do it." Sariah pulled back and tucked the device into her pocket. "How are you feeling?"

She couldn't move, she couldn't speak, she couldn't think.

"Oh, perfect. Let's get going, then."

Sariah slid the wheelchair up to the bed and undid her shackles. She grunted and groaned as she pulled Grace's helpless body across the bed to the wheelchair.

Once she'd gotten her seated, Sariah put her hands on her hips and took several gasping breaths. "Damn, you're heavy. All right, we're almost there."

She unhooked the shackles and wove them through the wheelchair's frame, then clicked them back into place around Grace's wrists and ankles.

"Shall we take a stroll up memory lane?"

Sariah pushed her down the hall and out the front door. She'd placed a large piece of plywood over the stairs, creating a steep ramp. "Hold on tight, Gracey." The wheelchair flew down the ramp and almost tipped over in the yard, but Sariah caught its handles and held it steady.

She giggled. "Well, that was fun."

Up the gravel road they went, the wheelchair swaying in one direction or the other as Sariah struggled to push it over the uneven ground. The wheels bogged down time and again. She panted and grunted, pushing the wheelchair out of one rut after another. Grace's mind was coming back to her, although her body was still out of the equation.

Brigham fell down around them, returning to the land. The remnants of fences stood like broken teeth, windows were shattered, doors hung open, and siding had fallen away in chunks. But at the top of the hill the temple and the Smith home still stood, dirt-covered but solid.

"Welcome home, Gracey."

Above their heads, birds circled and called out to them in song, and Sariah's voice rose to meet them. "'Twas grace that taught my heart to fear, and grace my fears relieved. How precious did that grace appear, the hour I first believed."

Tears leaked from Grace's eyes, making tracks on her cheeks that she could barely feel. Sariah panted between each verse, but continued to sing as she pushed her up the hill. She got her up the last steep incline and around the temple to the cemetery that lay behind it.

There were so many tiny tombstones back there, falling over with time and neglect. Beside them stood a giant mound of earth upon which the grass refused to grow, as though the poisoned bones that lay beneath couldn't sustain life. The mass grave.

Above them, the crags of the Rocky Mountains glistened with fresh snow. But down below, the sun warmed their shoulders with the last kiss of fall.

Grace could move her fingers in her lap, but that was it.

Sariah's voice rose in song toward the jagged peaks of the mountains and the blue sky above them. "Yea, when this flesh and heart shall fail, and mortal life shall cease, I shall possess within the veil, a life of joy and peace."

She squatted in front of the wheelchair, bringing her face level with Grace's. "I had to dig my own grave. But don't worry, Gracey. I won't make you dig yours."

She pointed at the jagged hole in front of them. The dirt mounded to the side was richly black and fertile.

"See? I already dug it for you." She stroked the hair away from Grace's forehead. "After all, what are sisters for?"

She still couldn't move anything but her fingers.

"Oh, Gracey, don't cry." Sariah wiped the tears from her cheeks. "You know, it turns out there was a lot of bullshit in the doctrine they taught us when we were kids. *A lot* of bullshit." She shook her head. "But there were a few nuggets of truth in there, too. Like that bit about blood atonements. Because sometimes you do something that's just so *bad*, and the only way to show you're sorry is to spill your own blood."

She pulled a small glass bottle from the pocket of her jeans and held it up in front of Grace's eyes. "But you're my sister, and I just can't stand the idea of seeing you suffer like that. So, all you need to do is take a few tiny little sips."

She uncorked the bottle and took a sniff. "It doesn't smell great. Do you want me to plug your nose like our mothers used to do when we had to take nasty medicine?"

Sariah held the bottle toward Grace's mouth and pressed her nostrils closed with the other hand.

Grace's ear screeched, and dozens of voices rose inside her head. Everyone shouted, drowning each other out and creating a cacophony of noise. But one voice rose clear above all the rest. It was Xander, her most loyal protector.

Go on now, Gracey. Mother's waiting to tuck you in.

"No!"

At first she thought it was the Grace part of her mind that had cried out. But Sariah's head flew up, her eyes wide and startled. She spun away from Grace, and a few drops spilled from the bottle onto Grace's lap.

"Back away, Sariah."

It was a man's voice, and not one that lived inside her head. He stepped forward. She could just barely see him out of the corner of her eye. He was tall and blond.

From a distance came the steady beat of an approaching helicopter. Moments later, it was joined by the wail of sirens.

Sariah froze, looking from the man to Grace and back again. Then she seemed to come to a decision. She bent down in front of the wheelchair. Her eyes were the sweetest blue Grace had ever seen. Sariah leaned forward and kissed her on the lips, stroked the hair away from her forehead. And then, like their father had done many years before, she smiled and lifted the bottle to her own lips.

FIFTY-ONE

As the helicopter lowered to the ground, Beau saw the plywood ramp covering the stairs of the abandoned DeRoche home. He saw the double wheel ruts leading up the road toward the temple. Were they from a wheelchair?

As soon as the helicopter touched down, he threw himself out the door and ran full bore up the gravel road toward the temple, following the wheel ruts and scanning his surroundings as he went. Where were they? Inside the temple? In the Smiths' house next door?

Emergency vehicles rolled up the road behind him, their sirens blaring. From somewhere ahead he heard shouting. Of course! They were in the cemetery behind the temple.

"Back away, Sariah!" A man's voice.

Beau skidded along gravel, banged a shoulder into the corner of the building, and kept going.

He rounded the corner just as Shelby — *Sariah* — bent to kiss Grace on the lips and stroke the hair from her forehead. Grace was strapped into a wheelchair, shackled at wrists and ankles. A freshly dug hole lay in front of her, the dirt piled to the side. A man stood between two rows of tombstones, aiming a deer rifle in Sariah's direction.

Sariah smiled and lifted a glass bottle to her mouth. Beau launched himself forward, hurdling one tombstone and then another.

"No!" Grace's voice sounded garbled and strange, like she'd had a stroke.

Ignoring her, Sariah tilted her head back and drained the bottle in one gulp. Beau rammed into her from the side, and the bottle dropped from her hands and shattered against the rocky ground.

He caught her as she fell and lowered himself to the ground, cradling her in his arms. He could hear emergency vehicles stopping on the other side of the temple.

"What was in the bottle? What did you drink?" he said.

She looked up at him with wide blue eyes, and her lips curled into a smile. "Oh, hi, Beau."

"Damn it, Shelby! What was in that bottle?"

"My name's …" A tremor ran through her body. "Sariah."

From the corner of his eye, he saw paramedics approaching. She saw them, too.

"Tell them … not to bother."

He stroked the curls back from her forehead and saw the pale brown hair at her roots. "Sariah —"

"The doctor … the real Shelby," she said.

"Yeah?"

Another convulsion rocked her body. Foam oozed from the corners of her mouth. "I'm sorry … about her."

"You killed her?"

She nodded between tremors. "She's … in the lake. Tell her family … I'm sorry."

"What about the rest? Did you kill them, too?"

Her eyes glazed over. Bloody foam trickled from her mouth, pink on her lips and chin. "I'm not sorry … about them."

With that, she was gone.

"No," Grace said. "Oh no."

Beau lowered Sariah's head to the ground. He scrubbed his hands over the stubble on his cheeks and pressed his palms against his closed eyes. "Shit. Shit-shit-*shit*."

Grace sobbed behind him. The paramedics lifted Sariah from his lap. He felt the weight of her go, but he couldn't look.

Gravel crunched as someone approached. "Grace, are you okay?"

"Clayne?"

Beau turned to watch. Clayne placed his hands over hers, squatted down in front of her. "Hey, Gracey."

"Oh my God, it's really you." Tears streamed down her cheeks. "For so many years, I thought you were dead."

He stroked her hair back from her face. "Not yet."

Beau climbed to his feet and moved away, giving them some privacy. At the corner of the graveyard he stopped an approaching paramedic. "Just give them a few minutes." He nodded at the covered body on the stretcher.

"Could you check her pockets for the keys to unlock those shackles?"

"Yes, sir."

He moved around to the front of the temple and wrapped his hands around the flagpole. He pressed his forehead against the cool metal and let the tears come. They burned in his eyes and turned to ice on his cheeks. Above him the Canadian flag flapped in the wind, both strong and free.

FIFTY-TWO

A car came up the gravel road. Grace stopped what she was doing and turned her good ear in that direction. Bella lifted her nose in the air with interest, but the goats didn't care. They brayed and nudged her hands for more treats.

It's the police. We should run.

But she held firm instead, waiting.

The car turned down the driveway, and moments later it nosed out into the clearing. It was a silver sedan, a Ford or maybe a Chevy, and not a car she recognized. It bounced across the yard and came to a stop beside her car. She wiped her hands on her pants and moved toward the driveway, Bella at her side.

He was tall and blond, his face ruddy with stubble. He was a man now, but she still saw him more clearly as the boy he'd once been. Memories were funny things. They could deceive both your eyes and your heart.

"Hey, Gracey." Clayne approached with a grin on his face, but he stopped with five feet or so between them. Old habits were hard to break.

"New car?" she asked.

"It's a rental. I've got to return it to Kamloops tonight. And then I'm heading home."

"Home."

He shrugged. "It's time to get myself sorted out. And if I'm there I can stop Boaz from running the business into the ground. He's got no head for numbers."

She smiled to cover the ache in her heart. "I'd like to see him sometime."

"Come out for a visit," he said. "You're welcome anytime."

"Maybe I'll do that someday."

"Yeah." He kicked at the gravel, stuck his hands into the pockets of his jeans. "How's Desiree doing?"

She looked behind her at the house. "Sleeping. But I can see she's getting restless for the big city. I think she'll be heading home soon, too."

"I didn't want to leave without saying goodbye."

"I'm glad you did. I never got a chance to thank you properly. I can't even think what would have happened —"

He put up a hand to stop her. "We protect each other, Gracey. That's what we always do."

She took a breath, summoning her courage. "You remember that last night in the forest?"

His eyes locked on hers, but she couldn't read the thoughts behind them anymore. Too many years had passed.

"I remember."

"I think about that moment a lot," she said. "It was one of the only times in my life I ever felt hopeful."

His smile was soft and wistful. "Me, too. But it was a long time ago. I'm a different person now, aren't you?"

She was many different people. But she kept that thought to herself, and said, "I suppose I am."

He stepped through the invisible barrier and kissed her on the cheek. His lips were warm and soft. "I hope you have many times ahead where you feel just the same way. You deserve it, Gracey."

"You do, too, Clayne."

As he moved back toward the car, she said, "Hey, Clayne?"

"Yeah?"

"Will you come back to visit sometime? I mean, once you've got yourself sorted out?"

His smile was slow to spread, but it grew until it lit up his eyes. "Yeah. I will."

She smiled back. "Then you've given me something to be hopeful about."

He climbed into the car and the engine roared to life. Before he could put the car in reverse, she knocked on the glass. He pressed the button to lower the window.

She leaned down and kissed him on the forehead. "That's just in case I never see your stupid face again. I love you, Clayne Johnson."

Acknowledgements

Thank you, once again, to the entire team at Dundurn Press. It is a joy to work with you, and to feel like my writing is both appreciated and honoured. Thanks to managing editor Elena Radic for believing in *Blood Atonement*; to project editor Jenny McWha for keeping everything rolling along so smoothly; to Kendra Martin and the stellar Dundurn marketing team, including publicist Heather Wood for her invaluable knowledge and guidance, and marketing coordinator Maria Zuppardi for constantly coming up with new and creative ways to highlight all of Dundurn's amazing books; to Shannon Whibbs for her insightful and eagle-eyed editing — this was a tougher one, wasn't it? And to Laura Boyle for once again knocking it out of the park with her cover design.

Thank you to Kim Lionetti at BookEnds Literary Management for being *Blood Atonement*'s biggest champion. I cannot express how much I appreciate your hard work and expertise.

My eternal gratitude to my first and most beloved editor, Hannah, who worked her magic on several early drafts of this book. I love you forevermuch.

And, as always, my deepest love and gratitude to my family: My husband, Jon, whose stated mission in life is to always find ways to make me laugh. Thank you for being calm, thank you for being steady, thank you for always being you. You're the best. Thank you to my mom, Sheryl, for being my loudest cheerleader and smartest reader. I'm still trying to slip one past you. And thank you to my two beautiful children, who are growing up way too fast. I'm so proud of you both for standing passionately and firmly for who you are and what you believe in, and for leaning into the world with compassion and kindness. You are amazing humans, and I'm so glad I get to share your journey.

About the Author

S.M. FREEDMAN studied at the American Academy of Dramatic Arts in New York and spent years working as a private investigator on the not-so-mean streets of Vancouver before returning to her first love: writing. Her debut novel, *The Faithful*, is an international #1 Amazon bestseller. It reached the quarter-finals in the Amazon Breakthrough Novel Award and was selected by *Suspense Magazine* as a "Best Debut of 2015." The sequel, *Impact Winter*, was published in 2016 and also became an international Amazon bestseller. She is also the author of *The Day She Died*. S.M. is a proud member of Sisters in Crime, Crime Writers of Canada, International Thriller Writers, and Mystery Writers of America.